MY BEST FRIEND'S MURDER

POLLY PHILLIPS

**SIMON &
SCHUSTER**

London · New York · Sydney · Toronto · New Delhi

First published in Great Britain by Simon & Schuster UK Ltd, 2021

1 3 5 7 9 10 8 6 4 2

Simon & Schuster UK Ltd
1st Floor
222 Gray's Inn Road
London WC1X 8HB

Simon & Schuster Australia, Sydney
Simon & Schuster India, New Delhi

www.simonandschuster.co.uk
www.simonandschuster.com.au
www.simonandschuster.co.in

A CIP catalogue record for this book
is available from the British Library

Paperback ISBN: 978-1-4711-9539-6
eBook ISBN: 978-1-4711-9540-2
Audio ISBN: 978-1-3985-0064-8
Export Trade Paperback ISBN: 978-1-3985-0130-0
Export eBook ISBN: 978-1-3985-0144-7

Typeset in Sabon by M Rules

Printed and bound by CPI Group (UK) Ltd, Croydon, CR0 4YY

MY BEST FRIEND'S
MURDER

For all my friends, both good and bad,
and for Alaric, the best of them all.

You're lying, sprawled at the bottom of the stairs, legs bent, arms wide. If I squint, you could be playing Sleeping Bunnies. Or maybe Twister. Or you might have flung yourself there in a parody of total exhaustion the way we did as teenagers. 'Stop the world, I want to get off,' we used to shout, tossing our school bags and collapsing onto the sofa. But tonight, your hair's covering most of your face and your neck's at a funny angle. And there's blood. So much blood.

The blood around the gash on your forehead is starting to crisp. I wish I could tell you how beautiful the tiny claret-coloured crystals are or that the blood pooling around your head looks like a halo. But you're past listening.

I should be beside myself. Instead, I find myself circling, careful to avoid the blood, acting like I'm trying to work out what happened. Even though I already know. I feel detached, like I'm watching this unfold on *CSI* or one of the other trashy TV shows we always used to watch together. I stop and wait for the waves of sorrow and regret to come rolling in. Nothing happens. I blink hard, trying to force tears into my eyes so I can palm them away. Nothing comes.

I lean in, so close the tips of my hair almost graze your skin. I need to see your face. It's the face I see in my head every time I go to the gym. The face that makes me run until my trainers burn against the rubber of the treadmill.

The face that makes me clench my thighs tighter every time I have sex.

This close, I can see dark hairs under the arch of your eyebrows. There are bags under your eyes and dried saliva on your lip. I want to wipe it away, tidy you up. But I can't disturb the scene. I cast my eyes up the stairs behind you. Polished wood, so shiny you could eat your dinner off it. Every homeowner's pride and joy. Lethal to a pair of stock-inged feet. The tiniest misstep could have catapulted you headfirst to the bottom.

I bend down again, my ear an inch from your mouth. There it is. The tiniest exhalation. You're breathing. The tears come now, a cascade of emotions I can't separate accompanying them. Wedged among them, the sharp sting of disappointment. I tamp it down and hurry to the door. I need to let the paramedics in. And then I have to be careful. Because as the energy trickles out of your body, it's pumping into mine. And while this could be a tragic accident, if anyone's got a motive to hurt you, it's me.

One

I stamp my feet and bang on the door again. I wish they'd hurry up and open it. I'm dying for the loo. And it's Baltic out here. The Porsche Cayenne is parked outside so they're definitely home. Aren't people with kids always saying they have to be up before dawn? So why aren't they answering? The old woman with the dog climbing the steps to one of the tall houses on the opposite side of the road keeps looking over. She probably thinks I'm breaking and entering. To the suspicious mind, my faded black leggings and dark puffa jacket are just what a burglar might wear. I want to call out something reassuring like, 'Don't worry, I'm a friend of the Waverlys', but I suspect that might alarm her further. I inspect my left hand – I was so excited to get over here I didn't think about getting a much-needed mani – and try to think warm, non loo-related thoughts instead.

3

It doesn't work. I shift from one leg to the other, eyeing the potted bay trees on either side of the glossy front door. If I have to wait much longer, I might end up squatting over one of them. Not quite the way I wanted to introduce the best thing that's ever happened to me. I should have called first.

I jiggle for a few moments, then give up and start rummaging through my bag. I'm digging past the sticker book for Tilly, Ed's car keys, three lip balms and a bag of dog treats when the door swings open. Standing in a cloud of the Issey Miyake perfume she's worn since school is Izzy, my best friend. She's a vision in Lycra. I thrust my left hand behind my back – I want this to be a surprise.

'Bec? What are you doing here? And why are you standing like a penguin?'

'Are you going running?' I feel a little guilty. I was so excited to get over here it slipped my mind that Izzy runs in the mornings. I remind myself that I'd be more than happy for her to turn up on my doorstep any time of the day or night. Though, given the state of my flat, it's unlikely she would.

'I was about to head up to the common. It's my morning to run while Rich watches Tilly. Is everything okay, hon?'

'More than okay. Just some good news to share. And –' I rustle the paper bag in my right hand '– I brought pastries.'

Izzy hesitates. Her Fitbit blinks like it's having a seizure. She looks at it longingly, then says, 'Go on then. I went to the gym while Tilly was at nursery yesterday.'

'That's the spirit! Now will you let me in already? I've been standing here so long your neighbour thinks I'm a burglar. And I'm dying for the loo.'

'I'll put the kettle on.' She stands aside so I can rush past. 'Then you can tell me this good news. It must be something big to get you out of bed before lunchtime.'

9.14 a.m.

I'm sitting on the buttercup-coloured Oka sofa next to the breakfast bar. It offsets its Farrow and Ball surrounds perfectly. I brush my fingers along the wall. 'Lamp Room Gray' with 'Elephant's Breath' for the feature wall. The Dulux colours of mine and Ed's two-bed don't lift the imagination in quite the same way.

She seems to be taking forever to plate the pastries. I play with one of the throw cushions to distract myself. This is exactly the kind of sofa I'd love to have if dog hair and my natural tendency to spill didn't prevent such a style statement. Not many three-year-olds could be trusted around such a beautiful piece, but naturally Izzy's daughter, Tilly, is super well-behaved. Not to mention well-policed; half her toys have nanny cameras in them and she's not allowed to go to the bathroom on her own. As if on cue, I hear her on the landing upstairs, her footsteps punctuated by Rich's heavier tread. I jump up. I want my news to have Izzy's complete attention. Apart from texting my brother, Rob, she will be the first person I tell.

'This is quite a haul.' Izzy offers me a plate as I come round the bar. 'Did you win the lottery?'

'In a manner of speaking.' I grin as I shoot my left hand across the marble counter splaying my fingers so fast I look like a demented Harry Potter character casting a spell. She can't miss the huge diamond sitting on my ring finger. 'Ed proposed.'

Izzy's so surprised she doesn't say anything for a second. Then her face breaks into a smile. She sweeps me into a hug.

'That's fantastic, Bec. Just what you've been waiting for. I'm so thrilled for you.'

She goes over to her double fridge and pulls out a bottle of Moet. She's so grown up. The only booze in my fridge is the stuff I'm planning to drink that night.

'Tell me everything.'

'Don't you want to see the ring first?' Izzy loves diamonds. I'm surprised it wasn't the first thing she asked about.

'I can see it from over here. It's massive!' She's fiddling with the champagne.

'What's massive? Hey, Bec.' Rich comes in, Tilly looped around his neck so her blonde plait sweeps across his broad chest. His dark hair's rumpled like he just got up. I concentrate on my cheese straw. I might have known him my whole life – we even had baths together as kids – but I still get tongue-tied when I first see him. Rich Waverly was captain of the rugby team while I was what you might call a 'late bloomer'. Izzy thinks my feelings are a throwback from when we were at school. She, of all people, should know there's a bit more to it than that.

'Ed proposed!' Izzy practically throws the champagne at Rich. 'Here, do this. I'm useless this morning.'

'Bec, that's great! He's a lucky man.' Rich deposits Tilly on the floor and pops the cork in one movement. 'Where is he?'

'On the common walking Missy.' I pull myself together.

'He thought I might want to tell Izzy on my own so we could – and I quote – "get all the screaming and crying" out of our systems.'

Rich laughs. 'A man after my own heart. And he walks the dog as well. Why don't we meet him up there? Take Tilly's scooter and make a morning of it?

Tilly's already at the built-in shoe rack, pulling shoes and boots off at random.

'What about the pastries?' Izzy's looking flustered. 'And the champers?'

'Bring them. I'll grab plastic flutes from the pantry.' Rich starts moving and I picture him at work, executing deals, a stream of minions in his wake. Not that I really know what he does. Something in finance. 'We'll bung the pastries in a carrier bag. What's left of them, anyway . . .'

He smirks as I blush. Now I'm engaged, I might need to rethink my pastry habit.

'Come on.' He grabs Izzy's hands and swings her arms. 'Where's your sense of adventure?'

'Okay. But only for an hour or so. You promised you'd get the Christmas tree this weekend and I've got to finish the Beef Wellington before your family comes over.'

'I'll do that when we get back. I only have to finish the chapter I'm working on then I'm free as a bird.' Rich starts to chase Tilly up the stairs, their feet clattering against the polished wood as Tilly's laughter bounces down the stairs.

'I'll text Ed and tell him to meet us at the bandstand,' I call.

'Already done,' Rich shouts back. 'See you up there.'

Their footsteps recede.

'How is his book going?' I ask while Izzy forcefully repacks her Anya Hindmarch 'mummy' handbag.

'Fine.'

'Are you okay?' I ask. 'You're a bit quiet. I'm sorry I derailed your run.'

'Don't be silly.' She stuffs another packet of wet wipes into the bag. 'I'm just knackered. I know everyone thinks I've got nothing to do now that Tilly's at nursery four days a week but I've actually got a lot on. Rich is working all hours and if he's not, he's holed up in his study trying to "write".' Izzy swipes her hands through the air to make inverted commas.

'Is his novel any good?'

'How should I know? He won't let me read it. And that's not the point.' Izzy sounds harassed. 'I've got a lot to manage. I'm trying to get Christmas sorted and Tilly's picked now of all times to have some sort of sleep regression. I could do without a big family lunch this weekend.'

I know she resents the time Rich's writing takes up but I can't help thinking that if she gave him a bit more freedom to pursue it, he'd be a lot happier. Not that I would ever dare say that. 'Can you postpone?'

'Don't be silly. You know I love seeing Rich's parents and they're so excited to have Henry back in town. This is the first time all their boys will be together since he got that job in Geneva.'

'Jenny will be in her element.' Rich's mum once told me that he and his brothers, Henry and Charlie, were named after kings of England, which is appropriate given that she treats them like royalty. As someone who's lost their own mother, it's touching to watch. 'Do you know, when they were little, she used to—'

'Anyway, hark at us.' Izzy changes the subject, oblivious to my attempted anecdote. 'Boozing on Clapham Common in the early hours of a Saturday morning. It's *almost* like nothing's changed in the last fifteen years.'

'Our terrible taste in blokes?' I play along.

'Speak for yourself. *My* taste has always been impeccable. Yours on the other hand . . .'

She's joking. But out of nowhere, the memory of a white rose, as bright as a fresh sheet of paper, and Rich's hand brushing my face tumbles into my mind. If things had been different that night . . . I steady my breath. I haven't let myself think about that moment in almost two decades. I will not start now.

'We can't all meet Prince Charming when we're sixteen,' I say lightly as Izzy switches off the kitchen light and holds out her elbow so we can link arms. 'Some of us have to wait a while.'

Two

9.30 a.m.

'So tell me how he did it. Did he whisk you out for a swanky dinner or get down on one knee in front of the Christmas tree? I want to hear every last detail. Even the naughty ones.'

We're at the traffic lights at the end of their road. Clapham Common's at the top of the hill, a swathe of green stretching the length of the road all the way down to the station. Normally it's packed with joggers and dog walkers but today the cold is keeping all but the most dedicated away.

'It was a total surprise.' I smile both at the memory and at the idea of being organized enough to have a Christmas tree already. 'Though I probably should have clocked something was up when he was home before me.'

'Don't tell me he missed Friday night drinks. *Sacre bleu*.'

Before she had Tilly, Izzy used to work at the same risk management firm as Ed. That's how I met him. Of course, at the beginning, I assumed he was interested in her. With legs up to her armpits, blonde hair and perfect features, most guys usually are. Thankfully I was wrong. This time.

'Exactly. Anyway I thought it was a bit weird when I saw his bike chained up in the front garden but he made some excuse about drinks not being on because it's December and everyone's so busy.' I breathe in, remembering the smell of cinnamon in the air. 'But he'd lit candles. And he was making curry as well. That was when I thought something might be up.'

'Candles and curry. Basic male seduction 101.'

'We can't all have Mr Romance.'

Rich has always surprised Izzy with gifts and treats. I remember the collective envy of our entire sixth form common room when he bought her a locket from H Samuel for their one-month anniversary. She's honed his taste in jewellery since then. He proposed with a family heirloom on a cliff in Cornwall. He'd got up at the crack of dawn and abseiled down to spell out 'Will you marry me?' in stones on the beach below. As grand gestures go, it's pretty hard to beat.

'Carry on,' Izzy urges.

The lights change and we start walking across the road. A car beeps, either at our leisurely pace or, more likely, Izzy in tight Lycra.

'Okay. So I was thinking maybe he'd got a pay rise or that he finally wanted to talk about moving house. I didn't think he was going to propose. I had my coat on! I was hanging it on the bottom of the stairs when he suddenly dropped to one knee in front of me. I thought he'd tripped on a loose floorboard at first.' I shake my head. 'I was so busy trying to help him up I didn't even see the ring box in his hand.'

'Only you would try and give a proposing man some assistance.' Izzy laughs. 'I'm surprised you didn't fetch his toolkit and make him a cup of tea while you were at it.'

'It has been said I do make a good cup of tea.'

'Must be all that practice you get at work,' Izzy quips. I laugh, but the comment stings a little.

She sees my face. 'Too close to the bone?'

I shrug. I've been the features assistant at the magazine where I work for the past four years and some days it does feel like all I do is make tea. That doesn't mean I want to be reminded of it.

'So anyway, I stopped trying to help him up.' I try to restore momentum. 'In fact I pretty much stopped breathing altogether. Then he looked at me and said, "I've known from the minute I met you I always wanted you in my life. Would you do me the very great honour of marrying me?"'

I wait for Izzy to point out that if he knew from the moment he met me, it shouldn't have taken him three years to ask. Uncharacteristically, she lets the comment go.

'That's so sweet, hon. These men pretend to be so macho but they're jelly when it comes to this. I remember Rich was so choked up he could barely get the words out.'

'Ed didn't cry,' I admit. 'But his voice did go a bit scratchy.'

'So romantic.' Izzy looks up at the shops we're about

to pass. 'I'm dying for a coffee and we're going right past Grind. Shall we pop in?'

'I thought you were off caffeine.' Izzy switched coffee for green tea about six months ago. She claims it's for health reasons but I suspect it's because she's thinking about getting pregnant again.

'I need something to keep my eyes open.' Izzy steers me into a café with a gunmetal grey awning and thumping bass. 'Last night was like something out of *The Night of the Living Dead*, I can't tell you. In the end, it got so bad I made Rich go and lie on her bed with her until she fell asleep. I better grab him one too.'

Grind turns out to be one of these trendy places that have turned coffee into an art form. The barista shakes his head condescendingly when I ask if they do hot chocolate. Izzy takes charge, ordering two flat whites while I lean against the wall, letting the smell of beans fill my lungs. It reminds me of my mum and her five-a-day habit. She would not have approved of this café, I think, looking at the men with man buns and designer stubble serving coffees in glasses. I swallow. It's been fifteen years but some days the loss feels so sharp it's like it happened yesterday.

'Ready?' Izzy's voice breaks in. She's holding a cardboard tray with three paper cups jammed into it. 'I thought about getting you a mocha but I figured if you've managed to avoid getting hooked on coffee this long, why start now? I got Ed a flat white as well though.'

'Thanks.' Luckily, I wasn't that thirsty anyway.

'Figure I've got to keep him on side now that he's going to

13

be a permanent fixture. Speaking of which, have you guys started making plans?'

'Iz, we've been engaged for less than twenty-four hours.' I don't mention I've already bought two wedding magazines.

'It's never too early,' she says. 'And I know it's going to be tricky planning it without your mum. So if there's anything I can do to help, I will.'

'Thanks.' I can feel a lump mushrooming at the back of my throat. Mum was never that convinced about Izzy. She thought our relationship had a toxic element to it (show me a teenage friendship that doesn't), but I'm sure if she saw us now she'd be glad we've stayed in each other's lives. I tuck the thought away. Thinking about Mum will only make me upset. 'We'd better get a move on or those coffees will get cold.'

9.51 a.m.

'Well done, you.' Izzy is already hugging Ed by the time I reach the bandstand. She started power walking as soon as we hit the common. I lean down and scratch Missy's long ears. She sniffs my hand to see if I'm carrying any treats then gives a disgruntled snort and lumbers off to investigate the bag of pastries. My brother, Rob, says she's more of a portable dustbin than a dog, but I love her. I let her go and pass Tilly her sticker book. The force of her hug nearly knocks me over. I ruffle her hair and tell her it's no big deal but really I'm chuffed.

'Let's have a toast.' Rich starts handing out the plastic flutes of champagne.

'Toast. Toast and jam and jam and toast,' Tilly sings, the wind snatching her words away as we raise our glasses.

'To the wonderful Bec.' Rich inclines his glass towards me. 'And to Ed, the man lucky enough to spend the rest of his life with her. Well done for pulling it off, mate.'

The plastic glasses snap as we tap them together. Ed clears his throat.

'Thanks for that,' he says. 'But we all know I couldn't have done it without a little help. I'd like to raise a toast to the other lovely lady in our company today. To Izzy.'

Izzy blushes and looks at the floor.

'Yes. Thank you for introducing us.' I nudge my glass against hers. 'And thanks to Rich for going AWOL at that dinner so that I got the chance to be your plus one.' I smile, remembering how Ed caught the seating plan after I nearly knocked it off its easel as soon as I arrived. 'Basic risk assessment,' he'd said with a chuckle, before swiping drinks off a passing waiter. I'd just had my heart broken by a sports journalist I'd been obsessing about for months but Ed made me smile. The rest, as they say, is history.

'We wouldn't be here without you guys.' I move closer to Ed and he wraps an arm around me.

'That's not all we've got to thank her for.'

'What do you mean?'

Izzy's face starts to look a bit strained. She's obviously worried about stealing my thunder. I smile to try and communicate that I'm more than happy to share it.

'Well when I decided to make an honest woman of you I

knew I needed a partner in crime, so I went straight to Izzy. I swore her to secrecy and she gave me all sorts of advice. She even helped choose the ring.'

Ed's grinning like he's won a prize but I stare at Izzy, who is still gazing intently at the floor. 'When I told you this morning you pretended to have no idea.'

The corners of Ed's mouth start to fold in on themselves. 'Darling, I'm afraid I made her promise. I hope you're not upset. I just wanted to get it right.'

'Why don't you help me give this a push, mate?' Rich nudges Ed towards where Tilly's discarded her scooter. 'Come on, Tills, let's see if we can really make you fly.'

Izzy waits until they're a safe distance away then says: 'I didn't want to spoil it for you.' She stares at me, eyes wide like a Disney princess. 'Besides, I had no idea how he was going to do it or when exactly. So really it was a surprise, if you think about it.'

'I feel like an idiot banging on like it was some massive bombshell when you knew all along.'

'I didn't want to spoil your moment. If you think about it, Ed put me in quite a difficult position. I could hardly say anything, could I?'

'I guess not,' I say doubtfully. My whole engagement now feels like a loop I was left out of.

'I wanted to make sure you got a decent ring.' She glances over her shoulder to check Rich is out of earshot. 'Not a hand-me-down like mine.'

I think Izzy's engagement ring – an antique square sapphire flanked by diamonds – is stunning, but I know she prefers her wedding and eternity bands.

'Did I do good?' Izzy looks like Tilly when she's done something she's really proud of. 'Do you like it?'

I look at the ring on my finger. The diamond blazes back at me. I always thought that if Ed ever got round to it, he'd choose something smaller, quirkier. This is so big I'm going to struggle to use a keyboard when I go in to work on Monday.

'I do . . . except . . .'

'What?'

'I keep waiting for the *Titanic* to call and say it wants its iceberg back.'

A cloud scuds across the sky and casts a shadow across Izzy's face and I worry I've offended her. Before I can check, Rich and Ed amble back around, Tilly and Missy sandwiched between them.

'So now Ed's finally popped the question –' Izzy claps her hands ' – we want to throw you an engagement party.'

'We can't let you do that,' Ed says. 'It's too generous.'

'We don't need to make a big deal of it,' I agree. Rob's the party animal in our family. Large rooms full of people I don't know stress me out.

'Don't be ridiculous. You know I love a party. We can have it at our place,' Izzy starts ticking things off on her fingers. 'If we get a move on, we can get it in before Christmas. It'll be Christmas-themed so we can save on the decorations. Oh, it'll be so much fun. Ed, Bec, can you get me the email addresses of the people you want to invite by the end of the weekend? That way I can get cracking.'

'You must let us cover the booze,' Ed replies. 'To thank you for the gesture.'

To my surprise, Izzy accepts. 'That would be wonderful,' she says. 'Plus that way you can make sure you like all the stuff we serve.'

I want to say that I've never met a glass of wine I didn't like – and that I don't really want an engagement party – but Ed's nodding.

Izzy grabs his arm. 'Come on. It looks like it's about to rain. We can talk about it on the way back. Guest list, band, that kind of thing. I need to head off now if I'm going to make this Beef Wellington in time.'

'I said I'd do that.' Rich flips Tilly's scooter over his shoulder as if it weighs nothing. 'I've only got a few pages to finish.'

'I'll believe it when I see it,' Izzy dismisses him. 'There was something else I wanted to talk to Ed about anyway.'

Ed hands me Missy's lead. 'I'm all ears. Bec, do you mind taking her round the bandstand one more time to make sure she's ready to go? I don't want her crapping in my car again.'

'She's only done that once,' I say, but they've already started walking off. A slight sourness creeps over me as I pack up the remnants of the picnic. Ed and Izzy are laughing, heads thrown back, teeth flashing as they walk. Perfect father Rich is bringing up the rear, his whole body inclined towards Tilly so he doesn't miss a syllable of what she's saying. And I'm back here, crumpling pastry wrappers into an old Waitrose bag. It doesn't feel much like an engagement celebration. Then I hear my name being called.

'Bec.' Izzy's cupped her hands over her mouth and is

hollering at the top of her voice. 'Hurry up. Ed's making all the decisions. And some of them are terrible. We need you!'

Just like that it's as though the sun's come out. I stuff the carrier bag in the nearest bin and set off at full pace after them, my resentment fluttering out onto the common behind me.

Three

I jiggle my leg on the bed while I wait for Ed to finish getting ready. For a man with relatively little to do (shower,
shit, shave), he seems to be taking an awfully long time.
Izzy says Rich is the same; in the mornings she has to use
the bathroom down the hall because he hogs the en-suite.
Not a problem Ed and I need to solve. I look through the
open bedroom door across the hall at the door to our sole
bathroom. The paint at the edge of the panels is starting
to flake. It's still the bland magnolia colour it was when we
bought the flat. I keep suggesting we repaint but somehow
we never get round to it. Maybe now we're engaged, we'll
move somewhere bigger. With Ed being a partner I'm sure
we could do better than a cramped two-bed. Before I can
start fantasizing about Clapham townhouses, Ed opens the
door and steps out in a cloud of steam. With the towel tight

20

around his waist like a mini-skirt, he looks like a modern-day Roman gladiator.

'You know that's the hand towel, right?'

He takes it off and whirls it around his head. He's trying to make me laugh but my mind's already flying ahead to tonight. I wait for him to start getting dressed then stand up and give myself a final onceover in the full-length mirror opposite the bed before it fogs up. I liked the way the navy Reiss dress hugged my hips when I bought it. Now I'm wondering if it's too tight. Or too short. I always underestimate how smart these things tend to be. I tug at the back and wonder whether there's time to change into something else. Not that I really have anything suitable.

'You look gorgeous.' It's as if Ed read my mind. Either that or my insecurity is written across my face.

'Really?' My mum always used to tell me off for fishing for compliments but I could use a boost.

'Really. You'll be the belle of the ball.' He leans forward and kisses me on the forehead. Then he finishes buttoning up his shirt and pushes his glasses back up his nose in a way that reminds me a bit of Clark Kent. 'Now, are you ready?'

'I think so.' I take a last look in the mirror. With the help of YouTube, I've managed to sweep my shoulder-length brown hair into a chignon and for once my make-up looks okay. My eyeliner's a bit wonky but I'm hoping Izzy will fix it.

I spot him tuck a piece of paper into the pocket of his jacket as he puts it on. 'You're not planning on making a speech, are you?' My stomach twists at the thought. 'Please tell me you're not making a speech.'

'Don't worry. I know you hate being the centre of attention. Relax.' Ed grabs me by the shoulders. 'I promise I'm not making a speech about you.'

I fiddle with my handbag. Ed's been acting 'surprise birthday party' funny all week. Tapping away on his phone constantly and going out of the room to answer when it rings. But if he tells me he's not going to make a speech, I believe him.

7.18 p.m.

Like most men, the Uber driver's idea of three minutes differs vastly from mine and he takes two wrong turnings while he's trying to find the South Circular. I'm drumming my fingers on the dirty window by the time we finally turn onto Izzy and Rich's road. Their house is lit up like Christmas. Izzy's studded the tall hedges at the front with fairy lights and hung enormous red bows in every window. It might be set back from the hustle and bustle of Northcote Road, on one of Clapham's more exclusive streets, but its festive embellishments could compete with any of the area's bars and restaurants. As we pull up outside, the first strains of Michael Bublé's 'Holly Jolly Christmas' waft down the front steps. Nobody throws a party like Izzy.

The front path is frosted with ice and I'm conscious of my heels so I totter up the front steps, gripping Ed's arm like he's a life raft and I'm drowning. I only let go to knock. The brass doorknocker is barely out of my hand when Izzy whips open the door. She's wearing a pale gold, floor-length dress that can really only be described as a gown. Rich fills the doorframe behind her, looking like James Bond. He's wearing a dinner jacket, for heaven's sake. I tug at the material around my hips. I knew I should have gone full-length. It's not until Ed coughs that I realize I'm standing on the doorstep with my mouth open. And it's freezing.

'Sorry, I was so taken aback by your gorgeousness that I forgot myself.' I reach forward to kiss Izzy. 'You should hire yourself out for weddings and bar mitzvahs.'

'Don't be ridiculous.' Izzy air-kisses me on both cheeks. 'You look pretty gorgeous yourself. I wish I were brave enough to get my legs out in this weather. And who is this silver fox you've brought with you? George Clooney, eat your heart out.'

I shoot Ed a sympathetic look. I know he's conscious about the grey hairs peppering his sideburns. But he's laughing along.

'You guys are among the first to arrive, which works perfectly,' Izzy carries on. 'Ed, come with me and choose what we should be drinking. There's champagne already open but I bet you can come up with something more imaginative.'

Izzy practically scoops Ed into the hall, leaving me standing on the threshold with Rich.

'You look lovely, Bec. I'm so glad we can celebrate this with you.' He leans down and I breathe in a waft of his aftershave. I hold the bunch of white flowers I've brought in front of me like a shield before he can hug me. I wonder if I'll stop needing a minute to regulate myself around him after I'm married. I hope so.

'Here.' I remind myself that I should be thinking about

Ed not Rich, then hand the flowers over. 'A little thank you from us.'

'You really shouldn't have. This is your party.'

'I couldn't come empty-handed but it seemed pointless to bring more booze. I'm sorry about the colour – I know pink roses are more Izzy's taste.'

'These are my favourite as it goes so you can stop apologizing. Honestly, you haven't changed. Do you remember that time when we were kids and you apologized to a paving stone that tripped you up?' Rich cracks up.

'I can't believe you remember that.' My shoulders start to loosen. 'But that paving stone probably did deserve an apology – it was about to feel the full force of my fat arse.'

'Moments like that you don't forget,' Rich shakes his head. 'If you want a proper trip down memory lane, my mum's coming. If you're lucky, she'll probably bring out pictures of the five of us in the bath together.'

'I'm hoping Rob'll pop along later. He'll love that,' I say with a dose of sarcasm. 'I'm pleased your mum's coming though. I was hoping to stop in and see her when she was last here but it didn't work out.'

'After Beef Wellington-gate, you mean.' Rich winks. 'Just as well you didn't. I was supposed to set a timer on my phone but I got carried away writing. It was ruined. I was in the doghouse all afternoon. I don't know who was more pissed off – Izzy, who'd been up since the crack of dawn making it, or Mum because she was starving. On the plus side, it did have them agreeing on something.'

'You're exaggerating,' I laugh. Izzy and Jenny get on like a house on fire.

'I promise you, I'm not. Oh and Bec? Stop putting yourself down. You didn't have a fat arse back then and you certainly don't have one now.'

I blush so furiously even my scalp is burning but, luckily, Izzy reappearing from downstairs saves me from having to reply.

7.31 p.m.

I'm loitering in the hall, drinking champagne when the doorbell goes again. I hear Rich's mum's – Jenny Waverly's – distinctive tones through the door declaring she could murder a gin and tonic while someone else, presumably David, stamps his feet against the cold. Izzy's patting her hair into place in the hallway mirror so I move to open the door and save her a job. She cuts in front and beats me to it.

'Hello, darling.' Jenny steps in and pats her on the back, while David nods a curt greeting and wanders down the hall looking for the bar.

'I'll have a gin and slimline,' Jenny calls after him. 'Isabel, the house looks gorgeous. You have been busy.'

'It didn't take long.' Izzy ducks her head modestly. 'Of course you remember my friend Bec?'

'Remember her? I'd know her in the dark. She was getting under my feet for the best part of her formative years.' Jenny beckons me into a warm embrace that quells the flicker of irritation I feel whenever Izzy tries to make out she knows the Waverlys better than I do.

'Rebecca, darling, lovely to see you. I'm so thrilled about

the engagement and I know your darling mummy would have been too.'

'Thanks, Jenny.' Normally I hate it when people reference what they think my mum would have thought about something. But with Jenny it's different. I'm glad she's here.

'I mean every word.' Jenny grips my upper arms. 'And is your father coming tonight?'

'The flights from Dubai are very expensive at this time of year. I did ask him but it wasn't possible.'

Jenny's mouth forms a moue of discontent as if she thinks my dad's excuse – or residential status – doesn't pass muster.

'And tell me, Isabel, Matilda can't be in bed already? I came early to see her.'

'It's past seven, Jenny. We didn't want to disrupt her routine.'

'If I crept in, I'm sure I wouldn't disturb her.'

I can see Izzy smiling through gritted teeth.

'Jenny, something about you is different,' I chip in. 'Have you had your hair cut?'

'I have.' Jenny pats the side of her silver chin-length bob. 'I'm so glad someone noticed. That's the problem with having sons.'

'And did I hear you saying something about wanting a gin and tonic? What a good idea – why don't we go downstairs and sort them out ourselves? I don't know about you but I find every time I wait for a man to get me a drink, I practically die of thirst.'

Jenny laughs as if I've cracked the joke of the century and

I flash Izzy a thumbs up behind her back. Perhaps tonight won't be so nerve-wracking after all.

'You two go on, I'll be a minute.' The doorbell rings again and Izzy waves us off. I follow Jenny, glancing up to see who's at the door as I turn the corner. But Izzy hasn't answered it. She's too busy staring at the roses I brought, lying wrapped in paper on the ornate side table where Rich left them. I know she's precise on colour schemes – you only have to look at her perfectly coordinated interiors to see that – but her next move shocks me so much I have to blink to make sure I'm not seeing things. And when I open my eyes, the white roses are still lying upended in the leather wastepaper basket, the bottoms of their green stems poking out. Izzy brushes her hands and goes to answer the door as though nothing's happened.

Four

7.45 p.m.

I'm so confused by what I saw that by the time I step into the kitchen, I'm starting to wonder if I imagined it. It takes me a second to get my bearings. They've pushed the dining table against the wall under the skylight to serve as a makeshift bar. The breakfast bar, which Izzy's usually militant about keeping clear, is covered in platters of food. I hang onto the stair railing and count to ten before I step down. There'll be a logical explanation, I'm sure. I just need to ask Izzy.

Jenny's already at the bar filling a glass that's more gin than tonic but I know a drink's not going to help my state of mind. I leave her to it and start to wander, trying to spot someone I recognize. Ed's talking to a couple of guys from work and there's a clutch of mums I remember from the times I've picked Tilly up from nursery. Looking around, I realize that I don't actually know that many people here. That's why I didn't want a big party. But when I tried to

28

tell Izzy that, she misunderstood and told me she'd help make up the numbers. Speak of the devil. She appears in the doorway, her dress shimmering under the lights. I know I need to speak to her. I'm screwing up my courage when I feel a hand on my arm.

'Bec, are you okay?'

'Jules! I'm so glad you made it. I wasn't sure you'd come.' I practically throw myself into her arms. Jules is the mag's beauty editor and my closest friend at work. In a room full of strangers, she's the person I want to see.

'We almost didn't by the time my husband had finally dragged himself back from football.' Jules disentangles herself and gestures at the gangly guy in glasses next to her. 'You remember Jonny.'

'Hey, Jonny.' I reach up and give him a quick peck on the cheek. 'Thanks for coming all this way.'

'Well you know I lose my super powers the second I cross the river,' he jokes. Jules rolls her eyes.

'Can I get either of you a drink?' Jonny can obviously see the way the conversation is heading.

'I'm all right but there should be some champagne knocking around somewhere.' I point at the bar. 'See that guy. That's Rich; he'll know where everything is.'

'Got it,' Jonny dips his head and makes his way towards Rich.

'So that's the famous Rich.' Jules squints in his direction. 'You never mentioned he's a dead ringer for Tom Cruise. If Tom Cruise were tall.'

'You probably only think that because he's behind the bar.' Rich says something that makes Jonny laugh then ducks under the table and reappears with a champagne bottle and two glasses.

'Probably. He is gorgeous though.' Jules starts looking around the room. 'More than a match for the beautiful Izzy.'

'When did you meet Izzy?' My voice is sharper than I meant it to be. But Jules is my friend, not Izzy's.

'I presumed she was the tall blonde in the metallic number who let us in.' Jules looks a bit taken aback by my intensity. 'She had a right face on her. Uber glam but a bit done, if you know what I mean.'

'She looks as good in joggers as she does tonight.' I shrug, trying to bring things back to normal. 'She's just one of those people.' I glance back at the doorway to see if I can spot her but Izzy's gone.

'Check out this house anyway.' Jules's eyes are wide. 'This basement conversion is insane. And don't tell me they sunk the garden so it was in line with the kitchen. That must have cost a fortune.'

'It wasn't cheap. Luckily, Rich is a banker and they had a bit of family money.' I look through the aluminium and glass bi-fold doors to the garden beyond the patio. The tips of the grass are glazed with frost, like a winter wonderland. Even the weather cooperates with Izzy.

'Is that our managing ed?' Jules interrupts her own running commentary to clutch my arm again. 'How on earth do you know Tony Maxwell-Martin?'

Izzy's dad. I look over. In a long silver dress with her blonde hair cascading around her shoulders, Izzy's mum, Glenda, has worked hard to look like an exact replica of her daughter. Her cheekbones are unnaturally prominent, and

I know she spends her life in the gym. Next to her, Tony looks bloated. He's supposed to be on a health kick but the skin around his eyes is pouchy and he could do with losing a few pounds.

'That's the family money,' I say. 'Tony's Izzy's dad. I'm surprised you didn't know. I thought everybody at work did.'

Jules frowns. 'I've never heard anyone mention it. Certainly nobody in beauty.'

'Really?' I recall the humiliation of walking into the loos on my second day to find two girls from the fashion department bitching about Tony dropping by my desk to say hello. I've been convinced everyone thinks I got the job because of him ever since. It's one of the reasons I keep such a low profile. 'Well, for God's sake don't tell them now.'

'Of course I won't. Anyway, I mustn't monopolize you. I should go and find Jonny and enjoy our forty-five minutes of freedom before we head back north.'

'Thanks for coming, Jules. I really appreciate it.'

'I wouldn't come to deepest, darkest south London for anybody else. Have an amazing night.'

Jules plunges into the party. I look around. Izzy's behind the breakfast bar now, pulling serving platters out of a cupboard. I could go over but she looks like she has her hands full and I'm not sure what to say yet. I look for Ed instead. He's over by the sofa talking to the same group of guys from work as before. I hesitate. It's not that I don't like Ed's colleagues; more that I'm worried they don't like me. They all love Izzy and I thought that being her friend would grant me automatic acceptance. But every time I see them, they crack inside jokes and I find myself either tongue-tied or spiky and defensive. Which means half of them probably think I'm a moron and the other half think I'm a bitch. But right now that group's my best option so I put on a bright smile and slip through the crowds towards them. Perhaps tonight's the night for a fresh start.

'Hi, guys.' I nudge my way into a space next to Ed.

'There you are.' Ed pulls me in. 'I've been looking for you.'

'We were just quizzing Ed about how he popped the question,' says the only girl in the group. She's got dark hair and a sharp face with a mouth that turns down at the corners. I think her name is Emma. 'Congrats.'

'Thanks.'

'Congratulations,' says the short guy with the goatee standing next to her. 'I'm Ian, by the way. I don't think we've met before.'

'Ian's joined us from Slaters.' Ed names one of their major competitors.

'Nice to meet you.'

'Are you in insurance as well?' he asks.

'God no.' Worried I sound rude, I add: 'I'm not nearly clever enough.'

'Bec writes for *Flare*,' Ed answers for me. 'It's one of the country's leading women's consumer magazines.'

'One of the leading women's magazines, is it?' smirks Ben, the self-anointed leader of the group. Ed says he goes out to lunch with clients at least three times a week. It shows; he's got the gut of a man ten years his senior. 'What's it leading women to, then?' He laughs and I force myself to join in.

'Better shoes,' I suggest and then, when nobody reacts: 'We're the usual selection of fashion, health and beauty, celebrity and lifestyle.'

'And current affairs,' Ed reminds me. 'There's a healthy mix of that sort of stuff in there too.'

'You'll be perfectly placed to plan a wedding then,' drawls Emma as if Ed hasn't spoken. 'I imagine you have a lot of contacts.'

'A few.' I don't mention that most of the connections are above my pay grade.

'Have it planned by the year end, will you?' Ben continues. 'Watch out, Ed, the net's tightening.'

He mimes a fishing rod reeling Ed in and this time they all laugh.

'I'm well and truly on the hook,' Ed says, but Ben's self-satisfied guffawing drowns him out. 'Anyway the point I was making about the new trade credit regs is pretty simple.' And off he goes.

'Izzy's offered to plan it for me,' I can't help saying when they've quietened down. No matter how churned-up my feelings are, I know she'll have my back with Ben. 'Were you at their wedding, Ben? It was amazing. I don't remember seeing you.'

Spotting her, I add: 'There she is. Shall I call her over?'

I can see Ben's Adam's apple bobbing as Izzy adjusts one of the canapés. She's paid local teenagers to come and waitress (I've already snagged a duck roll and a mini Yorkshire pudding from someone with thick eyeliner and hunched shoulders) but Izzy makes everything herself. As she turns around and bends over the oven to pull out the final baking tray, I can almost hear the saliva frothing in Ben's throat. It's disgusting.

'Don't distract her while she's cooking.' He sticks his hands in his trouser pockets. 'There's nothing that woman can't do. It was a sad day when that arse walked out of the office.'

Remembering himself, he takes his hands out of his pockets and folds them across his stomach.

'Speaking of which.' He nudges Ed. 'Isn't it about time you made that speech, old man?'

Ed shoots me a smile of apology before he steps forward. I tighten my grip on my glass. I thought he said he wasn't going to make a speech. Behind us, Emma's shushing people and Ben is braying for silence.

'Ladies and gentlemen.' Ed takes out the paper from his jacket and clears his throat with a soft click. 'Please forgive the interruption but I couldn't let the evening pass without thanking our wonderful hosts, Rich and Izzy Waverly, for throwing this fabulous party for us.' Aping a traditional wedding speech, he continues: 'My future wife and I thank you for your generosity and your friendship.'

Everybody cheers and the people closest to me lean in to clink their glasses against mine.

'We also want to thank the rest of you for coming – some from far and wide – to share in our celebrations. I think you'll all agree that Bec looks absolutely stunning tonight. The moment she said yes to me was the happiest of my life.'

I start to breathe more easily. That was lovely, and it feels nice to be appreciated. I make a mental note not to make such a fuss next time. But Ed hasn't finished yet.

'Second only, of course, to learning that we'd won the Credit Suisse account off Marsh, that is.' The insurance side of the room titters and Ed holds up his hand in acknowledgement. 'On that note, I'm sorry to take things from pleasure to business but with so many of you here, celebrating with us, I wanted to share some additional news. This time it's about a partnership of a different kind.'

Somebody near me – I think it's Ben – makes a suggestive catcall and a few people laugh. Ed waits for silence. I can't help smiling – it's so typical of him to revolve a party – even his own engagement – around his job. It's what makes him so successful.

'Earlier this week, SZR voted unanimously to ask Izzy Waverly to rejoin the firm and spearhead that account, this time at partnership level.'

What? My stomach drops like it's on a rollercoaster. Pushing a work agenda is one thing; using my engagement party to promote Izzy is quite another. I know I said I didn't want a fuss but I thought I would have at least this night to myself. And Ed's still talking. I try to catch Izzy's eye to see if she knew about this but she's staring at Ed.

'As many of you may recall, Izzy started as a graduate at SZR and rapidly worked her way up the firm to head of the banking division, a position she held for five years before deciding to take some time out to have a family. Now she's made the excellent decision to come back—'

His lips carry on moving but I can't take the words in. Different thoughts are firing across my brain so quickly I can't take any of them in. Izzy and Ed are going to be working together again? This is what all the secrecy was about.

I watch him beckon her over. Her cheeks are slightly pink but her smile is wide and broad like she's doing a victory lap. Just before she reaches Ed, she looks right at me. Am I imagining the edge to it? I shrink into the crowd. Why didn't they tell me?

There's a burst of applause. Ed must have stopped speaking. I clap along, hoping nobody can see the confusion splashed across my face. I don't understand why she didn't say anything before tonight. I feel a burst of resentment as I watch Ben and his cronies surround her, welcoming her into their circle. The memory of the flowers smashed in the wastepaper basket resurfaces.

Ed materializes at my side with two glasses of champagne. 'What did you think?' he twinkles at me. 'I told you I wouldn't make a speech about you.'

I snatch one of the glasses out of his hands and take a glug. 'Very clever.'

'What do you make of the news, then?' Ed smiles expectantly. 'Isn't it great that Izzy's coming back?'

'What I think is that it would have been nice to have heard it, say, about two hours ago before the rest of the masses.'

'Bec—'

'No, Ed,' I hiss. 'Don't you "Bec" me. I can't believe you didn't do me the courtesy of telling me this major life-changing news about my friend before everybody else found out. It's humiliating.'

'I wanted to.' Ed makes the same click in his throat he made before the speech. 'I'm sorry I couldn't. I never imagined you'd react like this. But it wasn't my place.'

'Isn't that exactly the point though? It is your place. Your place of work that she's coming to work at. Why didn't you say something?'

'Izzy asked me not to. If I'd known it would upset you, of course I would have said something. But I thought you'd be pleased for her.' He looks surprised and I feel bad. He's right. What kind of person am I who can't be pleased for her best friend?

'I am,' I manage to twist the words out. 'I just don't understand why she didn't tell me before tonight.'

'I expect she didn't want to steal your thunder. SZR made the offer just before we got engaged. She's been delaying telling anyone for weeks. I only announced it tonight because there are clients here.'

'Oh.'

'I'm sorry you felt out of it.' Ed wraps his arms around me. 'That wasn't my intention. It was one of the things Izzy was most worried about through the whole process. How it would affect you. She'd be horrified if she thought you were hurt in any way.'

I nod, though I can't help thinking that if she were that horrified she could have given me a heads up instead of letting me find out in Ed's speech at our engagement party.

'She really cares about you, you know.' Ed kisses the top of my head. 'And so do I. Now, can I get you another drink? I want you to have a good time.'

'Sure.' I finish my champagne. It tastes like sugary water. Maybe another drink will help.

I watch Ed wind his way back towards the bar with my glass. But when he gets absorbed into Ben's group on the way, I head over to the bi-fold doors. I yank them open and a welcome blast of cold air smacks me in the face. The gravel flicks against my heels as I skirt around the side of the house. I reach the corner of the side return and breathe a sigh of relief as the automated security light clicks off. I press my face against the brick wall and let the darkness envelop me like a cloak. I'm shuffling through what I want to say to Izzy when, out of the gloom, a voice says:

'Bec?'

It's Rich.

Five

8.42 p.m.

'You made me jump!' In the dim light I can barely make out his face. 'What are you doing out here – having a sneaky fag?'

He doesn't say anything. I start rummaging in my clutch, fingers tracing house keys, lipstick and a stray hairclip.

'That's what I'm doing. I just needed a break. Don't tell anyone.' My hand closes around the packet of cigarettes. In the flare of the lighter, I can see he isn't smiling.

'Are you okay?' I ask. 'I can move if you want to be left alone.'

'Give us a drag then.' Rich holds out his hand, avoiding the question. I don't think I've seen him smoke since we were teenagers.

He closes his eyes as he inhales. I let him have two long puffs then take it back.

'All right, Johnny Depp, you can have your own if you're that desperate.'

I rattle the packet at him but he shakes his head. I put the cigarette back in my mouth. Ed's never smoked in his life. He'd kill me if he saw me standing here, puffing away.

'That speech was a bit of a bolt from the blue, wasn't it?' Rich kicks his heel against the wall of the house and the stones under his feet scatter. 'Were you okay with it?'

'I was a little surprised.' I measure my words out. While I'm dying to unburden my doubts to someone, I learned my lesson about where Rich's loyalties lie years ago. 'Did you know?'

As soon as I ask the question, I want to kick myself. He's her husband. Of course he knew.

'I worry she's taking on too much.' It's as though he hasn't heard me.

'You mean going back? Tilly is at nursery pretty much full-time now.'

'It's not only that.' He pauses. 'Tilly will be starting school in September. That's going to be a huge transition. For all of us. With everything going on, I thought we'd agreed she'd wait a couple of years.'

'Maybe the offer was too good to turn down?'

'Maybe. But they've been asking for years. They'd have kept asking.'

'So why's she gone back now?'

'I don't know. I think she's got this crazy idea we need more money.'

He scrunches up his face and rubs his forehead. The gesture tugs on my heartstrings. With his dark hair flopping over his face, he looks like he did when we were teenagers. Being outside with him – alone – makes me think of *that* night. But what I missed out on, what was taken from me, isn't what I should be thinking about now.

I look across the garden and anchor myself firmly in the present. 'Really?'

By London standards, Izzy's garden is huge – a large wedge of grass begins where the patio ends and the whole thing is edged by flowerbeds on both sides – as is the house that looms over it. It might not be as big as the mansion in Dulwich Village that her parents live in, but with a house like this, Izzy certainly doesn't have to worry about money.

'Maybe it's an independence thing.' He shrugs. 'I've got my job and the writing. Perhaps she wants to have something of her own too. I thought the running was enough but … whatever makes her happy, I guess. And I want her to prioritize her family. I'm just worried she'll take too much on and stress herself out.'

'Don't worry about Izzy,' I nudge my shoulder against his. I'm so close I can smell the musk of aftershave on his skin. I force myself to step back. Literally and metaphorically. 'She can handle this. She always lands on her feet.'

'Thanks, Bec.'

'Oi oi, what do we have here?' The gravel crunches as Rob, my brother, stomps around the side of the house. I flick the butt into the bushes.

'Robbo.' Rich reaches forward to shake Rob's hand.

'Good to see you, Richie. And the blushing bride.' He shakes his head at me. 'Smoking like a chimney. You're all class.'

'Shut up.' I hug him. Rob's been funny about smoking ever since Mum's cancer. He doesn't get that I can have a cigarette at parties without being a smoker. 'It was only one.'

'Not interrupting a deep and meaningful, am I?' Rob looks between us. 'I can bugger off if I am.'

'Nah, you're all right,' says Rich. 'I should be getting back inside. Barman duties and all.'

'If you're sure.' Rob takes a swig from the bottle of beer in his hand. 'I would have thought with your missus going back to work, you could afford to put your feet up.'

'So you'd think.' Rich gives me a strained smile. 'I'll catch up with you later.'

'I wasn't really interrupting anything, was I?' Rob asks after the flash of the security light confirms Rich has gone inside.

'Don't be an idiot. This is my engagement party.'

'There was a time when you had a bit of a thing for old Richie though.'

'For about five minutes.' I make a point of rolling my eyes. 'Him falling in love with my best friend was kind of a turn off. Can we talk about something else? Like why you're so late.'

'I made it in time for the toasts. Sorry, Becster. You know what the life of a top personal trainer is like.' He's wearing a tight white top under a smart grey blazer and, when he flexes, his pecs stand to attention.

'Ugh, your boobs are practically as big as mine.'

'Bigger,' Rob laughs. 'I am sorry I was late, I've got a demanding new client. I'm a slave to her rhythm.'

'Don't tell me this is another one of your laydeez?' I make a face. Rob has a stock of demanding client-based stories, all of which seem to involve middle-aged women hitting on him. He's even had a few altercations with jealous husbands, not that it seems to put him off.

'This one's a bit different. She's a bona-fide A-lister. Referral from a regular client. Already in cracking shape but needs to get ripped for some fantasy movie she's shooting in London.'

'No way. Who is it?'

'If I told ya, I'd have to kill ya.' His smile is Cheshire cat wide. I can't remember the last time I saw him look this pleased with himself.

'Come on. We all know you're rubbish at keeping secrets.' It comes out more harshly than intended.

'What's eating you? Shouldn't you be in a good mood?'

'I am in a good mood. I'm just cold.' I rub my hands against my upper arms theatrically, noticing I've got goose-pimples. It didn't seem that cold when I was talking to Rich.

'Take this.' Rob shucks off his jacket. 'Now tell me what's actually wrong.'

'Okay. Fine. Izzy's going back to work.'

'So?'

'So I only found out when Ed announced it in his speech tonight.'

There's a beat while Rob considers this. Then he starts flicking through his phone. 'So?' He's lost interest already.

I consider telling him what Izzy did to the flowers but it sounds too crazy.

'It feels a bit off that she didn't tell me herself. And she asked Ed not to as well.' I feel like I'm telling tales at school.

'Look, I dunno. Maybe she didn't want to make a big deal

out of it. Though this is Izzy we're talking about.' He sneers and I regret mentioning it. Rob's always been funny about Izzy. He's the one who got my mum all het up about her too. I think it goes back to one bad date they went on when we were fourteen or so. He was so angry when she ended it that he punched a hole in his bedroom wall. I didn't tell him at the time but I was relieved. I prefer to keep things separate.

'Forget it,' I say. 'It's probably just a misunderstanding.'

'Probably. Now, do you want to hear about my new client or not?'

'I thought you were sworn to secrecy?'

'*You're* sworn to secrecy if I tell you. You can't even tell Mr Insurance.'

I roll my eyes again. 'You're going to have to stop calling him that now we're getting married. He's not really into celebrity culture anyway. Go on then, tell me.'

Rob looks over his shoulder to check the coast is clear.

'We're not in a John le Carré novel,' I snigger. But the name he whispers wipes the smile off my face.

'Sydney Scott. But she's—'

'Massive.'

'Massive doesn't even begin . . . She's on a whole different level. She's the only female to ever win an Oscar for best actress and best original screenplay. She's Ben Affleck and Matt Damon rolled into one. And she's a nice person too – she's done loads of work with street kids in Asia – the UN gave her some award for it, before she had that nasty break-up with the guy from *Prison Break* who looks like Justin Bieber. I think he's in prison or something now.'

'Thanks for the bio,' Rob cuts in smugly when I pause

for breath. 'She's actually really cool. And when the news breaks that I've been training her, my career will go stratospheric. I might even get a book deal.'

'You'll have to give *Flare* first rights to your genius.'

'Natch. I was talking to her about you as it goes. She said she might be looking to do some promotional interviews when it's announced she's doing the film. I bigged you up and she was quite keen to meet you.'

'No way.'

'Way.'

'Oh my god, Rob, you're the best.' I imagine letting slip in the next editorial meeting that I've scored an interview with Sydney Scott. Normally I don't even speak unless someone asks me a question.

'All right, I'll set up a meeting. I know they're looking at a bunch of magazines though, so it's no guarantee. But you can consider it an extra Christmas present if it works out. You still can't tell anyone though.'

'I won't.' Normally I'd be telling Izzy before Rob had even paused for breath. Tonight, I want to keep the news to myself.

'Speaking of Christmas.' I bat my eyelashes at Rob the way I used to when I was fifteen and we needed him to go to the off-licence for us. 'I don't know if you've bought my present yet?'

'Do I look like the kind of guy who buys anything before Christmas Eve?'

I smile. I knew he would say that. 'Why don't you swerve the hell that is shopping on Christmas Eve and shout me some free PT sessions instead?'

'Why the sudden interest?'

'Er, because I'm getting married. And –' I pluck the material around my stomach '– doesn't every bride want to look their best on their big day?'

'Bec, you've got the kind of figure most women would kill for. But if you want to get fit the best thing to do is take up running. I'll write you a programme then you need to do a park run or one of those 10ks Izzy's always boasting about on Facebook.'

'Maybe.' I can't imagine anything worse.

'Isn't there one on Boxing Day? She posted it the other week.'

'You're awfully clued up on what she's doing.' I arch my eyebrows.

'You can't help what you see on Facebook. It's all in the algorithm. I'll sign us both up. Now, can we get back to discussing my career as a celebrity training consultant? What shall I buy first – Ferrari or Porsche?'

11.05 p.m.

I use catching up with Rob as an excuse to stay outside for most of the party. He ferries me drinks from inside and a few people pop out – mainly for illicit cigarettes. At one point there are so many glowing ends dancing through the air, they look like fireflies. Rich doesn't come back though.

Just after eleven, Rob insists we go back inside.

'It's all right for you – wearing my jacket – but I'm freezing my nuts off. And you are supposed to put in a bit of an appearance at your own party.' He crosses the gravel and pulls open the bi-fold doors before I can argue. The kitchen's empty apart from a few sulky teenagers loading the dishwasher under Izzy's supervision. At the click of the door, she comes rushing over.

'There you are. Hello, Rob.'

'Izzy.' Rob waves his hand in a mock-salute, which Izzy ignores. She's too busy pursing her lips, which I know is to do with the smell of cigarettes. 'Have you been smoking, Bec?'

'I think there's a bonfire a few houses down.' I automatically trot out the excuse I used as a teenager even though right now I don't really care what Izzy thinks of me.

'Next you'll be telling us you were holding it for a friend.' Rob smirks. 'I'm going upstairs. I'll leave you to it. Laters.'

'Bec, you'd better come with me before you see Ed. I hope you haven't left any butts outside for Tilly to find.'

Izzy marches me down the corridor to the downstairs bathroom. She locks the door behind us and immediately starts burrowing in the cupboard under the sink.

'What are you like?' She moves a set of crisply folded monogrammed hand towels onto the tiles beside her and carries on looking. 'Lucky for you, I know I've got some old perfume back here somewhere.'

I scrutinize the back of her head. Now that we're alone, I've got no excuse not to confront her. I steel myself.

'Why did you tell Ed not to tell me you were going back to work?'

She bangs her head on the bottom of the basin. 'What do you mean?'

I fight my natural instinct to ask if she's okay. I don't

want to get side-tracked. 'When I asked him why he hadn't told me, he said you'd asked him not to.'

There's a clink then Izzy emerges, holding two different perfume bottles. 'I didn't ask him not to tell you. I simply told him his focus should be on the engagement party and my news could wait until afterwards.'

'Really?' I look at her. There's a pink mark on her forehead where it connected with the basin but other than that her whole face is perfectly smooth and guileless. I wonder if I'm being a total lunatic.

'I promise. Why would I tell him not to tell you? I would have told you myself but the last couple of weeks have been crazy. Tilly's had that horrible cold and trying to pull this party together at such short notice has been a massive strain. If you think about it, we haven't really had a chance to sit down together.'

She's right. She's cancelled our last two catch-ups.

'I was waiting until after the party because I wanted tonight to be about you. I had no idea Ed was going to mention the job. I was pretty embarrassed about the whole thing. The last thing I want is for you to think I'm keeping things from you.'

Izzy's eyes mist up and I feel a wave of guilt in spite of myself. 'I'm sorry.'

'Don't worry about it.' She sniffs and dabs at her eye make-up with the pad of her thumb. 'I just wanted tonight to be perfect.'

'Don't be silly, it is perfect.'

She looks so put out there's no way I can ask about the flowers now.

'You've got a new menu,' I say, to buy time. Izzy and Rich have the menus from all the Michelin-star restaurants they go to framed and displayed in their loo. I considered doing the same thing in our bathroom but the Pizza Express menu doesn't have the same kind of visual appeal.

'Yeah, Rich had a client lunch at Marcus Wareing at the Berkeley last week and I tagged along. The pudding was to die for.' Izzy brightens. 'Now, which perfume do you want? Issey Miyake or this old Number Seven that Jenny gave me yonks ago.'

'Number Seven.' I hold out my wrists. 'Issey Miyake's yours.'

Izzy sprays my wrists then dumps both bottles at the side of the sink. She starts examining her face in the mirror.

I bite my lip. I don't want to upset her again but I know the image of the flowers in the bin will keep nagging at me if I don't mention it. 'Izzy?'

'Yup.' She's pouting at herself.

'This is going to sound weird but did you by any chance chuck away the flowers I bought you? Only, I thought I saw them in the bin and I was wondering—'

In the mirror Izzy's face freezes.

'You saw that?'

'I saw it.'

Izzy puts down the lipstick she's been applying. 'I'm so embarrassed.'

'Embarrassed?' I try and keep my voice light even though I had to go to three different flower stalls to get the roses. And they cost a fortune. 'Why are you embarrassed?'

'I was embarrassed for you, hon. They were absolutely covered in bugs.'

'What?'

'That's why I chucked them. I'd never throw perfectly good flowers away. Especially since this house is in desperate need of brightening up. I was so caught up with decorating today I forgot to go to the flower market. But when I went to pick yours off the table, I spotted a mite at the edge of the paper. When I looked closer the flowers were riddled with them. You should go back to the florist and complain. It's not on. They looked expensive too.'

'They were.' My anger recedes, leaving a tidemark of humiliation in its wake.

'You didn't think I threw them away for the sake of it, did you?' Izzy's eyes bore into me.

I look away. 'I didn't know what to think.'

'You and your suspicious mind,' Izzy giggles. 'Do you remember when you were convinced your dad was having an affair with his boss because she kept giving him lifts home from work? Or when you thought your mum was . . . anyway, your little mind must have been going overtime on this one. Like a hamster on a wheel.' She dabs an invisible mark at the corner of her mouth. 'They were so gorgeous too. I love roses. It's been a long time since I had any. Now come on, you don't smell like an ashtray any more, we better get back out there. My parents are dying to see you.'

She flicks the bathroom lock and sashays into the hall leaving me no choice but to follow.

'You haven't seen Rich this evening, have you?' she says casually as I close the door behind us. 'He's been AWOL since about eight o'clock.'

'Not much.' I hesitate. I've got a feeling if she knows

Rich has been outside smoking with me, she won't like it. But the mention of Rich tugs something in the back of my mind. If the flowers were crawling with bugs, why didn't Rich notice them?

'He's probably holed up in his study trying to cram a few more words in,' Izzy carries on, oblivious. 'He's so caught up in that book some days he barely exists in the real world. The other day I caught him pouring Tilly's maple syrup on his cornflakes he was so distracted.'

Too distracted to notice flowers full of bugs? Rich won't even travel by bus because of the dirt on the seats. Bugs are the kind of thing he'd notice. But why would Izzy lie? By her own admission, the house is bereft of flowers. Long-stemmed roses would have made a nice centrepiece for their hall table. And she's my best friend. She's right about Rich, he has been distracted lately. He couldn't even finish his sentences outside. And he's a bloke. Why would he be peering at a bunch of flowers anyway?

'Sounds delightful.'

Izzy laughs and I file my doubts away. I let her take me by the arm and march me back towards the kitchen, our heels clicking against the wood in unison.

Six

I push open the door to the sitting room and breathe in the smell of cloves. The fire's roaring and it seems much warmer in here than the rest of the house. Rich and Rob are propped against the fireplace chatting while Ed sits in the armchair by the bay window, checking his emails. I feel a swell of affection. Only he would be working at a party. In the corner a couple of his co-workers are having a drunken debate about whether it would be quicker to call a cab or Uber home. The party's definitely thinned out. Even Jenny and David Waverly are shrugging their coats on.

'I'm glad we got to see you before we left!' Jenny says as she comes over, David in her wake. Staring at him is like looking at a snapshot of future-Rich. They've got the same wide rugby shoulders and mop of dark hair without a speck of grey. David even used to work at Rich's bank before he retired. He got him the place on the graduate scheme. And he never lets him forget it. Jenny is prattling. I think she might be a little drunk. Or maybe I am. It seems like every sentence that comes out of her mouth should end with an exclamation mark.

'Such a pleasure, as always! I had some photos I wanted to show you! There isn't time now! Never mind! I was talking to Robert about having the pair of you over for lunch with the boys when Henry's next back. And Richard and Charles, of course. Something of a childhood reunion! Wouldn't that be fun?'

'That would be lovely.' Funny to think we ran in and out of the Waverlys' house as children, as if it were our own. Now, aside from Rich, I barely see them. 'I was sorry Charlie and Laura couldn't make it tonight.'

'They wanted to,' Jenny says as David drifts away raising one hand in a lazy farewell. 'They've got a lot on. And if Henry hadn't just been over, I'm sure he'd have popped in. You know he likes a party. Now, don't be a stranger.'

She plants a kiss on both my cheeks then heads out of the door after David, leaving me standing on my own in the middle of the room. I wander over to the vintage drinks trolley parked by the enormous Christmas tree at the back of the room. As I'm walking, I notice the carpet in here is new. It's blush-coloured and heavily textured, already wearing the tiny smudges of people's footprints. Izzy clearly didn't ask people to take their shoes off like she did to me when she replaced the carpet in her bedroom. I smirk, imagining Jenny Waverly's reaction to being asked to remove her Tod's. Then I pour red wine into a glass the size of a fishbowl and take a gulp.

'Hey, you.' Rich materialises at my side. 'I wanted to say

thanks for the chat outside. You helped me see that Iz going back to work could be a good thing.'

'I didn't really say anything.'

'You listened. That helped me sort my head out.'

It's sweet of Rich to credit me but I know he'd have come to the conclusion on his own.

'I mean it. I needed someone to tell me Izzy could handle it and that I should wake up and smell the roses. I don't know what I'd do without you.'

I go to reply, and I don't know quite how it happens, but all of a sudden my wine glass is lolling on the floor, the contents seeping into the carpet. My hands are wet and Rich is covered in splatters of wine that make him look like a slasher victim.

'Oh my god, what happened?' Izzy's voice could cut glass. She hurries over to inspect the huge purple mark ballooning onto the carpet. Against the pale pink, it looks like a particularly vicious bruise blooming on the skin of a face.

'I'm so sorry,' I begin, but Rich cuts in.

'My fault.' He holds his hands up like he's being arrested. 'I lost my balance and knocked into Bec. Did I get you?'

'I'm sure there's no harm done.' Izzy sweeps her eyes across my dress. 'The one advantage of navy means nothing shows up on it.'

'Have you got any white wine?' Ed is on his haunches examining the stain. 'It might neutralize the discolouration.'

'I don't think white wine will stand a chance against this.' Rich nudges it with his foot. 'It's no biggie. We were talking about redecorating this room anyway, weren't we, darling?'

Izzy makes a visible effort to iron the frown out of her forehead. She doesn't mention that they've just finished redecorating this room, but the carpet and the new chandelier glinting overhead give her away. 'You know I never say no to a project.'

'Of course, we'll pay for a new carpet.' Ed brushes fluff off his trousers and gives me a squeeze.

'Don't be ridiculous, mate. It was totally my fault.' Rich insists.

'Nonsense. Bec's the one who dropped the glass. We don't want to put you out.'

'We can sort it out later. Let's not let it ruin our evening.' Izzy brightens. 'Can I get anyone another drink? Bec, you need a whole new glass, hon. Maybe you should stick to white this time?'

Despite Izzy furnishing me with another, smaller glass of wine, the party breaks up shortly afterwards. Rob has a client early in the morning and the other guests follow him out the door. Ed and I stay another half an hour but the energy's gone out of it, like flat champagne. When Ed says we should go because he might have to head into the office in the morning, Izzy makes vague noises about staying for one more but I can tell her heart's not really in it.

'I'm sorry about the carpet,' I tell her when we're standing in the doorway together. Ed's gone onto the street to flag down our driver so I don't have to walk in my heels.

'Don't worry, you can get me a new one for Christmas.' She's staring over my shoulder, tracking Ed's progress.

'I don't mind paying for it.' I start shivering. It seems to be getting colder.

'Oh, don't be ridiculous. I was joking. It's fine.' Izzy's face looks pinched. 'Now, I probably won't have time to see you before the big day but you're still coming, right? No last-minute plans to head north and celebrate with Ed?'

'Of course I'm coming. I come to you for Christmas every year.' I don't mention that Ed wasn't thrilled when I told him I wanted to continue the tradition this year. In the end, he conceded he'd hardly given Christmas with his family – particularly his feral nephews – the best sell. I told him I'd use the time by myself to do some wedding planning and promised to come with him next year. 'Are you sure I can't bring anything? I know you said chocolates but I could do starters as well. Or maybe a pud?'

'You know we don't do starters on Christmas Day. And Jenny's already doing the Christmas cake. Chocolates are fine. They're coming for twelve sharp, does that suit?'

'I can come earlier?' Last year, I went over at the crack of dawn and we got tipsy on Buck's Fizz before she started cooking. It wasn't the best Christmas dinner but it was a laugh.

'Twelve's better. I'm sure you'll want to spend the morning talking to your family and Ed. Speaking of which, that must be your Uber.'

She points at a black Lexus crawling down the street. It pulls up outside and Ed rolls down the window.

'Two secs,' I call. I turn to Izzy, needing to ask. 'Are you sure everything's okay with us?'

'Everything's fine.' The note of impatience in her voice makes me feel like a needy boyfriend.

'Positive?'

'Look, Bec—' Izzy's sentence is cut off by the sound of a small voice calling 'Mummy' from inside.

'For Pete's sake, it's like that child doesn't need any sleep at all.' Izzy grits her teeth. I look past her and see Tilly's heart-shaped face peering out from between the bannisters.

'Do you want me to come in and help?' I seize the opportunity to get things back on track. 'I could start tidying up while you put her to bed? Ed won't mind going home alone.'

'Thanks, Bec, but I've got this. Go home and have a lie-in. Ed's heading up north next weekend, isn't he? You should be with him.'

And with that, she steps back across the threshold and closes the door, leaving me standing in the cold.

Seven

Thursday 20 December

4.01 p.m.

On the last day before the magazine closes for Christmas, Tina, our editor, tells us we can all knock off at 4 p.m. I've spent most of the day looking up wedding venues and sending the links to Ed anyway. The issue before Christmas always goes to press early and the place is like a ghost ship. Normally I linger in the office, tidying my desk and making sure my inbox is empty. Today I'm first out the door. I leave the rest of the team cracking into a bottle of prosecco sent in by an advertiser and leg it to the lift. If I hurry, I can hit the shops and pick up a few last-minute bits before the after-work crowd floods the high street.

Clearly I'm not the only one to have this idea. I step out of the building into a tide of people with bright scarves and sharp elbows pushing and shoving their way towards Oxford Street. With five shopping days left until Christmas all the shops are open late and the whole street's rammed. Part of me is tempted to give up and go home. I've done all my Christmas shopping already. But I have something special in mind for Tilly. I'm so excited I don't think the day will be the same without it. I duck into the passageway that leads directly into St Christopher's Place to escape the tramping feet. It's not much quieter. The whole square's lit up like a fairyland and the restaurants are teeming with people and office Christmas parties. I duck past a crowd wearing particularly garish Christmas jumpers and cut up through the back streets towards Selfridges to pick up Tilly's present.

Despite having to jostle for space when I get there, I find myself pausing outside the entrance, staring at the window display. Mum used to bring Rob and I up here on the first day of the Christmas holidays to see the decorations. Sometimes Rich and his family would come and we'd get a milkshake in the American diner around the corner. Tonight's futuristic setting of Father Christmas on the moon, complete with shiny red space suit, is a far cry from the traditional windows we used to see in our childhood. But it makes me think of Mum. I smile. She'd be chuffed I was spending Christmas Day with Jenny and David. Which reminds me, I may as well have a browse to see if there's anything they'd like. I pull open Selfridge's shiny brass doors and step inside. Before I go to the children's department, I nip into the books section.

I find what I'm looking for almost at once, a trilogy of novels by Simon Sebag Montefiore, set in Russia during the war. I don't know what Rich is writing about but for some reason I imagine a World War Two epic. He loved history at school. While I'm there, I pick up a book on gardening for Jenny. For David, the latest doom-and-gloom analysis of the economy. I take a quick look on the 3-for-2 table for Izzy but she's not really a reader. Plus I've already got her present. I framed a picture of us in our early twenties, one of those rare ones where we both look nice, even though I'm slightly out of focus. I know she'll like the frame; it's a silver Vera Wang with a pretty bow in the corner. I'm planning on having them on my wedding list. I grab another sticker book for Tilly and take the books up to the counter. Armed with two distinctive yellow Selfridges bags, I make my way up to the children's toy department, where I have it on good authority (Jules got the press release) that there's an American Girl concession.

I smell it before I see it. Selfridges have cleverly positioned the pop-up next to a sweetshop, and the cloying smell of chocolate and melted sugar hits my nostrils as soon as I turn the corner. The American Girl awning makes the shop's front windows look like a dress rehearsal. Glittery snow falls over an alpine village, complete with ski lifts, polar bears and snowball fights. There's even fake snow piled up outside and a red carpet winding off the main shop floor. Inside the shelves are packed with rows of dolls in every colour, each clad in the latest winter fashions. In one corner, shop assistants do the dolls' hair, while in another, there's a spaceship almost as tall as I am. It's a world away from the Barbie-or-Cindy choice Izzy and I grew up with. I can't wait to see Tilly's face when she opens it.

I got the idea when I was round at the Waverlys' a few

months ago and Tilly had a friend from nursery over. The friend had an American Girl doll with her and both girls were obsessed by it. Jules confirmed the dolls are the hottest playground commodity going. When Izzy suggested that I might want to buy a basket or a bell for the bike they're getting Tilly, I told her fine but I had other ideas. I want this to be a surprise.

Tilly's a girly girl like her mum so I gravitate towards the girls with long hair and dresses. There are dolls in cheer-leader costumes, dolls that are dressed up for prom and ones that ice-skate. In the end, I'm torn between two. The first has long blonde hair, wide green eyes and looks not dissimilar to Tilly herself. She's wearing a skirt and jacket suit combination and carrying a briefcase, like the working-girl doll she's supposed to be. The other has dark hair and a fringe. In jeans and a hoodie, she's plainer but she has a dog on a lead that looks like Missy. Tilly loves Missy. I pick the dolls up and hold them side-by-side. If I squint a little, they look a bit like Izzy and me. Same types; Izzy all suited and booted and me slumming it. That decides it. I pick up the dark-haired doll and join the huge queue at the counter. If you don't choose yourself, how can you expect anyone else to?

6.28 p.m.

The drumroll thump of Missy's tail is the only thing that greets me when I get home. Ed must be working late. I consider going for a run but the programme Rob's set has me going tomorrow morning so I open the fridge instead.

It's like investigating a crime scene; drips of old food and what looks like the decaying carcass of old fried chicken at the back. I need to be more like Izzy, planning my meals at the beginning of the week. I call Ed and see whether he wants to get a takeaway when he gets back.

'Hey, sweetie.' I flip the lid of the bread bin. A pair of crumpets that have seen better days. 'What do you want for dinner?'

'Er.' There's static on the line. It sounds like he's outside. 'Did I not mention I'd be back late tonight?'

'You didn't say.' There goes our evening of watching Christmas movies together. Since Ed got made partner last year his hours seem to have doubled. I shouldn't complain, though; it's not as if he's enjoying himself. I cross the hallway into the sitting room and settle myself on the sofa, trying to ignore the stripes of grey paint on the wall above the TV. One of these days we really need to decide which colour we're going to paint this room.

'Sorry, last-minute client dinner –' more static '– be a late one, but don't worry, I know we've got dinner tomorrow. I'll make sure I'm not too wrecked. I want to be on good form for you before I go away.'

'No worries.' Perhaps I'll get a takeaway on my own. I'm about to hang up when I hear someone giggle in the background. It sounds like . . .

'Is Izzy with you?'

'She is indeed. We started going through some of the CS accounts so I flicked her a message to see if she could pop in. Then when the dinner got pulled together, it made sense for her to join. Do you want to speak to her?'

'No, you're all right. I've got to go. Try not to wake Missy up when you come in.'

'I'll be as quiet as a slightly tipsy mouse. Love you.'

I find myself frowning at the phone after Ed hangs up. I know it's stupid to feel jealous. She wouldn't mind if I spent the evening with Rich. Looking the way she does, she wouldn't have to. I don't like Ed's co-workers so it's not as if it's an evening I want to be on anyway. But Izzy's always complaining how busy she is. Ed only had to 'flick over' a message and she dropped everything. I sent Izzy three text messages today. She hasn't replied to a single one.

Eight

I stare into the dregs of my drink and think about ordering another. Given the time Ed crawled in last night,
I have a feeling he's not going to be up for a big night.
He didn't even stir when I got up to go for a run and he
spent so long in the shower I thought he might have fallen
asleep. I look at the door again but aside from the sturdy
bouncer fiddling with his earpiece, there's no movement.
At least I've got a seat. This place is down a side street
off Bank station and when I eventually found it, there
was a crowd of people milling outside. They must have
all been leaving though because inside is quiet. The ceilings in the restaurant are high and vaulted – I read online
that the restaurant was an old merchant bank until a few
years ago – and there are a few couples dotted around
underneath them. But the bar area is darker. Besides me,

there's only one guy, in his mid-fifties with a perma-tan. He looks a bit like David Dickinson and he keeps glancing over. The velvet French Connection dress I'm wearing is more low cut than I realized. I wonder if I should ask to go straight to my seat. I'd feel less conspicuous if I was sitting at a table with a white starched tablecloth instead of at a dimly lit bar. I finger my engagement ring pointedly and decide to wait it out. I'm probably imagining things.

I'm on the verge of ordering another drink when I see Ed framed in the doorway at the top of the stairs, a stressed look on his face and his laptop case slung over one arm. I try to get his attention. Izzy mastered the art of wafting her hand through the air in the sixth form common room. I, on the other hand, shoot my arm into the air like a rescue flare.

'Sorry I'm late.' Ed shucks off his coat and deposits his laptop case on the hook under the bar. 'One of our American clients didn't seem to grasp we're five hours ahead and that it was most definitely close of business. Do you want another drink? I'm getting a scotch.'

The man with the perma-tan throws the rest of his drink back and wraps his coat around his shoulders like a cape. He leers at me as he struts past on his way to the door.

'What was that all about?' Ed stares after him as he leaves.

'Nothing. Are you really having a scotch? You're brave.'

'What do you mean?' Ed waves the bartender over.

'It must have been about four when you finally made it into bed.'

'I'm hardcore,' Ed says, with a slightly fragile-looking grin.

'Was Izzy similarly incapacitated?'

'I hardly saw her.' Ed orders our drinks. He can say what he likes about being hardcore but his hands are shaking. 'Why, what has she said?'

'I haven't spoken to her today.' I don't mention that she hasn't replied to my messages. Is she really that hacked off about a carpet? There was that time at school she refused to speak to me for ages because I bought the same Jansport rucksack as her. So maybe she is. Ed's expression relaxes as he takes a sip of his drink.

'Shall we go to our table? I hope you'll like this place. One of the guys from work recommended it.'

I follow Ed to the lectern by the entrance where he gives our names. A moment later, the maître d', a man with the stereotypical slicked-back hair and pencil-thin moustache of a French waiter, leads us to a table by the window. I can see the dome of St Paul's Cathedral and the glitter of the city lights laid out before us.

'What a view,' I say.

'I second that.' Ed smiles at me and I blush.

'So how was your day?'

'Long and painful.' A waiter is hovering at Ed's shoulder. 'Red or white?' Ed asks me.

'Either.'

'We'll have a bottle of the Chablis.' Ed points at the menu. 'And can we get some bread to go with it?'

'I'm starving,' he says when the waiter's gone. 'I didn't even get the chance to leave the office at lunch today. Flat out. How was your day?'

'Good. I finished all our wrapping. I've put the stuff for

your family by your suitcase. I added some chocolates for your mum.'

'Thank you.' Ed takes my hand across the table. 'She's going to need the sugar to deal with the nephews.'

'I got an extra large box.'

'Superstar. Next year you can give it to her in person.'

I don't want to reignite that discussion. 'On another note, I think I might have found us a wedding venue.'

'Really?' Ed lets go of my hand to dive into the breadbasket.

'Okay, so it's in Surrey. I did look at London but everything seems to cost a fortune. I figured Surrey wasn't that far for people to come.' Ed looks a bit doubtful. 'It's this beautiful old stately home and they've got a chapel on site if we want. The grounds are gorgeous and you get the use of all the rooms in the hotel as part of the package.'

'I guess it depends on how much you reckon your dad's prepared to fork out,' Ed jokes.

He sees my face and winces. 'I'm sorry, baby. Bad joke. He might surprise you though.'

'Unlikely. You know he's always complaining about how much things cost in Dubai. Anyway, this place is surprisingly reasonable. I've made us an appointment to go and see it the second weekend in January.'

'You know January's going to be pretty busy for me at work.' Ed picks up the menu. 'I'm not sure I'll have that much time.'

'We can fit it around your work,' I know he's a workaholic but I shouldn't have to sell this. 'It'll only take a couple of hours.'

'Sure.' Ed starts flicking through the pages. 'But let's not become one of those couples who can't talk about anything but their wedding. I'm knackered. Shall we skip starters and go straight for mains?'

And he holds up his hand to order before I can answer.

9.54 p.m.

I wait until we get home to give Ed his Christmas present. I was going to do it at the restaurant, but he seemed distracted and I didn't want to spoil the moment. I don't like to blow my own trumpet but I'm sure he's going to love it. Ed's wallet was a gift from his dad before he died and it's falling to pieces. For Christmas, I got him an exact replica and had his initials embossed on the front. I can't wait to see his face. I wait until he's in the bathroom, then I lay the distinctive Smythsons blue box on his pillow and lounge on the bed next to it. In short shorts and a camisole, it's the best I can do seduction-wise on short notice. When he comes into the bedroom, wearing his pyjama bottoms, his face doesn't disappoint.

'What's this?' He comes to his side of the bed and picks it up.

'Open it and see.'

When he pulls the wallet out he can't stop stroking the leather, twisting it around and examining it at every angle.

'I noticed the one from your dad came from Smythson,' I explain. 'This should be an exact replica.'

'I don't know what to say.' Ed sounds almost choked. 'It's perfect. We'll have to get you a matching one.'

'You know I can't be trusted with something that nice. I lost my wallet twice last year,' I remind him. 'Why don't you switch all your stuff to it now? Or I can do it for you.'

I reach for his wallet but he moves it out of range.

'I'll do it in a minute. I need to thank you first.'

He starts kissing my neck, burying his nose in my hair. 'You smell so good.' He slips the strap of my vest off my shoulders and starts kissing my neck.

'Hey, what about my present?' I joke. But he dips his head lower.

'All good things come to those who wait.' He slips his fingers under my shorts, down into my knickers, pushing the flimsy cotton away. His breath is warm on my face as he whispers in my ear: 'I can stop if you want but . . .'

I pull him on top of me. I want to feel close to him.

'Who needs presents anyway?'

10.33 p.m.

'So do you want your present now?' Ed props himself up on his elbow. He seems to have cheered up since the restaurant.

'You mean that wasn't it?'

'Ha ha.' Ed gets up and goes over to the chair where his suit jacket is hanging. He fumbles in the breast pocket and pulls out a thin, white envelope. He hands it to me with a flourish. 'There you go.'

I look at the envelope. For our first Christmas together, he took me to Paris, but his current work schedule doesn't allow much time for romance. Last year he got me the same perfume as his secretary. I know not to get my hopes up. It's not his fault. I haven't been into Christmas since my mum died anyway. I slice open the envelope with my fingernail and two tickets fall out.

'*Les Mis*.' Ed beams. 'I remember you saying you've never seen it.'

'They're amazing.' I give him a huge smile. It's *Phantom of the Opera* that I've never seen but Ed looks so pleased with himself, I don't want to burst his bubble. 'I can't wait. We could make a real thing of it. Do dinner first and have champagne at the interval.'

'We can if you want.' Ed's expression suggests he'd rather do anything but. He's not into musicals. 'But I think you'd have more fun with a friend. You know I'm not really into musicals. I bet Izzy would love it.'

'Or Jules.' The childish part of my brain doesn't want to include Izzy in anything until she starts returning my calls.

'You don't have to decide now.' He yawns. 'Do you mind if we turn the light out? I'm shattered.'

'Don't you want to switch your wallet over?'

'I'll do it in the morning. I need to get some shut-eye.'

'I suppose you're going to need your strength to deal with those Wildlie nephews of yours.' I snuggle down, pleased with my *Game of Thrones* reference. While Ed's a huge fan, it's a bit violent for me.

'It's Wildlings, you dork.' Ed flicks out the lamp on his bedside table and pulls me to him. 'I wish you were coming with me. I'll miss you.'

'And I'll miss you.' I nestle against him. 'But think how perfect it will be to have our first Christmas together as a married couple next year.' I don't add that even with Izzy's froideur, the Waverlys' is a more enticing prospect than sleeping in Ed's old room while he bunks down with the nightmare nephews.

'I'm very lucky to have you.' Ed's lips brush my ear as he tries to find me in the dark. Then he rolls over, taking half the covers with him. I lie there, watching the shadows flicker across the ceiling. Normally I find the gap between the light turning out and sleep encourages destructive thoughts, but tonight I feel comforted. Ed's words have made up for his reluctance to talk about the wedding. Izzy says blokes are never interested in the details of a wedding anyway – all they want to do is turn up on the day. Even Rich didn't show much interest beyond the booze and the band. There's nothing to worry about. Ed will get to the wedding planning in his own time. And Izzy will be back to normal next time I see her. Nobody can stay angry at Christmas. Not even Izzy.

Nine

I'm sitting in my car outside Izzy's house like a stalker.
I woke up stupidly early and after I'd taken Missy for a
jog, I was left kicking my heels. I knew Ed wanted a lie-in
and I didn't want to ring and wake him up when he's been
working hard so I got in the car earlier than I needed to.
It's been so long since I was behind the wheel – Ed usually
prefers to take his Audi – that I completely overestimated
how short the drive would be.

It feels funny to be without him. This is the longest we've
been apart for months. I felt quite emotional when we said
goodbye on Sunday night. Ed did, too. I could tell from the
way he kept fluffing Missy's ears and checking and rechecking
he'd packed the boot properly. Maybe I should have agreed
to go to Leeds with him. This year, Christmas has started to
feel like something to be endured rather than enjoyed.

I check the clock on the dashboard. I'm twenty minutes early. Normally I'd have no qualms about barrelling up early but Izzy specifically said not to come before twelve. I glance around to see Missy staring at me reproachfully from the back seat.

I look up at the house. The shutters are down and there are no signs of life. Still too early, but I open the door anyway. I can't sit in the car forever. I put the bags of presents between my feet and wrap my coat around me. Even though the heater in my car's broken, the air outside is a good few degrees cooler. It's amazing how quiet the street is. I expect most people in this income bracket go away at this time of year – shopping in New York, ski chalets in Europe; that sort of thing – but it's quiet year round. The occasional dog walker might skirt their way up to either of the commons that this road is sandwiched between, but that's it. I guess that's part of the price tag. I never see anybody nipping out to buy the papers or grab a pint of milk. I suppose they all use Ocado. Northcote Road is far too full of artisan bakeries and boutiques for something as commonplace as groceries. The nearest Waitrose is back towards Clapham Junction. Which gives me an idea. I don't have to loiter outside Izzy's house like a spurned lover. I could do some window-shopping. I turn from the house and march back down the slope towards Northcote Road, tugging Missy behind me.

Some of the chichi boutiques have got their sale signs up already. I peer though the grates like a kid outside a sweet shop. It's probably all out of my price range. But there's a café across the street that looks like it might be open. I'm about to cross over to see if I can get a hot drink to warm me up when my phone rings. My dad. He's already tried to call twice but I went for a quick run when I woke up and missed them both.

'Hi, Dad.' I try to inject some warmth into my voice. I do love my dad but the distance between us isn't just geographical. We had a relatively normal relationship until my mum died. He spent the first few months afterwards in an extended state of shock, barely able to wash and dress himself. Rob and I did everything for him. Eventually he got himself together enough to attend some sort of grief support group. The next thing you know, he's 'met' one of the other grieving spouses. She had two young sons and he moved in with them and started playing happy families the minute I went to university. They call him 'Dad' now. The Dubai move came six months after that. I still haven't visited. I don't begrudge him his happiness but the time-line grates.

'Merry Christmas, Becky. And what are you doing with yourself today?'

Oh and he still calls me Becky, which I can't stand. I let it go. Correcting him will only prolong the call.

'Going to Izzy and Rich's. Same as usual.'

'Now that sounds grand. You must give them my best.' Dad's soft Irish burr is more pronounced on the phone. It makes me think of Christmases spent crammed around the kitchen table, the Pogues playing in the background and Mum laughing as Dad sang along. Back when we were a family.

'I will. What are you doing today?'

'Well Christmas is almost over here,' he chuckles. 'Judith and I have finished our lunch and we're about to go for a swim. The boys are sleeping off their hangovers. We'll be meeting friends by the pool and making sure we're back in time for the Queen's speech. And a little Jamesons to toast it with. Who knows what she'll have to say for herself this year?'

'Indeed.'

'Have you spoken to your brother?'

'Not yet.' I check my watch. Having been worried about being early, now I realize I am in danger of being late, which Izzy considers the height of rudeness. 'Look, Dad, I should probably—'

'I'd give him a call, Becky.' There's a roll of laughter in Dad's voice. 'If I'm not mistaken he's with a lady this year.'

'No way.' In spite of myself, I'm intrigued. Normally Rob goes away with a bunch of single mates at Christmas but this year he was cagey about it. Spending Christmas with someone is a big deal. 'Is he with her family?'

'I didn't get that impression, no. I think he's in the countryside somewhere. Give him a call.'

'I will. Look, Dad—'

'I know I should let you go. But I wanted to wish you a merry Christmas, Becky. Do give that fella of yours my best too. Judith and I are both very excited to hear what plans you'll be making for the wedding.'

'I'll let you know as soon as we have some. Merry Christmas, Dad.'

I hang up the phone and start walking quickly, dragging Missy behind me. The bag of presents I'm carrying knocks against my knees as I pick up the pace. By the time I reach the front gate, I'm practically running. My hair, which I spent ages pinning back, is plastered to my face and I'm out of breath. I fumble with the latch.

'Penny for 'em.' Rich appears on the front step and I jump out of my skin.

'God, you made me jump.'

'I seem to be making a habit of that.'

'Sorry, I didn't mean to sound so—'

'Don't worry about it.' He drops the cords of fairy lights in his hands, bounds down the steps and grabs my bags in one hand. 'Let me get these up the stairs for you.'

'Thanks. I won't get a ticket today, will I? Even parking inspectors take the day off on Christmas, right?'

Rich bends down to pat Missy with his free hand. 'You'll be fine. I don't like your chances with Izzy, though. Once she finds out you're not going to get stuck into the cooking sherry with her, you're going to be in big trouble.'

'What are you doing?' I look at the tangle of wires on the floor and try to ignore the warning.

'Fairy lights are out, bows are in, apparently.' He gestures at a stack of red velvet bows piled neatly next to the bay trees. 'I should have done it earlier but I got waylaid. Go right in. Izzy's in the kitchen and she's dying to see you. Thank God Missy can distract Tilly. She's been asking if she can open her presents since five a.m.'

'She's so sweet.' I pick up the presents and hurry down the hall, taking the steps to the basement two at a time. In the kitchen, Izzy's got the vintage Roberts radio I gave them as a wedding gift up loud and her back to me. Her hips are swaying as she slips a tray of sausage rolls into the oven and she's wearing a striped apron over her bright red Diane Von Furstenberg wrap dress. She looks like a stylish, modern Mrs Claus. The grey Jaeger jumper dress I'm wearing suddenly seems shapeless and dull by comparison, though I was pleased with it when I put it on this morning. I hover. I feel first-date nervous, which is ridiculous. This is my best friend. I take a step forward.

It's like Izzy can sense my presence. 'Bec, at last!' She unties the apron, tosses it on the breakfast bar and comes over to greet me with her arms outstretched. 'I don't know what I was thinking of saying twelve.' She hugs me tight. 'I've been missing you all morning. Let's get you a drink.'

Relief floods through my body. I feel light-headed, like I've been starved of oxygen. Then Missy's claws click down the stairs behind me.

Izzy snaps her smile shut. 'I see you've brought Missy.'

'I promise she won't be any trouble.' I pick up Missy's lead apologetically. Bringing her wasn't a problem last year.

'Will you give her feet a wipe? So that she doesn't track dirt across the floors.' Izzy turns her back and stomps back to the breakfast bar.

'Me do it.' Tilly appears from behind the Christmas tree. She runs over to the breakfast bar, leaving a trail of presents strewn in her wake. She grabs a drying-up cloth with a hand-painted Union Jack on it. 'I can use this.'

'That's for cleaning the things we eat from. And it's "I'll do it", not "me do it".' Izzy whips the drying-up cloth out of her hand. 'If you really want to, you can use kitchen towel. There's some on the table.'

'That should keep her busy.' Izzy watches Tilly unspool the entire roll. 'She's driving me mad. The only way to stop her sniffing round the presents is to read to her. If I have to open one more Julia Donaldson book today, I'll scream. Now, can I get you a drink?'

'You better let me know where to put these first.' I hold up the bags of presents, trying to delay the moment I have to tell Izzy I decided to drive. 'A few little bits. And the chocolates of course. They're at the top.'

'Just plonk the chocs where you can find a space.' Izzy sweeps a hand over the work surface.

The chocolates I bought are Charbonnel et Walker – the same brand I bought Ed's mum – and they cost an arm and a leg. Izzy doesn't look at them. 'You can shove the rest under the tree. We went a bit overboard this year, but there should be some space at the back.'

In addition to dwarfing the plastic number Ed and I stuffed into the corner of our sitting room, their tree is infinitely better decorated. I look for the types of squashed salt-dough shapes Rob and I used to bring home from school. There aren't any. I edge around the huge pile of presents heaped around the front and start unpacking my bags.

'Presents!' Tilly appears and starts fingering the packages as I unload them. 'Can I open them? I've been good.'

'I think you'll have to wait until Mummy says it's time.'

'Mummy says not before lunch.' Tilly's voice quivers at the injustice.

'Why don't you show me where I should put them instead? There's so many here already, I don't want to get it wrong.'

'Put them by mine part.' Tilly points towards the back and I crawl around, pine needles catching my sheer tights and laddering them as I go. Tilly touches a branch of tree straining under the weight of the ornaments adorning it.

'They wanted to be friends,' Tilly points proudly at a misshapen star, a bright blue Father Christmas and three bells, all of which clash with the rest of the tree's red and white colour scheme. My heart contracts with love for her.

'They look fab,' I say. 'You're such a big girl to do that all by yourself. Now, there's a bone for Missy in my handbag. Do you think you're grown-up enough to get it out and give it to her?'

I leave her burrowing in my bag and go over to the breakfast bar where Izzy's topping up two glasses of orange juice with a bottle of Moet. She holds out a plate of smoked salmon.

'Can I do anything to help?' I accept a glass and eye her warily. I've seen in the past how quickly Izzy's mood can flip and I'm not sure if I've been forgiven for Missy's presence yet.

'Not a thing. I've done all the veg, they need to go into the oven in a couple of hours.' Izzy seems to have recovered herself. 'The turkey is in already – Rich sorted it before you arrived. You know I hate dealing with the giblets. Why don't we sit down on the sofa and relax before Jenny and David arrive?'

She drops onto the sofa and pats the cushion next to her. I sit down.

'Did Ed get off safely?'

'He did, though it took him forever. There was an

accident on the M25 which caused about four hours of tailbacks.'

'Four hours? Ugh. That's why I'm glad we never travel at Christmas – unless we decide to go skiing, of course. I think Mum and Dad are mad going to New York. Though international's different – at least there's something worth waiting for at the end. How's he finding being back home?'

'His nephews are already driving him crazy. He told me he's counting the minutes till he gets back.'

'With three boys, I bet he is.' Izzy shudders. 'Though that's what Jenny had to put up with, of course.'

'I don't think Rich and his brothers were quite as feral as Ed's nephews. One of them draws on the walls.' I lean back into the sofa and start to relax. It feels like any other Christmas, even though Izzy's upped the dress code. A few Christmases ago, we spent most of the day in matching unicorn onesies. 'Thank you for having me, by the way.'

'Don't be silly. Christmas wouldn't be the same without you here.' As she rearranges the neckline of her dress, I spot a string of pearls I haven't seen before glowing against her skin.

'Christmas present?' I point.

'A total surprise.' Izzy purses her lips in mock-displeasure. 'Far too extravagant. I'd seen them in a shop a few months ago but I never thought Rich would remember. Lo and behold, there it was sitting on my pillow this morning when I got up. I told Rich he shouldn't be spending so much money on me but he wouldn't have it.' She's trying to sound disapproving but I can tell she's pleased.

'They're gorgeous.' As I reach out to finger the pearls, she flinches. There's a pink mark between her shoulder and her neck that looks sore. It's fresh. I'm surprised pearls would do that. When I open my mouth to tell her they're rubbing, she carries on talking about Ed.

'Tell me.' She inclines her head sympathetically. 'How was Ed when he got back from those client drinks the other night?'

'Pretty out of it, I think. Much as he tried to hide it.'

'What do you mean, hide it?'

'Well he spent most of the night on the sofa and he was in the shower before I got up, no doubt trying to wash the fumes off him. Was he pretty bad?'

'I was surprised by quite how candid he was being. But I left early. At one point I thought—'

Before she can finish, the sound of 'Jingle Bells' fills the room.

'What the hell?'

'It's our new Christmas doorbell.' Izzy grimaces. 'Rich put it on for Tilly this morning. She loves it. I don't.'

She stands up. 'That'll be Jenny and David. Can I get you a top-up before they come in and drink it all?'

'Wait, were you going to say something about Ed being a massive drunken reprobate?'

'Forget it.' Izzy picks a dog hair off the front of her dress. 'Too late.'

'Hello, girls,' Jenny bustles in with her arms full of brightly wrapped packages. 'David's got the cake. Now, where do these go? There's hardly any room under that tree!'

'Why don't you pop them down at the front to save you

crawling around looking for space?' Izzy goes over to the freezer and pulls out the ice tray in anticipation. 'What can I get you to drink? G&T?'

'I'd murder a Bloody Mary since it's Christmas.' Jenny grabs a triangle of smoked salmon from the tray and settles herself onto the sofa next to me. 'Tell me how the wedding plans are going. I see you've brought the dog with you. How gorgeous. Matilda must be thrilled. Matilda, where are you? Wait until you see what Granny's got for you.'

'One Bloody Mary extra Tabasco.' Izzy reappears in double-quick time. She must have had it pre-prepared. In the corner I can see Rich at their drinks cabinet, pulling out a bottle of Tallisker whisky for David. Izzy grabs the bottle of Moet from the marble work surface.

'Come on, Bec, you've hardly touched your mimosa.'

'What's a mimosa?' Jenny takes a sip of her Bloody Mary and nods approvingly.

'Champagne and orange juice.' Izzy holds the bottle near my glass, waiting for me to neck it.

'In my day, that was a Buck's Fizz.'

'They're pretty much the same thing,' I take a small sip, hoping to appease Izzy.

'A Buck's Fizz is two parts champagne to one part orange juice while a Mimosa is equal measures, so it's weaker.' Izzy butts me with the bottle. 'Which means there's no excuse for not drinking it more quickly. Come on. Jenny's nearly finished hers.'

'Actually, I'm driving.' The words creep out of the side of my mouth. I know I shouldn't be embarrassed but somehow

I feel like I'm spoiling the fun. Not that Izzy even drinks that much herself.

'You're what?' Izzy's eyebrows inch upwards while her forehead stays smooth. We've always said we'd never do Botox. Looking at the smooth plane of skin makes me wonder if she's reconsidered.

'Driving.' I try and inject a bit of 'nothing to see here' nonchalance into my tone. It works to some extent because Jenny picks up her glass and goes to check what the men are up to.

'But why?'

'There wasn't really another way to get over here.'

'Couldn't you have got a bus?' Izzy says the word 'bus' like it's dirtying her mouth. It's like the hours we used to spend gossiping on one to and from school belong to a different lifetime.

'They don't run on Christmas Day.'

'Couldn't you have got an Uber?'

'They don't take dogs.'

'Are you sure this isn't just some big elaborate excuse and really you're—'

'I'm not pregnant.' Sometimes how well I know the way her mind works scares me. 'I promise you'd be the first to know if there's ever any news on that front. Aside from Ed that is.'

Izzy opens her mouth again but I cut her off. 'I promise it's not a big deal. I can have a couple of glasses over the course of the day and not be over the limit. And don't forget we've got that run tomorrow.' I don't want to admit that's the main reason I'm driving. It's not as if I'll win but for once I'd like to be in the race.

'Oh yes, I'd completely forgotten.' She puts her own glass down. 'Perhaps I shouldn't drink either. I haven't run for weeks.'

I nod as though I didn't see her running trainers neatly paired in the hall, grass on the soles still wet.

'Why don't we both take it slowly then?'

Ten

It's gone four by the time Rich declares the turkey is ready. He and Izzy have had several whispered discussions in front of the oven about whether to serve Tilly something separate, culminating in Izzy defrosting an additional batch of homemade organic sausage rolls to keep Tilly going, half of which Tilly has wolfed down and half of which she's fed Missy. I hope neither of them is sick. By the time we sit down, Izzy's chignon is starting to unravel and Rich looks like he'd rather be anywhere but here. I pile my fork high with food. My new running regime means I'm starving all the time. I'm waiting for Izzy to take her first mouthful when Tilly starts jabbing my elbow with her cracker.

'Can we do the crackerjacks?' She's bouncing on her Stokke Trip Trapp high chair. 'Me pull yours.'

'Tilly, we need to wait until we've finished otherwise the streamers will go all over our food.' Izzy leans over from the other side to try to take the cracker. Tilly's hand tightens like a vice.

'I want to do it now. I haven't had any presents and I'm so hungry.' Tilly's three-year-old logic contradicts itself but her bottom lip is starting to quiver.

'There are plenty of presents under the tree. For when we finish our food.' Izzy presses her lips together.

'But I want a hat.'

Izzy opens her mouth and I know she's about to parrot her favourite 'I want never gets'. But Tilly finds an unlikely ally in David, who's been jabbing at his iPhone for the past half an hour and only put it down when Rich started carving.

'Surely the sooner we do the crackers the sooner we can actually eat,' he pipes up in a put-upon tone as if he's spent the morning on a starvation diet rather than thumbing through last week's Sunday supplements with a plate of mince pies at his elbow.

'Fine,' Izzy says in a voice that suggests it's not. 'Let's pull the crackers.'

Of course the crackers that Izzy's bought are far too sophisticated to contain anything like streamers. They're covered in stylish monochrome chevrons (to match Izzy's black and white place settings), and when they're pulled, they contain things like caviar spoons and crested thimbles. There are riddles instead of jokes and the hats, when we put them on, are subdued. Looking around the table, our expressions match them. Izzy won't put her hat on until she's redone her hair and David refuses to wear his at all. Discovering hers is too big and neither pink nor purple,

Tilly looks like she might kick off again until Rich distracts her with an extra roast potato. Christmas at the Waverlys' seemed so much more fun last year. It's hard to know whether it's them that have changed, or me. I take a gulp of the ration of wine I've allocated myself and decide not to consider it too closely.

Rich has barely taken his first mouthful when David asks him about work. Although he's not quite as successful as Izzy's dad (which you can tell kills him), Rich's dad is super driven. At school he was the kind of dad other parents dreaded lining up behind at parents' evenings because he interrogated the teachers and ran over time. Old age hasn't mellowed him.

'I heard from Steve Ogden that they're looking at setting up a new division at your shop,' David says. 'Would you be in line to run it?'

'It's a possibility.' Rich concentrates on cutting up his turkey.

'That's exciting,' Jenny pipes up, clearly determined to be cheerful. She was the only one who laughed at any of the cracker riddles and she's still wearing her hat. 'But let's not talk about work today. It's a time for family.'

'When will you know?' David acts as if she hasn't spoken. This is unusual. Normally the senior Waverlys are perfectly in unison. Today they seem slightly out of sync. Everybody does. 'Something like this could be a pivotal moment for you.'

Rich is practically mincing his turkey now. 'I'm not sure.' Anyone who knows Rich can tell from his tone that he doesn't want to talk about it. Jenny opens her mouth, presumably to steer the conversation away, but David ploughs on.

'Don't you think you should make it your business to find out? I know when your brother was making the Geneva move he was in on every conversation. You should be ahead of this if you want to stay in contention to head it up.'

Rich puts down his knife and fork and rests his elbows on the table. 'To be honest, I'm not sure I do want to be in contention.'

'Calm down.' Izzy puts a restraining hand on Rich's forearm, though he seems perfectly calm. Stressed. But calm.

'Excuse me?' David looks as if he's swallowed something unpalatable. It can't be the turkey. 'And what do you mean by that?'

'I'm already breaking my back for them. The way things are now, Tilly just about recognizes me. I manage to see my family on evenings and weekends and still carve out the tiniest modicum of time for myself. If I take on anything else, that won't be possible.'

'Time for yourself?' David's tone oozes disdain. 'That's very new age, if you don't mind me saying. In my time, men didn't worry about things like "time for yourself". We climbed the ladder as hard and as far as we could go.'

Rich shrugs as if he's not bothered by the implied slight on his masculinity but there's a vein throbbing in his forehead that gives him away. I look at Izzy, expecting her to intervene. But she's chopping up Tilly's carrots for her. David follows my gaze.

'And what do you make of this, Isabel?'

Izzy looks at Rich. 'If Rich feels department head isn't a good fit, I trust him.'

As defences go, it's muted. I wait for her to carry on, to point out how hard Rich works, how much he does for their family. But she simply pats Rich like he's a well-behaved pet and goes back to chopping Tilly's carrots. Hardly a ringing endorsement.

'Humph.' David settles back into his seat. He looks like he's got more to say but this time Jenny jumps in ahead of him. 'This turkey is absolutely delicious. Perfectly moist. And the potatoes. Sublime. Did you use goose fat?'

'Yes,' Rich says shortly.

'And the stuffing. Is it Heston?' Jenny's attempt at conversation peters out when Rich doesn't reply. For a few minutes, the clink of cutlery against china and wine glasses being refilled are the only sounds to break the awkward silence.

'Definitely the best turkey I've had all year.' I decide to have a stab at jollying things up. This could be my last Christmas lunch at the Waverlys'. I don't want it to go down in flames. 'If you ever decide banking's not for you, Rich, you can always chuck it in and become a chef.'

The silence I've tried to interrupt is swelling. I look around the table. My comment might have been inane but surely someone wants to grab hold of the conversational lifeline. David's gone such a deep shade of red he looks almost purple and Jenny's staring at her plate like Christmas has just been cancelled. Only Rich is smirking. I'm about to ask if I've said something wrong when Tilly knocks her beaker over. Milk cascades across the table and everyone jumps up. There's a flurry of activity as everyone hands their napkins to Izzy. I flick my eyes over her face. She's clutching the wad of napkins in her hands so tightly she's practically shredded them. From the way her lips are pressed into a thin line, I can tell that while Rich might have appreciated the joke, she did not.

Eleven

'Why don't you all sit down and relax while I clear this up?' Izzy is now attacking the spilt milk with a roll of kitchen towel, trying to stop it seeping into the floorboards. They're reclaimed wood, all the way from Denmark, and they don't handle stains well. 'Rich, you could flick the box on; see if there's a film on or something? There's a TV schedule in the *Radio Times*, I think.'

'Anna and Elsa?' Tilly pushes back her chair with a scrape. 'I want to watch Elsa and Anna.'

'I'm not sure everyone wants to watch *Frozen*, kiddo.' Rich ruffles Tilly's hair as he walks past. As everyone else files into the living room, I pick up the kitchen roll and hand another sheet to Izzy.

'I'm sorry I dropped such a clanger. I had no idea I was hitting such a sore spot for you.'

'It's not a sore spot for me.' Izzy's practically scouring the table. She looks over her shoulder. 'It's Rich's parents.

91

Careers are a touchy subject for them. Jenny's in bits, if you must know.'

I follow her gaze. Jenny's perched on the edge of the sofa next to Tilly, feigning interest in the screen. But her gaze keeps flicking over to David and Rich, who are sitting in a pair of armchairs, opposite each other. Neither of them is speaking.

'Why? Are they worried about you going back to work?'

'Don't be silly. It's nothing to do with me. It's Charlie. He's decided to quit his job and retrain as a teacher. Can you imagine? The son and heir. The golden child. They're beside themselves. Thank goodness baby boy Henry's making obscene amounts of money in Geneva or all the pressure would be on Rich, and you know how he'd take that.'

'Why are they so upset about Charlie?' I ask. 'It's not like he wants to become a pimp. In some circles, teaching is more respectable than being a lawyer.'

'There's no money in it though.' Izzy sniffs. 'I can't imagine how Laura feels.'

'I suppose.' I thought Charlie's wife had her own interior design company. 'What does that have to do with Rich?'

'It's obvious, isn't it?' Izzy looks over her shoulder again. 'Rich saying he doesn't want to go for a promotion has given them the jitters that it's going to happen all over again. And you make some crack about him being a chef. Honestly, it couldn't have been worse timed. David's been on at him for months about this new department. Offering to have a word or pull strings with someone on the board.

That sort of thing. Rich won't have a bar of it. Loses his temper every time David even mentions it.'

I think Izzy's overreacting but I'm not going to tell her that. 'David should be proud he wants to stand on his own two feet.'

Izzy ignores this. 'Anyway, that and Rich banging on about his book all the time has them both quaking in their boots. Jenny's wondering where it all went wrong . . .'

I glance over at Jenny again. The wrinkles around her eyes do seem more pronounced than when I last saw her.

'You're not worried he's going to chuck it in, are you?' I ask Izzy.

'Don't be silly,' she scoffs. 'Rich knows the score. He may harbour dreams of being the next JK Rowling but money is what makes the world go round. And with his expensive tastes . . .'

I don't like to point out it's Izzy that's dripping in jewellery and designer labels.

'JK Rowling? Is he writing a children's book?' I look back into the sitting room. Rich has abandoned his armchair and is now sprawled on the floor next to Tilly, singing along to the opening credits. 'I bet he'd be really good at that.'

Izzy shrugs. 'He could be writing the next *Fifty Shades of Grey* for all I know.'

'Gross. Aren't you curious?'

'Marginally. I better get this Christmas cake sorted out or we'll be here at New Year. Do you want to give me a hand getting the plates out?'

'I might give Ed a ring. His last few messages sound like he could use a breather.'

He actually sounded surprisingly spritely in his last message but I need an excuse.

'Give him my love.' Izzy tosses the wadded-up kitchen roll into the top of their Brabantia bin. 'And don't be long. I told Tilly we couldn't open any presents until we'd finished pudding. If we leave it much longer, she's going to go nuclear.'

I call Ed from the corridor but his phone goes straight to voicemail. His family has their Christmas meal in the evening so they've probably only just sat down. I pull up his last message – a picture of his whole family in matching red and green pajamas in front of the tree – and send him a jokey response suggesting it might be time to get dressed. I suggest we chat when he's finished eating then I kill a few minutes staring at the canvases on Izzy and Rich's walls. Izzy's dad made his money in art before he got into magazines and he's gifted Izzy some amazing pieces. I know I promised I wouldn't be long but with that atmosphere I'm not rushing to go back. I could call Rob but I suspect he won't thank me for interrupting his romantic Christmas and I don't need the aggro. I'll see him at the race tomorrow anyway. I'm toying with trying Ed one more time when the most terrible screech, like the sound of someone being killed, rips through the air. I thrust the phone into my pocket and practically run down the corridor, my heart pounding with every step. I fling open the door and see Tilly lying in the middle of the floor, kicking her legs in the air and sobbing at the top of her lungs. Rich is crouched next to her while Izzy slams plates in the kitchen. David's flicking through the papers, Jenny's eyes are glued to Tilly.

'Is everything okay?' I ask Izzy, but she bangs another plate in response.

'Tell me what's wrong, sweetheart.' Rich tries to put his arms around Tilly but she continues to wail. There are chunks of snot coming out of both nostrils and I can hear the phlegm rattling in her throat.

'You know what's wrong.' Izzy smacks a bowl onto the counter. 'She wants to open her presents and I've told her she has to wait until we've finished dessert.'

Tilly increases her volume. Her sobs are so loud she's almost choking.

'There you are, Bec,' Izzy says as if nothing's going on. 'How's Ed's Christmas going?'

'I think he's still eating. I'll try later.'

'Probably knee-deep in family politics.' Rich has to raise his voice to be heard over Tilly's shrieks. 'Look, why don't we get cracking on the Christmas cake and then we can do the presents. Mum, can I start you off with the first slice?'

But Jenny's gaze is fixed on Tilly.

'Jenny?' Izzy prompts.

'Isn't there some way to calm that child down? I'm worried she'll do herself a mischief.'

'Ignore her. She'll tire herself out soon.'

'If you say so, dear.' Jenny purses her lips. 'Having boys, I never had to deal with this sort of thing. And with Charlie and Laura's being that bit older . . .'

She looks at David and her voice trails off.

'What about if we let her open one present before pudding?' Rich suggests. 'Would you like that, Tills?'

Tilly stops mid-wail and starts nodding so hard it looks like her head might come off. 'Yay! Daddy's the best.'

'I said she had to wait.' Izzy's hand tightens around the cake knife she's holding. Tilly's face crumples and she buries her face in Rich's chest.

'I'm sure one present couldn't hurt, could it?' Jenny intervenes. 'What if it's just a little one? Granny's got you some ninny nonnies, Matilda. Would you like me to fetch one?'

I can't help smiling. 'Ninny nonny' is such a Jenny Waverly phrase.

'I want Auntie Bec's present.' Tilly jumps to her feet. 'The one in the box with the white ribbon.'

'Mummy hasn't said you can open anything yet.' Izzy's voice is tight.

'I don't mind.' I don't think my nerves can withstand another Tilly tantrum. 'I mean, only if it's okay with you.'

'Please, Mummy,' Tilly beseeches. 'I've been good.'

'Go on, Iz, you remember what it was like when you were little. Christmas Day seemed to go on forever.' Rich gets up and goes to Izzy. He stands behind her and starts massaging her shoulders. 'And she has been pretty good today.'

'I always let you boys open your things on Christmas morning,' Jenny gives an indulgent chuckle. 'We weren't nearly as strict as your generation.'

'Fine.' Izzy shrugs off Rich's hands and picks up her phone to capture the moment. 'I hope it's a small one. I want the B-I-K-E to be the first big thing she opens.'

The back of my throat knots.

'Maybe you should start with Granny's present, Tilly,' I

suggest. But she's already dragged the American Girl box out from behind the tree. It's nearly the same size as she is.

'Honestly the packaging these days,' Izzy huffs. 'It's such a waste.'

But nobody's listening. They're too busy watching Tilly tear the paper like she's trying to free something trapped inside.

'There is a card, Tilly. Look at that first,' Izzy prompts, but Tilly's beyond hearing. She's reached the layer with the American Girl logo on it.

'An American Girl,' she bellows. 'Like Amelie's. And it's got a dog!'

She starts clawing at the plastic casing surrounding the doll. 'I love it. I love it.'

'We need scissors or she's going to lose a finger,' Rich laughs.

'I think it's a hit,' Jenny comments. 'Clever of you to know exactly what she'd want.'

I smile weakly.

'Iz, where are the scissors?' Rich asks.

'In the top drawer of the island. Bec, can I have a quick word?' Izzy raps out the words like an order.

'Sure.' I feel a bit wobbly when I stand up. I recognize her tone from my schoolgirl transgressions. I remind myself we're not at school anymore.

'Outside.'

Before I can move, Tilly throws herself at me and wraps herself around my legs.

'This is the best present in the whole world. I love you, Auntie Bec.'

Izzy's eyes narrow into slits.

'Mummy, can I have the dog kennel for my birthday?' Tilly is clinging to my legs, unknowingly sealing my fate. 'And the grooming kit?'

'I'm going to need my legs back, Tills,' I croak.

'Let's get some scissors,' Rich says. 'That way we can get the rest of her stuff out.'

'And the dog.' Tilly releases me and rushes after Rich. Izzy yanks the doors open. She waits for me to walk through then steps out and shuts them hard behind her. I start shivering immediately. The temperature's dropped again. But it's still not as cold as the look on Izzy's face.

'What are you playing at, Bec? Those dolls cost a ridiculous amount of money.'

'They're not that much.' I trace a circle in the frost on the patio with my foot.

'They're at least a hundred. And that's before you get started on their ridiculous accessories. I know because I looked into getting one but I decided it was far too extravagant. From me. Her mother. What on earth are you doing spending that much money on her?'

'I wanted to get her something good. She means a lot to me.'

'She's three. You could have got her something nice from the pound shop. If it glitters, it's a hit. Or you could have bought her something nice to go with the bike we got her like I suggested. The bike that she's now going to think is a piece of crap next to that stupid doll.'

'I'm sorry. I was trying to pay you back.'

'If you want to pay us back, offer to babysit or something.

Don't throw money you haven't got around. And leave Tilly out of it.'

Something about the way she's pacing tells me this isn't about the money. 'I was trying to do something nice.'

'Bec, not even her godmother will spend that much on her. Laura probably won't even remember with what's going on.'

I flinch. Izzy bowed to family tradition and asked her sister-in-law to be Tilly's godmother. It still stings.

'You can take it back if you want. I've got the receipt.'

Izzy snorts and her breath comes out in a cloud in front of her – it reminds me of huddling over cigarettes together as schoolgirls. That seems like a long time ago now. 'And give Tilly ammunition for a lifetime of therapy? You saw how she was with it. You know we can't take it back.'

'I'll babysit for you guys then.' I grasp at the suggestion. 'Like you said. Anytime you want, call and I'll come. Any time of the day or night. You don't need to give me any notice. You can call me Mary Droppins.'

I'm hoping to make Izzy laugh but she barely manages a smile. 'You may live to regret that.'

'I won't. I want to make this up to you. I genuinely didn't mean to upset you.'

'Don't people always use the word genuine when they're being anything but?'

'Oh, Iz, please don't be like that. Look, I haven't got her anything for her birthday yet. Shall I leave it and this could be a joint thing. Would that make it better?'

'Just run any presents past me in the future. Or better yet, buy me a new carpet.'

I gulp. I knew she was still annoyed. I glanced into the sitting room when I came in earlier and my red wine stain glared back at me, like a bloodstain.

'You know Ed was serious about us replacing it.'

'Well I'm glad he's got time to be serious with all the fun he's having.'

'How do you mean?' I'm confused by the tangent. And Izzy's snide tone. Normally she's Ed's biggest fan.

'Here.' Izzy passes me her phone. The screen's open on Ed's Facebook page. I can't remember the last time I was on Facebook. And Ed rarely posts anything. But today he's been tagged in a flurry of photos. In the first he's standing in the street outside a pub in the middle of a massive group of people. He's got his arms around a blonde girl wearing a pair of reindeer ears and the skimpiest of strappy dresses, even though there's snow on the ground. The date says last night, which is weird. He didn't mention he was going out. In the next picture they're all sitting round a table piled with drinks, the lights of a slot machine blurring in the background. In the final picture everybody's disappeared except for two of his best mates, who are making kissy faces behind him. The blonde girl is sitting on his lap. Ed is wearing the reindeer ears.

'Looking cosy, isn't he?' Izzy's eyes are bright.

'You know that's his best friend Jonno's wife, right?' I thrust the phone back. 'She's like a sister to him.'

'And there I was thinking three's a crowd.' Izzy laughs. But there's an edge to it.

'What are you trying to say, Iz?'

'Nothing, hon.' But she has the same look that Missy gets when she's working out how to steal food from the table. Calculated.

'If there's something about Ed—'

'Don't worry, I wouldn't dare spoil the fairy tale.'

For the first time, it occurs to me she might be jealous. Ed and I are at the beginning of forging our lives together. Making exciting plans. She and Rich are halfway through. My eyes fall on the house behind us; Rich's doting parents framed in the expensive kitchen conversion. A flash of gold as Tilly runs back into the room, Rich's broad shoulders moving into shot behind her. I'm being ridiculous.

'Is it something else?' I persist. 'You've been acting funny with me all week. If I've done something to—'

'For goodness' sake, stop being so self-centred. Has it ever occurred to you that I might have other stuff going on? The world doesn't revolve around you, you know. I'm going inside. I suggest, when you've come off whatever paranoia trip you're on, you do the same.'

I watch her strut down the garden. Like a child who hasn't been paying attention in class, it dawns on me. Finally. Izzy enjoys making me feel bad. How has it taken me this long to notice the casual venom in all of her putdowns? My mind flashes back to the engagement party. The look of triumph on her face during Ed's speech, the exaggerated pity when she told me about the roses. When did our relationship hollow out? I tell myself it must be a recent thing. I don't want to face the thought that our entire friendship has been like this. I don't know how long I stand there, taking it in, but by the time I make my way back to the house, I can't stop my teeth chattering.

'All right?' Rich looks up as I pull the door shut behind me. He's helping Tilly lay all the American Girl outfits on the carpet. Izzy's sitting next to them, her long legs tucked beneath her. Behind them, Jenny's sitting on the sofa, squinting at the rules of a board game that's obviously just been unwrapped. The TV flickers in the background, sound on low. It's the perfect family tableau. I walk over to the dining table to pick up my things.

'I think I might make a move,' I say. 'Early start and all.'

'Don't be silly,' Jenny protests. 'You haven't had any cake.'

'I was about to crack open another bottle of wine,' Rich adds. 'One of that Merlot you like.'

'No, really.' I untangle my handbag from where its strap is caught on the chair. 'I should let you have some family time.'

'You're part of the family, silly girl,' Jenny says. 'Now come and sit down.'

Izzy's voice is noticeable in its absence.

'Honestly, I better go.' I click my fingers for Missy, who lumbers up. 'It's getting late.'

I wait to see if Izzy will say anything, but she opens *The Gruffalo* and starts reading to Tilly instead.

I slip Missy's leash on. I have to work to keep my voice level. 'Thank you all for having me. It's been so nice for me to spend it with you.'

'And us with you.' Jenny levers herself off the sofa and clasps me to her. 'I don't like to think of you going off into the night alone.'

'Are you all right to drive?' Rich comes over. 'You two weren't necking cheeky shots in the garden, were you?'

'Those days are gone.' I give my best impression of a smile. 'I'm fine. I should go.'

'David's just in the sitting room on the phone to Henry,' Jenny says. 'Will you wait and say goodbye?'

'I'll poke my head around on my way up.' I won't.

'Well at least we'll see you at the party on Saturday.' Jenny pats me on the shoulder and goes back to her place on the sofa.

'Tilly's party,' Rich prompts when I don't say anything.

I feel like two hands have reached into my chest and are slowly compressing my lungs.

'I'm four,' Tilly shouts out as if I didn't know. 'I'm having a bouncy castle. And a unicorn cake. And unicorns!'

'Petting zoo.' Rich winks at me, eyes twinkling. But I can't look at him.

'I didn't think it would be your sort of thing.' Izzy uncoils herself like a snake and stands up. 'Screaming kids hyped on sugar. You've had a lucky escape.'

I nod, as though I haven't been to all of Tilly's birthday parties. First to arrive; last to leave as it happens. I don't say it. But this feels like the end of something.

'Got it,' I manage and my voice sounds strangled, even to me.

'Oh and Bec?' There's a fleeting moment when I think Izzy might extend the invitation after all, say something nice to wash this whole mess away. Instead, she wrinkles her nose the way she's been doing to express distaste ever since we were teenagers. She used to practise it in the mirror. 'I think you'd better take those chocolates you brought home with you. They must have oxidized or something because they've gone off. You haven't had much luck with hostess gifts lately, have you?'

Twelve

Wednesday 26 December

9.47 a.m.

At first I think the pounding is in my head. Then the door-bell goes and I realize the noise is someone banging on the door, not the result of the bottle of wine I finished off as soon as I got home yesterday. I try to get up but my hip hits something hard. I fumble under the covers and pull out my phone. Did I call someone last night? Before I can check, the pounding starts again. I haul myself up and stumble down the stairs. Missy trails me to the door and I open it, praying I didn't drunken dial anyone embarrassing.

'Rough night?' Rob's rocking back and forth on the balls of his feet. He's wearing exercise shorts and a wind-breaker as if it's the middle of summer and he's got the kind of healthy glow that makes me feel like I've climbed out of an ashtray.

'What are you doing here?' I blink. Thank God the sky's

covered in clouds the colour of dirty snow. I don't think I could deal with sunlight today. I'm never drinking again.

'And a merry Christmas to you, too! After I got your messages, I thought I'd better swing by and make sure you hadn't topped yourself.'

'Did we talk last night?' I screw up my face.

'No, but you had a lengthy conversation with my answer machine. Some might even call it a rant.'

'Was it about Izzy?' I'm almost afraid to ask.

'Among other things. Now, are you going to let us in or what?'

'Us?' Squinting past Rob, I realize there's someone wearing a black Canada Goose parka and a beanie standing behind him. Is this Rob's girlfriend? He never introduces me to who he's dating. My eyelids are pasted together with sleep dust but there's something about her mass of curls that looks familiar. Suddenly, I'm very aware that I'm wearing a pair of Ed's boxer shorts and a t-shirt that came free with a magazine.

'Bec, I'd like to introduce you to Sydney Scott.'

Oh God. There's an A-list celebrity standing on my doorstep and I'm almost certain I didn't brush my teeth before I went to bed.

'It's a pleasure to meet you.' Her American accent is softer than it is on-screen and her voice sounds like honey. Her hand, when she holds it out, is soft and her nails are perfectly manicured. I shake it, then, as subtly as I can, slide my hand up to my mouth to check my breath. Rob catches me.

'Yup, you smell as bad as your dog,' he tells me cheerfully.

'Go and have a hot shower and I'll make you a smoothie. You need to get some fluids into you before you run this race.'

Ugh. With everything that happened, I'd almost forgotten about the 10K.

'Haven't we missed it?' I check my watch hopefully.

'You wish. It doesn't start till eleven – plenty of time to get you race ready.'

'I don't know if it's such a good idea.' All I want to do is crawl back under the covers.

'You're not wriggling out of it.' Rob ushers me down the hall. 'I left Soho Farmhouse at the crack of dawn for this. Now go and shower.'

I take my phone into the bathroom and check it while I peel off the clothes I slept in. It doesn't look as if I called anyone else last night. I imagine disturbing Ed at his mum's, trying to drunkenly tell him Izzy had accused him of sleeping with his friend's wife. At least I only called Rob. It could have been a lot worse. The hot water makes me feel human again. I turn my thoughts to the fact that Sydney Scott is currently standing in my kitchen. My best friend seems to hate me and my brother is dating an Oscar-winner. The world is going mad. I pull on an old pair of leggings and a sports bra and throw one of Ed's t-shirts over the top.

'So do you want me to tell you how to thrash Izzy at this race, or what?' Rob's leaning against the kitchen doorframe, smirking.

'What did I say last night?' I groan just as Sydney asks: 'Who is Izzy?'

I look at her properly for the first time. She's draped her

107

parka and beanie over the back of one of my wonky chairs. Now I can see her clearly, she's just as gorgeous as she is on-screen. All jutting cheekbones and pouty lips. Even in a loose black t-shirt and jogging bottoms her waist is the size of my inner thigh and she's got the sort of glow you can't get out of a bottle. She's the kind of girl that Izzy would hate. But the way she bends to crouch on the floor and pet Missy makes me warm to her.

'Who is Izzy?' I echo. 'Good question.'

'Don't get all metaphorical, Becster.' Rob hands me a glass of something green that smells like vomit. I cover my mouth with my hand.

'Stop being such a baby. Drink it. Izzy is Bec's best friend slash worst enemy. They've been friends since they were about twelve and it's taken Bec this long to work out Izzy spends half their friendship being a total cow to her.'

'Eleven.' I stare at the glass. Is that grass floating around the top? 'We met on the first day of senior school.' I think of my short hair scraped into a stubby ponytail held by a million hairgrips; the way the pleated skirt dwarfed me. How nervous I was. Until Izzy, hair loose and halfway down her back, skirt already two inches above the knee, crossed the hall and smiled. From then on we were inseparable. How different my life might have been if she'd smiled at someone else.

'So she's a frenemy.' Sydney gives Missy a final stroke and stands up. 'Drink it. It doesn't taste as bad as it looks and it really will make you feel better.'

'We're going through a bad patch at the moment.' I take a small sip of the shake. She's right. It's not as bad as I thought.

'Can you call two decades of emotional abuse a bad patch?'

'Rob!' Sometimes I wonder if Izzy did something worse than just dump Rob. Of course, now's not the time to ask.

'Look, I'm not getting involved. But I think not inviting you to Tilly's party is pretty low. She knows you're devoted to that kid. And it's not the first time she's done this sort of thing.'

'Can we change the subject?' I focus on the drink. 'I'm not up to dissecting my friendship with Izzy on an empty stomach.'

'Whatever. Just remember you don't owe her anything just because she hung around after Mum died.'

I look away. We never talk about that time. How the other kids at school treated us as though the death of a parent was contagious. Izzy was the only one who didn't melt away. Until you've lost a parent, you can't imagine how every tiny facet of your life changes at the same time as remaining painfully the same. How intensely that hurts. Even now, I've blocked the whole period out because it hurts to remember. I thought Rob had done the same.

'She was a good friend,' is all I can manage.

'Maybe. But what about when—'

'I said I didn't want to talk about it,' I snap.

'Why don't we talk about this interview you and I are going to do together instead?' Sydney interrupts smoothly.

'Oh my god, are you sure?' The offer displaces all other thoughts. My first full interview for the magazine (getting quotes from a *Coronation Street* star making a fitness video hardly counts) and it's with an Oscar-winner. I can't believe it. My hands are itching to text Jules but I suspect it would be a bit uncool to get my phone out right now.

Sydney nods. 'This one showed me some of your stuff. You may not have done a lot of interviews but what you write is good. I'd love to have you talk with me.'

'This is amazing.' I want to jump up and high-five someone. But acting like a crazed fangirl might make Sydney change her mind. I settle for noting the affectionate use of 'this one' and messaging Jules later.

'It was a hard sell with my press team. They think your demographic is a little older than where they wanted to pitch the movie but I talked them round. Tash, my head of press, will give you a call next week. Here, take my cell. If you key your number in, I can pass it on.'

'I don't know how to thank you.' I can't believe Sydney Scott's mobile phone is sitting in my palm. It feels heavier than normal. It's probably made of gold or something. I flip it over. The screensaver is a close-up of my brother's face. Surreal.

'Don't be silly, anything for Robbie,' Sydney is saying. 'And I get something out of it too. Now, can I use your bathroom?'

'It's the first door at the top of the stairs.' I can't believe Sydney Scott is going to use my bathroom. Of course we still haven't redecorated. I turn to Rob as soon as I hear the bathroom door squeak.

'Robbie?' I raise my eyebrows. 'My god, you guys *are* dating. Tell me everything.'

He blushes. I've never seen him blush before. 'I don't want to put a label on it, but we're seeing how it goes.'

110

I look at him objectively. I've always known he was good-looking from the fact he went out with Izzy and how giggly my friends used to get around him. And of course he's been stacked since he started personal training. But *Sydney Scott*?

'You know you can't tell anyone, right? Not even Izzy . . .'

Reality comes crashing back in.

'I doubt she'd even take the call.'

The aprons on the back of the kitchen door rustle as Sydney comes back in. It's not clear how much she's heard but she gives me a sympathetic look.

'You know I had a relationship a bit like the one you're describing when I was in college,' she says. 'Dionne was my roommate. We pledged the same sorority, took the same classes, had the same friends. But in our second year, I got into theatre. We were still close but she started organizing things and purposely not inviting me. I didn't think anything of it. I'd gotten cast in this big production and I was busy. Then this rumour went across campus that I was only doing so great because I was sleeping with the theatre director.' She stares into the distance. I watch her, transfixed. 'I never in a million years would have thought it came from her until some guy we both knew told me what she'd been saying. I wish I'd been brave enough to confront her but I wasn't as confident back then. I cut her out instead.' She smiles sadly. 'You harden up pretty quickly in this business. The show went well and I ended up getting an agent and not going back the next semester. But the whole experience taught me that sometimes the people around you have an agenda.'

'That's awful.'

Sydney half-smiles. 'It's more common than you'd think. Especially in Hollywood. Dionne tried to contact me before my first Academy Awards ceremony. She'd ended up getting kicked out of college and couldn't seem to hold down a job or pay her rent. I guess karma can be a bitch. Anyway, forget it. I have. But I'm thinking maybe your friend's jealous of you.'

'Izzy, jealous of me?' I laugh. 'Fat chance. She's got everything.'

'You'd be surprised.'

'She's going to be jealous today when you go flying past her on the final stretch.' Rob claps his hands. 'Speaking of which, we'd better go. I want to get you warmed up before the start.'

'You know I'm not going to beat her, don't you?'

'You will if you believe in yourself the way she does.'

I grab Missy's lead and say nothing. Maybe now is finally the time I start backing myself instead of Izzy. I've waited long enough.

Thirteen

Given that it's Boxing Day, I didn't expect a big turn-out. But apparently lots of people think this kind of self-flagellation passes for festive fun. Clapham Common is heaving. The race start is marked out with red and white balloons and banners and there must be over a hundred people milling around it. Rob has to go around the block twice to get a parking space. Missy's circling the boot like she's testing the perimeter by the time he finds somewhere. As he pulls in, I notice Sydney shift in her seat.

'You can switch your beanie for my cap if you're worried about being recognised?' Rob reaches around the back of his seat and pulls out a baseball cap with a faded Nike logo on the front. Sydney shakes her head.

'Would you guys mind if I passed? That crowd looks pretty big.'

'You sure you'll be okay in the car?' Rob looks concerned.

'I'll be fine.' Sydney gives a small smile. 'As long as you guys don't mind me missing the big moment.'

We shake our heads.

'I might see if I can grab coffee,' Sydney muses. 'Do you know anywhere local that'll have soy?'

'There's a place on the corner by Izzy's called Grind,' I volunteer. Then I realize Sydney won't have a clue where that is. I need to stop using her as a benchmark for everything. 'About halfway down the hill towards the junction. I'm pretty sure it has all that stuff. I don't know how busy it'll be though.'

'It sounds perfect.' She pulls her beanie down lower. 'I'm wearing my civvies so I should be okay as long as I keep moving. Perhaps I can take Missy with me?'

'That would be great,' I say. 'She's not brilliant with crowds either.'

'Sounds like a deal.' Sydney scratches the top of Missy's head. 'We'll keep each other company.'

'I don't mind staying,' I say half-seriously.

'Bec, you're doing this. You might even enjoy it.' Rob hands me a water bottle and jumps out of the car. 'Now, come on.'

'Let me check my phone.' I scroll through my messages to see if there's anything from Izzy. For all I know she might not even be coming. I don't know how I'd feel about that. Much as I don't want to admit it, I do want to beat her. Maybe that would even the score and we could go back to normal. But there's nothing except for a good-luck message from Ed. I shoot him a quick response and put my phone back in my bag.

114

'Stop dawdling.' Rob holds the car door open and stands there until I get out.

'You go, girl. You've got this.' Sydney smiles at me and reaches forward to squeeze Rob's hand. 'See you later, babe.'

'Babe?' I tease him as we walk off.

'Shut up,' Rob says. But I can see him grinning to himself.

I feel myself start to tense as we get closer. Every flash of blonde makes me flinch. But none of them are Izzy. Rob leads me over to a table where two ruddy-faced women in their mid-forties are handing out race numbers. As I point to my name on their list, my eyes scan it for Izzy's. I notice she hasn't been checked off yet. Maybe she's not coming and I can go home and curl up in bed with a hot chocolate and a bacon butty instead. I remind myself that I'm not running this race for Izzy, even though part of me knows I am. I'm pinning my race number to my t-shirt when Rob shouts, 'Rich, mate, over here', and I stab myself with a safety pin.

He points through the crowd and I see them. Izzy's wearing a pair of running shorts that barely cover her backside and her hair's pulled back in tight plaits. She looks like a Nordic Lara Croft. Catching sight of us, she stops to do her laces.

'You not running after all, mate?' Rob gestures at Rich's jeans and Barbour jacket as he and Tilly come up. Tilly looks cute as a button with huge pink earmuffs and her hair pulled back like Izzy's – the perfect fashion accessory.

'Nah. My running days are long gone. And we've got to cheer on Mummy and Auntie Bec. Show them your sign, Tills.'

Tilly holds up a ragged piece of paper with 'Go mummee go' daubed on it in multi-coloured letters. She flips it round. 'Yay Auntee Bec' is written on the other side.

'Sorry, mate, wasn't enough room for you on the sign.' Rich punches Rob on the arm and he laughs.

'What an amazing sign.' I bend down to give Tilly a hug. 'I love the colours.'

'They're teaching them to spell phonetically these days.' Izzy comes up behind me. I hold my breath, not sure how she's going to receive me. 'Nice to see you, Bec. Did you get home okay yesterday?'

She sounds like she's talking to a stranger.

'I did. Thanks again.' Part of me wants to lean forward and hug her, brush all the ill-feeling aside. But this time I can't.

'I'm just going to check the start.' Rob looks at his watch. 'I'll be back in two secs.'

Izzy waits until he's gone. 'Heard from Ed today?'

And this is why.

'A quick voicenote,' I say defensively. 'He's still in bed, sleeping off the Christmas excess. I don't blame him. I'll chat to him later.'

'As long as it's his own bed, eh?' Izzy laughs. Rich doesn't join in. My desire to beat her crystallizes.

'What?' She widens her eyes. 'I was only joking.'

'It was a bit harsh,' Rich says.

'Sorry.' Izzy throws the apology out without looking at me. She could be apologizing to Rich for all I know. 'Another sleepless night at the Waverlys'. I guess I have a tendency to be snippy without my eight hours.'

'Don't worry about it.' I pretend it doesn't matter. 'I think we're about to start in a minute. That guy with the megaphone is getting up on the podium.'

'Come on, Tills, let's go get a good spot,' Rich says. 'Good luck, guys. And, Iz, take it easy, especially if you get tired.'

'Over here, Bec,' Rob calls. 'I've found us a space.'

Izzy follows me as I work through the crowd to where Rob's standing a couple of rows back from the start line. He moves to the left to let me in and Izzy elbows her way into the space next to me.

'Remember what I told you.' Rob presses a handful of Jelly Babies into my hand and I shove them into the pocket of my running jacket.

'Talking tactics, are you?' Izzy leans in. 'It's only a fun run.'

But I notice her jaw is set as she bends down to touch her toes.

'I'm afraid we're going to be another few minutes while we sort out the timing chips,' the organizer calls out on the megaphone. 'I'm sorry for the delay.'

A groan goes up around us.

'What a faff.' Izzy starts jiggling on her feet. 'Especially in this weather. It's colder than New York here, you know. I spoke to Mum and Dad last night and they said it's mild there.'

'How are they?' I try to sound interested while keeping my eye on the man with the megaphone. I want to make a good start.

'Mum's fine, loving the shopping, but Dad sounded stressed. Mum's got him on this diet to lower his cholesterol so he can't eat any of the things he wants and I think he's been working the whole holiday.'

'Well he'll have good news coming his way shortly, won't he?' Rob nudges me as he hooks one foot behind the other and stretches. I do a double take. I thought we weren't supposed to be talking about Sydney Scott.

'What's this?' Izzy whips her head around like a Velociraptor.

'His ace reporter standing right here happens to have secured a world-class, exclusive interview with Sydney Scott.' Rob nudges me again.

'The actress?' Izzy frowns. 'Didn't she get an Oscar last year?'

'And the year before,' Rob adds.

'How did you pull that off?'

'She had a film she was promoting.' I flick my eyes towards Rob. I'm not sure how much I should be saying. 'It sort of fell into place.'

'Well that's wonderful.' I can see the corners of Izzy's mouth jerking but she can't quite make herself smile.

'Clear to start in two minutes,' the man with the megaphone cuts in. I can hear the relief in his voice. 'Last chance to warm up – or duck out.'

There's a ripple of laughter across the crowd. Now Izzy's face is creased with concern.

'It's really great news, hon,' she says. 'What a scoop. But will they let you do the interview?'

'What do you mean?'

'Well she's a big name, isn't she? Won't the editor want to do it?'

'I think because I brought the interview in, they'll let me do it.' I dig my nails into the palm of my hand. The idea that Tina might take the interview never occurred to me.

'I could have a word with my dad, if you like?'

'Don't bother,' Rob butts in. 'Bec's the one with the relationship with Sydney Scott. I imagine she'd stipulate that she wouldn't do the interview unless it's Bec asking the questions.'

'I'm sure it will be fine,' Izzy carries on in a tone that suggests the opposite. 'I remember my dad saying Tina sometimes likes to write up the bigger interviews herself. I just hope she doesn't take it off you.'

'I don't think she will,' I say, trying to sound more confident than I feel.

'Ten, nine, eight, seven . . .' Around us the crowd join in with the countdown, drowning out Izzy's response. Then the pop of the gun splits the air apart and everyone surges forward. Izzy sprints off. Runners are tearing past on either side but I keep my focus on the back of Rob's red windbreaker and don't try to keep up. He said most people burn themselves out in the first few kilometres and not to try to catch her until the end. I turn my music up and try to zone out. Before I know it I'm nearly at the end of the first lap and I'm almost enjoying myself. More importantly, I'm getting quicker rather than slower.

'You're doing really well.' Rob drops back briefly to talk to me. 'You're nearly halfway. Just keep going and remember you've got the Jelly Babies if you need a sugar hit. Don't worry about Izzy. She backs herself too much – she always slows down for the second half.'

I love that we've both abandoned any pretence that this race isn't about Izzy. I can't believe Rob's gone the extra mile to analyse all her previous race splits. It must be a personal trainer thing. The course is a double loop of Clapham Common, skirting its perimeter and circling the bandstand before crossing the road to round the swimming pond and the church on the other side. I don't see Izzy until I'm passing the church for the second time. The other runners have thinned out and I see her blonde plaits swinging about 200 metres ahead, up by the 9km sign. I watch her, envying the way her legs seem to kiss the ground as she lopes along. I, on the other hand, feel like each of mine weigh a tonne. I don't know if I'll ever catch her. I think of her face when she suggested Tina might write the interview for me – and all of the other things she's taken off me through the years – and I pick up my feet.

My lungs burn as I pass the 9km sign but I block the pain out. The gap between us is closing. If I keep going at this pace, I might catch her. Then she glances back. She gives no sign of having seen me but I'm near enough to see her press her teeth together before she turns back round and speeds up. If her legs looked long before, they seem endless now. I shove a handful of Rob's Jelly Babies into my mouth and stick with her, although I have to take two steps for every stride of hers. There's a rutted section, surrounded by long grass, before the course widens into the final stretch. As she turns onto it, I'm on her back. She turns again and I see her eyes narrow. She sticks her elbows out slightly, forcing me to drop back.

I feel a final pulse of energy as we come into the open.

The soles of my feet are burning but I keep thumping them down on the ground. I'm so close to Izzy that I can smell a faint whiff of Issey Miyake. I pull alongside her. Muscles I didn't know I had are stinging and I can feel the chafe of my sports bra against my ribcage. I don't care if it's red raw by the end; I have to keep going.

At the start of the finishing chute, I brush past her and see the look of surprise on her face. There's the shadow of something else there too: is it resentment? Respect? I never get to find out. I screw my face up and put everything into the final few metres. Rob's already at the finish line munching on a banana and giving me a thumbs-up. I find a final sprint. I can't help focusing on Rich towering above those around him with Tilly on his shoulders as I'm about to cross the line. The look on his face is my first clue something's wrong. His mouth is slack with shock. I wonder briefly whether it's that much of a surprise that I might beat Izzy – then Tilly's shout whips the thought from my mind. There are volunteers holding medals and a camera flashing in the corner. I turn away from them all. Instead, I look around. Halfway down the finishing chute, right at the point I overtook her, Izzy is lying on the ground, clutching her ankle.

Fourteen

12.10 p.m.

Two medics are huddled over Izzy by the time I get to her.
They've taken her trainers off and they're watching as she
points her right foot like a ballerina. Rich is standing beside
her, shielding Tilly.

'Oh my god, what happened?' I crouch next to Izzy. 'Did
you trip?'

'You can put your sock back on now, love.' The medic
who has been rotating her foot hands back her trainers.
He's got a thick white beard that's so fluffy it's on the tip
of my tongue to ask him if it's real or just for the occasion.
But with Izzy sprawled out like an injured footballer, now's
not the time. 'It's not sprained and I can't see any signs of
a tear. You may have bruised it. The best thing to do is to
ice it when you get home and stay off it for the rest of the
day. Use it as an opportunity to put your feet up.' Behind
the beard I can see his cheeks crease into a smile.

'It's really sore.' Izzy's face is scrunched in pain.

'If it's still giving you trouble in a few days, see your GP. But honestly, I don't anticipate you having any more problems. Here, let me help you up.' He puts out a meaty hand but Izzy shakes her head.

'I think I'll sit here until I'm feeling a bit stronger.'

The man tugs on his beard – which stays firmly in place – and glances back at the race. 'I'm afraid I am going to have to ask you to move. You're on the course and we've got other runners coming through.'

He holds his hand out again but she refuses.

'I can manage.' She puts her hands on the grass beside her to pull herself up and winces.

The medic hesitates. 'Look, the van will be around for another hour after the race finishes. If it's feeling sore when you're ready to leave, come back and see us.'

'Thank you,' I say. Izzy, trying to pull herself up from the ground, ignores him.

'Rich.' She snaps her fingers and he rushes forward. I take a few paces back so I'm not in the way.

'Bec,' I hear a small voice at my side. I look down to see Tilly's worried face staring up at me.

'Hey, Tills.'

'Is Mummy going to die?' Tilly's face crumples up.

'God, no.' I pull Tilly close. 'She's got a little ouchie on her foot, that's all. Why on earth would you think that?'

'Harry's daddy had an ouchie on his head and he died.'

'Well that's very sad for Harry but your mummy's going to be just fine. Look over there, can you see that squirrel?'

Tilly looks unconvinced.

'Shall we go and see if Mummy's feeling better?' I ask Tilly. 'I bet one of your magic hugs would really help.'

Tilly skips the few paces to where Izzy is standing, swathed in Rich's jumper and jacket, bracing herself between him and an oak tree. The way he's rubbing his hands together and digging his neck into his t-shirt makes me glad I'm wearing a jumper. When we get closer, Tilly stops skipping and jerks back.

'Oh, Tilly, don't be silly,' Rich says. 'Come and see Mummy.'

'I don't want to.' Tilly hides behind my legs.

'I promise you won't hurt me.' Izzy grimaces as she straightens up and holds out her arms. Tilly throws herself into them. Two seconds later she asks Rich:

'Can I have my ice-cream now?'

'There was a van over on the corner by the pond. I said she could have one when you finished.'

'We're going to have lunch in about …' Izzy goes to check her watch, then stops. 'Fine.'

'I'll make sure it's a small one. Can I get either of you anything?'

Izzy and I shake our heads and watch Tilly scamper away. Rich strides across the grass to catch up, the wind whipping at his t-shirt.

'What happened out there?' I ask.

'Like you don't know.'

'Did you catch your foot against one of those stumps sticking out of the grass? I only just managed to avoid them.' The sour look on Izzy's face makes me wonder why I'm even bothering. I'm like one of those old dogs that pine for the owner that beat them.

'You know it wasn't the logs that tripped me up.'

'Sorry?'

'You tripped me when you passed me.'

'What? You can't think I tripped you?'

'I don't think it. I know it, so pack in the innocent act. Nobody's around to see it.'

'Izzy, I have absolutely no idea what you're talking about. I would never want to hurt you.'

'Perhaps you did it subconsciously then. It's not like you haven't been waiting your whole life to trip me up.' She mutters the last words out of the corner of her mouth but I hear them. Like I'm supposed to.

'You're the one who had your elbows out.' My voice is louder than I realized. A couple of racers, clutching medals in one hand and bananas in the other, look over. Izzy pastes a smile on her face until they walk off. She hates a scene. I stand there, waiting for her to take it back. Instead, the grass squeaks as she adjusts her feet. 'I'm going to catch up with Rich before we both say things we regret.'

She flips her plaits over her shoulders and marches off without turning around. As she rounds the pond to catch up with Rich and Tilly, I notice her limp has disappeared.

12.35 p.m.

I sit under the tree for a few moments, feeling winded. I've spent years working hard not to mind how easily things come to Izzy. Or how much she takes them for granted. She has no idea what it's like to walk into a room behind her and see people's smiles dip. I never complain. But this is it. I'm done. I pull my jacket tighter around me. The sky is threatening rain. I want to go home. But Rob's chatting to the organizer over by the finish.

'You ran a good race,' the guy says as I come over.

'Thanks.' I expect he tells everyone that. 'Rob, are you about ready to make a move?'

'Don't forget to rate us on Facebook,' the organizer calls after us.

Rob waves a hand in acknowledgement. We start to walk back to the car. Aside from a few stragglers, the race is finished and the crowds have dispersed. Rob checks his phone to see if Sydney's called, then puts it away. 'He's right. You did run a good race. How come you're not wearing your medal?'

I look at the brass disc slapping against his chest.

'I forgot to collect one.'

'You forgot? Bec, the medal's the whole point of doing the race. Don't let anyone tell you it's for the satisfaction of competing.' He cuffs me on the top of the arm. 'Do you want to go back?'

'Never mind. I just want to go home.'

'Does this have something to do with Izzy's dramatic collapse?'

'You saw that? Why didn't you come over?'

'I thought she had enough of an entourage. What did she do, break a toenail?'

I laugh hollowly. 'If only.'

'What happened?'

'She accused me of tripping her.' I wait for Rob to have

the same horrified reaction as I did. He strokes his chin instead.

'Interesting.'

'Is that all you're going to say? You could try being a bit more supportive.'

'Look, I know you'd never trip her. Mainly because you're so mal-coordinated that you'd end up tripping yourself up in the process.' He stops smirking when he sees my face. 'Bec, *she* knows you'd never trip her. But I'm not surprised she said you did.'

'Why would she do that?'

'Duh. To save face. She needs to stay one step ahead of you, pardon the pun, to feel like she's worth anything.'

'That's crazy. She's the one with the perfect life.' Which she doesn't even appreciate.

'That she has to work like a Duracell bunny for. I saw her face when she found out you were interviewing Syd. She looked like she'd swallowed shit. She can't stand it when you do well. She was the same at school. She was never going to let you win that race. And if she wasn't going to win . . .'

'You think she tripped herself up deliberately?'

'I wouldn't put it past her. She's manipulative. You know that.'

I look at him. 'You're either a genius or a total nutter. How did you come up with all that stuff?'

'It helps when you're going out with an American. They have a lot of therapy.' Rob grins. 'And I've had front-row seats for the way you two are with each other for years.'

We've reached the edge of the common. I can see Rob's

Alfa Romeo glinting on the opposite side of the road. Missy's sprawled halfway across the passenger seat onto Sydney, who has Rob's cap pulled so low over her face she looks like a PI on a stakeout. It seems incongruous that my brother is dating her but somehow they fit together. Part of me envies the ease they have with each other. I wonder whether people think that about me and Ed. I hope so. Our relationship might not have the glossy novelty factor that theirs does, but we look out for each other. I glance at Rob to see if he's noticed Missy on the front seat but he's looking at me.

'Look out for yourself, Bec,' he says. 'You heard what Syd said about her roommate. These kinds of friendships can get nasty.'

'This is Izzy we're talking about,' I laugh. 'She's hardly going to stab me in an alleyway, is she?'

'I'm only saying—'

'I'll be fine.'

'Look, why don't you come have lunch with us?' Rob suggests. 'Syd knows this great vegan deli in Notting Hill. It'll be fun.'

'I never thought I'd hear you utter the words "vegan" and "fun" in the same sentence. I'll pass. My legs are killing me. I think I'll head home.'

'Need a lift?'

'You're the opposite direction. I'll be fine.'

I don't want to tell him that I want to be on my own.

'If you're sure.' Rob gives me a quick hug. 'Don't be a stranger.'

'You sound like Jenny.'

128

'Waverly?' Rob rolls his eyes. 'Give me strength.'

'There's nothing wrong with Jenny.'

'Bec, the whole lot of them are up their own arses. Rich used to be all right but even he's changed.'

'What do you mean? You seemed pretty pally with him earlier.' My voice goes up an octave. Rob's too busy waving at Sydney to notice.

'He's so pretentious these days. Did you see the Gucci loafers he was wearing today? On the common. And all this talk of writing the great novel? I bet he hasn't written a word. He probably sits in his office watching porn.'

'You're wrong. I bet it's really good.'

'Whatever you reckon.' Rob taps on the car window and Sydney lowers it. 'You must be baking in there with all these windows up. And what is that dog doing on the front seat?'

9.43 p.m.

I've eschewed the usual festive selection of *Only Fools and Horses* re-runs for back-to-back episodes of *CSI* when the doorbell rings. Do Jehovah's Witnesses work over Christmas? I'm not expecting anyone and I'm not in the mood for company. Given that Boxing Day is the calendar's official built-in post-Christmas hangover day, I've never expected much from it. But what with the race and Izzy, this one has been particularly rubbish. I consider not answering but it rings again and Missy clatters down the hallway and starts whining like she knows who it is. For a fleeting moment, as I hobble down the hall, I wonder if it's Ed. He didn't mention leaving early when I spoke to him after the race but I know his family is doing his head in. I didn't tell him what happened with Izzy but maybe he heard something in my voice and decided to surprise me. That would be one way to turn this mess of a day around. But when I pull the door open it's Izzy on the doorstep. And there are tears running down her face.

I'm so surprised I stand there with my mouth open. Izzy hasn't been here in months. 'Izzy, what's wrong?'

'Oh, Bec.' She launches herself at me, practically choking me as she flings her arms around my neck. 'I've come to say sorry.'

Izzy's tears have made her cheeks shine. When I cry my eyes shrivel up and my nose looks like somebody's punched it.

'For what?' When we've fought in the past, she's never come round to apologise in person before. In fact, I can't remember the last time she said she was sorry for anything.

She dabs at the corners of her eyes. 'I know you would never trip me intentionally. I must have got disorientated with all the pain. I wasn't thinking straight. Can we forget it ever happened?'

I hesitate. I was going to take a step back. Make myself a little bit less available. Until the toxic atmosphere cleared. But it's not as simple as that. Looking at Izzy is like looking through a kaleidoscope. Fragments of my childhood whirl around us. Her teaching me to smoke at a bus-stop when we were fourteen. The night she held my hair back when I vomited all over her parents' kitchen. The moment we laughed so hard during a *Friends* marathon that I snorted Diet Coke over the sofa. Her hair might be glossier and her face thinner but she's still the one I called the moment I lost my virginity. The guy had barely left the room before I picked up the phone. Then there's how she held me up after my mum died. We've got so much history that sometimes I wonder where Izzy stops and I begin.

'Go on. You'd better come in.'

'When did you get the same floors as us?' Izzy points at the floorboards as she tramps down the hall into our tiny sitting room.

'About six months ago.' I bite back the urge to point out half the houses in south London are carpeted in the same blonde wood as her place.

'They're everywhere these days.' Izzy never usually admits to being part of a crowd – she's on her best behaviour, too. 'Must be because they're wipe clean – you can get rid of the scene of the crime. Shall we have a glass of wine? It's been ages since we had a drink, the two of us. And it is Boxing Day.'

After the state of my head when I woke up, the last thing I feel like is a glass of wine. But I've never been able to resist Izzy when she wants something.

'I'll get a bottle.'

Izzy's running her hands across my bookshelf when I bring the wine in.

'Rich has got this, I think.' She plucks at the spine of a popular history book. 'I couldn't get into it at all.'

'It's Ed's.'

She drops the book.

'Look, I didn't mean what I said about Ed and that girl.'

'Forget it.' I put the glasses on the coffee table.

'I was trying to look out for you but when you spend as much time as I do with Tilly, you lose your filter about what's funny or not.'

Her mention of Tilly brings back what happened on Christmas Day. Despite her apology, she still hasn't invited me to Tilly's party. It seems so ridiculous that our friendship could unravel over something as insignificant as a kid's birthday party. But it's not just that. It's the roses; the engagement ring; any number of other tiny slights. Death by a thousand paper cuts. Izzy must sense she's said the wrong thing because she sits down then immediately jumps up again. 'Were you sitting here? Where do you want me?'

'Sit where you like.' I flop onto the chair with the wonky leg in the corner. We got it from Ed's granny's house after she got moved into sheltered accommodation. I've always hated it. But I don't want to sit on the sofa.

'Are you watching *CSI*?' Izzy gestures at the TV. 'I haven't seen it for ages.'

'I think it's a re-run. Look, Iz, don't take this the wrong way, but what are you doing here?'

'How do you mean?'

'Normally you're tucked up in bed by this time. It's not like you to make a midnight dash. Is everything okay?'

'Don't be silly. Everything's fine. And it's not that late.' Izzy takes a sip of wine then winces. The bottle's been open a few days. 'Rich's going for that promotion after all. He realized it made sense. David practically did a jig when he found out. Hardly even mentioned Henry once. Or Charlie.' She makes a fake sad face. 'Anyway, he's a shoo-in so that'll take the pressure off. And work's going pretty well for me. Ed probably said? I wasn't supposed to be starting until after the New Year but it turned out the position couldn't wait. It's been tough fitting it all in but I'm glad I went back. But it means we're going to be very busy this year. You must be the same. You've got the big interview coming up, haven't you?'

'In a couple of weeks.'

'You must be excited.'

'I am.'

'I'm really proud of you, you know.'

There's a silence I know she's expecting me to fill. Normally I'd tell her all about meeting Sydney, how smitten Rob seems. But there's a wedge between us. I look at her, perching on the edge of the sofa, acting like nothing's wrong. Trying to work out if she's genuine or not is exhausting. I turn back to the TV.

'I dread to think how many hours we've whittled away watching these shows together. I'm even getting Rich into them now. In fact, I might snuggle up in front of one of them when I get back tonight.' Izzy takes another sip of wine, this time without wincing. 'Something comforting about how predictable they are, isn't there?'

She settles back onto the sofa, making a point of avoiding the takeaway stain on the arm. The familiarity of the movement lights the touch-paper in me.

'Actually, I can't stand how same-y they are. Horatio gets shot but survives to save the day. Same old tired storyline every week. I don't know why we bother. Let's watch something else.'

I flick the channel without waiting for Izzy to reply. The rest of the evening passes in silence.

Fifteen

Monday 7 January

10.04 a.m.

'You've got to be kidding me.' I haven't seen Jules this excited since she found out Rihanna was launching a make-up line. Her eyebrows are in her fringe and she's about to tip a fifth spoon of sugar into her tea. 'And your brother is seriously dating her?'

'Keep your voice down.' The kitchenette might be empty but the doors out onto *Flare*'s office are wide open. 'He swore me to secrecy.'

'Imagine if they got married.' Jules takes on a faraway expression. 'Think of the wedding. And yours! Isn't she BFFs with Reese Witherspoon?'

'And Jennifer Garner, I think.' I say it as if I haven't been compiling a mental celebrity guest list ever since I saw them together. Ed can't see what the fuss is all about. He looked at me so blankly when I told him that for a moment

I wondered if he even knew who Sydney Scott was. I knew Jules was the right person to tell.

'Tina's going to go crazy for this. You should tell her at the beginning of the meeting. Don't even give her a chance to sit down.' Jules looks down at her mug and realizes it's coated in sugar. 'Rubbish. Hang on a tick, I'll make another.'

'Are you sure I shouldn't hold back? I don't want to seem too cocky. She might have loads of ideas for the issue already. Come on, are you nearly ready?'

'Bec, she could have ten thousand ideas and none of them are going to come close to Sydney Scott. She's one of the most famous people on the planet.'

'I guess you're right. When we were in Clapham the other day she could hardly even get out of the car in case she got spotted. Imagine. It must be a bit miserable if you think about it.'

'You didn't tell me you'd met her already.' Jules' eyes are goggling like a spaniel's. 'What's she like?'

Thinking about the weekend reminds me of Izzy. She's sent a couple of messages since the night she came over but the tone's always off. When she asked what we were doing for New Year's Eve, I feigned a headache and didn't tell Ed she'd asked because I knew he'd insist on going. We had prosecco and a Chinese takeaway in front of the television then went to bed at midnight so Ed could get up and cycle in the morning. He made me breakfast in bed when he got back – the perfect start to a new year. It might have been less glamorous than the drinks party Izzy was planning but at least it was real. I couldn't face having to pretend everything's fine.

'Is she all zen and health foody?' Jules puts the biscuits she's holding back in the cupboard.

'She's pretty normal.' I tuck Izzy out of my mind. 'Though she did get my brother to go to a vegan café, which is a first for someone who thinks eating chicken is going vegetarian. Hurry up, will you? I don't want to be late for the first meeting back.'

When we get out of the kitchen, the office is empty apart from a gaggle of work-experience girls stuffing clothes into plastic bags near the fashion cupboard. I feel a ribbon of tension. Everyone else must have gone in. I knew waiting for Jules to make a second cup was a mistake.

'Don't worry, the first ten minutes is always chat,' Jules reassures me when she catches the look on my face. 'And Tina was running late herself.' She struts down the corridor surprisingly quickly for somebody in vertiginous heels and I follow suit, trying not to worry.

'Sorry we're late,' She yanks the door open and plops into the seat next to Tina. I scurry into one of the empty chairs at the other end of the table. 'Kettle's on the blink.'

'Right, now that everyone's here, let's make a start.' Tina rolls the sleeves of her Stella McCartney silk shirt up and frowns around the room. 'I hope that you're all feeling invigorated and ready to get cracking on what promises to be a great year.'

There are a few groans. The first few days after New Year always have that horrible 'back to school' feeling. Usually I'd be joining in with the rest. Today I can't stop my leg jiggling under the table.

'Thank you for your enthusiasm, ladies.' When Tina smiles

she looks less like Anna Wintour, more like someone you could have a coffee with. 'Now if everyone's finished groaning, shall we get down to it?'

'Tina?' Jules raises her hand. I shake my head at her but she grins.

'Yes, Jules?'

'Sorry to interrupt before you kick off but I was chatting to Bec in the kitchen and I know she's got an amazing feature to pitch.'

Every head in the room turns to face me in a single movement. They're all so chic and polished in their designer knits and trendy alpine-wear. I remind myself I have a right to be here.

'Go on.'

'It might be nothing.' Great intro. I force my eyes from the table to meet Tina's. 'Over Christmas, I learned that the actress Sydney Scott is in London working on a new fantasy film. They're looking to secure her some press before the release and ... I've managed to get an interview with her.'

'On what terms?' Tina leans back in her chair, appraising me.

'How do you mean?'

'Is she doing press junkets for everyone or is this on an exclusive basis?'

'Oh. Well I'd have to check but I'm under the impression she'd only be talking to us. I mean –' I hurry to remember what Rob said '– she might be doing press junkets nearer the release, but at the moment, she's talking exclusively to us.'

'Isn't it fantastic?' Jules claps her hands like my own personal cheerleader.

'It's very impressive,' Tina agrees. 'Fenella, have a look

through the freelance roster, will you? I'd do it myself but I'm afraid the Terekovsky interview won't leave me the time. If Chrissy's free, she'll do a great job. Bec, do we have an idea of timeframe?'

This is what Izzy said would happen. But now I'm prepared. I dig my nails into my palm again, remembering the response Rob crafted. 'I think they're keen to get it done in the next couple of weeks. But there's a stipulation.'

'Isn't there always?'

'It's nothing major.' I press my nails in deeper. 'But because I'm the one with the relationship, they've said that they need me to be the one that does the interview. And to write it up,' I add for good measure.

'Indeed?' The corners of Tina's mouth twitch. 'And *they've* stipulated this, have they?'

'Yes.' I hold her gaze. Across the table, Jules flashes me a subtle thumbs up.

'How solid is the connection?' Tina looks like she's weighing something up.

'Rock solid.' Unless Rob and Sydney break up. I make a mental note to ring Rob up and tell him to be nice to her.

'Can you expand on that?'

'Er.' My mind pedals. How do I make my brother's shagging her sound professional? 'I have close links with someone who is a key member of her inner circle.'

Jules snorts into her mug of tea and I regret my choice of words. 'I've met Sydney already. We just have to firm up a date.'

'Fine.' Tina makes a note in her diary. 'Come back to me when you've got that date in writing. I can pencil it in for

April/May. Normally I wouldn't give this to someone at your level but you're a valuable member of the team, Bec, and your writing is strong. I'd like you to run your questions by me and if you have any concerns, I'm sure Fenella will be on hand to offer support. If this works out, it could make the cover.'

She widens her gaze to include the rest of the room.

'This should be a lesson to everybody around this table. Bec has shown real initiative here. I don't need to tell you that times are tough in publishing at the moment. Many of this company's magazines are losing market share and are facing closure. *Flare* is not under threat, but we're under great scrutiny.' She pauses. 'Now, did anyone bring any biscuits?'

7.13 p.m.

'And she said if it works out it could make the cover. Ed, you're not listening?'

'I am listening.' Ed lifts his head from the Jamie Oliver cookbook next to the hob. 'It's brilliant news. But I'm also checking to make sure you haven't forgotten any of the ingredients. You forgot to tell me to add the mushrooms last time.'

'It tasted fine without them.' I pout.

'It's a chicken and mushroom risotto.' Ed flicks a tea towel at me.

'Whatever. As long as Rob and Sydney don't break up, I'm golden. Think, if they carry on going out, we might have a Hollywood A-lister at our wedding.'

'Well when you put it like that, who needs risotto? I'm glad you're getting the recognition you deserve, though. You'll do a brilliant job of this interview and then, who knows? The sky's the limit.' He looks up and smiles at me then goes back to nursing his risotto.

'How was your first day back?'

'Not as exciting as yours. Lots of emails to catch up on; policies that need renewing. The usual. Oh and I've got a bit of bad news on the wedding front.'

I stiffen. 'What's wrong?'

'Nothing major, you don't have to look so worried.' He dips a spoon in to taste. 'One of the other partners has dropped out of next week's conference and I've been drafted in to go in his place. It means I won't be able to check out the venue you booked.'

'The viewing is on the Saturday.' I try not to show how disappointed I am. 'Couldn't you get back for it?'

'I wish. There's a whole lot of tedious team bonding on the Saturday. I'd much rather skip out but I need to be there. I don't mind if you want to go on your own. I'm not sure I'm much use anyway. I don't know what we should be looking for. It's a shame you can't ask Izzy but she'll be at the conference with me. She's speaking.'

'I'll see if I can reschedule.' This is by far the best venue my online trawling has turned up. I want to experience seeing it for the first time with Ed. Plus I can't imagine anything more tragic than turning up on my own. 'Why's he dropped out at the last minute? It's not very fair on you.'

Or me, I add silently.

'His wife's having a baby. I couldn't really say no under those circumstances, could I?'

'Where is the conference? If it's somewhere nice, perhaps we could make a weekend of it?'

'It's in Norwich.'

'Or maybe not.'

'At least you can comfort yourself by knowing I won't be having any fun.'

'Fair point.' I brighten. 'Perhaps I'll get cracking on making some dress appointments. I feel like everything else depends on setting a date though. Like I shouldn't do anything until we've got the venue. When do you think you'll next be free to check this one out?'

'Give it a couple of weeks. Work's going to be slammed until then and if we're going to try for the weekend away we talked about—'

'I'd rather get the wedding venue pinned down than go on holiday.' I try to keep my tone even. I know planning is traditionally the bride's domain but it would be nice if Ed showed more interest. This wedding is not going to plan itself and I can hardly rely on Izzy to help now.

'I'm sure we can do both. I saw Izzy today, by the way.'

'Oh?' I open the fridge and get out a bottle of wine.

'I didn't realize they'd invited us over for New Year's Eve?'

'Damn, can you pass me a cloth? I spilled a bit.'

'Here.' Ed leans over me and wipes the wine up. 'Yeah, I didn't realize we were invited to go over there for New Year's Eve.'

'It was a last-minute thing. Do you remember I had that headache? It seemed to make more sense to stay in.'

'I'm not fussed. We had a great time on our own. I'm just surprised you didn't mention it, that's all.'

'It must have slipped my mind. Watch out, the risotto's bubbling over.'

'It's fine.' Ed gives the rice an affectionate poke. Risotto is his pride and joy. 'I think we hurt her feelings a bit by not going. Sounds like they had a great night though. And luckily for you, I've found a way for you to make it up to her.'

'What's that?' I put my hand to my head. It's as if talking about my fictional migraine has made it appear.

'I told her you'd babysit for her during the conference.'

'You said what?'

'Not for the whole conference.' Ed chuckles at my reaction. 'I said you wouldn't mind filling in the gap between Tilly's pick-up from nursery and Rich getting home from work on the Thursday. She mentioned you'd offered to help out over Christmas and I said I thought you were free. Jenny's going to do the Friday. Izzy'll call over the next few days to get the details sorted.'

'Great.' I don't even try to muster up a smile.

'You don't sound that happy about it.'

'It's not that I'm not happy.' I bite my lip. I deliberately haven't told Ed what's been going on with Izzy as it sounds so petty, and now they're working together, I don't want to make things awkward. 'Things have been a bit strained between us lately.'

'How so?' Ed abandons the risotto and comes to stand next to me. 'Has she said something to upset you?'

Seeing the concern in his eyes makes my mind up. I don't want to drag him into all this.

'It's nothing. I went a bit overboard with Tilly's Christmas present and she was a bit pissed off. She didn't invite me to Tilly's birthday party either.' I don't mention the stuff at the engagement party. I don't want him to think I'm having a go at him.

'I'm sure she was trying to do you a favour. The last one was a bit of a scrum, wasn't it?'

'It would have been nice to be asked.'

'Well I'm sure she didn't mean any harm. She was singing your praises when I saw her. Saying what a lifesaver it was that you'd offered to babysit over Christmas. You're really helping her out by agreeing to do this.'

'I haven't exactly agreed—'

Ed's face closes down. 'I can get you out of it if that's what you really want.'

He turns back to the stove; his shoulders are stiff.

I bite back my annoyance. The last thing I want is to fight over this. I wrap my arms around him from behind.

'Of course I'll do it. I don't know why I'm making such a fuss.'

'I should have checked with you first. I assumed 'cos it was Izzy you'd be only too happy to step in.'

'Normally I would be . . .' I nestle into him. I don't want to be on the outs with him as well.

'I know she can come across as a bit overbearing but she's a good friend to you,' he reminds me. 'To both of us. She's got me out of a few holes already since we started back.'

'I just feel a bit funny around her at the moment.' In the past I've purposefully kept Ed out of any ups and downs with Izzy because I didn't want to put him in the middle.

Now I realize it doesn't matter that she knew him first — he's my fiancé. He should be on my side, not in the middle. 'There have been some things—'

'Why don't we have them over for dinner when I get back?' Ed's turned back to the food. 'I'll cook. I'm sure it'll have blown over by then. Everybody's a bit busy and stressed at the moment. We just need to sit down together.' Ed kisses the top of my head and hands me the wine glasses. 'Why don't you take the plates and glasses through?'

I take everything across the hall to the sitting room, wishing I shared his optimism. What Ed doesn't realize is that it's not about whether or not this row will blow over or how busy Izzy is. It's about whether or not Izzy and I have ever had a friendship at all.

Sixteen

Despite Izzy's five reminder texts, I'm the last to arrive at nursery pick-up. Tasha, Sydney's press agent, rings as I'm closing down my desktop, wanting to talk interview details. I rush the call and run all the way from the station to the nursery but I arrive, red-faced and panting, at least ten minutes after everyone else.

'I'm so sorry,' I say to the girl on the door. 'I came as quickly as I could.'

The girl, who looks about seventeen, frowns. 'At Oak Tree our day runs from 7.30 to 6 p.m. We ask our parents to be considerate of those hours. Any late pick-ups do incur an additional fee.'

'I am sorry ...' I peer at her nametag. 'Kayleigh.' Normally I instinctively kowtow to authority figures but the backless rabbit slippers she's wearing on her feet make it hard to take her seriously. And there are at least half a dozen mothers still shepherding their children into black four-by-fours outside. The street looks like a presidential cavalcade. 'I'm picking up someone else's child and I wasn't quite sure how long the journey would take.'

'Who are you here to pick up?'

'Matilda Waverly.'

Kayleigh visibly starts to thaw. 'On this occasion, I think we can make an exception. Mum did explain a few months ago that she'd be going back to work so we expected a few teething problems. We thought we might see a little more of Dad instead though. What's your name?'

Much as I'd like to point out that Izzy and Rich aren't Kayleigh's parents, I keep my face neutral. 'Rebecca Maloney. I should be on her list.'

'One moment.' She closes the door in my face. I try to peer in after her but the glass door is frosted and emblazoned with the nursery's name and a pretentious-looking crest. I can't see a thing. When she comes back, she's holding a clipboard and wearing a disappointed expression. She cracks the door an inch.

'I'm afraid your name isn't on the list.'

'What? I've picked her up loads of times and there hasn't been a problem. Perhaps I'm there under Bec? That's what I generally go by.'

'There's no Maloney here at all.'

'Could it be misspelt?'

Kayleigh bristles at the implied criticism. 'I'm afraid the only two names I have down for Tilly are Jenny Waverly and Glenda Maxwell-Martin.'

I grit my teeth. I was there when Izzy filled that form out just before Tilly started nursery. I can't believe she's been petty enough to change it. This is the last time I do her a favour. 'Well, *Mum's* on a conference so she asked me to pick Tilly up. I can show you the messages if you need.'

'That won't be necessary.' The woman holds up the phone in her hand. 'We'll give Mum a call.'

Ed never answers his phone at these conferences so I doubt Izzy will. 'You might be better off trying *Dad*.'

'I'm trying Mum now.' Kayleigh holds the phone to her ear and turns away. After a couple of minutes, she hangs up, refers to the clipboard and taps in another number. She holds the phone out so we can both hear.

'Hello.' Even through the tinniness of the receiver, I recognize Rich's deep baritone. He'll sort this out.

'Mr Waverly?' It's as if Kayleigh's swallowed helium. 'I'm sorry to bother you at work but I've got a Rebecca Maloney here to pick up Tilly. Only she's not on the list. Can I release Tilly into her care?'

'You most certainly can.' I can hear Rich chuckling. 'She should be top of the list. Please could you give her my profuse apologies and tell her I'm finishing up here in the next half an hour. I won't be too long.'

Kayleigh hangs up, looking considerably friendlier than she did when I arrived. 'I'm happy to say we can release her to you. And Dad says—'

'I heard.'

'I'll call upstairs and get somebody to bring Tilly down. I'll need to see some ID first, though. It's nursery procedure.'

Only when I've dug around in my wallet for my driving licence does she let me in. I guess you expect them to be this security conscious with the fees that Izzy and Rich pay. I nearly choked when Izzy told me; a year of nursery, five days a week, is almost equivalent to my annual salary. Before tax.

The foyer's painted the colour of custard and plastered in framed artwork. I'm scanning it, trying to find something of Tilly's, when she appears at the double doors on the other side of the foyer. She's togged up in a coat so padded it looks like a mattress and she's holding a picture slick with wet paint. She runs over as soon as she sees me and throws her arms around me.

'Hey, Tills.' I try not to wince as the painting connects with my favourite indigo jeans. I need some new ones anyway. 'What have you painted?'

'Spring.' Tilly says it like it's the most obvious thing in the world.

'Oh.' I look again at the picture, which seems to consist of little more than green swirls of paint. 'That's excellent. Are these leaves?'

'It's the inside of a seed.'

'Of course it is.' Fearing I'm at risk of being intellectually outclassed by a four year old, I nod my thanks at Kayleigh and open the door. 'Shall we head for the hills? What do you want for tea?'

Tilly prattles on about her day all the way home but she doesn't answer the question. I probably shouldn't have asked. Izzy's fairly militant about what Tilly eats. I'm sure there will be a veritable smorgasbord of healthy options available. When it comes to cooking, I need all the help I can get.

What I'm not expecting when I open the front door is so many Post-its stuck to the walls it looks like the house has been engulfed in a snowstorm. *Beware the yellow snow.* I finger the closest one, tacked next to the alarm. Instead of telling me something useful like the code, it reminds me to wipe my feet and leave my shoes on the rack. Down the hall there's one advising us to 'eat your snacks downstairs'. There's more lining the stairs but I don't bother to read them.

The kitchen is worse. I can't even open the biscuit cupboard without being reminded to 'eat fruit first'. It's as if Izzy thinks I'm the same age as Tilly. I resist the urge to rip them down and set Tilly up on the sofa in front of CBeebies even though the Post-it next to the TV dictates 'no screen time'. This one's underlined. I put the kettle on, making sure to fill it to the brim as instructed, then I pick up the laminated piece of paper headed 'Instructions' lying on the breakfast bar.

According to the sheet, I should have fed Tilly by 6.15 at the latest so that I can do 'bath and bed' on time. It doesn't say what she should be eating or what will happen if I'm five minutes late. Heaven forbid Tilly miss out on her beauty sleep when she needs to be as pretty as Mama. I think of Glenda's tight face and unnaturally plumped cheeks and wonder if Izzy will feel the same competition with Tilly that Glenda displays towards her. Maybe that's what drives her relentless search for perfection. If I wasn't feeling so put upon, I might be able to eke out some sympathy for her.

Instead I open the freezer, feeling harassed. Given that it's almost half past six, I'll be pushing it to hit bath and bed on time but if I bung some fish fingers and chips in the oven I should just make it. Aren't fish fingers kiddy crack? Izzy must have some knocking around for playdates. I dig around in the freezer but it's full of Tupperware containers, labelled things like 'béchamel' and 'stock'. Not a fish finger in sight. I try the fridge instead. There's a plate covered in tinfoil with Tilly's name and 'heat in oven not micro!!' printed on it. I can almost see the condescension poking through her neat lettering. I nudge the tinfoil back to see salmon, rice and what looks like mung beans.

'Right, Tills. Will you go and wash your hands? I'm going to heat up some salmon for your tea.'

'I don't want salmon.' Tilly throws herself on the floor.

'But it's delicious. And it'll be ready in two ticks.'

'I hate salmon. It's all mushy.'

'Mummy made it specially. Think how happy she'll be when you've eaten it.'

'Please don't make me.' Tilly's eyes start to go glassy. 'I had it before. It's so yucky.'

I hesitate. I don't want a repeat of Tilly's Christmas Day meltdown. I also feel sorry for her. When Izzy and I were young, everything we ate was covered in bright orange batter and came out of a packet.

'Tell you what. Why don't we order a pizza as a treat?'

Tilly's eyes go as round as a pizza. 'Really?'

'Yes. But let's make it our secret.' Aware that my words are those of a child abuser, I rush on. 'Mummy and Daddy would much rather hear about what you did at nursery than what you got up to with me.'

'You sound like Daddy when Mummy goes for a run and he lets me watch his iPad.' Tilly giggles. 'And do you know what?'

'Tell me.' I'm already scrolling through Deliveroo options but I pause. My interest is piqued. What other secrets might Rich be keeping from Izzy?

'Sometimes he gives me *chocolate*!' Tilly collapses in hysterics.

'Let's get this pizza ordered then. Shall we have some doughballs too?'

8.13 p.m.

Tilly's in bed by the time Rich gets home. The high ceilings down here make for great acoustics so I hear the rustle as he takes his coat off, followed by what sounds like paper ripping and a scrunch of something hitting the wastepaper basket. I shove the pizza box under the sofa. The process is repeated for several minutes before his feet hit the stairs. I guess he isn't a fan of the Post-its either.

'Bec, I'm so sorry for the mix-up at the nursery.' Rich rubs his forehead then sweeps his hands through his hair as he comes over. 'What a nightmare. Of course you were on the list but a couple of months ago Glenda kicked off about not being included and Iz had to change it. Predictably she hasn't been near the place since.'

'These things happen.' I stand up and reach for my bag, wondering whether I should try and sneak the pizza box out now or leave it for the cleaner to find in the morning.

'How did Tilly settle?'

'She went down really well.' I gesture at the monitor on the table. 'I think she was tired.'

'You're not going straightaway, are you? Say you'll stay and have a drink.'

'Well . . . maybe a small one.' Being so irritated with Izzy seems to have made me feel less edgy around him.

'Thank God. I've been staring at screens all day. Really, you're carrying out a mission of mercy.'

'Well when you put it like that, maybe you can make it a medium.' I settle back on the sofa. I'll stay for a quick one. Rich and I haven't hung out on our own since we were teenagers. We haven't been allowed. I watch him open their state-of-the-art wine fridge and pull out what looks like an expensive Shiraz.

'There's an open Sauv Blanc in your actual fridge,' I protest.

'I know you prefer red.' Rich's thighs tense as he puts the bottle between his legs and pulls the cork. 'Here you go. Now, if we leave that to breathe for a few minutes, it should be good to go. God, I sound like a pretentious twat, don't I?'

I push Rob's comments to the back of my mind. 'No, you don't.'

'Do you remember the days when we used to drink anything as long as it was wet?' Rich undoes his shoelaces, takes off his shoes and throws himself into the armchair opposite me. 'In fact, screw that. Let's drink it now. It's Penfolds. It's going to taste good whether we drink it now or leave it open all night.'

He grabs the bottle and fills the two glasses to the brim.

'Cheers.'

'Cheers.'

'So how are you, Bec?' Rich takes a slug then puts the glass on the table and steeples his hands together.

'You look like your dad when you do that.' I regret it as soon as I say it.

'You sure know how to bring a man down.' All the warmth disappears from Rich's voice.

'Sorry. I didn't mean to—'

'I guess you heard I'm going for the promotion after all?' His voice sounds harder than usual.

'Izzy mentioned it. How do you feel?'

'Like I want to get hammered.' He takes another gulp of his wine. 'Cheers again.'

'Do you want to talk about it?' I take a smaller sip to be sociable.

'I'd much rather talk about you. How are the wedding plans going? Izzy's hardly said a word.'

'I haven't done as much as I'd planned to.' I gloss over Izzy's lack of involvement. It's nice to talk to someone who's interested. 'Looked at a few dresses online, that kind of thing. But nothing major. We were going to look at a wedding venue this weekend but now Ed's at the conference and . . . I didn't fancy going on my own.'

'I'll come, if you like?'

'What?' I allow myself the fleeting image of turning up with Rich on my arm. A taste of how it would feel to be Izzy for the day. I shake the idea away before it takes root. I can't go to a wedding venue with Rich Waverly. 'You'd be bored out of your skull.'

'Don't underestimate what I'd do for free champagne. You know most venues give it to you, right? It's one of the best bits. The only problem is, people might think I'm the groom.'

We take matching gulps of wine. I almost choke on mine.

'Do you want to grab something to eat? I'm starving.'

My mind returns to the remains of the pizza currently congealing under our feet. 'I'm all right, thanks. I think Izzy left some salmon in the fridge. She mentioned it on a—'

'Post-it note? I saw. In amongst telling me not to burn the house down and reminding me to breathe at regular intervals. I better take the rest of them down before Mum arrives and spits the dummy. I don't really fancy salmon though.'

'There's a tonne of stuff in the freezer.'

'Yeah, Izzy stocked me up for a nuclear winter. Anyway, what do you fancy? Anything you like. On me.'

'I'm not really hungry.'

'Sure I can't tempt you to something like a ... pizza?'

He nudges the corner of the box out from under the sofa with his toe and creases up.

'How long have you known?' I cringe.

'Bec, the place reeks of pepperoni. I could smell it as soon as I came in. Plus I know you're a pizza demon. Is there any left?'

I pull the box out and flip the lid. 'Two slices.'

'One each?'

'Nah, you're all right.'

'Don't make a man eat alone.'

'Honestly, I'm stuffed. Any more pizza and I think I'll burst out of these jeans.'

'Don't be like that.'

'Like what?'

'You're supposed to be one of the normal ones. The one I can sit and have pizza and a beer with without you getting all paranoid and girlie about it.'

'That's me, always one of the lads.' I finish my wine then refill it. 'Shall we see what's on the box?'

Rich picks up the handful of the remote controls on the coffee table and points them haphazardly at the flatscreen mounted on the wall. 'Any preferences?'

'Something unchallenging.'

'Right you are.' He flicks channels, stopping intermittently to check if there's anything that grabs me.

'How many channels do you have anyway?'

'Too many. Netflix, Sky, Amazon Prime. Anything to drown out the silence.' He settles on the rerun of a 90s quiz show. 'Can I interest you in some vintage *Catchphrase*?'

'My mum used to love this. We watched it every Saturday night. It was on before *Baywatch*, do you remember?'

'*Gladiators* was before *Baywatch*. *Catchphrase* was before that. Ah, the glory of a misspent youth.'

We grin at each other, complicit, as the sound of the contestants' buzzers pipes out from the television.

'Any progress on the great novel?' I ask companionably as one episode rolls into another.

'I didn't really have a chance to work on it over Christmas. I'm hoping it'll pick up now the holiday is over. Once I start the new gig, I've got no chance. If I put in the hard yards this weekend, I might get it done.' He tops up my already full glass so the wine nearly slops out of the top. 'My dad is probably weeping at the very prospect.'

'I bet he'd be proud if he did read it.'

'I don't think being proud of me is in his range of emotions.'

Rich is trying to smile but the vein in his temple is pulsing the way it did at Christmas. When he sees me looking, he takes a swig of his wine to cover it. I follow suit, embarrassed to have been caught watching him.

'It's fine,' he says, but his voice burns with resentment. 'I know he loves me. He just wishes I was someone else.'

I always thought that Rich had won the parental lottery. I want to tell him that he can confide in me, that I'll always listen. But it's not my place. I opt for jokey instead.

'Families – who'd have 'em? At least your dad is actually in the country. Although maybe that's not such a good thing.' I knock my glass against his. 'Forget him. You've almost finished writing a novel, Rich. How many people actually do that? It's major.'

'Only the first draft. Apparently that's when the work really begins.'

'Most people don't even get that far. You should celebrate.'

'Speaking of which . . .' Rich picks the wine bottle off the floor. I can hear the dregs rattling at the bottom when he shakes it. 'Shall I open another?'

'I dunno. It's getting late.'

'Come on, live a little. We don't have to finish it.'

I've never been able to say no to Rich. Perhaps I'm not that different to Izzy after all. 'Fine. But don't let me have more than one.'

The door to the wine fridge makes a smooching sound as he tries to open it. I dig my back into the sofa. I can feel the alcohol gliding through my veins, loosening my muscles. Rich sloshes wine into both glasses and flops down on the sofa next to me. *Catchphrase* has been replaced by some random Japanese game show where the contestants seem to be attempting to kill each other. We reach to turn it off at the same time. I let my hand fall back. I'm trying to remember the last time I felt this comfortable when he asks me, 'Have you ever thought about writing a book?'

'Me? God, no. I don't have the patience. Or the talent.'

'Don't put yourself down. You're insanely talented. Even the stuff you used to write for the school magazine was on a different planet to the rest of us. I was going to ask you to cast your eye over my stuff, once I'd plucked up the courage.'

'You want me to read it?' I take another sip, absorbing the compliment.

'Why's that such a big shock?'

'Izzy says you won't let anyone read it. She says even she doesn't know what it's about.'

'That's because it's not finished. When it is, I'll need all the help I can get.'

'Go on then, tell me what it's about.'

'This and that.' He waves his hand vaguely and his wedding ring clinks against the rim of his glass.

'Sounds gripping.'

'Ha ha.'

'Seriously, if you want me to read it, you've gotta tell

me what it's about. Imagine I'm your agent. Give me an elevator pitch.'

'This is stupid.' Rich's cheeks flush.

'Sorry, I didn't mean to—'

'It's about two people trapped in an unhappy ma— relationship, if you must know.' Rich puts his glass to his lips. I watch the wine recede into his mouth. 'Entirely fictitious, of course.' He puts his glass on the floor.

'Of course,' I echo. Meeting his eye would feel too intimate so I stare into my alarmingly empty glass instead.

'I'm thinking of changing it anyway. Nothing's set in stone.'

'You probably couldn't handle my feedback anyway.' I do my best imitation of a verbal swagger to cover the awkwardness. 'I can be pretty harsh.'

'I don't buy that. You're too nice.'

'Now who's bringing who down?'

'What's wrong with being nice?'

'Nothing.' The word feels thick in my mouth. I'm drunker than I realized. 'I should go soon.'

'Seriously, what's wrong with being nice?' Rich tries to pat my shoulder but ends up hitting the sofa instead. 'It's a good thing.'

'As long as you don't mind people walking all over you.'

'Who's walking all over you?'

The comment makes me snigger into my wine glass. The fact that I'm here in the first place should make it perfectly obvious who's walking all over me.

'Nobody respects me,' I say instead. It's one of those thoughts that, despite never having thought it before, seems instantly true.

'I respect you.' He's close enough that I can see the sincerity in his eyes. He thinks he does but he doesn't. Otherwise he wouldn't have picked Izzy over me. Not that she gave him much of a choice. And I don't want to make him feel bad.

'That's because you're a nice guy.' I try to fob him off but my 'nice' and 'guy' run together. I put my glass down and stand up. It's time to go home.

'It's because you're worth respecting. Now sit down and finish your drink. Then I'll call you a cab.'

He tugs my arm again but I'm more unstable than he realizes and I stumble, landing in an undignified pile on the sofa. On top of him.

This is the time I should get up, brush myself down and be on my way. But the feel of his breath on my face unlocks something. I can almost hear the hum of the music spilling out of the house party; smell the roses in the air. The last time we were this close, a trio of boys from the year below were trying to rap along to Backstreet Boys. I feel his hand on my cheek. Like he did that night. I move my face an inch closer. The moment – which in reality is probably only a few seconds – stretches. I'm acutely aware of the smell of congealing pizza, the whir of the dishwasher and the soft velvet of the sofa. Then we're kissing like teenagers, his lips as soft as I remember. The years fall away. I can feel him hard against me. His hands on my shirt. His tongue in my mouth. Nothing and nobody to stop us this time. Has there ever been a moment when I've stopped wanting this? The dishwasher beep jolts me back to reality.

I force myself to pull away. 'I'm so sorry, I don't know

what happened.' I stand up and start rebuttoning my shirt. My heart is beating so hard I can feel it beneath the buttons. My legs are shaking. This must be what earth-shattering feels like.

Rich grabs a sofa cushion and shoves it on his lap. His cheekbones have gone pink, which only serves to make him look more attractive. 'I'm the one who should be sorry. I don't know what came over me. Other than two bottles of wine.'

'We both had too much to drink.' I back away, feeling suddenly achingly sober. In all my endless teenage fantasies, I never considered this would happen after he was married. 'I'm going to go.'

In my haste to get out, my foot catches the lip of the pizza box and it sends me sprawling. I put my hands out and manage to right myself before I hit the deck. It's a reminder. Izzy is the girl who gets to lie on the sofa, snogging the guy of her dreams. She's the one who married him after all. Not me.

'Are you okay? Let me call you a cab.'

'I'm fine, I'm fine. I'll get the bus.' I stagger towards the stairs, ignoring the pain in my knee from where it connected with the wooden floor.

'Will you let me know you got home safely? I don't like to think of you on the bus on your own.'

I keep moving. I can't bring myself to normalize the situation by replying to such a mundane request.

'Bec?'

I pause, barely allowing myself to hope.

'I hate to be that guy.' Rich looks genuinely pained. 'But can we agree not to tell—'

'Right. Don't worry. I won't say a word.' The cliché of it feels like a slap in the face, although I don't know what else I was expecting. It's just like that night – he's choosing Izzy all over again. I force the words out of my mouth. 'It's not like it meant anything.'

'If things were different—'

My heart does a silly little leap. I'm trying to unpick whether he means it or if it's just another platitude when he adds:

'Ed's a lucky guy.'

I feel a hot rush of shame. I haven't thought about Ed since Rich sat down on the sofa next to me.

'Izzy's the lucky one.' I run upstairs and out of the front door. Only when I'm halfway down their road do I let the tears at the back of my throat wash over me.

Seventeen

'What a beautiful space.'

Ed is showing unnatural levels of enthusiasm about the wedding venue. He's been like this since he got back from the conference. I thought he'd be able to smell the guilt burnt into my skin. It's the opposite. He couldn't be more attentive. Clare, Bramley Hall's on-site wedding planner, can't get enough of him. She keeps shooting me little looks from behind her glasses as if to check I know how lucky I am. I do.

'It's nice.' I can barely look at him. I was so excited about this venue but as we looked at the on-site chapel, the banqueting hall and the guest bedrooms, I kept my eyes on the floor the whole time. Now they're walking across the lawn that runs towards the lake in the middle and I'm trailing behind, like a lost dog.

'I know it might be difficult to imagine at this time of year but we've even had some of our more nautically-minded couples choose to arrive by boat,' Clare pointed out with a little tinkle when we first passed it. Ed made the right noises, even though he hates the water. I could barely muster a smile.

'Others choose to pitch their marquee in the area over there in front of the Orangery.' Clare pitches her voice louder so I can hear as we round the other side. 'In the summer, those flowerbeds are teeming with roses. They really bring it alive. Will you be considering a marquee for your big day or would you prefer to take advantage of our banqueting rooms? I can show you a mock layout of one of those rooms if you're interested.'

'We haven't looked into that part yet,' Ed tells her. When we turn the corner to see the croquet lawn he mouths, 'Are you okay?' at me.

'Just tired.' It's true; I haven't been sleeping. Ed thinks it's because I'm nervous about the Sydney Scott interview. He has no idea it's actually guilt that is keeping me tossing and turning every night. That and the memory of Rich's mouth pressed against mine.

'I thought we might finish off in the Orangery? You can ask me any questions you might have over a cup of tea. And perhaps a biscuit?' Clare clasps her hands together and beams. If wedding planning doesn't work out for her, she's definitely got the relentless perkiness for a career in children's TV.

'Sounds great.' Ed waits for me to start walking again so he can fall into step with me. He keeps looking at me and then away again as if he wants to say something. I have to stop acting like a zombie. Ed's not an idiot. I need to focus on the guy that did choose me, not the one who didn't. I had my chance with Rich years ago. Or at least I nearly did.

I haven't heard from him since that night and I don't deserve to. Whatever Izzy may or may not have done to me, what I did is unforgivable. When he said it, the fact that his book was about an unhappy couple seemed to have such personal significance. Now it just seems like a fairly well-worn topic. I'm reading something like that at the moment. Isn't every book a bit like that? It means as little as our kiss did. The Waverlys are impenetrable. Izzy hasn't been in touch either. Not even a thank-you for babysitting, which normally I'd think was pretty rude. After what I did, I can hardly complain.

3.20 p.m.

'So have you talked about dates?'

I blink. Clare's stirring her green tea and smiling at me. We're sitting in the Orangery, a rather chintzy-looking brasserie whose only connection to citrus seems to be the glass bowl of lemons dumped on the counter by the coffee machine. I need to stop being so negative.

'Not really—' I start at the same time as Ed says:

'Perhaps early next summer?'

I look at him. A month ago, he couldn't even commit to looking at the venue. Now he's practically skipping up the aisle. I shouldn't have doubted him.

'Sounds like you've got some talking left to do together.

I must say it's nice to see a groom taking such an interest. Some of these fellows just sit there and play with their phone.'

Fellows? Is she from the nineteenth century? I try to catch Ed's eye but he's drinking her in.

'But I'm afraid it's time for me to lay my cards on the table.' She makes a sad face. 'As you can imagine, summer is Bramley Hall's most popular time and I have to tell you every single Saturday is booked from now right through to next October. And as you know we don't hold Sunday weddings.'

'How disappointing,' says Ed.

'There are, however, plenty of other options.' She hurries to reassure him. 'You could look at later in the year and think about a winter wedding. Or we are finding that it's becoming increasingly popular to get married on a Thursday or a Friday. Sometimes even a Wednesday. We're able to offer slightly reduced rates for weekdays and we do have a handful currently available.'

'I don't think we want to make our friends use up their holidays to celebrate our wedding,' I say before Ed can say anything.

'How about one of the bank holidays?' Ed suggests.

'Unfortunately our bank holidays are our most popular times of all. People do love the chance to extend the party. What about looking at a Friday earlier in the first half of the year? If you went for a late afternoon wedding, you'd only be asking friends to take a half day. And we often have some of our best weather in March or April.'

Ed looks eager. 'Could you check your availability?'

'I'll go and get the diary,' Clare practically purrs. 'That way we can have a good look and see where we are.'

I stab a spoon into my hot chocolate as she sashays off, her heels clipping against the tiled floor.

'What do you reckon? Fancy being a March bride?' Ed circles an arm around my shoulders.

'I hate going to weddings when you have to keep your coat on all day.' I know I sound snarky but I can't help it. Ed's enthusiasm is having that effect on me. I hate myself for it.

'So we'll have heaters. You're the bride,' he points out patiently. 'You won't be wearing a coat. Plus you heard what she said. The past few years have been wall-to-wall sunshine.'

I can't believe how nice he's being. It should bring out the best in me. It seems to be bringing out the worst instead. 'You can't guarantee that.'

'You can't guarantee the weather any time of year. I thought this was the place you liked?'

'It was. It is. I'm sorry. I'm tired and my headache's back.'

'Are you sure that's all it is?'

I freeze. 'What do you mean?'

'Maybe you're coming down with something?' Ed presses his hand to my forehead, totally failing to notice when I flinch. 'You haven't been yourself all week.'

'I'll feel better when this interview's out of the way.'

Ed nods. He takes everything at face value. That's one of the things I used to like about being with him. It lacked the dark subtext that defined some of my other relationships. I try to recall how happy I was when he proposed. The

167

cinnamon in the air; the candle reflecting in his eyes. The relief of being chosen at last.

'You're right. This place is fab. And it's definitely going up in my estimations.'

A man in a dark green waistcoat comes over with a bottle of champagne. Clare is strutting behind, carrying a thick blue diary.

'This is very generous.' Ed motions to the champagne as Clare sits down and starts flicking through the diary.

'Oh no.' Clare flushes and starts flicking harder. 'I'm afraid I can't take the credit for this. A friend of yours called earlier this week and arranged to have it sent over at the end of the tour. It's one of the reasons I suggested we end in the Orangery.'

'Who was it?' Ed asks.

I remember the curve of Rich's lips when he said getting the champagne was the best bit. A twisted bubble of possibility builds in my chest.

Then Clare says: 'A Mrs . . .' and the feeling fizzles like someone's stubbed out a cigarette. Of course.

'Waverly? Izzy Waverly?' Clare asks. 'I took the call myself. What a nice gesture. In all my years as a wedding planner, it's the first time someone's done such a thing. She's even left a note. I have it here.'

She clears her throat like she's about to make an announcement.

'It says, "A toast to cherishing each other and forsaking all others, you lovebirds". Isn't that nice?'

It feels like a shot across the bow and I wonder for a crazy moment if Rich has told her what happened. But no sane person would send champagne to a woman who'd just snogged her husband. This should exacerbate my guilt but Izzy's pomposity irritates me instead. Who even uses the word 'forsake' anymore? With that and Clare's 'fellows' it's like we've wandered into the set of *Pride and Prejudice*. Minus Darcy. Even Ed looks like he thinks she's gone over the top. He's shifting in his seat like he's ready to go home. Only Clare looks charmed.

'Should I be "mum" and do the pouring?' she asks.

I suppress a scowl. I've always hated that phrase.

'Can we offer you a glass, Clare?' Ed's recovered his solicitousness.

'You're very kind but I'd better not. I've two more couples to show around before I'm finished for the day. Now, where did we get to on those dates?'

Eighteen

4 p.m.

'If you're not feeling well, perhaps we should head straight home?' Ed suggests as we get in the car. As designated driver, he stopped drinking after one. I choked down half a glass to be polite but in the end we left Izzy's champagne almost untouched. I hope Clare ferrets it away to drink after her shift. She didn't look the type though. 'You could cancel your drink with Rob and we'll have a night in front of the telly.'

'I'm not "having a drink" with Rob. I'm meeting Sydney to discuss the last few details of the interview before tomorrow. It's a work thing.'

'It was only a suggestion,' he says mildly.

'I feel like nobody takes my work seriously.' I stare out of the window, watching the green give way to grey as we hit the motorway.

'I take your job seriously.' Ed takes his hand off the wheel to squeeze my knee. 'If it's important I'll take you right there. I was only thinking of you.'

I can't believe he's being so reasonable. I wish he'd snap back and take the bait. But he doesn't. This is why we never fight.

'Make sure you don't stay out too late. I think you need a rest.'

'I'll be fine.'

'So what did you make of Bramley Hall? I have to say I was impressed. And Clare did say they had a couple of days in April.'

'She did.'

'The broker in me says it makes sense to view a couple of other places but Bramley Hall is definitely the benchmark. Don't you think?'

'I guess we could tell our guests to put their thermals on.' I try for humour but even to my own ears it comes out begrudgingly.

'I bet we'll have a scorcher. Tell you what, I don't have much on this afternoon. Why don't I park up and come in and have a drink? A soft one, of course.'

'I'm literally going to go in, go through the questions with Sydney and bugger off. I probably won't be home much after you.'

'Do you want me to wait?'

I know Ed means well but the way he's fluttering around is bringing out the worst in me. I need to get away for a couple of hours. I take a deep breath. 'Go home and put your feet up. You were at the conference all last weekend. You deserve some time to relax.'

I'm trying to put Ed at ease but my reference to rear-ranging the viewing makes him redouble his efforts. 'Why

171

don't I pop by Sainsbugs and whip up something nice to eat when you get back? I could get some of those bath bubbles you like too.'

I close my eyes. I've never realized how much it annoys me when Ed says Sainsbugs instead of Sainsbury's before. 'I'm not that hungry.'

'I'm sure I can whip up something to change your mind. Here we are.' Ed reverses into a space outside Rob's flat. 'You sure you don't want me to come in?'

'Positive. I'll see you at home.'

I peck him on the cheek and jump out of the car. I give myself a little pep talk as I walk up Rob's uneven front path. I need to shake off this horrible funk. I can't keep punishing Ed for not being Rich.

The concrete's warped and I jump over the cracks, adhering to schoolgirl superstition. I've checked my questions are inside three times. There's a lot riding on this. Sydney may be Rob's girlfriend but she's a megastar. It's just what I need to take my mind off things. When Rob opens the door, I've got my most professional smile on.

'Hi, Rob. Is Sydney ready to get started?'

Rob tugs his earlobe the way he used to if he was in trouble when we were younger. It's so dark inside it looks like he's holding a séance. This doesn't bode well.

'Er, about that—'

'Tell me she's here.' I look past him to see if I can catch a glimpse of her. Despite the dim light, I notice he's finally hung some pictures in the hall. He's been here five years without bothering and the canvases – three small squares with huge blue splashes of colour – look too sophisticated to be his taste. It must be Sydney's influence. That's a good sign at least.

'Tell me you guys haven't broken up.' I push my way in. There's no sign of her in the kitchen at the end of the hall so I open the door to the tiny den where Rob spends most of his time. The curtains haven't been drawn and it's fairly dim but I can make out the coffee table is piled high with takeaway cartons. 'Has she dumped you because you live like a pig?'

'Thanks for the vote of confidence. She's upstairs as it goes.'

'Oh. Sorry. Should I go up?'

'Better not.' He looks shifty.

'Is she coming down?'

'Not exactly.'

'She's not ill, is she?' I look at the takeaway containers on the coffee table. I thought Sydney was vegan but I can definitely see bacon hanging out of one of them. 'The questions will only take five minutes.'

'Look, why don't we go to the pub down the road and I'll go through the questions with you? She's given me some pointers.'

'I'd rather do it with her. She is alive, isn't she? You haven't killed her and dismembered her body.'

'She's alive. She's just indisposed.'

Rob's coyness collides with the pressure of having held it together all day and I snap.

'We're not in the 1930s, for God's sake. Can you stop being so bloody cagey and tell me what's going on?'

'Jeez, don't take your bad mood out on me.' Rob looks affronted. 'If you must know, she's pregnant, all right?'

'What?'

'She's vomming her guts out. Has been for days. If it's not fried, she can't eat it. And even when she does, it comes straight back up. I wanted to call and cancel this but she wouldn't let me. She didn't want to let you down.'

'Shit, Rob.' I stare at him.

'I know.' But Rob doesn't look like he thinks it's shit. His eyes are shining and the corners of his mouth are twitching.

'So this is . . . good news?'

'The best.'

'Is she pleased?'

'Through the roof. Studio's furious though.'

'I can imagine. What does this mean for—'

'The film? She's going to have to drop out. She can't do any of the stunts if she's pregnant.'

I'd meant what did it mean for the interview but I can't see a way of asking that now without seeming selfish.

'Do you want me to head off then?' I try to temper my disappointment.

'Don't be stupid. You and I are going to the pub.' Rob grabs his keys from the ledge above the radiator. 'I'm celebrating.'

5.50 p.m.

'Obviously what I've told you is top secret.' Rob puts down his pint. The pub we're in is deserted and we're huddled in the corner by a rather paltry-looking log fire. But he keeps looking over his shoulder like he's being hunted. 'You can't even tell Mr Insurance.'

'I won't.' I'm reeling. I can't believe my brother has impregnated a Hollywood star. It's definitely taking my mind off my own problems.

'It also means there are a tonne of questions you can't ask her when you see her tomorrow.'

'Can she even do the interview at all?' I cross my fingers under the table.

'She shouldn't. Her press officer's a bit of a pitbull and she pretty much nixed it. But Syd stood her ground.'

'So she'll do it?' I let out the breath I didn't realize I was holding.

'She might be a bit green but she'll make it. Ironically her morning sickness is better in the mornings. It's the afternoons she can't handle.' Rob turns business-like. 'Obviously you can't mention the film or the pregnancy. But she's given me a list of things she thought might make good talking points.'

He gets out his phone and starts scrolling through. 'Here we are. Exercise regimes, getting old in Hollywood, the MeToo movement – she's got a lot to say on that. Things like that. Keep it more general.'

'Can I talk to her about you?'

'Have you listened to a word I've said?' Rob frowns.

'I don't mean blatantly. I mean, can I ask her about relationships and stuff?'

'See what she's happy with. She'll shut you down if she's not. Or Tasha will. The good news for you is that because she's got to drop out of the film, yours will be the only mag she's talking to. So that's a win. But enough about that. Weren't you looking round a venue today? Found a winner?'

My phone pings before I can answer. My eyes nearly fall out of my head when I see that the message is from Rich.

I hope your venue hunting went well. You deserve the best. Thanks for the other evening, by the way xxx.

'That loverboy?'

'What? No. It's just a message from Rich.' I drop the phone back on the table. I can count the number of times Rich has texted me before on one hand. None of them have ever had any kisses. My mind is reeling. What did he mean, thank you for the other night? Curled up in the corner of my mind is the fledgling idea that maybe Rich doesn't regret what happened. I can't let it out. I try to focus on Rob. 'Tell me about the baby. When's it due?'

But Rob's eyes are pinning mine. 'What did ole Richie boy have to say?'

'Nothing really.'

Rob grabs the phone and reads the message out loud in a breathy voice that makes me want to punch him. I scratch at his hand to get it back. For a moment we're teenagers again.

'He's taking a pretty keen interest for a heterosexual man you're not engaged to.' Rob relinquishes the phone. 'And what happened the other evening?'

'Nothing.'

'Be careful, Bec. I'd watch yourself.'

'What are you trying to say?'

'I think it's a bit weird he's texting you. Izzy's your friend – if you can call her that. Not him.'

'You forget I knew him before they even started going out.'

'I remember. I was there. I was the one who mopped you up when they did start going out.'

'Whatever. I wasn't that upset.'

He looks at me.

'I wasn't.'

'Look, I'm not saying this to be a dick—'

'Could have fooled me.'

'I'm saying it because I give a shit about you.'

'How sweet.'

'What does that message mean? Bit cryptic, wasn't it?'

'I was talking to him about the venue when I babysat the other night.' I watch the embers of the log fire glowing. What *does* the message mean? 'He's being nice.'

'He doesn't sound nice; he sounds weird. And you know Izzy wouldn't like it. Look, I know I haven't always been the biggest fan of Ed.'

'Understatement of the century. You called him the most boring man alive the first time you met him.'

'He's a good guy, Bec. If you love him you need to stick with him.'

'I know.' I shift in my seat. The bottom of the chair is digging into my thighs. 'Can we talk about something else now? Like do you even know what to do with a baby?'

'It's your funeral. I'm going for a slash. Don't say I didn't warn you.'

I pick up my phone after Rob goes to the loo and stare at the message. Before I can help myself, I start typing a reply.

I know we said we were going to forget—

Before I can finish typing, another message pops up.

Doh, I didn't say in the last message, this is Izzy. My

177

*phone's bust so if you need to reach me call R. Thanks
again for babysitting. We owe you one xxx*

I drop the phone like it's about to bite me. As if Rich
would ever text me. He made his choice fifteen years ago. I
can't believe I've been so stupid. If I'd finished that text and
sent it, I would have jeopardised everything I have. When
Rob comes back from the loo, I'm grabbing my coat.

'I'm going to head.'

'You all right? You look like you've seen a ghost.'

'It's nothing.' I shake my head, yanking the belt of
my coat tight. 'You were right, by the way. I need to get
back to Ed.'

Nineteen

Monday 28 January

10.33 a.m.

I spot Sydney straight away. In a sea of pastel coordinated athleisure wear and perky ponytails, she's wearing dark baggy jogging bottoms with her hair scraped back. Her face is pale but she still looks gorgeous. Pregnancy aside, I wish I looked as good at the gym, though this place is a far cry from the Fitness First I pay sixty quid a month to almost never use. The sign-in process felt like I was trying to break into a government building. The membership list is so exclusive even Sydney can sit in the bar space without her cap on. A few people look over but nobody approaches.

'Hi, Sydney.' My voice trembles. Somehow she seems more famous when Rob's not with her. 'How's it going?'

'Bec.' She jumps to her feet and slides her arms around me. 'Great to see you.'

'You too.' I disentangle myself slightly awkwardly. I point

at the smoothie she's nursing and put my bag on the chair next to her. 'Can I get you another? I'm on expenses.'

'I'm okay. You knock yourself out. And put it on my account. You can't use cash in here.'

I cross the room, making sure to record every detail of the wraparound bar and ergonomically designed seating for Jules. Normally this kind of place intimidates me but I remind myself I'm here with Sydney Scott. I order a hot chocolate off a man with biceps the size of my thighs and try to ignore his look of distaste as he hands it over.

'So, how are things?' Sydney asks when I sit down.

'Wait a minute, shouldn't I be asking you that?' I set my mobile on the table. 'How are you?'

'Forget about me for a second. You look a bit stressed.'

'Do I?' I shouldn't. I don't have anything to complain about. Ed and I have booked Bramley Hall. April 10 next year. Clare emailed the confirmation through this morning. The countdown is on. He spent last night mocking up 'Save the Date' cards on his laptop, to make sure they were perfect. Each change in font and colour made me feel more guilty.

'I think I just had a bad commute. Let's talk about you. Are you feeling any better? You look great.' I fiddle with my mobile to make sure I'm not recording. 'Don't worry, this bit's off the record.'

'I'm good. Hanging in there, trying to take it easy and whatnot. I'm sorry I couldn't make yesterday. I had no idea this would take so much out of me.'

'Don't worry. I really appreciate you doing the interview at all.'

'Wouldn't miss it.' She flashes a smile, her teeth glinting. 'So hit me.'

'Okay, so I'll start recording. But if I ask anything you don't want to talk about, let me know and I'll turn it off straightaway.'

'Sure.'

'So I guess my first question is; how are you enjoying London?'

'I'd rather not answer that on tape, all things considered.'

I nearly knock the phone to the floor in my haste to turn it off. 'Of course, I totally understand.'

'I'm kidding, I'm kidding. I'm sorry, that was mean.' Sydney shoots me a mischievous smile. 'Ask me anything. I even got rid of Tasha so we could talk freely.'

'Really?' Fenella always complains that celebrities hide behind their press officers.

'Sure. Between you, me and the neighbourhood cat, I think she's pissed at me.'

'Because you told her not to come?'

'And, you know . . .' Sydney flicks her eyes down to her stomach.

'Right. Of course. Sorry. So, tell me how it feels to be in London.'

From that moment on, she doesn't stop talking. She answers all of my questions, giving me half a dozen quotes I know would make great headlines. She even says some sweet things about Rob, though she doesn't mention him by name. By the time we've finished, I know the interview is going to be a smash.

'I think that about wraps it up.' I flick the voice notes off and try to sound professional. 'Unless there's anything you want to add.'

'I think you covered it.' Sydney stretches her arms over her head. Her t-shirt rides up. Underneath, her stomach's smooth and taut. No sign of a bump yet. She catches me looking.

'It's been kind of fast, hasn't it?'

'A bit. Are you okay with all of it?' I don't want to offend her. 'I mean it must have been a bit of a – surprise?'

'Total.' She laughs. 'I'm good though. I always throw myself into things head on. I keep meaning to look before I leap, but I guess I'm too impetuous.'

'I admire that. I can't think of the last time I did something spontaneous.' Apart from kissing my best friend's husband. I push down the sick feeling that rises. I can't let myself think about Rich.

'Yeah, Robbie said you've always been the one who played it safe.'

She catches my expression.

'He didn't mean anything bad. I mean it obviously works for you. Here you are, about to marry the man of your dreams and ride off into the sunset. Robbie said you guys booked a venue. You must be super excited?'

'I am. Did Rob say anything else?'

'Honestly, he didn't. But he's so proud of you. He's always talking about how smart you are.'

'Really?'

'Why do you think I'm doing this interview?' Sydney twists her mouth into a sideways grin. 'Tasha was adamant that I not do any press in case it leaks. She wants to control the narrative. But Robbie said it was important. And we know we can trust you.'

'Thanks.' I try to process the idea of Rob being proud of me. Mum used to say things like that all the time. But Rob and I don't share those kinds of feelings.

'By the way, Tasha needs you to email her the digital recording of the interview and send the write-up and what not over when it's done.'

'No problem.' I have no idea how to send over a digital recording but I'm sure someone in production will. If all else fails, I'll ask Ed. He's good at tech.

'And obviously you won't mention the—'

'Baby.'

'Film.' Sydney stiffens as the biceps guy approaches our table.

'Can I get you ladies anything else?'

'We're fine.' I wait until he goes away. 'I'm so sorry. Do you think he heard?'

'It's fine. Everyone here signs a non-disclosure agreement. It's a safe space. You could confess your deepest darkest secrets in here and nobody would even bat an eyelid.' She winks. 'It's where all the bodies are buried.'

I busy myself with my bag so she can't see my face.

11.55 a.m.

I'm on the train on the way back to the office when my phone rings. Caller ID says it's Ed's office.

'Hello?'

'Not that version, the updated one. Sorry, Bec. Give me

two seconds.' My heart plummets. Of course Izzy and Ed have the same number now they work together. It's weird how normal her voice sounds when we haven't spoken in weeks. Probably because she's in her natural element: giving orders.

'Sorry about that. We're run off our feet today. No, not this one. The red line one with the tracked changes. If you can't find it just look for the most recently saved document. Honestly.'

I reach over and pick up a copy of the *Metro* from the seat opposite. Clearly I could be here a while.

'Now, Bec, are you still there?'

'I'm here.'

'I wanted to call and thank you for babysitting Tilly the other night. It's awful of me not to have called before now. I really appreciate it.'

'No worries.' I feel a surge of guilt, parcelled up with anxiety.

'Rich says you guys had a real laugh.'

She sounds overly casual. My hand tightens around the phone.

'It was nice to see him.' I read somewhere liars get caught out by giving away too much detail so I dole my words out sparingly.

'I think you must have reminded him of how miserable it is being single,' she tinkles, dousing out any last residue of guilt. 'He was very family orientated – going to the dump, taking Tilly swimming, cooking dinner. He even did some of our tax returns. It was wonderful.'

'You remember I'm not actually single?' I try to keep the

hostility out of my tone. I don't want to give her the satisfaction of a reaction.

'You are until you have kids. You know what I mean.'

'Sure. Anyway, Iz, I'm coming back from an int—'

'Oh yes, it was the big interview today, wasn't it? Here
you are at last. Now, I'm going to need you to make two
copies. In colour. Sorry, Bec, it's so frantic here. You were
saying . . .'

I'm so irritated by the fact that she's called me only
to direct her minions down the phone that I speak without thinking.

'It went amazingly. She said loads of really nice things
about Rob and asked me if I wanted to hang out again.'

As soon as I've said the words, I want to call them
back. Her keyboard is clacking in the background.
There's a chance she won't notice. But she's on it like a cat
on a mouse.

'Why would she say loads of nice things about Rob?'
Pause as she pieces it together. 'Wait, don't tell me he's
shagging her.'

I do what I should have done earlier: say nothing.

'He is, isn't he? God, that's hilarious.'

'Why's that so funny?'

'Didn't she just get totally dumped by that guy who looks
like Justin Bieber? The one from that prison series who's
now up on some tax-evasion charge? Don't they think he's
going to be the next Martha Stewart-style celebrity behind
bars? And didn't he cheat on her before he got banged up?'
She gives a pitying laugh. 'Now she's dating her personal
trainer as revenge. What a cliché. Do you want me to have

a word with Daddy to make sure your interview gets published before it's all over?'

'Your dad doesn't have anything to do with editorial,' I say through gritted teeth. Only Izzy could make having a celebrity girlfriend sound like a bad thing.

'I'm sure he could if I needed him to. Shall I ask? You don't want to miss your moment.'

'It's serious between them.'

'Of course it is,' Izzy laughs. 'Until it isn't. You wait. She'll go running back to her budget Bieber and it'll be like it never happened.'

'She won't.'

'I know he's your brother, hon, and granted he is quite good-looking, but what's he really got to compete against a Hollywood A-lister?'

'She's pregnant.'

In the silence that follows, I feel a brief fizz of satisfaction that I've managed to shut her up, before the enormity of what I've done slams me in the face.

'She's what?'

Shit. 'Izzy, promise me you won't say anything to anyone.'

'That's one heck of a whoopsies. I didn't think he had it in him.' Her laugh sounds like a cackle. 'What a joke. There goes her career.'

I look around to see if anyone can hear me. But apart from two teenage boys in school uniform huddled over a mobile, the carriage is empty.

'Izzy, seriously. Please. If you say a word to anyone – even Rich – I could be in all kinds of trouble.'

'Why would Rich care?' There's an odd intonation in

her voice when she says his name. It makes the back of my neck prickle.

'Er—'

'Don't you think Rich has got enough going on in his own life to care about what's happening in yours?'

'I'm sorry. I didn't mean—' I'm itching to ask her why she's being like this but I can't afford to rile her up.

'He got the promotion, by the way. What with that and me going back to work, he's got far too much on his mind to worry about what your family's up to. He can barely focus on his own.'

Her tone changes again, like it's all a big joke.

'Mind you, he does go on the *Mail Online* more than I do. He even knows which Kardashian is which. I despair sometimes.'

I'm gripping the phone so tightly my knuckles have turned white but I strain my voice to inject some jollity into it. 'You know you've got to worry if he gets into the Jenners as well, right? Seriously though, Izzy, please don't tell anyone. Not even your dad. It's more than my job's worth. And Rob would literally kill me.'

'Don't worry, you can trust *me*.'

There's the weird emphasis again. What if she knows something happened? I tell myself I'm chasing shadows. If Izzy knew something there's no way she'd keep it to herself. In the past I've watched her eviscerate people for even daring to talk to Rich. On our last day of school, when the whole year went wild with water pistols and I ended up on the Maths corridor with Rich, dousing each other at point blank range, she didn't stop flaring her nostrils until she pushed me into a puddle outside the sports hall. I fell flat on my face. What I've done now is so much worse. I would definitely know if she knew anything.

This is the point where I should say: 'And *you* can trust me.' Instead I squeak. 'Thanks, Iz. It means a lot. I'd better go. We should meet for drinks when things have calmed down. A proper night out. Like we used to.'

'That'd be nice.'

She sounds wistful. I breathe more easily. I'm being paranoid.

'Right, well I—'

'You don't need to worry so much, Bec. I'm good at keeping secrets. Ask Rich.'

She hangs up.

There's a slim chance she could have meant Rich knows she's good at keeping secrets because he's her husband. She could be referring to the innocent secrets that glue together every relationship; the gifts you pretend to like, the surprise occasions you fake astonishment for. But I think back to the way her voice faltered when she said Rich's name earlier in the conversation. As if she didn't want to say it to me. The *Metro* flutters from my lap to the floor. If there's a chance, no matter how small, that Izzy does know what happened, I've given her a weapon to destroy me. And Rob. I fumble over to the train doors. If I get off at the next stop, I can get the tube into the City. I know I shouldn't. I promised myself I'd forget about him. But much as I don't want to, the best way to find out what Izzy knows is to ask Rich.

Twenty

12.14 p.m.

I stare up at the building. City workers in dark suits and regulation Hackett overcoats cross in and out on their way to and from lunch. The plate-blue glass is glinting in the winter sun and the lifts look like tiny bugs scaling the building from the outside. There's a fountain in the lobby that people have dropped one- and two-pound pieces into instead of coppers. Gold-plated wishes.

Izzy was annoyed with me the first time I came here. It was just after we'd left university. Rich's bank was doing welcome drinks for its new graduates. Izzy spent the evening fending off job offers while Rich drank free champagne with me at the bar. At the end of the night she left me flicking coppers into the fountain and herded him into a taxi without asking if I needed a lift. It took me three night buses to get home.

Three night buses will be the least of my troubles if Izzy finds out what happened between me and Rich. She's a human wrecking ball when it comes to protecting what's hers. I hurry into the building, brushing past two Antony Gormley statues that guard the glass doors like sentries. The circular reception at the centre of the room is so buffed I can see my reflection in it. I drum my fingers against it, leaving greasy marks, as the receptionist prints me a visitor's pass.

I have to type the number of the floor I want into a pod by the bank of lifts to call one. My fingers are so sweaty I get it wrong twice before a set of doors open for me. I step in and immediately feel as though I've left my stomach in the lobby. I try to ignore the traffic on the ground getting smaller and focus on what I'm going to say. I don't want to sound accusatory. Or desperate. I try to recall exactly what Izzy said on the phone, what made me so sure she knew, but my memory's shredded the conversation. Maybe I'm overreacting. I can't be sure. By the time the lift lands on the 57th floor, my chest feels tight. What am I doing here?

There's another reception desk beyond the lift. The woman behind it has an expression like a prison guard. The patterned scarf around her neck looks like a rope tied around a tree. I smile, trying to suppress my nerves.

'May I help you?' She appears to speak without moving her lips. No chance of a smile back.

'I'm here to see Rich Waverly.'

'Is he expecting you?'

'No but—'

'I'm afraid without an appointment . . .' She looks back at her desk as if I've ceased to be of interest.

'He'll see me.' I point at the bank of telephones in front of her, hoping he's not out to lunch. 'If you tell him Bec is here, he'll see me.'

The receptionist's expression changes and she sits up straight in her seat. I pat myself on the back mentally for not backing down to someone who looks like Kathy Bates in *Misery*. Then I realize she's looking at the space behind me.

'Bec, what a nice surprise.' Rich is striding down the corridor, holding a coffee in one hand and a chocolate muffin in the other. 'Don't tell Izzy. We're on a health kick.'

It's the first time I've seen him since that night. The moody lobby lighting makes him look tanned and he's taller than everyone else in the vicinity. When he smiles, his dimples dance in his face. I make a point of thinking about Ed, who doesn't have dimples, but makes a mean risotto and has been putting up with my bad mood for weeks. I'm done being flustered over Rich Waverly.

He turns to the receptionist. 'I'll take it from here, Jean.'

I square my shoulders and follow him back down the corridor, resisting the urge to stick two fingers up at Jean on the way.

He ushers me into a huge office at the end of the corridor and sits down behind a desk the size of a front door. He leans back in his chair so he's at a forty-five-degree angle. The Thames shines like a sheet of metal through the window behind him.

'What can I do you for? Do you want a muffin? I can get someone to bring you one.'

Normally I'd tease him for having a corner office, a

huge desk and a minion prepared to bring him muffins. Today, I dispense with the niceties and blurt out my worst fear.

'I think Izzy knows what happened between us.'

'What?' The tan seems to slide off Rich's face. 'How do you know?'

'I just got off the phone to her. There are some things she said . . . that made me think she knew.'

'Like what?' He lurches forward in his chair. 'What exactly did she say?'

'She said she was good at keeping secrets. But it was the way she said it. And she was really funny about you. The way she said your name it was like . . . she didn't want to share it with me.'

'What else?'

'That was it. But it was the way she said it . . .'

The corner of Rich's mouth starts to twitch. 'Should I be flattered that you were talking about me?'

'It's not funny. This is serious.'

'I know it is. But in the nicest possible way, I think you're running away with this. Have you seen Jean?'

'Jean on reception?' I frown. What has she got to do with this?

'The lovely Jean. One of the perks of running this new team is we get our own floor. Jean was the twenty-third candidate we saw for that job.'

'I'm not following.'

'Izzy sat in on the interviews, Bec. She insisted. Jean was the only one who passed muster. Probably because she bears more than a passing resemblance to my grandfather.

My wife is possessive. If she knew, there's no way you and I would still be standing, having this conversation. Or if we were, I'd be talking in a much higher voice.'

'You didn't hear how weird she sounded on the phone.'

'If she knew, she'd say something.' He shakes his head. 'You know she would. She'd murder us in our sleep, but she'd say something first.'

'So what did she mean about being good at keeping secrets? Then she said "just ask Rich". Don't you think that means she knows you're keeping secrets?'

'I don't. Look, Bec, I know it's a weird thing to say but there's loads of things she could have meant by that. I'd go into them but they're very boring.'

'She sent me a WhatsApp pretending to be you.' I pull out my trump card. 'It was like she was trying to catch me out.'

'What did she say?'

Rich puts his hands behind his head and leans back in his chair again. I feel like he's indulging me.

'She said she hoped I liked the venue and that I deserved the best. But it was from your phone. She didn't say it was her until the next message.'

'Oh that.' Rich waves it off. 'Don't worry, I was there when she sent that. Tilly had done something to her phone and she felt bad she hadn't thanked you.'

The idea of them sending the text message together makes me feel embarrassed, like I'm back on the outside. Which is ridiculous. Rich and Izzy are married. Obviously I'm on the outside. I go on the offensive, to cover up.

'You shouldn't have let her send that message without saying it was from her. I could easily have replied with something that … gave away what we did.' It sounds so tawdry. I wish there were a more eloquent way to put it.

'You're right. I screwed up. I'm sorry.'

'I still think something's off.'

'I don't know how to say this without sounding like I'm totally up my own arse.' He pauses like he's trying to figure out how to fit the words together. 'But have you considered maybe you're reading too much into things because you feel guilty about what happened? Not that you have any need to … what happened was far more my fault than yours. But I'm saying it because I was the same at first. Every time Izzy said something I was convinced it was because she knew and she was angry. When I calmed down, I realized she was the same old Izzy. Nothing had changed except my reaction.'

I can see his point. Izzy was funny with me weeks before what happened with Rich. That's the whole reason it happened. Or that's what I've been telling myself anyway.

'Look, you know Izzy's been pretty stressed out. It's not hard to see why.'

He gazes at me as if he's expecting me to contribute. I don't say a word. I can't see what Izzy's got to be any more stressed out about than the rest of us. He frowns.

'I know she's told a few people how good her work–life balance is—'

I try to hold back a snort. Izzy's been telling anyone who'll listen how great her life is for as long as I can remember. And for that brief moment, when I got to lie on her sofa and pretend to be her, I could see her point.

'But she's struggling to juggle it all. Tilly's playing

194

up – probably cos of the change – and I think it's a lot harder than she thought it would be. That's probably why you think she sounded funny on the phone.'

'Do you really think that?'

'I really do.'

What he's said makes sense. Mainly because I know how vicious Izzy can be when she's wronged. 'Then I'm sorry for bursting into your office like this. And for bringing the whole thing up again. I feel like a total moron.'

'Don't. It's always a pleasure to see another human being. Particularly one with a personality. God love Jean but most of the time, I'm staring at screens.' He gestures to the computer monitors on his desk, all of which are filled with columns of figures. 'Have you met the four horses of the apocalypse? Famine, Plague, Pestilence and what was the other one?'

'Do you really hate it that much?' I notice that, apart from the monitors, his desk is completely empty. No books, no photographs, nothing that gives a hint to the kind of person he is. His bookshelves are the same. Lined with heavy books bound in red and gold that look as though they've never been read. The office could be anybody's. Where's his personality?

'More than life itself.' Rich's smile doesn't reach his eyes and my stomach twists. He looks like an abandoned dog. I hate seeing him so miserable. 'You don't want to hear about the boring life of a wanker banker. What else can I do for you? Are you hungry? Do you want to grab lunch? Save me from my sad little muffin.'

I want to say yes but I know I shouldn't. 'I can't. Ed's

mum's in town so it's going to be a big dinner.' Invoking Ed's name reminds me of my priorities. I make a point of looking at my watch. 'I'd better get back. I'm on a deadline.'

'Of course, the interview.' Rich smacks his hand to his head. 'I can't believe I forgot to ask. How did it go? I bet you absolutely knocked it out of the ballpark.' He puts on a surprisingly authentic American accent. 'Is that the kind of thing she said?'

I can't help laughing. 'She said some really nice things. I just have to write it now.'

'You'll nail it. I can't wait to read it.'

'Thanks, Rich.'

'Any time.' He turns back to the computers. When I get to the door I look back. He's already clicking his mouse so frantically it's like he's trying to resuscitate it. My heart constricts with sympathy. Even a six-figure salary and a Clapham townhouse isn't worth staying shackled to a job you hate.

'Rich?'

'Yup.' He looks up from the screens.

'Hang in there. Things can only get better.'

1.30 p.m.

The *Flare* office is in uproar when I get back. Every desk is filled, even though it's lunchtime. Nobody's looking at each other. There's a knot of people examining proofs and talking in low voices by the production desk and Tina's standing up in her office, bellowing down the phone.

'What's going on?' I sidle over to Jules's desk, trying to look as though I've been there the whole time.

'Marina Terekovsky's been arrested for doping. It's all over the news.' Jules shakes her head. 'Which means our cover interview with her—'

'Has gone down the drain. God. Tina must be—'

'Absolutely losing it.'

I sneak a glance into Tina's office. Her face is puce and she's shouting. This is bad news. Marina Terekovsky's the best female tennis player in the world. She combines her career on court with her own fashion line and five-year-old twins. She's the poster child for 'having it all'. Fenella and Tina worked for six months to get her to be our cover star.

'So we can't use any of it?'

'Not a word. BBC News is saying she might be banned from sport for life. We can't touch her with a bargepole.'

'We've already had the proofs back though. I thought the magazine was ready to go.'

'Not without a cover.'

I look at the production desk. The whole issue is laid out on a whiteboard over by the computer; a miniature copy of each page tacked up to the board. But the box where the front cover was pinned is empty.

'And that's where it gets interesting.' Jules does a little shimmy at her desk. 'Because she was looking for you earlier. Quite urgently.'

'What's interesting about that? She probably wanted to bollock me for coming back late.'

'Doubtful. Think, Bec. Who have you just interviewed?'

'Sydney Scott.'

'And what did she say about the interview in that meeting?'

It takes me a minute to make the connection. 'She said it might be a cover story.'

'Give the girl a prize. My bet is the second she gets off that phone, she's going to come marching over here. She's going to tell you she wants that interview written up now and that it's going to be this month's cover.'

'No way. Do you really think we can turn it around that quickly?'

'We don't have much choice. Here she comes now.'

We both watch as Tina slams the phone down and scrapes her hands through her cropped hair. She starts scanning the office with a frown on her face. When she sees me, she marches over to the door and yanks it open.

'Give me your phone,' Jules hisses. 'I'll get one of my work experience girls to transcribe the interview for you while you start going through your notes.'

'You're a star.' I hand the phone over, watching Tina approach. Could this be my big chance? I try to read into her face but her mouth is a thin line. She's giving nothing away.

'Bec. At last. Can I have a word?'

And it unfolds the way Jules said it would. Which is why I find myself ringing Ed to apologize profusely for skipping dinner and sitting at my computer finishing off the interview long after everyone else has gone home. Lucy, the picture editor, is still here, pulling up old photo shoots of Sydney Scott, and Tina's pacing in her office. Other than the monitors on the production desk and the desk lamp in Tina's office, my computer is the only light in the room.

'Have you finished yet?' Tina pokes her head out of her office. It's the third time she's asked.

'Finishing up now.' I've been typing so long, tuning and retuning the same words, that my hands feel like claws.

'Send it over as soon as you're done. We still need to run it past her people.'

Pressing send feels like I've got my hands on the nuclear button. I remind myself I'm pleased with the piece. I might not have been able to linger over it as I'd planned, but Sydney said some nice things about ageing and sexism in Hollywood. I've even managed to include some opaque references to a new romance without giving anything away.

I watch Tina through the glass window after I've sent it. She stoops over her computer, tapping her nails against her desk as she reads. She frowns, types something, smiles, types, frowns again. I watch her, reading her corrections, head moving from side to side as she follows the words down the page. After about five minutes, she picks up her phone. The receiver on my desk rings.

'Bec, I've finished reviewing. Can you pop in?'

I'm in her office before she has time to hang up the phone.

'It reads well.' Tina looks up from her screen. 'Only needed a few changes. We don't have time to do a shoot – all the other pages are gone. This has to go to the printers tonight or we'll miss the deadline. But if we use stock images, we'll be able to recoup some of the costs from the Marina debacle, which should get management off my back. I don't mind telling you this has been a colossal cock up. Your interview might just have got us out of a hole.'

She breaks off to check her emails. 'I'm waiting for approval from her press team. Tasha, is it? Very friendly. Production are working on the layout as we speak. As soon as we hear back from her people, we'll send it to print. You don't have to stay. Go home. You've done the hard yards.'

On my way out of the office, I can't resist detouring via the production desk. Rob was a bit reluctant to be mentioned so I think it's worth checking the text. Lucy, the production editor, looks up when she sees me coming.

'I thought you might be hanging around like a bad smell. Do you want to have a squiz and see how it looks?'

She tilts the screen so I can see it. I gasp when I see the first page. Sydney's lying in the shallow end of a swimming pool, wearing an emerald green ball gown that floats ethereally around her in the water. On the opposite page, the words 'Great Scott' are scrawled. Lucy taps the keyboard to show me the rest of my interview laid out.

'It looks amazing.' I can't take my eyes off *Rebecca Maloney* under the headline.

'Headline's provisional at this point. Would be nice to find something less generic but we're pressed for time.'

I skim the text on the screen. There's nothing in there that Rob will find offensive. Tina's only made two changes. Inwardly, I glow. I can't believe how well this is going. I should buy Sydney flowers. Or maybe something for the baby. I definitely owe her.

'She might not say it but Tina's chuffed,' Lucy continues. 'This interview's going to be amazing. Someone from the board's even coming down. Apparently they are a big fan of the actress. I'd better get back to it.'

'Which pictures are in contention for the cover?' I don't want to tear myself away.

'There's another ballgown one and a swimshoot one. That's the one I prefer but Tina's worried it'll make us looks like *Women's Health*. I'd show you but I don't have time. She's in there, deciding now.' Lucy jerks her thumb at Tina's office where Tina's leaning over her drafter's table with her reading glasses on. 'She's only got about five minutes, though. We're way over deadline. I'd go home if I were you.'

I linger by my desk, fiddling with something in my bag in case Tina decides to call me in. But she doesn't even look up. My stomach's rumbling. Jules thrust a Mars bar on my desk as she was leaving but other than that I haven't had anything to eat all day. I check my watch. If I hurry, I could catch Ed and his mum for dessert. The restaurant he's chosen isn't far from here. Then again, Ed's mum has the tendency to revolve her conversation around people I've never met and all I want is a hot bath and a takeaway. I decide to head straight home. After what's happened today I think I've earned it. I sidle past Tina's office at a snail's pace, trying to see the images she's examining. I'm so busy staring that I don't realize I've walked into a wall of flesh until it's too late. My bag drops to the floor and the contents fly out.

'I'm sorry.' I stuff my keys, Oyster card, a leaking biro and a copy of last month's magazine inside and stand up. I feel a familiar shoulder grip.

'Oh, you've got nothing to be sorry about, Bec.' Tony

Maxwell-Martin relinquishes his grip and makes a gesture like he's tipping his hat. 'Nothing at all. From what I hear, you're the woman of the hour.'

I watch him waddle in the direction of Tina's office. In eight years working at the magazine, this is the first time I've ever exchanged more than two words with him that haven't involved Izzy.

Twenty-One

Tuesday 5 February

8.04 a.m.

The Tuesday the magazine hits the shelves I'm up even earlier than Ed. It's going to be a long day – Jules has offered
to take me to some beauty reception tonight so we can have
free drinks and celebrate the front cover, but I wanted to
see the magazine as early as possible.

'Don't wait up,' I shout as I leave the house. I hear him
grunt in response. I think he's still a bit miffed I missed
the dinner with his mum. She was only here for the day
and I haven't seen her since before Christmas. But I'll
worry about that later. Today is a day for celebrating. As
I walk to the station, I can smell spring blossom in the air.
It's one of those perfect days that trick you into thinking
summer's already en-route. I'm practically skipping by the
time I get to the newsstand outside the underground. I'm
too early. It's not open. I try to peer through the heavy

plastic covering the rack but I can't see *Flare*. I decide to get off the tube a stop early to pick up a copy but it's sold out at the newsstand by Bond Street station. I feel a fizz of excitement, even though I'll have to wait until I get into the office to see it. It being sold out has to be a good sign. This could be my first front cover of many. That will show Izzy.

8.59 a.m.

At first I think I'm the only one in. Then I notice the lights on in Tina's office. The velvet chaise longue in there must double up as a bed; she never seems to go home. There's no sign of her now though. There's a stack of issues against the wall, bound in brown paper from the printers. I ditch my bag on my desk and approach the stack cautiously. Tina normally distributes them and I don't want it to look obvious I've taken a copy without waiting. I peel back a corner of the paper and ease out the top copy.

'Bec? Can I have a quick word?'

Tina is standing behind me holding a mug of coffee and a plate of brown toast.

'Of course.' I drop my hands to my side guiltily. 'Let me just—' I mime taking my coat off and trot over to my desk. I wonder what she wants. To tell me I've done a good job and she's happy to send more interviews my way? Perhaps she'll even promote me. I put my bag on my desk, telling myself to stay realistic. She's probably got admin to go through. I'm looping my coat over my chair when my phone starts ringing. I fish it out of the pocket and look at caller ID. Rob.

It's not like him to call this early. And I've missed two other calls from him. I look up. Tina's sitting at the drafter's table next to her desk, looking at me expectantly. He's probably bored between clients or ringing to thank me for the flowers I sent Sydney. I press reject. I'll call him back later.

'You don't have to look so anxious,' Tina says when I rap on her door. 'Come and take a seat. I wanted to go through the piece with you.'

I take the seat opposite. She's got the magazine open on the interview. I scrutinize it from this angle. She went with the ball-gown shot. The colour of the swimming pool really pops against Sydney's long limbs. 'Great Scott,' I read the strapline upside down. 'Sydney Scott talks life, love and those . . .' But Tina moves her hand so I can't see the rest.

'As I was saying, I thought it made sense to go through the piece with you,' she says. 'We've had some great feedback from our subscribers, dozens of emails already. I'm convinced and management seems to agree –' she allows herself a triumphant smile ' – that this might be our fastest-selling magazine of the year. I'd like to see a lot more writing from you going forward.'

'That sounds great.' I try to act as though I get feedback like this all the time but I can't contain the grin spreading across my face.

'There is, however, a small problem. It's really nothing to worry about . . .' My smile falters. When people say there's nothing to worry about, it usually means the absolute opposite.

'What's happened?'

'As I said, we've had some very positive comments from

our subscribers and I've no doubt it'll be flying off the shelves. And Scott's press team are happy too.'

'That's great. So—'

Tina closes the magazine and looks up at me. 'The issue is the actress herself is not particularly happy with us.'

'Sorry?' I shake my head. I must have misheard. Sydney loved the interview. She said she wanted to do it again sometime. In fact I owe her a call. My eyes drop down to the magazine. That's when I see the headline on the cover. Set against the azure of the pool in orange letters so bright they're almost glowing scream the words, 'Maybe Baby?'

My stomach drops like a stone. The words are a play on a popular film Sydney did a couple of years ago but the meaning is clear. I reach for the magazine, clawing at the paper as I turn to the interview. 'Great Scott,' the strapline reads. 'Sydney Scott talks life, love and those pregnancy rumours.' In the corner of the page, right at the bottom, is a grainy picture of Sydney walking with someone who may or may not be Rob. The back of my throat fills with bile. I put my hand to my mouth. How did this happen? An alarm rings at the back of my brain.

'It's really nothing to worry about.' Tina's watching me closely. 'Her team approved this before it went to press. I wanted to let you know because you mentioned you had a personal connection to her.'

'Where did this stuff come from?' I trace the pages with my fingers. Rob is going to kill me. I think back to the missed calls from him and feel even sicker. They're going to think I betrayed their confidence. 'She didn't say any of this on the recording.'

'That's why there's a question mark.' Tina doesn't look at all worried. 'But her press team confirmed it.'

'Why would they do that if she's not happy?'

'Come now, don't be naïve. You know what the publicity machine is like. They need to keep her in the news now she's dropped out of her latest film. And they need public opinion on their side before it comes out she's abandoned filming. The studio will be out to smear her.'

'But she's not happy?' I bite my lip, telling myself maybe Tina's exaggerating. After all, if Sydney's press team approved it, she can't be that annoyed. But even as I'm thinking it, I know I'm kidding myself. I remember the protective look on Rob's face when he swore me to secrecy. There's no way they wanted this news out so early. They haven't even had their twelve-week scan yet.

'It's really nothing to worry about.' Tina pulls her lips together in what I think is meant to be a sympathetic smile. 'It will blow over in no time. These things always do. And legally, Scott hasn't got a leg to stand on.'

What about morally, though? 'Thanks for letting me know, Tina.' I force a wobbly smile. 'Did you need anything else?'

'That was it.' Tina holds my gaze. 'You did a good job on this. It's been noted at all levels.'

The way she looks when she says it makes everything click into place. I can't believe I didn't see it straightaway.

'Tina?'

'Hmm . . .' She's already flicking through the issue again, folding back corners and making pencil marks at the edge of the pages.

'Where did news about the pregnancy come from in the first place?'

She gives me a half-smile. 'You of all people should know a good journalist never reveals their sources. Let's say it came from a "friend" to the magazine.'

I picture Tony Maxwell-Martin's corpulent form bustling towards Tina's office. I know exactly who the source was. Izzy. The only question is whether she did it to punish me for what happened with Rich or whether she did it simply because she could.

'If you'll excuse me.' I fumble for the door-handle. 'I need the bathroom.'

I barely make it into the cubicle before I'm violently sick.

10.04 a.m.

I stay in the bathroom longer than I need to, dabbing at my mouth and rinsing my hands repeatedly. As long as I'm in here, I don't have to deal with the real world. My phone is on my desk. I'm uncontactable, like I'm marooned on a desert island. Albeit one that smells of overly floral air freshener with a back-note of stale vomit. I splash cold water on my cheeks. It doesn't help. My eyes are puffy and my skin looks like day-old porridge. But I can't stay in here forever.

Back in the office, Jules is waiting by my cubicle. There's a shiny new copy of *Flare* on the desk beside her. She's wringing her hands together.

'You saw it then,' she says.

'I am in such deep shit.' I sit down and put my face in my

hands. 'Deep, deep shit. This might be the last day you get to see me happy.' I think of the implications of Izzy spilling the beans as an act of revenge. 'Or alive.'

'Surely it won't be that bad?'

'No. It'll be worse.'

'We don't technically say she's pregnant—'

'We may as well have.' I notice someone's put a Post-it note on the copy on my desk with 'Nice job' scrawled on it. The sight of the yellow square reminds me of that night at Izzy's. *I can't believe she's done this*.

'If you explain her PR is the one who okay'ed it—'

'I'm the one who wrote it. Rob's going to be furious and he's got every right to be.'

Jules's mouth flaps open as she gropes for something comforting to say. When she can't think of anything, she squeezes my arm. My mobile starts ringing. It's the Darth Vader theme – the tune Rob programmed to play whenever he rings.

'Right on cue.' I pick up the phone and squeeze my eyes tight shut. 'I'm sorry,' I whisper. 'I'm so sorry.'

'You're sorry? What the actual fuck? You're sorry?'

'They put the headline in after I left for the day.'

'Oh not on my watch, guvnor. So that makes it okay, does it? What about all this other Mills and Boon crap about her stroking her stomach wistfully and looking dreamily out the window. I suppose they put that in without you as well?'

It's worse than I thought. I didn't realize they'd tampered with the text as well.

'They did. I know it doesn't make it any better but—'

'Damn right it doesn't make it any better. Do you know where I am right now?'

'No.'

'I'm in some scuzzy hotel in fuck knows where because Sydney's hotel is surrounded by paparazzi. The whole of Charlotte Street is a write-off. Thank God they're all too thick to realize we made it out the fire exit. Do you have any idea what you've done?'

'I'm so sorry.'

'That doesn't make it any better. This isn't kids' stuff, Bec. You don't say you're sorry and get a do-over. I've got Sydney ranting and raving and crying her eyes out on the bed. I've had to cancel all my clients this morning because I can't leave her.'

'Maybe it'll blow over?' Even as I'm saying it, I know it won't.

'Nice try. It's an absolute clusterfuck.'

'I know.' Out of the corner of my eye, I can see the picture of Rob and I that I've got pinned up on the wall of my cubicle. We're at some festival – I'm wearing a sombrero and he's got my heart-shaped sunglasses on. There's a wisp of blonde hair in the corner of the shot. Izzy. I rip the photo down.

'I swear I didn't tell them. It was Izzy.'

'You what?' Rob's voice sounds quiet. Dangerously quiet.

'She must have told her dad and they would have changed it after I went home for the night. I'm really sorry but there was nothing—'

Then comes the explosion. 'How the hell did that poisonous bitch find out in the first place?'

'I—'

'*You* told her. Of course you did. I said this would happen, Bec. I bloody warned you. I said someone would get hurt. I just didn't think it would be me. But you couldn't let her go, could you? You're like a fucking addict and you just threw me under the bus to get your fix.'

'It wasn't like that—'

'It was exactly like that. One thing I asked you. One thing.'

'Tell me what I can do to make it up to you. I'll do anything.'

'You've done enough.'

'There must be something.' My voice cracks.

'All right, there is.' There's a pause and I think he's going to relent. Then he says, 'Tell that bitch she's going to get what's coming to her and stay the fuck away from us.' He hangs up the phone.

I press redial but it goes straight to voicemail. I put my head against my computer. The back of my throat feels full. I don't care who is watching. I want to cry but the tears won't come.

'How did it go?' Jules is hovering again.

'Imagine the worst and multiply that by a thousand.'

'I'm so sorry. Is there anything I can do to help? I know you probably don't feel much like celebrating but if you want to bin the launch and go for a drink and talk about it, I'm still around tonight.'

'That's really kind, but I'm okay.' I twist my mouth into a smile that's more of a grimace. 'And I'm going to be busy tonight. Very busy.'

'What are you going to do?'

'I'm going to go and see Izzy.' After Jules has walked away, I add under my breath: 'And then I'm going to kill her.'

Twenty-Two

5.50 p.m.

The rest of the day passes in a kind of blur. Jules keeps coming to check on me like an anxious parent and a few people stop by to say well done. I call Rob repeatedly and even try Sydney but both go straight to voicemail. I don't blame them. I don't leave my desk, even to get lunch. I think Tina realizes something's wrong. Normally she makes a little speech about each new issue but today she stays in her office. I keep staring at the clock, waiting for the hands to inch their way towards 6 o'clock. When the minute hand stabs ten to, I can't bear it any longer. I push back the chair with such force it nearly falls over and leave the office without saying goodbye to anyone.

As the tube rattles towards Clapham, I lay out the facts against Izzy, like a lawyer trying to clinch a case. She was the only person I told about the pregnancy. And she's been out to get me since I got engaged. Since before that, really. When I look back at all the things she's done – the

213

engagement ring, the party, the flowers – they all seem like an elaborate game of one-upmanship. I can't think of the last time she was genuinely on my side. Even Ed's gone off her. He's hardly mentioned her since that conference. That reminds me. I need to message him when I get off the tube to say I am going to be home tonight after all. Thanks to Izzy. Celebratory drinks are one more thing she's robbed me of.

When I get to Izzy's house I can see she's left the shutters wide open. The lights are blazing. I can see right into her sitting room. The armchair in the bay window squatting beside an antique side table, dripping in Diptyque candles. A glass of white wine on the table next to them, the condensation glistening. On a coaster of course. Most people are protective of their privacy. I've no doubt Izzy does this on purpose so everyone can see her perfect life.

I'm stomping up the front path when my phone rings. Unknown number. Normally I don't bother with these – they're uniformly either life insurance or calls about PPI – but after everything that's happened today, a sixth sense tells me to pick up.

'Hello?'

Heavy breathing on the other end.

'Hello?' I say again.

'Bec?' Even tear-drenched, I recognize Sydney's American twang.

'Oh my god, Sydney, is that you? I'm so sorry. Are you okay?' My words come out in a rush, falling over each other. There are a thousand things I want to say. I don't get the chance.

'Have you seen Robbie?' Her voice sounds hoarse, like she's been crying for hours.

'Sorry?'

'Robbie? He went for a walk an hour ago – he was so mad – and he hasn't come back. I need him.'

'I haven't seen him.' She sounds frantic. I understand she doesn't want to be on her own but this is quite extreme. It makes me feel even worse. 'I'm sure it's nothing to worry—'

'Someone pushed me,' she croaks, 'when I was trying to leave the hotel. I thought I was safe going out the back but there was a guy with a camera by the dumpster. He got up in my face and when I tried to push past, his camera was right in my face and I . . . I stumbled. And now I think I'm losing the baby.' She breaks down completely.

'Oh my god, Sydney.' I feel sick. 'Where are you now? You need to get to a hospital.'

'How can I leave the hotel?' She's sobbing again. 'They're all out there. I just want Robbie.'

'Get the hotel to get you a cab. You can tell him to meet you there. I'll call him if you like. I'll keep calling till I get through. Are you bleeding?'

'No,' she says and her voice sounds small, like she's stopped talking into the receiver.

'Okay, that's good.' I try to recall every pregnancy saga I've ever seen play out on *ER* or *Grey's Anatomy*. 'That's a really good sign. Did you land on your stomach when you fell?'

'I didn't fall.' Sydney's less hysterical now. I can hear the fight coming back into her voice. 'He pushed into me but

I didn't fall. I don't need to go to the emergency room. I need to see Robbie – I want to make sure he's doing okay.'

'He'll be fine. It's you I'm worried about.' At the back of my mind, I dare to hope this might be the conversation that brings us back together. If Sydney and the baby are okay, this could be the moment that we heal the rift.

'You didn't see how mad he was.'

'He gets like that. He'll have gone for a run to burn it off.' I try to sound reassuring. 'But you need to get to a hospital, just for a check-up. Where are you registered?'

I look up the path towards the house, remembering Izzy's insistence on giving birth at Chelsea and Westminster hospital, despite being closer to St George's. All for the sake of a better postcode. My whole body is thrumming with rage.

'Don't you tell me what I need.' The tears have gone. Sydney's voice has hardened. It's as though even by letting Izzy into my thoughts for one second, the gap has widened.

'Sydney, please let me explain.' I try again. 'It wasn't—'

'I could care less, Bec.' There's a bite to her tone now. 'I trusted you. But you crossed the line. So I don't want to hear you're sorry and I don't want to talk it out. I just wanted to know if you'd seen Robbie. And you haven't. So there's nothing more to say.'

The dial tone serves as her goodbye. Unlike Rob, Sydney didn't shout at me. Somehow that makes it worse. Every bone in my body oozes with shame. And fear. What if Sydney is losing the baby? How will Rob ever forgive me? I may as well have pushed her. The paparazzi outside their hotel are my fault. Not just mine though. I march up the remaining stairs, put the pad of my index finger flat against the doorbell and press. When she doesn't appear, I start slamming the doorknocker against the door, imagining I'm driving it into Izzy's face with each knock. She must be hiding, waiting for me to give up and go away. I'm not going anywhere. Finally, after five minutes of solid pounding, I hear footsteps clipping down the hall and the door swings open.

Izzy looks exhausted. There are purple shadows under her eyes and she looks paler than I've ever seen her. Gone is the usual pristine orderliness. Tilly's stuffed animals and the remains of a tea-set are strewn across the hall. The house is a mess. Six weeks ago, I might have been worried. We're past that now.

'Goodness, Bec, are you trying to wake the dead? What are you playing at? Tilly's in bed.'

'No, I'm not.' A shrill voice floats down from upstairs.

'What am I playing at?' I can't believe her.

Izzy holds up a finger like she's marking a page. 'Wait. Tilly, if I have to come up there again, I'm going to take away a privilege.'

'Don't know what yet,' she mouths at me. Like we're friends. Like this is a social call. 'Anyway, what are you doing here?'

'What am I doing here?' My voice gets louder with each word. 'What do you think I'm fucking doing here?'

'Calm down, Bec.' She frowns then glances over my shoulder. She doesn't seem concerned at how angry I am. Probably thinks she can talk her way out of it like she usually does. 'Have a nice walk, Mrs Rudge,' she calls cheerily to the old woman on the other side of the street. She looks back at me. 'Are you coming in or what?'

This is just typical. Even when I'm standing here shout-ing in her face, I can't hold her full attention. My blood starts to boil.

'I'm hungry.' Tilly calls down again. There's a pause, then she adds: 'Fucking hungry.'

Izzy knits her hands together and gives me a reproach-ful look. She's the type of parent who says 'sugar' instead of 'shit'.

'I warned you—' Izzy goes over to the bottom of the stairs, almost tripping over a particularly ragged-looking elephant. She stomps halfway up and calls, 'If I have to come in there, there'll be no swimming with Daddy on Saturday. Do you really want that?'

'No.'

'Then get into bed.'

Tilly's door slams shut and I hear the sound of bed springs squeaking.

Izzy must be tired because when she turns back, she wobbles. For one glorious moment, I imagine her losing her footing entirely and crashing down the stairs face first. She puts a hand on the wall to steady herself and I give myself a mental shake. I can't believe my thoughts could be so dark.

'Sorry, I feel a bit light-headed. I didn't eat lunch today. Now where were we?'

I look at her, standing in the middle of her perfectly dec-orated Clapham townhouse. There's a series of pictures set against the wall next to her, each one a smug memorial to her perfect life. It makes me hate her even more.

'You were about to tell me why you've been such a fuck-ing bitch.'

Twenty-Three

6.40 p.m.

'Have you gone mad?' Izzy flares her nostrils. The gesture takes me right back to school. But this time is different. This time I'm going to stand up to her.

'I know what you've done.'

'I don't know what you're talking about.' She stalks down the stairs. Up close, her features may be perfect but there's an iciness about them. I can't believe I've never noticed how cold she is before.

'Why did you do it? You must have known it would hurt them as much as it would hurt me. Or was that the point? Did you want to hurt Rob as well?' My voice rises like a piano scale. 'For what? Because it didn't work out when you were fourteen?'

Izzy looks at me as though I'm insane. 'I dumped him, as you recall. Not that he took the hint, not that it matters. Unlike you, I don't spend my life obsessing over what was going on when were fifteen.'

'What do you mean by that?'

'I should think it's perfectly obvious. Go on, humour me. Tell me what I'm supposed to have done this time.'

'You're really going to pretend you don't know?'

'Know what?'

'That the whole world is talking about Sydney's pregnancy and she nearly lost the baby thanks to you.'

Izzy shrugs. 'I'm sorry to hear that but I don't see what it's got to do with me.'

'So the fact that *Flare*'s front cover has a huge headline blaring on about Sydney Scott being pregnant is news to you as well?'

'I haven't had a chance to buy it today.' Izzy glances upstairs as if she's worried Tilly might still be up. But I know it's because she can't look me in the eye.

'I gave you a subscription for Christmas, Izzy. You don't buy it. It appears on your doorstep every month.'

'I haven't had a moment to look. I have more important things to worry about than a Maybe Baby headline.'

'So you have seen it.'

'It's an expression.'

I can't believe she's going to deny it. It's like when she copied my GCSE coursework and looked our teacher in the eye and swore I was the cheat. Even though my notes were found in her locker. She's like Teflon. Nothing sticks.

'You couldn't bear to see things going well for me, could you?'

'Oh for goodness' sake, Bec, stop playing the victim. Change the tune. It's boring.'

'Excuse me?'

'You've been playing this record since we were about fifteen. Ever since your mum died, you've acted like the world is out to get you. You use it as an excuse to sit around in the same rubbish job, in the same tedious relationship. Doing nothing to change it. You act like everything comes so easily to me. I work at things, Bec. That's why good things happen to me. Whereas all you do is sit around and wait for me to sort out your life for you.'

'What, so now you're my hero? Don't make me laugh.'

'You're making my head hurt. I'm tired, I'm not feeling well and Tilly's being a pain. All I want to do is have a glass of wine and a bath and go to bed. So can you unravel your latest little conspiracy theory and we can all go to bed?'

'My life is falling apart because of you and you want to have a fucking bath? Are you even human at all?'

'Bin the histrionics, Bec. You remind me of Tilly.'

'You told your dad Sydney Scott was pregnant and he put it in the magazine.'

'I haven't spoken to my dad all week. And even if I had, I've better things to do than pass on crappy Z-list celebrity gossip. Unlike you, I've got a serious job to hold down and a family to look after. When you've achieved either of those things, come back and talk to me. Until then, you can take your accusations   '

'I do have a serious job.' I feel my fists clench. 'And Ed is my family.'

'Ha. Why don't you give Mr Family Man a call right now and see what he's up to. It might not be as PG as you think.'

'How dare you? You wouldn't even *have* a job if it weren't for Ed, and all you do is put him down.'

'I got that job because I was the best candidate.'

'If you're so brilliant, why did Rich tell me you couldn't handle it?'

Izzy stops dead.

'Rich would never say that.' But there's doubt in her eyes.

'Really? Why don't you ask him?' I feel something vicious take hold of me. I wasn't planning on detonating this because I didn't want to get Rich in trouble. But I can't help myself. 'He told me he was worried. I guess he felt he couldn't talk to you.'

'Why were you talking to Rich?'

'It's a free country. I can *talk* to him when I want. I knew him before you even existed.'

Izzy gives a loud, theatrical groan. 'Are we really going to do this again?'

'Do what?'

'Give your tragic crush on Rich some more air time.'

'I . . . don't know what you're talking about.' I feel hot and flustered.

'You think I don't know that you've been obsessed with Rich since the night he and I got together? Cornering him in the garden like that even though it was obviously me he liked. So tragic.' She takes a step forward, backing me against the wall. She's standing so close the smell of Issey Miyake clogs in the back of my throat. 'Oh, hon, we've been laughing about it for years.'

I flinch and for a moment I'm right back there. She was wearing Issey Miyake that night too. The night Rich and I were supposed to get together. He and I had been circling each other all night, finding excuses in shots and song choices all designed to bring us together. We were in Izzy's parents' back garden, next to the rose bushes, standing so close together, the front of our shoes were touching. His lips had just met mine when Izzy appeared, handed me a phone and told me to order a pizza. By the time I'd finished the order, she had her tongue so far down his throat she could probably taste what he'd had for breakfast. They were a couple from that point on. None of us has ever discussed what happened since. And while I know it didn't happen the way Izzy said it did, her confidence has cast a shadow across my memory. She's taken my most precious thing and smashed it.

'It's pathetic,' she jeers. 'You've spent your whole life lusting after a man who doesn't even know you exist.'

So she doesn't know. Which means this whole thing hasn't even been about revenge; it's simply been another power trip. I don't know whether that makes it better or worse. I take a breath. I'm going to savour the next words that come out of my mouth. 'If Rich doesn't know I exist, why did he kiss me the other night?'

'You're deluded.' Izzy doesn't even blink.

'I'm not. He kissed me the other night when I was babysitting Tilly. And I'm willing to bet it would have gone a lot further if I hadn't pulled away.'

'You're a fantasist.'

I look at her standing there, perfect white teeth shining like tiny pearls, and I wonder what she finds more difficult to believe: that Rich cheated. Or that he cheated with me?

'I don't need to fantasise. It was right after he'd ripped

down all your Post-it notes. See. This one left a mark.' I point to a speck of white in the grey paint on the wall next to my head.

'We had a lovely time actually. Told me all about his book. You might want to have a flick, I think you'd find it illuminating.'

'You haven't read it.' At last a note of doubt is creeping into her voice.

'No, but he asked me to. He wanted to know what I thought. Right before he kissed me. I'd forgotten how soft his lips were. Oh, and Tilly and I had pizza. With pepperoni. She was practically crying with happiness. At least I'm not stupid enough to try to feed mung beans to a four-year-old.'

Izzy slaps me so hard my ears ring.

'You leave Tilly out of it. I made you. I. Made. You. You were nothing before me; a quiet little mouse with frizzy hair and a monobrow. I found you your job, your fiancé, everything. And this is how you repay me.'

I put my hand to my cheek. It's stinging and something feels wet against my palm. Izzy must have caught me with her nail. She's not finished yet.

'I hope she loses that baby,' she snarls. 'And the whole thing ruins your career. And your relationship with your pathetic brother. By the way, you can tell him if he's so happy with his Hollywood floozy, he should stop stalking me on Facebook.' She gives a hysterical high-pitched laugh that makes her sound unhinged. 'And if it doesn't, I'm going to ring the *Daily Mail* and tell the world. Then I'm going to call my dad and tell him what you've done. Don't bother going into the office on Monday. Or trying to find another job in journalism. You're finished.'

She's so angry she's panting. 'And if you see your precious Rich, tell him not to bother coming home. I'm changing the locks. If he wants his clothes, he'd better scour the charity shops. And he can whistle if he thinks he's going to see his daughter again.'

'You can't do that.' I start to falter. I wanted her perfect world to come crashing down but I didn't stop to think what would happen when it did.

'Watch me. By the time I'm done, he's going to wish he'd never been born. He's not such a prize, you know. Not that you'll ever get to find out – he's only ever gone near you to make me jealous. I bet he's been gagging for you to tell me. Oh, and on that note, Ed's been trying to shag everything that moves and whining about it to me since Norwich. I almost fucked him myself just to put him out of his misery, but sloppy seconds aren't my style, they're yours. Now get out of my house.'

She spins around so quickly I get a mouthful of her hair. I reach out to pull her back but she marches towards the stairs, her back so straight she could be balancing books on her head. It's a performance. She knows I'm watching but she keeps going towards the stairs. She's so secure she's never felt the need to watch her back. She's always assumed somebody else – her parents, me or Rich – would do it for her. She should be more careful. I take a step forwards. All I can hear is my own ragged breathing cutting through the air.

'That's not true, Izzy,' I rasp. 'None of it's true.'

I'm so full of rage I can barely see straight. In one conversation, she's laid waste to my entire life. I take a step forward. She doesn't turn. But I'm not finished with her yet.

'Izzy.' I say it more forcefully. This time her head whips around and she stops midway up the stairs.

'Get out of my house, you fucking loser,' she spits. 'If you come near me and my family again, I'll kill you.'

Without waiting for a response, she turns back and resumes her pace up the stairs, leaving me at the bottom, itching to follow.

Twenty-Four

8.14 p.m.

I'm shaking when I get back to my house. I don't remember the bus journey home. When I open the front door, there's music playing. That should be my first clue that something's wrong. But my head's so busy turning what just happened over I barely hear it. I go into the kitchen to put on the kettle and clear my head. Missy's shut in there, whining. I feel a creep of doubt. Ed and I give her the run of the house. I pat her absently on the head and she quietens down. That's when I hear the sound of giggling.

I put down my bag and head towards the stairs, already knowing what I'm going to find at the top. He hasn't even bothered to close the bedroom door properly. I can see his shoulders thrusting and the fingernails gripping his back from the top of the stairs. They don't hear me coming. It's not until I yank the door open, pulling down the jumble of towels that hang on the back, that they see me. Ed jumps out of bed. He scrambles into his clothes, while a girl with a sweep of black hair covers herself up with the duvet.

'I can explain.' Ed pulls on his trousers so quickly I'm surprised he doesn't chafe. He reaches for his glasses and stabs himself in the cheek with the frame. It would be funny if it wasn't so tragic. 'This isn't what it looks like.'

'Spare me the clichés. Emma, isn't it? Fancy meeting you here. I haven't seen you since my engagement party.'

Emma blushes crimson and stares at the ceiling.

'Bec, I—' Ed finishes buttoning up his trousers and comes towards me with his hands outstretched. I jerk away.

'Don't touch me.' I can see Emma wriggling into her clothes under the duvet. Her hair's got longer. In spite of itself, my brain registers that the length suits her.

I march into the corridor. Ed's feet shuffle against the carpet as he follows. I look at him, shirtless and bare-footed. The parody of a man caught out. I think back to when I first met him. He seemed so stable. Reliable. What a joke. And the laugh's on me. All the energy I've wasted feeling guilty about a five-second kiss with Rich. For what? I should throw it in Ed's face, but what's the point? He doesn't deserve to know.

'I'm sorry.' He bows his head like he's following a script. 'I never meant to hurt you.'

'What was this supposed to be then? An ego boost?' But I don't have the energy for another fight. I feel numb. The fact that this pales into insignificance compared to what just happened with Izzy tells me everything I need to know.

Inside the bedroom, there's the sound of a zip being fastened. The door inches open and Emma creeps out, clutching shoes and a Coach handbag to her chest. Ed stares at the floor until the front door closes behind her. I don't know if his failure to acknowledge her makes me hate him more or less.

'How long has this been going on?' I stare at him.

'It only happened once.' He shifts on his feet like a guilty schoolboy. 'I didn't think you were coming back.'

'Sorry to inconvenience you. Next time I'll call ahead.' I can tell from the fact that he can't stand still that he's lying. A new thought occurs. 'Were you shagging her when you proposed?'

'No.' He sounds aghast. 'I would never do that to you. Bec, I'm so sorry—'

'Oh but this – this is okay.' I rap out the words. 'How could you?'

'I'm sorry. It's just ever since we got engaged—'

'You're the one who asked *me* to marry *you*.'

'Because I knew it was what you wanted.' He sounds plaintive. 'I thought I did, too. But then it just took over everything. All you wanted to do was look at venues and talk about dates. I got freaked out.'

'You could have talked to me about how you were feeling.'

'I should have done.' He nods furiously like agreeing with me is going to make things better. 'But Izzy said I shouldn't—'

'You went to Izzy? You told *her* you were having doubts about *our* wedding instead of talking to me?' As if the betrayal couldn't get any bigger. Suddenly I don't feel numb anymore. I'm fuming.

'It wasn't like that, I promise,' Ed rushes on. 'I just had too much to drink at that client dinner over Christmas, remember? The one she came on. And she's so easy to talk to. She seemed to really care about how I was feeling. I only mentioned I was worried that it was all moving a bit quickly and that I was going to talk to you and she said . . . anyway that doesn't matter.' He gulps. 'What matters is we're going to fix this.'

'What did she say?' I carve the words up with my tongue.

Ed pauses before he answers. 'She said I shouldn't bother you.' He looks at me earnestly, like he's actually expecting me to understand. 'She said everybody gets pre-wedding jitters and they'd go away if I stopped thinking about them. She said I could call her anytime I felt them.'

'That was good of her.' Ed doesn't even seem to notice the sarcasm. He's too busy trying to unburden himself.

'I tried, I really did. But you wanted to talk about venues and dates and I felt more and more suffocated. Then she said—'

He breaks off as though he's just remembered I'm his fiancée not his therapist.

'Don't stop now. Tell me what the great Izzy Waverly said to solve your next problem.'

He looks stricken. I know I'm not going to like what he says next.

'Well?' I demand.

'She said maybe I needed to get it out of my system. It was in Norwich. We'd all had a lot to drink. I think she was joking but Emma arrived and, er—'

'Let me get this straight. You decided to go out and shag someone else because Izzy told you to?' I'm disgusted. I can't believe he'd be so weak.

'It wasn't like that.' He's starting to sound whiny, as if he's the victim in all this. I notice the slope of his shoulders, how pigeon-toed he is. Everything about him seems diminished.

'So what was it like then? For you and your pimp,' I shout so loudly I surprise us both. I bet he didn't think I had it in me.

'You've been so happy over the past few months,' he pleads. 'I didn't want to ruin it.'

I stare at him like he's grown an extra head. Happy? Where has he been?

'I'm so sorry. I can't believe I've done this. To you. To us.' Ed's voice thickens and I think he's going to cry.

'Don't.' I hold my hands up. 'You need to go.'

'But I love you.'

'People who love each other don't cheat on each other.' I yank the ring off my finger and hold it out. Rich's face pops into my head and for a moment I feel like a hypocrite. Then I think of Emma's nails on his back and Ed, with his head close to Izzy, confiding in her instead of me, and my feelings harden.

'Keep it.'

'If you don't take it, I'm going to throw it in the bin.'

His hands fold around the ring. I look at him standing there, his glasses askew, a hangdog expression on his face. I should feel worse than I do.

'Bec.' There's a wheedling tone in Ed's voice. I wonder if he's going to make another bid for forgiveness.

'What?'

'Please don't be too hard on Izzy. She was trying to help.'

For a second I think I've misheard him. The look on his face leaves no room for doubt.

231

'Do you know where I've just come from? I've come from seeing Izzy. She told me you'd been banging everything that moved since that conference.'

'What?' Ed jerks his head like I've hit him. 'But she promised not to—'

'Tell?' I spit. 'Turns out she doesn't keep her promises either. Tell me, how long have you two been conspiring behind my back? Did you go to her for advice, ask her for help in selecting a suitable candidate for you to work out your doubts on?'

'It wasn't like that. She was trying to look out for you.'

'Izzy's never tried to look out for me.' I shake my head bitterly.

'I can't claim to know the ins and outs of your friendship with Izzy.' Ed's got his hands out again. Like I'm a wild animal he's trying to calm. 'But she was furious on your behalf. Told me to break it off.'

'Well she did a good job of that, didn't she?' I sweep my hands through the air, gesturing to the unmade bed, the remnants of Ed's clothes crumpled on the floor. 'I couldn't give a shit about Izzy, Ed. You did this in my own house. In my own bed. How could you?'

'It wasn't supposed to – Emma just came round to . . .' Ed's mouth is flapping like a goldfish. 'I broke things off. Like Izzy said. But then you were so wrapped up at work. That interview was taking over your life—'

'So first I'm too obsessed with getting married, then I'm not obsessed enough?' When I laugh, it doesn't sound like me. It sounds hard. 'You need to go.'

He hesitates.

'Just leave.'

I hold my head up as he walks past but I slump to my knees when he's gone. Even in his pathetic groping apology, Ed was trying to stick up for Izzy. I can feel the anger pressing behind my eyes, tightening my skull. I can hardly think straight. I'm not going to sit here and take it. This ends tonight.

Twenty-Five

8.29 p.m.

I storm into the kitchen and open the fridge. There's no wine left. Undeterred, I reach into the top cupboard and pull out the bottle of whisky. I discard the idea of a glass. She couldn't even let me have Ed to myself. Taking Rich wasn't enough; she had to get involved with Ed as well. The ironic thing in all this is that Rich is actually the one who liked me first. We spent our childhoods together. At school we hung out in different crowds but he always had a smile and a wave whenever we bumped into each other. I never thought anything of it. He was just Rich. He wasn't on anybody's radar then. I don't think Izzy even knew who he was. Then one Thursday afternoon, he turned up late for double Maths. One of the few subjects Izzy and I were in different classes for. I moved my record bag to make room for his without looking up. I was barely awake. It was a warm day and the teacher had one of those droning voices that make your eyes close of their own accord. We were doing the trapezium rule, which I still don't understand. I was sliding my eyes shut when a piece of gridded paper, neatly folded into quarters, landed on my desk. I shot a look at Rich. He was staring at the blackboard. I opened the note.

Wake up ☺

I take a swig of the whisky straight from the bottle and gag. I take another. I'd scrawled, *I'm bored* on the paper, flicked it back and tuned out again. That's when Rich started drawing pictures of trapeziums doing increasingly stupid things and lobbing them at me. I'd caption them and flick them back. By the end of the lesson I had a stack a foot high.

'Who knew the trapezium rule could be so much fun?' He waited while I stuffed the last of my lever-arch files into my bag.

'How come you were so late?'

'Rugby coach wanted to see me.' He rapped his knuckles against the desk. 'Told me he was considering me for captain next year.'

'That's awesome.'

'Pretty cool day all round, as it goes.'

'Yeah?' I remember looking up. The moment felt charged. The sun streaming through the window had caught his face. He had the kind of smile that makes your stomach do somersaults. He still does.

'Yeah.'

'Maybe you should be late for Maths more often?'

'Maybe I should.' He made it sound like a promise.

The next day there was a piece of paper stuffed inside my locker with a picture of two trapeziums kissing on it.

I still have it. Nestled between cringy love letters from a particularly verbose university boyfriend, A-level exam papers and old photographs. Even after he married Izzy, I couldn't bring myself to throw it away.

I hugged our encounter to me like a comfort blanket. Cancer had my mum in its clutches by then. That moment with Rich was a bright spot in the dark. I started looking out for him at school, taking back routes through corridors I didn't need to be in, hoping to catch a glimpse of him. I imagined taking refuge in his house after school, doing homework, staying for tea. Letting Jenny fuss over me in a way my mother no longer could. I didn't tell Izzy. I liked having something for myself. Would it have changed anything if I had? I doubt it. Rich had a target on his back the moment it was announced he'd be captaining the rugby team the next year. Izzy's always been drawn to success.

The whisky doesn't taste so bad when you get used to it. It's the smell more than anything – like dirt and horses. Maybe that's this brand. I squint at the label. It looks cheap. I feel a creep of self-pity. I take another glug to neutralize it. I'm sitting at the wonky kitchen table of a flat I'll probably have to sell because I can't hang onto the man I bought it with. Drinking whisky that could strip paint with no one but my dog for company. I think of the set-up at Izzy's: her Diptyque candles, her chilled white wine and her roaring fire. Rich on his way home to tend to her every whim. *Oh crap. Rich.*

I fumble for my phone, nearly knocking the whisky over. It goes to voicemail. He must be on the tube. I'm about to send him a message when I remember what Izzy said about how they've been laughing at me for years. I stop. I know Rich wouldn't laugh at me. She must be lying. It wouldn't be the first time.

I throw my shoulders back so sharply I feel a crick in my neck. Who is Izzy anyway? She might tell everyone how successful she is, combining her high-flying job with her perfect marriage, but she works in insurance. Even Ed admits it's dull. And if her marriage is so perfect, why was Rich kissing me? Who's the loser now? I grab my handbag off the chair opposite. I'm going back.

When I open the front door, I see the 37 bus pulling away from the stop. I jam my hands in my pockets and start walking to the next stop. The walk might sober me up. The streets are deserted but I hear chanting as I pass the local pub. There must be a football match keeping everyone inside. That and the wind – this morning's spring promise has hardened back into winter. Not that I can even feel it. My rage is keeping me warm. Perhaps I'll walk the whole way. It's peaceful out here. It gives me time to think things over. After about ten minutes, my left foot starts to hurt. I'm trudging by the time I pass the Hootananny pub on the corner. It was called the Hobgoblin when we were at school. It's changed names about a hundred times since. It's always stunk of weed. If I keep walking I can get the bus from outside the Town Hall. Most of them go on to Clapham. I can see the Ritzy cinema on my right and the yellow 'M' of the McDonald's glowing like a beacon on the corner. Not much further. There was a shooting in that McDonald's when we were at school. It's one of the reasons Izzy won't bring

Tilly to my house. She'd have to drive through Brixton to get to me. The area's been totally gentrified since then but she says it makes her uncomfortable. Unless she's eating at the Franca Manca with her mummy friends.

I feel a pang of sadness as I get on the bus, thinking of Tilly. I'll miss that little heart-shaped face and the feel of her arms clasped tight around my waist. After tonight, I might not see her again. It's a price I'll have to pay if I'm going to get Izzy out of my life. I pull an old Bobbi Brown compact out of my bag. I look terrible, as expected. My pupils are darting around like I'm on something and there's a nasty scratch on my cheek from where Izzy caught me with her nail. I pick at it with my thumb. I know it'll make it look worse but there's something comforting about gouging into my own flesh. I can barely feel it.

9.01 p.m.

The bus gives an enormous lurch as it turns off Battersea Rise onto Northcote Road and I smack my head against the metal bar. That pain takes me out of myself and I wonder what on earth I'm doing. I've already seen Izzy tonight. Why am I coming back? I glance out of the window as the bus pulls into the stop. I could just go home. But the bus stop on the other side of the road is empty. I must have just missed one. A familiar set of shoulders huddled behind the glass catches my eye. His fringe might be hanging across his face but I'd recognize that stance anywhere. I ding the bell, jump to my feet and hurry down the stairs. The doors are already sliding shut. I hurl myself through them just in time and weave across the road, narrowly avoiding a collision with a Deliveroo driver swerving to overtake the bus.

'Rich?' He's in a world of his own. He jumps like a startled cat.

'Bec?'

'Are you okay?' I peer at him. I know I'm not looking my best, but Rich looks awful. Under his hair, his face is drawn and he's shaking despite his winter coat.

'It's Izzy—'

The whisky starts churning in my stomach.

'She was all over the place. Told me she wants a divorce. She said she called my mum and told her she's going to make sure I never see Tilly again.' He bends over, hands on his knees. He looks like he might be sick. 'Somehow she must know what happ—'

I squeeze my eyes shut. 'Rich, it's my fault. I'm so sorry, I told Izzy that we kissed.'

'What?' He looks like a rabbit caught in the headlights. 'But why?'

'There's no time to explain it. You need to go and see her. She can't take Tilly from you. You haven't done anything wrong.'

'She said she told my mum everything.'

'What does your mum say?'

'I don't know. I turned my phone off. I knew if I kept it on I'd say something I'd regret.'

'You've turned your . . . okay, that doesn't matter either. You need to go and talk to Izzy. She's only lashing out.' I bite my lip. 'She loves you. She won't want a divorce. You just need to go home and sort it out.'

'I can't face it.' He shakes his head. 'I've been sitting on the common for the last ninety minutes since I spoke to her. You have no idea how angry she sounded.'

'I have some idea.' I think of Izzy's face when she tried to throw me out. Anger sparks again. She's never deserved him. 'It will all be fine. I'm so sorry I got you into this. You must hate me.'

'I don't hate you. Obviously I'm not thrilled it's come out like this but . . .' He looks at me, like he's weighing something up. 'There is one thing you can do for me.'

'Anything.'

'Come back there with me now.'

Anything but that. I shake my head. 'You and me going back there together is not a good idea.'

'Why not?'

'Er, are you mad? Last time I saw Izzy she threw me out of your house. She told me if I came near her family again, she'd kill me. Me being there will just make things a thousand times worse. I'll write her a letter or something, telling her that we only kissed, that nothing else happened. I'll say whatever you want me to say. But I can't come back with you—'

'Please.' His voice catches. 'I need you. And you owe me.'

There's nothing I can say to that. And he's already started walking. I fidget with the strap of my bag. Then I pick up my feet and go after him. I can't match his long strides so I end up trailing him all the way up Northcote Road to the turn off for their street. He waits at the garden gate for me to catch up. If I didn't know him better, I'd say it was a delaying tactic. His face is creviced in the streetlights.

He looks a decade older than he did last time I saw him, and I've done this to him. He's right. I do owe him. Even if I'm only here as cannon fodder.

'After you.'

He stops on each step like a man going to his execution. I don't blame him. This isn't going to be pretty. About half-way up, we see an Amazon delivery guy on the doorstep of the house next door. Rich stops. 'Nobody's in, mate,' he says. 'They've got a chalet in the Alps. They're away until the snow melts.'

The delivery guy grunts and punches something into his keypad.

'How the other half live, eh?' Rich continues, oblivious to the fact the delivery guy clearly wants to be on his way. The own-brand trainers he's wearing and the scrappy goatee scratching at his chin indicate very little in the way of a natural affiliation with Rich. 'The ones on the other side winter in Florida. Keep hoping they'll extend the invitation but so far nothing doing.'

He barks out a laugh that sounds more like a cough. The delivery guy's halfway down the front steps now, eyes on his van. Zero interest in prolonging the exchange. I feel sorry for Rich. He's got more to lose than me. But he can't delay the moment any longer.

He hesitates again, checking his watch at the top of the steps. He's got one of those complicated athletic ones and he fiddles with the screen. He's playing for more time. Izzy's drawn the curtains since I left so we can't see what's going on inside. I wonder if he's going to bottle it. But he grits his teeth and puts his key in the lock.

'I'm glad I'm not coming back alone.' He turns his head back to meet my eyes. 'I couldn't have faced this without you.' He pulls open the door and flicks on the hall light.

That's when I start screaming.

Twenty-Six

9.15 p.m.

There's so much blood around Izzy's head it's seeping into the cracks in the floorboards. The rest of the house looks exactly the same as it did a few hours ago. Stuffed animals and cushions; the remnants of the teddy bear's tea party still strewn across the floor. It makes the sight of Izzy lying crumpled like a rag doll at the bottom of the stairs even more surreal. For a moment, I feel as though my feet are welded to the floor. I couldn't move even if I wanted to. All I can do is stand there and take in the scene, my mind processing tiny details – the angle of her neck, the way her arms are spread angel-wide.

'Is she breathing?' I cross to where she's lying, careful to avoid the blood, and start circling her. I'm trying to see it from every angle. I keep waiting to feel something but I'm on autopilot. I feel jittery, wired, like I've had too much caffeine. Perhaps I'm in shock.

Images of Izzy at various points of our friendship crowd

my mind. They're so vivid I have to blink them away. I lean over her, trying to be useful, looking for signs of life. Rich carries on standing there, his back against the front door. I wait for him to move. I would have thought he'd be better with blood. He played rugby for ten years. But this is Izzy. The thought twists my stomach.

'You need to call an ambulance,' I urge. He looks at me like he can't understand what I'm saying. 'Call an ambulance.' I enunciate each word.

'But she's, she's already—' He covers his face with his hands and his shoulders start to shake. 'She must have been lying there for hours,' he keeps repeating, like it's some kind of mantra. He looks like he's going to collapse.

I look down at Izzy. The bits of her face that aren't covered are the colour of concrete. I get up and cross the hall.

'Everything's going to be okay.' I put my arm around Rich. I'm being so calm. When my mum died, I went to pieces. Perhaps when you've already lost the only person that really matters to you, everything else pales. And I know I need to be strong for Rich.

'Think of Tilly,' I say. 'She's going to need you. So what we need to do is call an ambulance—'

I've said the wrong thing.

'My god, Tilly.' Rich looks stricken. 'What if she saw—'

'Tilly's fast asleep.' I cross my fingers and pray it's true. 'Izzy put her to bed hours ago. Now let's—'

'She might have woken up . . .' Rich's face is now paler than Izzy's. 'My god, what if she's come down and seen—'

'You know what a deep sleeper she is. I'm sure she hasn't—'

'How do you know?' He practically shouts. 'How can you know that?'

'The monitor.' My eyes focus on the white receiver on the side table. 'There. See.' I've always secretly mocked Izzy for persisting with Tilly's baby monitor when she's due to start school in September. Today I couldn't be more grateful. I point to the screen, glowing like a beacon. Rich snatches it up.

'If Tilly was awake you'd hear it,' I say. Rich is scouring the screen. 'Or see her moving. She's fast asleep. But we need to check if Izzy's—'

I can't bring myself to finish my sentence. I've just noticed the socks Izzy's wearing. Everything else in her wardrobe is tasteful. Camels and greys: soft, muted shades. These socks are bright purple with unicorn faces on the toes. Their nylon flies in the face of the cashmere or silk she prefers. I helped Tilly choose them for Mother's Day last year. Izzy loved them. I have to look away. Someone needs to stay in control.

'She's fine,' Rich calls, and for one heart-stopping moment I think he's talking about Izzy. Then I see him put down the monitor. The sight of Tilly sleeping peacefully seems to have helped Rich get back in control. He taps 999 into his mobile and starts talking. 'I need an ambulance. Straightaway. My wife's fallen down the stairs. You've got to hurry.'

I can't hear what the dispatcher is saying though I can guess from Rich's responses.

'I don't know, I don't know.' Rich shakes his head. 'I just came back and found her. She's on the floor.' He gulps. 'No. I don't think she's breathing.'

I go back over to Izzy. I'm not squeamish like Rich but the sight of the blood clumped and matted in her hair turns my stomach. I breathe back the nausea and put a finger forward, scooping a hunk of it out of the way so I can get to her face. Her eyes are closed. I put my hand above her mouth the way they do in *CSI*, testing to see if there's an answering breath. There isn't. I lean in. Nothing. I look back up the stairs. It's a long way down.

'I don't know how to do CPR.' Rich comes up behind me. His voice is panicky again. 'I don't know if I can.'

He's close enough now that I can hear the response.

'Yes, you can. We'll do it together. I'm with you every step of the way.'

Despite everything, I wish I'd thought to say that.

It's as I'm moving to let him get closer that I see her lips move. I see her take a breath. For one crazy moment, I hesitate. Then I'm pushing back Izzy's hair, digging like a dog in sand to uncover the rest of her face. She exhales again and it's like a dam has burst. Having not felt anything, now a tangle of emotions threatens to overwhelm me. One of them being guilt.

'She's still breathing.' Tears sting my cheeks.

'What?'

'She's breathing. Look.' I point to her mouth. Rich is there so fast, I barely see him move. He dips his head low over her face then jerks back.

'My god. She's breathing.' He almost shouts into the receiver. 'Okay, tell me what to do?'

But the sound of a siren wailing cuts through the air.

'They're here.' Rich's head is so close to Izzy it looks like he's praying. There's an intimacy to the gesture that makes me feel like I'm intruding.

'I'll open the door for the stretcher.' I feel dizzy as I run over to the front door and pull it open. I can hear the blood pounding in my ears. Outside, the ambulance is navigating its way into the space between Izzy's Porsche Cayenne and a random Beemer. I wait until the paramedics have stepped out of the ambulance.

'She's in here,' I shout, and I can hear the relief in my own voice. 'And she's breathing.'

9.35 p.m.

I can see Izzy's breath misting up the oxygen mask. She's wearing a neck brace and a wad of gauze covers the cut on her head. There are wires snaking up her arm, doing God knows what. Although her face has regained some of its colour, she looks about a hundred. Her hair seems thinner and the bones of her chest stick out where they've pulled down her top to get the brace on. I can't help thinking of the jolly paramedic at the race, winking as he told Izzy to put her feet up. These paramedics aren't smiling.

'Is she going to be okay?' It's a variation of the same question I've been asking since they came in the door. I have to know. 'Her head—'

The paramedic who patched up her head looks up from unfurling the straps of a backboard.

'We've stemmed the bleeding but they'll need to do a CT scan when she gets to St George's. The team are prepping for her already.'

'So she's going to be okay?'

'She'll be in good hands. With hematomas—'

'We're taking her now,' his crewmate interrupts. 'To me.'

They scoop Izzy onto the backboard and raise it in a single movement. They take her towards the front door, Rich at their heels, his hip jostling the stretcher as he tries to get close enough to take Izzy's hand.

'I'll stay with Tilly,' I call. But nobody's listening.

They've barely been gone five minutes when Jenny sweeps through the doorway. She's not wearing any make-up and her pyjamas are peeping out from under her coat. But there's a strange energy coming off her and her eyes dart around the room, not meeting mine.

'Oh my dear lord, what's gone on here? Richard called me from the ambulance and asked me to come and see to Matilda,' she continues when I don't say anything. 'I'll stay here and you can go on to the hospital.'

'I can't.' I gouge my feet into the floor. After having to watch the life leech out of my mum in a cubicle barely bigger than a shop changing room I swore I'd never set foot in another hospital. Izzy begged me to come when Tilly was born but I wouldn't. How can I go now?

'Are you all right, dear?' Jenny's trying to be soothing but, like me, she can't seem to take her eyes off the bloody smears where Izzy's body lay.

'She was right there.' I grope through the air to point at the stairs again. 'Just lying there.'

'What a horrid shock it must have been for you.' Jenny sweeps across the room to scoop me into a hug. I let myself go floppy in the firmness of her grip. 'A mercy you found her when you did. She must have slipped. Poor thing wasn't in her right mind tonight.'

In a flash I remember what Rich said at the bus stop about Izzy calling Jenny. About how she said she was going to take Tilly and make him pay for what he did. What we did. A fist of guilt socks me in the stomach. That's why Jenny won't look at me. This is all my fault.

'What did she say when you spoke to her?' I ask. But still, Jenny won't meet my eye.

'Oh this and that. She's been under a lot of pressure with going back to work and minding Matilda. I don't think we realized how much she'd taken on. Now, speaking of Mat—'

'She's asleep. She slept through the whole thing. Did Izzy tell—'

'I don't think we need to worry about all that now.' Jenny shakes her head. 'Let's wait until she's out of theatre before we go down that road. Speaking of which, why don't I give the hospital a call and see if I can find out if there's any news. Perhaps you could check on Matilda?'

She takes a few steps away and busies herself with her phone. I'm amazed at how calm she's being. Izzy's her favourite daughter-in-law. Given the fact that one son quitting a lucrative position was enough to send her into a tailspin, I thought she'd be more frantic. She's not even crying. For me, fear is starting to set in. Even though Izzy's fit and healthy, whatever drugs the paramedics gave her weren't enough to wake her. And there was so much blood.

I don't think I can bring myself to go upstairs. I don't want to walk past all that blood. And how can I look

Tilly in the face? I get out my phone instead. Seeing Jenny clucking around makes me feel the pull of my own family. I'm worried about Rob, out there on his own. And Sydney and the baby. Both their phones ring out. The tap of knuckles against the front door startles me. I look round to see Jenny marching over to the open front door. Two men in police uniform are on the step. I feel a prickle of unease. This was an accident. What are the police doing here?

'Can I help you, officers?' Jenny's trying to smile but her lips are tight.

'Sorry to trouble you, Mrs . . .'

'Waverly. Jenny Waverly.'

'Mrs Waverly.' The taller one on the left nods his head. 'We've had a report of an incident of someone sustaining serious injuries after falling down a flight of stairs.'

'That's right.' Jenny wrings her hands. She looks more upset now. Maybe reality is sinking in for her too. 'My daughter-in-law, Isabel. My son is with her at the hospital right now.'

'Of course.' He nods again. His colleague, a younger man with a pronounced widow's peak, takes a step forward.

'Would you mind if we came in and asked you a few questions? We just need to build up a picture of what happened here tonight.'

There's something about the overly casual way he says that that makes me feel nervous, but Jenny stands aside to let them past.

'Perhaps I should get off to the hospital,' I suggest. Jenny fixes me with a razor-sharp glare.

250

'Don't be silly, Rebecca. You're the one they need to hear from. You were the one who found her.'

The thought that she's deliberately trying to erase Rich from the scene crosses my mind. He was there too. But when it comes to protecting her boys, Jenny is the definition of a tiger mother.

'Is that right?' Both policemen turn their attention to me and I nod, feeling instinctively as though I've done something wrong.

'I'll just put the kettle on. Why don't you go into the sitting room and make yourselves comfortable?' Jenny is trying to act like this is just a social call. But I can tell from the speed her heels are clicking against the floor that she's stressed.

I lead the two men across the hall into the sitting room. I can hear the tall one – he said his name was Tallis – talking into his radio but I can't make out what he's saying. My brain can't take anything in anyway. I can't stop my eyes flicking to the wine stain. Izzy must have been at it with the bleach – it looks smaller. Or maybe I made it into something bigger in my head.

'So.' Tallis stretches his long legs out and leans forward in his seat. 'Jenny mentioned you were the one to find Isabel? Can you tell us what happened?'

His colleague with the widow's peak gets out a notebook and stubby pen and for a moment I'm struck dumb. Grey box rooms with two-way mirrors straight out of *The Bill* swim before me. They said they just wanted to have a chat. I didn't think they'd be writing everything down. Is this the point I should be monotoning, 'No comment'? I tell myself

I'm being ridiculous. Izzy's going to wake up any minute and make all this redundant anyway.

'That's right. Rich and I came in and she was just lying there ...' I break off, remembering the sea of crimson around her. 'She must have fallen.'

'Had you and Rich Waverly spent the evening together?'

'No, we bumped into each other in Clapham Junction.'

Tallis obviously senses my discomfort. 'I can imagine it must have been very upsetting to see your friend like that,' he says. 'But we have to look at what happened from every angle. So while it might look like some of our questions don't seem to make sense, remember we're just trying to build that picture.'

'Okay.'

'So did you notice anything out of the ordinary when you came in – anything out of place or where it shouldn't have been.'

'I don't think so.' I rack my brains. Aside from Tilly's toys, everything looked interiors-magazine perfect. 'You'd have to ask Rich though. He obviously knows the place better than me.'

'Oh, we will.' The one with the widow's peak is about to write something else when we hear raised voices in the hall. The first is Jenny's. While her voice is loud, she's speaking slowly, as though she's talking to a child. I get ready to spring up in case Tilly's awake.

'Now, I think you need to calm down,' Jenny is saying. 'It's obviously been a huge shock for us all but I think it'd be best for Isabel if you went back to the hospital.'

The answering voice, while high-pitched, is too nasal for

Tilly. I feel a click of recognition just before Glenda shrieks, 'How dare you have the audacity to tell me what's best for my daughter after what's gone on tonight?'

Glenda bursts in, Jenny right behind her. I notice that in contrast to Jenny's pajamas-and-mac look, Glenda has taken the time to coif her hair and put on the full face of make-up she's never without.

'I want to see the person in charge of the investigation,' Glenda says, the sinews in her neck taut with the effort of spitting out the words.

'It's not an investigation,' snaps Jenny as Tallis stands up.

'Well, it should be. My daughter's lying in a hospital bed and I want to know what you're doing about the person who put her there.'

'I can understand your concern and I want to assure you—' Tallis begins but Jenny cuts him off.

'You don't know anyone put her there, Glenda. She had her mind on other things and she slipped, that's all. Those floorboards are murder.'

'You know exactly who put her there,' Glenda hisses with such venom that Jenny takes a step back. 'Your precious son, that's who.'

'Don't you go hurling wild accusations like they're facts.' Jenny's voice flattens in warning. 'Richard would never hurt Isabel. He's devoted to her.'

'So why did she ring me two hours ago and tell me she was terrified of him?'

Twenty-Seven

10.06 p.m.

Tallis's partner takes Glenda out of the room. He closes the door but snatches of the conversation float through it. Glenda keeps repeating that Izzy said she was scared but when he asks her what else Izzy said, she falls silent.

'You know she's talking rubbish,' I tell Tallis. 'If anything it's the other way round – Rich was scared of putting a foot wrong. Izzy definitely wears the trousers in their relationship. Tell them about the Post-its, Jenny.'

But Jenny doesn't say anything. She's too busy straining to catch what Glenda's saying.

'Why don't you tell me about the Post-its, Rebecca?' Tallis leans forward in his chair.

I bite the skin around my thumb before I answer. 'I'm not trying to say anything bad, I'm just saying Izzy can be a bit of a control freak – she'd be the first to admit it. Last time I babysat for them, she left about a hundred Post-it notes all over the house telling me exactly what to do and when to do it.'

'Sounds helpful.'

'It was, I suppose.' My mouth puckers. 'But it was kind of overkill. Like there was one telling me to take my shoes off before I went downstairs. That kind of thing. As if she hadn't already asked me a thousand times, every time I come round. Don't get me wrong; I love Izzy. I'm just saying she'd never be scared of Rich.'

'Are you round here a lot, would you say?' He sounds so casual I know he's asking me something important.

'A fair bit. Izzy's my best friend.' The words stick in my throat. I hope he doesn't notice.

'And am I right in thinking you were round at the house earlier in the evening?'

'How do you know that?' I bet it was the old bat opposite with the dog that looks like her. She should be in bed but this is probably the most exciting thing that's happened to her since she set up Neighbourhood Watch.

'One of the neighbours was quite insistent.'

When he smiles, I can see his teeth pressed together, like a shark. I wonder whether I should be less concerned about protecting Rich and more worried about myself. 'That's right.'

'Any particular reason you came back?'

'I wanted to tell Izzy she was right about something.'

'Can I ask what?'

I take a deep breath. 'When I came to see her the first time, she told me my fiancé was cheating on me. I got home and found out she was right and I wanted to come back and thank her for being honest with me.'

When I say it like that, I can almost believe it. It could still be true. I could go to the hospital; kneel down and beg forgiveness. But even as I think it, I know I can't. Not now she knows I kissed Rich. I'm surprised Glenda didn't hurl that in my face when she came in. She hasn't mentioned it to the police either, I don't think. Izzy can't have told her. Yet Jenny knows. Why not Glenda?

'I'm sorry, I didn't catch that.' I snap my attention back to Tallis.

'I said that's a nasty-looking scratch you've got on your cheek. How did you manage that?'

'Er . . .' I touch my hand to my cheek, flustered. It's wet. The scab must have opened up again.

'Sorry to interrupt, Tom.' The door swings open and the other police officer pokes his head around. 'I'm going to take Glenda here back to the hospital. I'll check in with Ditton while I'm there.'

'Right you are.' Tallis waves him off then whips his head back to me. 'You were saying . . .'

The swiftness of his head movement makes me panic.

'My dog scratched me.'

'Your dog?' He raises his eyebrows.

'Missy.' I nod in agreement with myself. Now I'm trapped. 'She's a basset hound. She needs her nails cutting. Normally she grinds them down when she walks or I take her to the vet but we haven't been getting out much lately.' I don't know why I'm still talking. It must be obvious I'm lying. Why didn't I tell the truth?

'Hmm . . .' Tallis makes a note of something. 'I've a lab myself. If he were ever to swipe me, he'd leave track marks two inches thick. You might want to clean it up a bit. It looks nasty.'

256

'I can help you,' Jenny pipes up. I'd almost forgotten she was in the room. 'I'm sure Isabel will have some antiseptic in her medicine cupboard.'

'Why don't you go on by yourself, Rebecca? There are a couple of things I want to go over with Jenny. Then I'd like you to walk me through the rest of the evening from your perspective.'

Jenny sits back down again and I get up.

'Absolutely devoted to each other.' I can hear her warming to her theme as I walk out into the hall. 'Childhood sweethearts.'

I'm concentrating so hard on what she's saying that I nearly trip over Tilly's stuffed animals. I grab the offending elephant and the tiger sitting next to it and tuck one under each arm. Izzy won't want to come home to a mess. I dump them on the kitchen table and open the medicine cupboard. It's bursting at the seams. I grab a few bottles and some cotton pads and head to the downstairs loo so I can see what I'm doing in the mirror. The scratch is deeper than I thought. I have to swipe it half a dozen times with designer-looking antiseptic before it looks better. But the break from the intensity does me good. I'm feeling lighter as I come back up the stairs. They always say head wounds look worse than they are. Izzy will be fine. Maybe we can claw our friendship back. I could tell her I made up kissing Rich to get back at her. Lies seem to be tripping off my tongue lately. It would be in his interest to back me up. And hers to believe me. I should go down to the hospital. Being there when she wakes up would show her how much I care.

Tallis is in the hall when I turn the corner. He's ramrod

straight and he's got his police radio so close to his mouth it looks like he's snogging it. Through the open door behind him I can see Jenny curled into herself on the sofa like a bit of crumpled paper.

'What's happened?' I look at Tallis first but he's talking into the radio. 'Jenny?'

'It's Isabel.' Jenny looks up at me and I can see her eyes are ringed with tears. She sniffs noisily. 'She's passed.'

'Passed what?' I say idiotically. Then it hits me and my legs buckle. Hysteria bubbles at the back of my throat. I grope at the wall to stop myself falling down. She can't be gone. Not Izzy. She's always so full of life; so much more vivid than the next person. Except for tonight. I try to flush the memory of her grey face out of my mind. It lingers. Why didn't I call the ambulance sooner? A huge wave of guilt washes over me as reality starts to seep in. Izzy's gone. We'll never split another bottle of wine, finish each other's jokes or collapse into giggles over something only we found funny. What am I without her? When Jenny folds me into her arms, I realize I've started sobbing.

'There, there.' Jenny rocks me like a child. 'Hush now.' She shuffles me closer to Tallis, who turns his back to shield the call. Even through my grief I register he's speaking almost entirely in acronyms so eavesdropping is hardly worth the bother.

'ETA? And the SOCOs? How many? Roger that.' He nudges the radio back into its holster.

'I'm afraid I'm going to have to ask you to wait in here.' Tallis holds up his hand. 'Some forensic officers will be coming to take a look at the scene and we need to make sure nothing's disturbed.'

'And have you asked the permission of the house owner?' Jenny draws herself up to her full height. Her outraged tone is so reminiscent of the one she used when we were teenagers that under any other circumstances, I'd smile. Tonight I don't know if I'll ever smile again.

'I'm sorry?'

'Have you checked that my son's okay to have his house invaded? And can you assure me that it will all be done quietly so as not to disturb my granddaughter? I think that little girl will have enough to deal with in the morning without being disturbed by an army of men in uniform tramping through her house.'

The thought of Tilly waking up to a world without a mother is enough to set me off again. Izzy adored that little girl. I swipe at the tears running down my face and feel a stab of pain as my fingers jab the cut.

'What sort of dog did you say you had again, Rebecca?' Tallis addresses me. 'Only that does look pretty nasty. It looks like the kind of scratch that takes a lot of force.'

The scrape of the front door saves me from having to answer. Rich comes in, his head hanging, his face pale. The sight of him looking so shattered awakens something in me. I remember that feeling of hopelessness when my mum died. I swore I'd never feel that way again. The door opens wider and two policemen follow him in. One picks his way across the hall and heads upstairs while the other waits with Rich. I start to feel a sense of foreboding.

'Darling.' Jenny moves towards the door but Tallis blocks her way.

'I'm going to have to ask you to stay put for now,' he says.

'In that case, you'd better come in here,' she calls to Rich in her most put-out voice. He ignores her. 'Richard?'

Rich stares straight ahead, his eyes clouded. He looks like a statue. I notice his shirt is smeared with blood from where he cradled Izzy. In spite of myself, I shudder. I can't believe this is happening.

'What's going on?' Jenny calls out again. It's not clear whom she's asking so nobody responds.

'Will someone please tell me what's happening? A good job your father's in Portugal. If he were here—'

'They're taking me down to the station to answer a few questions, Mum.' Rich doesn't sound like himself. He sounds broken.

'This is harassment.' Jenny gets out her phone and starts hammering the keys. 'I'm calling your father. He'll know who to talk to. I know he's got an old client who's a QC.'

'It's just a few questions.' Rich shrugs like he's already defeated. 'And I've asked my own lawyer to meet me there.'

'Under what grounds, that's what I'd like to know.' Jenny turns the full force of her rage on Tallis. 'If it's because of that utter rubbish Glenda Maxwell-Martin was spouting, I'll have you know she's been on medication ever since I've known her. You can't trust a word she says.'

'We are duty bound to look into every complaint,' Tallis tells her smoothly. 'As your son says, it's just a few questions at this point.'

I look at Rich. His shoulders have rounded into themselves

and the expression on his face reminds me of Tilly. She's always been the spitting image of Izzy but tonight she's all that I can see in the purse of his lips. I think of her asleep, oblivious to what's unfolding. There's a thump as the third officer comes downstairs carrying a stack of Rich's clothes.

I stand up. I can't let this go on any longer.

'I don't understand why you want to speak to Rich when you know I was with him when we found her,' I say. 'Surely that excludes him from your enquiries.'

'You mentioned you met him in Clapham Junction and walked back here together. It's earlier in the evening that we're now trying to get a picture of.' Tallis dismisses me.

'I was with him then as well.' The words are out of my mouth before I can stop them.

'Bec.' The muscle in Rich's forehead is pulsing again, the way it does when he's about to lose his temper. He doesn't understand that I'm trying to help.

'I met him in Clapham Junction like you said but I didn't say we walked straight back.' My mind's sifting through the details, remembering what Rich said at the bus stop and the questions Tallis has already asked me. My eyes alight on Rich's damp trouser legs. I feel righteous as the story builds. Rich and Tilly should not have to go through this on top of losing Izzy. 'We went up to the common. Rich said he wanted to think but I thought I'd better keep him company because he was pretty upset.'

Tallis is writing everything down so quickly his pen is scratching through the paper.

'Which common was this?' I can tell by the way he says it that Rich has given him an answer. The skin on the back of my neck begins to tingle. Both Clapham and Wandsworth Commons are a walk from that bus stop. I look at Rich but he's staring at the floor. The stress muscle in his jaw is pumping. He must be furious with me for doing this. But I have to – for him and Tilly. I'm still scarred by the nights I cried for my mum and nobody came. It's why I attach myself so tightly to people. I can't bear for Tilly to feel the same. I look at Rich again and think of all the parties and festivals we've been to on Clapham Common; the afternoons we all used to spend lolling beneath the trees, tucking into packets of Pringles and sculling cheap wine. There's no way he'd go there to think. I take a deep breath and look Tallis squarely in the face.

'Wandsworth,' I say, and from the look in his eye I know I've got it right.

Twenty-Eight

Friday 22 February

1.27 p.m.

I dither over what to wear like I'm going to a job interview.
The last funeral I went to was my mum's. Today I feel like
I need to put on a suit of armour. I'd prefer an invisibility
cloak. But since I can't have that, I need something to hold
me up. Some days I feel like Izzy's still here – the way those
who lose an arm or leg report feeling the missing limb long
after it's been removed. Then I remember. I find myself
waking in the middle of the night, panting, wondering what
I could have done differently. But at the back of my mind,
the thought that life feels easier without her is blossoming.
And that makes me feel worse than the fact she's gone.

In the end I settle on a fitted black knee-length dress with
full sleeves. It gapes a little around the neck and there's
at least an inch spare at the waist. I haven't eaten today –
I've been finding food hard to stomach since that night. I

remember how cock-a-hoop Izzy was when she got food poisoning on her honeymoon. I picture her in the kitchen, standing under the skylight, pulling her jeans away from her waist to expose her bronzed abs. On me, weight loss just makes clothes look gappy.

The wake is being held back at Izzy's house. I'm not sure it's the best idea – Tony and Glenda won't go and after what happened was splashed all over the local papers, I doubt people will feel comfortable there. But Jenny's got a crack team of caterers who bring everything from the food to the crockery and cutlery and take it all when they go. No more local teens with wonky eyeliner. She's determined to make an event of it. I don't know if I can manage seeing people; imagining what they must think of me. Or if I can face Rich.

He was so furious with me for lying to the police. He never thought they'd charge him. He's an eternal optimist. He said that me jumping in had painted him into a corner; that they couldn't have held him on the back of something as circumstantial as a phone call. It worked though – the police released him without charge. In the inquest, the coroner ruled death by accident or misadventure, despite what Glenda said. She was furious.

I'm hoping if I sit at the back and don't hang around, I won't have to face Izzy's parents today. I know they haven't forgiven me for standing up for Rich that night. Not that they know the half of it. They just want someone to blame.

My hands shake as I try to do up my dress. If I don't hurry I'm going to be even later than I wanted to be. I yank the zip so hard the metal bites into the skin of my back. The sting feels like a release. I slip my feet into my least battered pair of black heels, shrug on a dark coat and go into the sitting room to get my bag. The flat looks shabby without Ed's stuff. The wall still bears the stripes of paint from when we were trying to choose a colour and the carpet's coming up in the corner where the sofa used to be and you can see the skirting boards are patchy. There are gaping holes on the shelves where his books used to be. Like a mouth missing half its teeth. It should make me miss him, I suppose. He's called a few times in the weeks since it happened, trying to see if I'm okay. But I feel nothing. All I can think about is the last time Izzy came here. How she said she was trying to look out for me. She was right in the end. And I didn't listen. One more thing in the ballad of our friendship to feel guilty about. I'm developing quite a list.

I'm halfway out of the front door when I see Rob leaning over the hedge, trying to reattach the gate to its hinges.

'Don't bother,' I say sourly. 'It's been like that for weeks.'

I turn to check I've closed the door properly, blocking him out of view. This is so typical of Rob. He used to explode in fits of rage when we were kids and then disappear until the dust had settled. If he thinks he can waltz in and act like nothing's happened, he's got another thing coming. 'What are you doing here? You haven't come to fix the gate.'

He digs his hands in his pockets and scuffs the floor with his feet. 'I've come to say sorry.'

'For which bit? Sorry for the fact that my best friend

died and you didn't even bother to call me back? Or sorry about the fact that my engagement broke down and you didn't call then either?' It feels good to get angry. 'Or could it be that you're finally sorry that you got so wound up about something so stupid in the first place? I mean, last time I checked the world was still turning. The sky didn't cave in just because it got out that your girlfriend's pregnant.'

In fact, Izzy's attempt to get the news out fell flat. Other than Sydney's official confirmation of the pregnancy (her stumble luckily didn't have any ill effects) and a blurry shot of her in the airport, the story totally disappeared. It helps that one of the One Direction boys impregnated someone around the same time. I wonder if Izzy would be disappointed if she knew.

'When you put it like that I've been a right bender, haven't I?' Rob puts out his hand to stop me as I brush past. 'I'm sorry. I've been away. I only just listened to your messages.'

The skin on his nose is peeling. It looks incongruous when the sky's stacked with clouds. Rob gives me a hopeful smile.

'Where did you go on holiday? Mars?'

'Come again?'

'You couldn't check your messages where you were?'

He looks defiant – he's never been one to back down. 'I was too upset.'

'*You* were upset? Rob, I've lost everyone. I needed you.' I suddenly feel close to tears. I shouldn't have to explain this.

'I know, Bec. I'm sorry. I'm sorry I wasn't there. I'm here now.' He wraps his arms around me in a clumsy hug. I try to push him away but he holds tight.

'I feel so guilty,' I mumble into his chest.

'You've got nothing to feel guilty for.'

'You don't understand. The last things I said to her were so horrible.' I don't know how many hours I've wasted, going round in circles, wishing I'd never fought with Izzy, that I'd never gone round to see her at all. But then if I hadn't I couldn't have saved Rich. I'd still be with Ed. I suppose I should be grateful to Izzy that I'm no longer trapped in a lie. The debt just makes me feel worse.

'There's no point torturing yourself. She was horrible to you too. It's the way you two were.' He puts his hands up to my face and thumbs away the tears. 'You don't want to smudge your mascara before the funeral, now do you? Hop in the car and let me give you a lift.'

I inhale. 'Is that why you're here?'

'It is, as it goes. Car's right there.'

My breath comes out in a blast of relief. I won't have to walk in alone. 'Oh, Rob, I didn't think you'd come.'

'Hang about, I'm not coming in.'

'What?'

'You've got the wrong end of the stick, Bec. I've come to give you a lift – didn't want you having to make your way there on your tod, especially when it starts pissing it down. But I can't come in. It wouldn't be right.'

'Why not?'

Rob starts hacking at the hedge with the heel of his hand. 'Because funerals are for mourners. I don't qualify. I'm not sad that the biggest nightmare in our lives took a nosedive down the stairs.'

'I can't believe you.' I'm shocked at how callous he is. 'Whatever Izzy did, nobody deserves that.'

'Let's not fall out about it.' He jiggles the keys to his Alfa Romeo. 'Let me run you there. It'll be much quicker.'

It's starting to spit now and talking to Rob has cut into my time. I don't have much choice if I don't want to be late. But what he said and the way he's acting – edgy, jumpy – bothers me.

'There's something I wanted to talk to you about,' he says as he starts the car and the engine roars to life.

'Go on.' I'm not really listening. I'm trying to process what he said. He was oddly specific about Izzy's fall.

'Sydney and I are moving back to the States.'

'What?' Rob's announcement brings me back to reality.

'I know,' he laughs. 'She wants to be closer to her family. I think all this stuff with the paparazzi freaked her out a bit. They're not as bad in the States. And there are more opportunities for us as a couple over there.' Rob starts to detail all the ways in which the States is better, but my mind slips out of focus. I know I didn't mention the stairs when I called Rob. I told him that she died, but I didn't say how. It made it too real. Then there's Sydney's call that night. I don't know how long Rob was missing for but at least part of his evening was unaccounted for. I don't want to think it but—

'Rob, where were you the night Izzy died?'

'What?'

'Sydney was trying to get hold of you. You were missing.

And she'd fallen.' Each detail feels like it could be a tiny fracture in our relationship. I wonder if Rob will read the implication behind them.

'Becster.' He side-eyes me. 'Are you asking me if I pushed your best friend to her death?'

It sounds ridiculous when he puts it like that. He's trying to embarrass me into dropping it. But I can't. The idea that he might have done something is starting to take root. He's always had a temper.

'Should I be asking you?' I counter.

There's a long pause, broken only by the sound of horns honking as Rob zips through an amber light on the verge of flicking red.

'Jeez, Bec,' he says eventually. 'You think you know someone.'

'Just answer.'

'No, of course I fucking didn't. I couldn't stand the witch but I wasn't going to do time over her.'

'Then where were you?'

'If you must know I went for a run and then I was so hacked off, I went to Nandos.'

'Nandos?' It's so ridiculous I hiccup out a giggle.

'All right, all right.' Rob's jaw clicks. 'Sometimes when I get really stressed, I go for a cheeky Nandos. Doesn't really fit with the business I'm in but there you go. And before you ask, when I realized I had about three hundred missed calls from my pregnant girlfriend, I hotfooted it back to where she was. I didn't even get a custard tart.'

'So how did you know she fell?'

'I read it online. I googled her after I got your message.

269

Any more questions, Miss Marple – or does the prosecution rest?'

I just nod sheepishly. Rob wouldn't lie to me. I don't know what I was thinking. It was an accident. 'I'm sorry,' I say. 'But I had to ask.'

I'm worried he'll be angry but – with the exception of Izzy – Rob's got an amazing capacity for forgiveness. And he knows he still owes me for ignoring my messages. 'Forget it.' He bats my apology away. 'You're a woman – you're all crazy. It's genetic.' He grins. 'What do you make of the news, then? Me in the big US of A.'

'Pretty big.' First Izzy leaves, then Rob. I try to sound interested instead of abandoned. 'When are you going?'

'As soon as. Syd's got a few things here she can't get out of so we'll be back and forth for a couple of months. Then we'll pack up for good.'

'Why such a rush?'

'No real reason.' He keeps his attention on the road.

'What about your clients?'

'They'll live. Right, there we are. Church is just on the left after the lights, isn't it? I'll park by the gastro pub.'

He peels away from the lights too quickly, tears down the side street and swings into a resident's parking space outside the pub. I want to ask more about why he's leaving but he keeps the engine running. I can tell he wants to go. I don't move from my seat. I haven't been to this church since Izzy and Rich's wedding – I remember the crowd clustered outside the church and people peering out of the pub as the wedding cars rocked up. Today the street is post-apocalypse empty. Everyone must already be inside.

'I'll be about if you need picking up afterwards.' Rob leans over me and opens the door. 'Give us a bell.'

Izzy and I used to give him such a hard time about his mockney accent when we were younger. It wouldn't be right to tease him without her. 'Thanks, Rob.'

'Anytime.' He shoots off so fast his tyres leave marks on the road.

Twenty-Nine

1.58 p.m.

The rain is coming down in sheets before I've crossed the road. I stand there and let it seep into my coat even though I know it'll make the wool smell. I can't go in until I'm sure there's nobody else coming. I don't want to talk to anybody and I don't want anybody to see me. I wait until the clock on the bell tower starts chiming and then I slide into the vestibule. Through its glass doors, I can see the mourners have divided into two clear sides, just like at a wedding. Izzy's side is so crammed, people are sitting shoulder-to-shoulder. I spot Ed in a pew towards the centre, wedged between Ben's pudgy shoulders and one of the church's columns. Another person to avoid. My eyes find the front of the church. Tilly, dressed in Sunday best, is bouncing up and down in the front row, like she's at a party. It reminds me of a Christingle (which she insists on calling Kris Kringle) a couple of years ago when she had to be taken out because she wouldn't sit still. Today, she's flanked by

Glenda and Tony, with a host of lesser relatives stuffed in on the end. Both of her grandparents are ignoring her and I long to swoop in and snatch her away. No four-year-old should have to endure this.

By contrast, Rich's side of the church gapes. Jenny and David have Henry and Charlie next to them in the front row, then the pews are almost empty until you get to the back five, which are full of non-descript people I don't recognize. It's possible they are the overspill from Izzy's side. They don't seem connected to Rich. He's at the front, scuffing his feet into each other and standing to the right of the large glossy photograph of Izzy laughing into the camera that's mounted on an easel. It's there in lieu of a coffin. Izzy was cremated earlier today. I wasn't invited. Close family only.

The vitality in the photograph makes it hard to look at so I turn my eyes to Rich instead. Even from behind, he looks thinner. His wide shoulders look like coat hangers and there's a stoop to them that wasn't there before. He looks so alone. I don't know why neither Jenny nor David is standing with him. I want so much to go in and walk up to him but I know it would be wildly inappropriate. Glenda and Tony are suspicious enough of me already and I haven't seen Jenny since it happened. I think back to Rich's face, contorted with rage the last time I saw him, and I stay put. I wait until the organ starts and people stand up. Then I open the doors just enough to slip through and find a seat in the corner of the last pew on Rich's side.

I hold in my tears during the service. I don't have the right to the kind of loud sobs Glenda is emitting from the front row. She only quietens down when Tony heaves himself up to the podium and makes a speech about Izzy's accomplishments, half of its content lifted from his father-of-the-bride speech. He can't finish it. Rich puts out a hand to help him down from the podium but Tony ignores it and hefts himself back into the pew. Then Rich starts to speak. Even from the back row, I can see Glenda twitching in her seat, like she wants to leave. Rich can't meet anyone's eye. His voice dips in and out as it bounces off the crenelated stone columns. When he sits down, nobody puts a comforting arm around him the way they did for Tony. Jenny shifts in her seat to make room, but that's it. I feel desperately sorry for him. He looks so lost.

At the end of the service, Tilly stands up in a black dress at least two sizes too big to put a pink rose by Izzy's photograph. My tears fall so hard and fast they trip off my nose. I bury my head in my order of service. There can't be much call for funeral attire for a four year old. There shouldn't be. I swipe viciously at my tears and refuse to look up until everyone has filed outside. Only when the church is totally empty do I get up.

I hover by the doorway, trying to make myself inconspicuous while I find the best escape route. Glenda and Tony have laid on champagne and canapés inside the church hall so that's the direction most people are going in. Jenny's standing by the churchyard gate, trying to drum up people to go back to the house in Clapham. Most are making their excuses and swerving around her. Although it's stopped raining, the weather is still aiding a quick getaway. Rich is nowhere to be seen.

I duck along the side of the church, not sure if I'm trying to find him or avoid him, and nearly collide headfirst with Tilly.

'Whatcha doing back here, Tills?' I can't believe nobody's watching her.

'Puddle jumping,' she says in a *duh* voice, like it's the only thing in the world she could be doing. I love her for it.

'You're pretty good.'

'I got new shoes.' Tilly sticks one sopping foot out in front of her. 'They've got big-girl heels.'

I look at the black patent Mary Jane she's wiggling in front of me. They're smeared in mud. Izzy would have a fit.

'Do you think you should go back and find Granny now?'

'Do you think Mummy will like them when she comes back?'

She looks so hopeful that I have to press my hand to my mouth and step away so I don't lose it in front of her. Of course she doesn't get the concept of death. She's four. I feel wrung out. This weather doesn't help. My sleeves are clinging damply to my arms and my dress is pressing against my chest. The air feels like it's pushing against me. I wish it would start raining again.

It was scorching at my mum's funeral. I remember how weird it felt to do something as mundane as sweat when my mum was dead. Izzy, wearing something that resembled a cocktail dress, positively glowed. Some of my dad's friends did double takes until their wives elbowed them in the ribs and moved them along. Not that Izzy hung around. She'd been a rock in the run-up but when it came to the funeral she stayed long enough to neck three champagnes in a row and went to go and watch Rich play rugby instead. That was Izzy. Always there for me – when it suited her. That's what makes missing her so complicated.

'We're heading back to the house now.' I don't see Rich at first. He's leaning against the plinth dedicated to the parish's war dead and his face is half in shadow. 'Tilly wanted me to come and get you, though personally I can't think of anything worse. Tempted to skip the whole thing and check in to a hotel.'

'Aren't people expecting you?' I try to get a feel for whether he's forgiven me.

'To be honest, I think people would be glad if I bailed.' His tone gives nothing away. 'I'm the reason most of them are swerving it.'

'They just don't know what to say. That's what they were like when my mum died, too.'

'Or it's a case of guilty until proven innocent. Even my own family doesn't seem to believe the official version of events. Mum can barely look at me.'

I feel a thump of guilt in my chest. 'I'm sorry I jumped in and said you were with me. I was only trying to help.'

'I know. But sometimes I can't help thinking it would have been better if they had taken things further. Then I'd have had the chance to show I didn't do it. So that people don't listen to Glenda.' He jerks his head back towards the churchyard. 'She's gone home, by the way. Had to be helped into a cab. So it's safe to come out.'

'Honestly, I'm sure nobody believes you did anything bad for a second. Anyone who knows you knows you'd never do anything to hurt Izzy.'

'Do they?' He tries to hitch his mouth into a smile but his eyes are hooded.

'Well they should do. And if they don't, they'll have me to deal with.'

'Thanks.' He doesn't smile but he does move a step closer, into the light. It's a start. 'Anyway I'd better get going.'

I take a chance that his need for support will outweigh his anger. 'Why don't we nip into the pub before we head back to yours? You look like you could use a drink.'

Thirty

Monday 4 March

10.10 a.m.

Everyone in the office is avoiding me. I've been working from home a lot and this is my first real day back. I remember this blanket of silence from when my mum died. People think if they ignore the situation, things will go back to normal. They don't understand that once you've lost someone important, there is no normal. Jules is the only person in the office who still talks to me. And even she's jittery.

'You don't have to treat me like I'm in mourning,' I remind her after she's asked me if I'm okay for the third time. 'Sorry. I can't stand everyone looking at me.'

'Don't worry, it'll die down.' Jules screws up her face at her choice of words. 'Lucy from production's getting that much-needed nose job next week and then everyone will be looking at her, not you.'

'How do you know that?' I can't help glancing over. I'd

278

never noticed her nose before but from this angle it does look prominent.

'She's doing a feature on it for us. They're giving her a discount. Anyway, I didn't come over for that. I came to see how you are.'

'I'm fine,' I say, once again. I turn back to my keyboard and try to look busy.

'You must miss her.'

'I do.' And I do miss her. But also, I don't. Not that I can tell Jules that.

'Do you want to go for a drink tonight?'

'I can't. I promised I'd pick Tilly up from nursery.'

'That's the third time this week.'

'Are you counting?' It's snappier than I intended and Jules's face falls.

'I didn't mean to—'

'No no, I know you didn't. I'm sorry I snapped. You sound like my brother. But I'm happy to do it. Rich doesn't want to get a nanny right away. We think it would be hard for Tilly to have someone she doesn't know in the house.'

I feel a stab of pleasure at the casual way I can use the word 'we'.

'How's she doing?'

'She has her good days.' I think of the nights she refuses to go upstairs; how she kicks and flails in Rich's arms until he calms her down. 'Rich is wonderful with her.'

Jules frowns. 'It's all very well when she's at nursery but what's he going to do when it's the summer holidays? He'll need someone. I know some good sites if he's looking for an au-pair – they might be a bit north London-centric though.'

'Nurseries don't have holidays,' I remind her. 'They run all the way through. Of course, it'll be different when she starts school in September. But I'm sure we'll have figured out what to do by then.'

Jules looks like she might burst into tears. 'Of course. She's not even at school yet. God, so little.'

'Are you okay?' I eye Jules, wondering why she's having such an extreme reaction.

'Do you want to come to the vending machine? I'm starving.'

'I should really get some work done. Especially if I'm leaving early.'

'Please. I need to talk to you in private.'

I stand up and grab my wallet, my interest piqued. Usually Jules is like a public service announcement. She can't keep anything to herself. 'The vending machine it is.'

We pass Tony's office on the way. The blinds are drawn. I try to peer through the slats. He hasn't been in since Izzy died. There are rumours he isn't coming back. Then again, it's a magazine – rumours are what we do. But I have to admit I hope he doesn't. I don't want to bump into him. What if he blames me?

'So?' I say as Jules peruses the shelves. 'What's up?'

She keys in the code for a Mars bar. 'I'm pregnant.'

'Jules.' I reach out and give her a hug. 'That's great news. I'm so happy for you. You should have told me before and I could have bought the Mars bar!'

'You can buy the next one. This baby's going to be the size of a small house if its brother is anything to go by. I'm hungry all the time.'

I don't point out that Jules is always starving, pregnant or not. I don't know where she puts it. She's about the size of a gnat.

'How far along are you?'

'Fourteen weeks last Tuesday. I was going to tell you earlier but . . . that's not why I wanted to talk to you.'

'It's not?'

'Well, it is, but it isn't. I was talking to Tina – she knows, by the way – and I suggested you might want to do my mat leave cover.'

'You're joking, right? I don't know anything about beauty.' I pull at a strand of hair coming loose from my ponytail. 'Look at me. Hardly the epitome of glam.'

'Don't be silly, you're gorgeous. Anyway, you don't need to know about beauty to edit it. I barely do any writing these days. Tina was really impressed with your interview with Sydney Scott. Plus it'd be great news for her budget if she doesn't have to get someone in. She needs a bit of convincing, but I'm on it. So are you up for it?'

'Gosh, I don't know.' I try to imagine myself as acting beauty editor. 'It's a big step up.'

'You'd be fab.' Jules takes a bite of her Mars bar. 'Don't know what it would mean for your nursery pick-ups though. But, you know you can do it.'

'Maybe you're right.' I decide to ignore Jules's nursery comment for now. 'Only if you promise to show me exactly what to do and not to pop until I've got it.'

'Deal.'

'Well let's get back in there then. I can't be loitering

out here with the likes of you if I'm going to be the next beauty editor.'

I make a face at Jules so she knows I'm joking, but there's a definite spring in my step as we go back in.

5.29 p.m.

Although there are a few four-by-fours parked up, mothers tapping away on iPhones behind the wheel, I'm the first to knock on the nursery door. I left the office well before five. Nobody said a word – grief has its benefits – and I was determined not to be late. This time, it isn't Kayleigh that opens the door. It's a woman in her fifties with Deirdre Barlow glasses and the loose, flowing clothes of a former hippy. She makes a sad face when I explain I'm there to pick up Tilly.

'I should be on—'

'We're aware of the circumstances. I'll go and get her.'

The Tilly that greets me isn't the exuberant child that came flying through the doors a few months ago. This Tilly has a pout and her head is bent low. Kayleigh's marching by her side like a prison warden.

'Tilly, can you just wait here a moment?' Kayleigh motions at the coatrack. 'I need to have a quick word with Mu—. My friend Rebecca over here.'

I can't believe she nearly said 'mum'. My dislike for her intensifies. Tilly's head sinks lower.

'We've had a bit of a problem with Tilly today,' Kayleigh says in a stage-whisper when she reaches me.

'What kind of a problem?'

'I'm afraid there was an incident with another child.'

'What did they do?' I glance over. Tilly's chin is on her chest and her lips are quivering. Heaven help the kid that hurt her if I get my hands on them.

'I'm afraid it was Tilly that was the aggressor. She bit another little girl and refused to say she was sorry. We understand . . . there's been a lot going on at home, but we needed to bring it to your attention.'

'Did she say why?' I know I sound aggressive but I don't care.

'I'm sorry?' Kayleigh looks taken aback.

'Did Tilly say why she bit the other girl? I imagine she was provoked.'

'It's our policy not to ask. We think asking for a justification normalizes the behaviour. At Oak Tree we believe there's no excuse for any acts of violence.'

'It's hardly an act of violence, is it?'

'I'm sorry?'

'I mean; they're four. Four year olds bite, don't they?'

'Not at Oak Tree.' Kayleigh says it with a grandiosity that makes me want to bite *her*.

'How nice it must be to live in Utopia. I think we're done here.' I hold out my hand to Tilly. 'Come on, darling, shall we have a McDonald's on the way home?'

I can't bring myself to eat in at the horror show that is McDonald's in Clapham Junction so we get a takeaway. I refuse to let Tilly eat it until we get home and I cut up a flaccid-looking cucumber so that her entire plate of food isn't beige. Tilly's wolfing down the nuggets when the front door slams and we hear Rich thundering down the stairs.

'Where's my monkey?' He picks her up and flips her

upside down just like he used to. I can't believe how strong he's being, shouldering all this alone. 'Just checking for loose change.' He pretends to rattle her and she curls up in giggles. It's the first time she's smiled since we got home. 'Nothing here – did you spend it all at Maccy D's?'

'I thought she could use a—'

'Relax. I was just wondering if there was enough for three.'

'I can run back if you've got a Maccers craving.' He looks like he could use a good meal. His face is gaunt and the contents of the fridge weren't particularly appetizing when I got the cucumber out.

'Don't worry about it. You're our guest. I'll knock something together later.' He rubs his hands together in a mock-sinister way. 'If you're feeling brave, that is.'

'You can't be as bad as me. I only worked out how to use a tin opener last week.'

'Now that is bad. We'll have to have a cook-off to see who's the worst and Miss Tilly can judge.'

I smile. I'm so glad things are back to normal between us. Although Rich made it clear he didn't approve of what I did when we went for that drink, he started to thaw when he realized why I did it. For Tilly. Me helping with her has also smoothed things over, though in my more insecure moments I've wondered whether he's only being nice to me because he has nobody else. I shake those thoughts away. They don't do anyone any good. He scoops Tilly up and carries her back to the breakfast bar. 'We're going to need some sustenance first though. Can I tempt you to a chip?'

He grabs a handful of Tilly's chips and hands me one.

She immediately tries to prise the rest from his hands. 'They're mine, they're *mine*!'

'Can't Daddy have one little chip? This little one's dying to be eaten.'

He walks the smallest chip off the plate, up his shirt and towards his chin. I think Tilly's going to laugh but to my horror, she bursts into tears.

'Mummy says chips are bad for you. I want her to come home. Why hasn't she come back?'

I feel like I've been smacked in the guts. Rich snatches Tilly up and holds her close. Over her shoulders, his eyes meet mine. 'I'm going to take this one upstairs. I think the cook-off will have to wait.'

'I don't want you to take me upstairs.' Tilly cries harder. 'I'm scared.'

'Shush, shush.' Rich strokes her hair. 'There's nothing to be scared of. Daddy's here.'

'Every night,' he mouths over her shoulder as he turns around and starts towards the stairs. I hover in the kitchen after they've gone. I'd planned to go home and have a bath and a large glass of wine – and luxuriate in the possibility of being beauty editor – but I think Rich could use someone to talk to. It doesn't feel right leaving him on his own.

I take a pan out of the cupboard next to the Aga. An omelette is about the only thing I can make. I crack some eggs in a bowl and hunt through the fridge to see if there's anything else I can throw in with the milk. But the ham is curling up at the corners and the mushrooms look wrinkled. Rich needs to look after himself and Tilly better. Perhaps I should be doing more. Clearly nobody else is pitching in. I pull out the butter dish and pop it next to the hob, ready to go. By the time Rich comes down, the butter's melted into a golden pool.

'That took longer than I expected.' He rubs his eyes. 'Is there any wine?'

'Let me get you a glass.'

'I'd prefer a bucket. You didn't make an omelette, did you?' He's staring at the bowl of congealing eggs and milk like it's got a Michelin star.

'Honestly, it took five minutes.' I decide not to mention the ten minutes I spent picking eggshell out of my first attempt. 'How is she?'

'She's asleep.' Rich sighs heavily as he reaches around me to grab two wine glasses from the cupboard above the hob. 'Finally.' He gives me a wobbly smile that makes me want to hug him. He's being so brave but I know he's suffering, too. 'We've got a very confused and miserable little girl on our hands.'

The way he says 'our hands' makes me want to freeze the moment and commit it to memory so I can replay it later and untangle my feelings about it. Pleasure that he sees us as a team undercut by the usual guilt that it's at Izzy's expense. I could definitely use some therapy. But right now Tilly and Rich are more important. 'You're doing an amazing job, you know,' I tell him. 'The fact that you can get her smiling again after everything that's happened ... not many people could do that.'

'I think that's what upset her. She feels like she's not allowed to be happy anymore. It breaks my heart.'

I think of Tilly's pinched face when I picked her up. 'And

mine. It's so unfair that she has to go through this.' I turn back to the hob. I don't know if I should tell him what happened at nursery but I don't want to keep secrets from him either. 'She had a bit of a tough day at nursery too.'

'Oh God, what now?' Rich groans.

'Nothing major,' I hedge. 'The nursery blew the whole thing out of proportion . . . but she bit another child.'

'Oh crap, who? I hope it's not the spawn of one of the more litigious parents.'

'They wouldn't say.'

'I forgot they don't. Data protection or something ridiculous. As if the kids won't spill the beans. Last time I asked Tilly she sang like a canary. Turned out the boy had given her a whack with a toy so she'd taken a chunk out of his arm. Fair enough in my book. Not that we told her that.'

His smile fades and I know he's thinking of Izzy.

'I'll get these eggs on.' I turn back to the Aga. I don't want to see the loss on his face.

Thirty-One

Friday 22 March

8.31 p.m.

'Have you considered taking Tilly to see someone?' We're outside on the patio, taking advantage of the mild weather and sitting at the distressed wooden table-and-chair set Izzy bought at the end of last summer but never used. For someone with such a huge presence, it's amazing how normal it's starting to feel without her. Missy's curled at my feet as if she lives here. I pick an olive from its plastic container and bite into it, slurping out the tang of the feta inside. I picked them up from Waitrose on the way over. Rich had offered to cook me dinner to thank me for all my help but in the end he was running late so we decided chips and dips would do instead. When he doesn't reply, I think Rich hasn't heard the question. I repeat it.

He pauses, a handful of Doritos halfway to his mouth. 'What do you mean?'

'I thought maybe if she had someone to talk to—'

'She can talk to me.'

'Of course she can, I'm not saying that. I was just . . . Did you know I saw someone after my mum died?'

'Did you?' Rich's tone isn't encouraging but I persist.

'I did. My dad insisted on it.' I want to tell him how unpacking my thoughts every week was the only way to make sense of what had happened, that sometimes talking to someone paid to listen is the only way to feel heard. But I can tell from his closed expression that he doesn't get it. 'What I'm trying to say is that it might help for her to see someone outside, someone she can say anything to. It definitely helped me.'

Rich picks at a gap in the table where the wood has split. 'Tilly's different.'

'How?' I want to sound non-judgemental. Rich is doing an amazing job of parenting Tilly, but it's a lot for one person. And there's clearly something bubbling away inside her that needs dealing with. I'm surprised he can't see it.

'She's not a teenager for one.'

'No, I know that. I just think there are a lot of complex emotions surrounding the death of a parent, whatever age you are. Talking to someone about it—'

'She's got me. I don't want to be cruel about your dad, Bec, but he was always a bit of a non-entity, wasn't he? You've always said how detached he was, even before your mum died. I'm not like that. Tilly knows she can count on me.'

I should defend my dad, tell Rich that it was the aftermath of my mum's death – and his relationship with

Judith – that pulled us apart, and that's what I don't want to happen to him and Tilly. But he doesn't seem in the mood for listening.

'I know she does,' I say soothingly. 'And I get what you're saying and why you might have reservations. I'm just saying that—'

'I don't want her talking to a stranger and raking the whole thing up, all right.' Rich bangs his fist against the table and makes me jump. I've never seen him like this. 'I've seen this kind of shit on TV – the way psychologists are with kids. They'll have her going over and over it, make her think she feels things she doesn't. Some things are best left well alone. She lost her mum. Of course she's sad and broken. She just needs to work through it. I'll help her. She's got me. She doesn't need some bloody shrink.'

I hop off my chair awkwardly. He couldn't have made it any clearer that I've overstepped the mark. That after all I've done, it's still them and me. 'I should get going.'

Rich is on his feet so quickly the gravel crunches beneath him. 'No, don't. I'm sorry I snapped. It's been a shitty day with work and Tilly. But that's no excuse. Please stay.'

'It's okay.' I reach under the table for my handbag. I don't want him to see that he's upset me. He's got enough to manage without my emotions. And I shouldn't have pushed it. 'I get you've got a lot on your mind.'

'I shouldn't take it out on you though – especially since you're the one person in my corner.'

'Has something happened?' He hasn't been himself since he came in this evening. He was even short with Tilly earlier, snapping at her when she asked for another bedtime story. I should have picked up on it. I was too focused on the pleasure of sitting down and relaxing together.

'HR suggested I take compassionate leave.' Rich sounds bitter. 'It's a joke. They just want me out of the building because I make people feel uncomfortable.' He shakes his head. Under the bitterness, he sounds defeated. 'I've only just gone back. They'll be angling for voluntary redundancy before long. If they can get it in before the end of the tax year in April, all the better. It's not like the department is doing well.'

'Oh, Rich.' He looks so lost. Without thinking I reach out and squeeze his arm. It's the first time I've touched him since the night we kissed. I snatch my hand away. I shouldn't be thinking about that moment right now.

Rich has got his face screwed up. He hasn't even noticed. He's too busy fighting tears. 'It's fine. I couldn't give a toss about work. It's Tilly. I worry I'm doing it all wrong. The crying; the biting.'

'But that's perfectly normal. She's sad. She just needs to work through it. You said so yourself.'

'I say a lot of things.' Rich gives a rueful smile. 'Some of them I even mean. But I haven't got a clue what I'm doing. What if I'm totally fucking it up?'

'You're not. Tilly's brilliant. Because you're a brilliant dad.'

'But I don't know how to do it on my own.' I can see tears bubbling in the corners of his eyes. In all the time I've known him, I've never seen him cry.

'You're not on your own.' I try to infuse my words with

the strength I know he needs. There's so much more I wish I could say.

This time he's the one that reaches for me. He puts his arms around me and I pull his head onto my shoulders. I can feel his tears seeping into the top of my dress. He's hugging me so tightly I think he's going to break my ribs. I'm just absorbing how it feels to be needed this way when he takes a shuddering breath and pulls his head back, breaking the connection. I tense. He's going to tell me that as much as I want to help I'm not a parent and I have no idea what he's going through. He's right. I gather the corners of my mouth into a smile so that I can pretend the rejection doesn't hurt. But Rich doesn't say a word. He dips his head and kisses me instead.

I feel like my knees might slide out from under me. I know this is a terrible idea. But I can't help myself pushing closer to him, sweeping my hands down his back. I've waited so long. If it weren't for the faint smell of Doritos on the breeze, this would be one of the most romantic moments of my life.

'Bec.' He stops and I know it's all going to come crashing down.

I squeeze my eyes shut. If I say it first at least I can retain my dignity. 'I know, we shouldn't be doing this.'

'We shouldn't.' He sounds torn. 'But I can't help it.'

I open my eyes.

'I know it should feel wrong but it feels so right.' His cheekbones flush. 'Sorry, that sounded like the lyrics to some nineties song, didn't it? Cheesy.'

'It didn't.' I reach for him again, barely daring to hope. 'It's exactly how I feel, too.'

He buries his hands in my hair and pulls me close. It's as if we're right back to that night by the rose bushes. And things had happened the way they were meant to. When I close my eyes, it's like falling into a dream.

Thirty-Two

Friday 19 April

7.20 p.m.

The smell of burning fat stings my nostrils and hits the back of my throat as Rich puts the steaks on the skillet. They immediately start to spit.

'Salt?' he says, and I pass him the salt. 'Pe—' I hand him the pepper mill.

'Am I that predictable?

'Adorably so.'

He puts the arm not holding the spatula around me and flips the steak. We're starting to anticipate what the other needs and wants automatically. I already feel more in step with him than I ever did with Ed. It's like we've been together for years, not months. The way we could have been if only . . . I duck out from under his arm. I wonder if Izzy pops into Rich's head as often as she does mine.

'Everything okay?'

'Fine. I don't want to get anything on my dress.' I smooth down the material, inspecting myself for marks. The dress I'm wearing is so much more expensive than what I'd usually buy; I might still take it back to the shop after I've worn it.

'Where is the leaving do again?'

'Some private members' club Sydney's part of. I think it's near Piccadilly.'

'I'm sorry I'm not coming. I don't think I'm up to public scrutiny quite yet.'

'I get it.' I don't mention that I haven't told Rob about my relationship with Rich yet. I keep meaning to. I tell myself I haven't had the opportunity. Really, I don't want to jinx it and I'm nervous of Rob's reaction. After that first night, I was terrified Rich would wake up and think it was a huge mistake. I laid there for about an hour watching him sleep. I had to get up and start doing something else in case he woke up and thought I was some kind of pervert. Even now, I find myself touching him whenever I go past. To prove it's real.

'Why don't you come back here later?'

I'm dying to say yes but I force myself not to jump in too quickly. 'What about Missy? She'll have been on her own since the dog-sitter dropped her off.' I hesitate, not wanting to seem presumptuous. 'I can't leave her overnight.'

'I'll drive over and pick her up after dinner. It won't take long.'

'You'd do that?'

'Only if you promise to do the washing up.'

'Deal.' And just like that we reach another milestone. We

talk about the usual things during dinner; Tilly, how much he hates his job, who might be at the party tonight – but inside I'm glowing.

7.40 p.m.

I contemplate putting on more make-up after Rich goes to fetch Missy. He's used to having someone who looks effortlessly camera-ready after all. But I don't want to end up looking like a clown so I wander around looking for something to do instead. The house is spotless – he's upped the amount of times their cleaner comes – but already signs of Izzy's absence have crept in. No fresh flowers on the side or designer handbags hung on the back of the chairs. There are coloured pens scattered all over the dining table. I spot a lid on the floor and reunite it with its owner. Finally the house looks like a child lives here.

Not that it's having a positive effect on Tilly's behaviour. She screamed blue murder when Rich put her to bed tonight – and came down twice – and there have been two more biting incidents, both of which the nursery handled badly. I've grown to dread pick-up. Oak Tree has a school attached to it, which I know Tilly's name is down for. I'm not sure she should go. After the way he took my head off about counselling, I haven't voiced this to Rich.

I've caved and started putting on another coat of lipstick when Missy comes clattering down the stairs. She greets me like a long-lost friend, throwing herself at my legs and head-butting me in the knees. I feel a pang of guilt. I've been neglecting her.

'Keys.' Rich slides them along the breakfast bar. 'Your place is looking a bit sorry for itself, isn't it?'

I cap the lipstick with a click. 'I haven't been there much.'

'I wasn't having a go. It got me thinking.'

'About what?' My heart rate speeds up.

Missy chooses this moment to squat on the floor and let out a torrent of urine. '*Missy.*' I yank her towards the bi-fold doors. 'I am so sorry. Where's your kitchen roll? I am so embarrassed.'

'Don't worry about it.' Rich is totally unruffled. 'These floors have seen far worse. We potty-trained Tilly in this kitchen, remember?'

I do remember. Tilly did not take to potty training naturally and for months Izzy and Rich used to find the evidence of this hidden behind sofas and curtains. But it's not my memory to share.

'Yeah – well.' I change the subject. 'That's no excuse for Missy. Anyway, what were you going to say?'

'What do you mean?'

'You said you were thinking?'

'I can't remember now. My brain is in power-down mode.'

'Oh.' I try not to sound too disappointed. It's typical. Every time I think we're moving forward, Izzy pops up in some guise or other. Usually I end up feeling guilty for resenting that, but tonight I can't quite manage it. I think it must be the prospect of seeing Rob and Sydney; it's putting me on edge.

'Don't you need to get a move on? Robbo will be gutted if you miss it.'

'I'm not sure he'd care that much.' I try to prolong the moment.

'Play nice. You've only got one brother. The fact that he actually wants you around means you're one up on me.' He tries to sound flippant but I know him too well.

'Still nothing from Charlie or Henry?'

'Apparently Laura is finding it difficult.' Rich makes a face. 'She was very fond of Izzy. And you know what Henry's like. If it's not right in front of his face he doesn't give a shit.'

'So what? They should—'

'Forget about it.' Rich sounds bone tired. 'You should get going.'

'Maybe I should stay behind. Especially if Missy's playing up.'

'Bec, I can handle an incontinent basset hound.' Rich puts on the 'firm dad' voice he uses with Tilly. It makes me smile. 'Now go. Just hurry home.'

I leave reluctantly and hug his use of the word 'home' to me all the way to the party.

8.30 p.m.

'You've got to be kidding.'

'You sound like John McEnroe.' Since Rob's been dating Sydney, I've noticed American terminology creeping into his speech. I keep picking him up on it and he doesn't like it.

'Sod McEnroe.' Rob looks incredulous, which is hypocritical given his own dating rap sheet. 'Are you telling me you've shacked up with Rich Waverly when Izzy's not even cold? That's a bit sick.'

'We haven't shacked up.' I glance round. We're standing

by the bar, under a heater shaped like a hair drier on the club's roof terrace and I've already seen two BAFTA-winners and a minor rapper walk by on their way inside. I wouldn't have told him if I thought he was going to make such a scene. 'We've just started seeing each other.'

'You mean shagging. If you were *seeing* him, he'd be here.'

'He couldn't face the crowd. And after your reaction I can't say I blame him.'

'Guilty conscience, more like.'

'I thought you'd be happy for me,' I snap. 'You never liked Ed.'

'Happy you've ditched Mr Insurance and found someone new, yes. Happy that person happens to be the husband of your dead best friend on the rebound? Not so much.'

'Rich isn't on the rebound.' I grab a canapé from a passing waiter and chomp it down.

'No, he's high on life. His wife just died and he's already banging the babysitter.'

'It's not like that.' Rob's always been able to zero in on my weaknesses and exploit them. And he's never liked anyone I've dated. The joys of having a sibling. I try to brazen it out. 'This has been years in the making, you must see that.'

'Then why did he marry Izzy?'

The question is like a slap in the face but Sydney glides over before I have to find a response. She's wearing a midi-length cream dress that accentuates her bump and manages to make the rest of her look tiny. From behind you'd barely know she was pregnant. Her calves, flashing in the roof garden's mood lighting, are more slender than mine. She's even rocking a pair of fierce white Louboutin shoes with wings at the heel and a feathered trim. She looks like an avenging angel. I shrink back. Rob and I might have made up but I haven't spoken to her since that angry phone call.

To my surprise, she throws her arms around me. 'Bec, you're here at last. I thought you weren't coming.' Before I can even absorb that she's not angry anymore, she turns to Rob. 'Did you ask her yet?'

'Ask me what?' I turn to look at Rob but he's busy grabbing two orange juices from a tray on the bar.

'Drink this, babe.' Rob ignores me. 'You've been running around all night. You've got to keep your energy up.'

'My feet are killing me,' she concedes.

'If you will wear those ridiculous shoes . . .' He bumps his hip against hers.

'Hey, no fair. Don't come between me and my Loobies. You know you'll lose.' She bats his arm and I study the mirrored bar. Seeing someone flirting with your sibling is never a comfortable experience.

'So did you ask her?' There's a touch of impatience, as if she's not used to repeating herself.

'Not yet.' Rob looks sullen.

'I'll do it then.' Sydney turns to me and gives me her widest smile, the one she used when she won the Oscars. It's amazing how quickly she can change her expression. And how special her smile can make you feel. 'So, Bec . . .'

'Yes.' I try to concentrate but her enthusiasm is slightly overwhelming. And Rob's question is still gnawing away at me.

'Now that my press officer has vacated her post—'

'Wait? Tasha left?'

Sydney puts her hands on her hips. 'Honestly, don't you guys talk at all? Yes, Tasha left. She made some calls I wasn't happy with.' She looks at Rob like she expects him to finish her sentence. He doesn't say anything.

'Okay, I'll say it. She was the one who gave your magazine the pregnancy story. Now she's gone, we're a person down and we wondered if you might like to—'

'Tasha was the leak?' I croak. It feels like someone's squeezing my windpipe. It's hard to breathe. *Izzy didn't betray me.*

'She won't want to do it,' Rob's saying. His voice is just background noise.

'I'm sorry about what happened.' Sydney looks genuinely upset. 'It all got out of control. I've been looking for a way to make it up to you—'

'So you want me to come and work for you?' I struggle to focus.

'I thought the piece you wrote was awesome.' She grimaces. 'Before the changes were made. Now I know you had nothing to do with them, it seemed to make sense. And I know Robbie would love to have you close. Especially when the baby arrives.'

Rob snorts. I can tell he's still annoyed about the Rich thing. He hasn't apologised for blaming me for everything either. Much as he'd hate me to say it, he's similar to Izzy that way.

Sydney ignores him. 'So what do you say?'

For a moment, I picture myself in New York, fielding calls from her trendy brownstone. I think of Jules saying

Tina still had to be convinced about the beauty-editor role, the shopping list of complaints I get every time I pick up Tilly from nursery and the For Sale sign outside my cramped London flat. How easy it would be to leave all that behind. But then I think of Rich.

'I can't.'

'I knew it,' Rob sneers. 'Nothing can compare with the power of the Waverlys, can it?' He frowns at me then – glossing over the three-week period when he refused to take my calls – he delivers his final comment like it's a character assassination. 'Not even your own family.'

And that's the last thing he says to me that evening.

Chapter Thirty-Three

10.05 p.m.

Rich is curled up on the sofa with a stack of papers in his hands and Missy snuggled next to him, her head on his lap. He dumps the papers on the floor as I come down the stairs. 'You're back early.'

I wiggle out of my heels and slump next to Missy. 'It wasn't that much fun.'

'Did something happen?'

I bury my fingers in Missy's fur. Where to start? I never talk to Rich about the magazine. I haven't even told him about the beauty-editor role because I want to save it until it's official. And he doesn't know anything about the pregnancy leak. But if I'm honest, neither of those things are what's really bothering me.

'Do you remember the night you and Izzy got together?'

Rich does a double take. 'Not what I was expecting.'

'This might be massively random.' I have to keep going. 'And you won't remember and this probably sounds totally crazy but there was a moment at that house party. We were standing by the rose bushes and you leaned in and I thought there might have been a . . . that we might have . . .'

I break off. I was hoping he'd swoop in and finish my sentence. Instead the silence stretches. He's obviously fumbling for a platitude to make me feel better. Even if it was just about tonight, that would mortifying. But it's worse. Izzy was right. I've been holding onto a moment that doesn't exist for the better part of two decades. I scrunch my head down into my shoulders. I don't think I can ever look him in the face again.

'Of course I remember kissing you,' he finally says softly. 'I'd been crazy about you all year.'

'Crazy about *me*?' A wash of relief, disbelief hot on its heels. 'Why?'

'You were smart, funny.' He ticks the reasons off on his fingers. 'And you had the biggest boobs in the class.'

He attempts a roguish smirk. I have to laugh. We're on a sofa so expensive it has its own insurance policy, two mortgages between us. Rich has a child; he's a widower, for God's sake. My best friend's dead. And still it comes down to boobs. I should hold onto this moment of levity but I can't help myself. 'So why—'

'Why did I end up with Izzy?' His words unconsciously echo Rob's and my smile fades. 'There it is. The big question.' He splays his hands in supplication. 'I suppose I was flattered. I got swept up. I couldn't believe someone as good-looking as her was going after me.' He chuckles. 'My brothers couldn't either.'

I nod, trying to act as if it doesn't hurt. He sees my face.

'I know that sounds bad but you don't know what it was like growing up with Charlie and Henry. Everything I did, they'd already done it better. But neither of them had ever gone out with anyone who looked like Izzy.' He pauses. 'I'm sorry if that's not what you want to hear. But I don't want to lie to you. Izzy and I did a lot of things wrong in our marriage, first of which was not being honest with each other. I don't want it to be that way for us.'

'I shouldn't have asked.' I pick at a cushion cover. 'It's probably the last thing you want to talk about.'

'You're right. It doesn't feel particularly good remembering the highs and lows of my marriage. But it's time we had the conversation. If we're going to do this, that is.' He flicks a glance at me. 'Do you want to do this?'

I'm not sure if he means 'do I want to have the conversation' or 'do I want to do "us"?' So I nod, not trusting myself to speak.

'Then I guess we'll do it.' He lets out a deep sigh and I feel bad for putting him through this. 'As you know, us becoming a full-blown couple was a foregone conclusion. She'd decided. At first it was amazing. It wasn't just about the way she looked. We had so much in common and she had this way of making everything seem easy. Sixth form, all the way through uni. Everywhere she went, she just fitted in and, as a result, I did too. Even my own family seemed to like me better when I was with her. It was easy to get hooked.'

His voice sounds lighter now he's started talking about her. My stomach twists. I don't want to see his face while he tells this story. But I'm like one of those drivers who slow down when they pass an accident. I can't help it. I look at him. 'I remember.'

'I wasn't really thinking about the future. Life was one long party. Then I started to realize it was never us on our own; there were always other people around. Like we needed an audience. I'd worked out finance wasn't for me by then and I'd started to think of jacking it all in. Ditching the job and going travelling; seeing the world. Then she got pregnant.'

'What?' My mouth must be goldfish wide. Izzy went on the pill a month after she started dating Rich. She had zero tolerance for the accidental pregnancies that occasionally lit up the school switchboard. She was adamant she didn't want kids until after she was married. This doesn't fit.

'You didn't know? But she said she . . . Of course she did.' He rubs his forehead. 'Yup, she got pregnant. She told me her parents would kill her if she had a baby before she got married. There went my plan to see the world.'

'I don't understand. She never—'

'She lost the baby two days before our engagement party.' He's matter-of-fact, like it doesn't hurt. But he's squeezing his hands together so tightly all the colour's leeched out of them.

I try to temper my expression. I don't know what to say to this. Izzy wore a pair of blue and white Dolce and Gabbana hot pants to her engagement party and danced on the bar of the trendy club it was held at. And she never mentioned the miscarriage to me in any of the years that followed. Not once.

'I was in by then. I couldn't leave her. So we got married.

She wanted the house, so we got the house. And the crippling mortgage.' Rich hasn't noticed the sceptical look on my face. I pull my features back into line. 'And there was Tilly.' He breaks into a grin. 'And she was amazing. I wanted another one straight away! Izzy said she did too – but that we should wait a little while. It got longer and longer. Then she went back to work.' He pauses. 'I feel like a total bastard saying this to you ...'

'Don't. I asked the question.'

'I don't think she ever wanted another kid. After Tilly was born, she made it clear I was a massive disappointment. I couldn't do anything right. Obviously I wanted what was best for Tills from the get go, but I couldn't see why she had to have three prams and an interior designer to do her bedroom. None of that crap matters.' He shakes his head. 'The nursery's a case in point. We only signed Tilly up to it because there was a rumour one of the minor royals was going. Now she's not even happy there.'

I wonder whether this is the time to raise my concerns about Oak Tree. 'Maybe you could—'

It's like he hasn't even heard me. 'Probably a moot point. I doubt I'll be able to send her there much longer.'

'What are you talking about?'

He jabs his foot at the papers he was reading. 'Do you know what these are? Details about voluntary redundancies that HR so kindly sent over. On a Friday night.'

He looks at me like I'm supposed to get it. I don't.

'They're pushing me out, Bec. The department's tanking and they're going to pin it on me. If I don't take this deal, I'll probably find myself out on my ear in six months.'

'Is it a bad deal?'

'It's not a *bad* deal. It's just what do I do after the money runs out?'

'Write your book and sell it for millions?' I try to jolly him up.

'If only.' He doesn't even crack a smile.

'Don't you guys – I mean you – have some family money to tide you over until then?'

'All of Izzy's money is held in trust until Tilly's twenty-one. I thought there was a way of getting round it but there's not. And I'm sure as hell not going to go cap in hand to Mum and Dad if I can help it. I suppose I should start looking elsewhere. I just don't know if I can bear to.'

I refuse to let him wallow in self-pity. He's worth more than that. 'So what would you do if you could do anything?'

'Win the lottery.'

'Ha ha. I'm serious.'

'So am I.' At last, the ghost of a smile.

'I mean it. Close your eyes. Do it.' I take his hands and shake his arms, trying to loosen him up. We did this kind of visualization technique on a team-building day at *Flare* once. I thought it was new-age bullshit then. I'm hoping paraphrasing it might help now. I've got nothing else to offer. 'Imagine you're in a vacuum. Let your worries go. You can do absolutely anything; you have no financial pressure, no responsibilities and whatever you choose, you're not committed to. You just have to try it. What would you do?'

His forehead is concertinaed with the effort. I watch his eyelids flickering as he thinks it over and I feel a rush of pure affection. I want to look after him.

'Some time this century.' I give him a gentle nudge in the ribs.

'Maybe I'd teach.' He opens his eyes. 'I mean write, obviously, but if my book didn't work out, maybe.' He blinks the thought away. 'Wow, I never thought I'd say that.'

'Then I think you should take the redundancy.' I surprise us both by saying it.

'Unfortunately I don't exist in a vacuum.' He chuckles. 'Unfortunately life gets in the way.'

'I mean it. You hate what you do. Changing company isn't going to help. Take the redundancy; buy yourself some time. Finish your book. Look into teaching. Just give it a shot.'

'There is the small matter of paying for things like school fees.' But I can tell by the pull of his mouth that he's thinking about it.

'You said yourself Tilly's not happy at Oak Tree.'

'But all the schools around here are shit. I'd have to pay fees somewhere.'

'So move.' I shrug.

'What?'

'You heard me. Sell up. Rent if you have to. Do what it takes.'

His eyes skate over the sprawling basement room. 'You wouldn't miss it?'

'Rich, I don't even live here.' My pulse speeds up. This is the perfect opportunity.

His eyes linger on the double fridge, the gleaming appliances. 'And you wouldn't care?'

'Care about what?'

'That I wasn't pulling in six figures?'

'Rich, I'd lo— like you if you were emptying the bins.' I backpedal frantically. 'So what do you think? Are you going to do it? Take the redundancy?'

'I don't know. I'd probably have to leave London.' My declaration has totally passed him by. I don't know whether to feel pleased or disappointed. 'Which might not be a bad thing. I feel like people stare at me wherever I go. I'd like to go somewhere where nobody knows me or Izzy.'

'Right.' Izzy again.

'Could you handle it?'

'Handle leaving London?' I say it slowly. I want to make sure I understand what he's asking so I don't fluff my response.

'I know it's a big ask, what with work and everything.'

'Not that big.' Mentally I gloss over the beauty-editor role. There was no guarantee I was going to get it. And we could always move somewhere commutable. Aren't Surrey and Kent supposed to be packed with decent schools? 'I could use a change.'

Rich's dimples widen as he grins at me. 'You'd really pack up and leave it all behind?'

'Isn't that what you do when you believe in someone?' I take a punt. He's basically just asked me to move in with him, after all.

'I guess I'm not used to it.'

'You better get used to it.' This time I push past Izzy. Enough moments have been about her. Not this one too.

'I guess that settles it.' Rich says it as casually as if we've decided on nothing more than a dinner menu. 'We're moving. Oh and Bec? I'd lo— like you if you were emptying the bins too.'

Chapter Thirty-Four

Monday 3 June

4.00 p.m.

I unwrap a blue and white porcelain mug and pop it on the counter next to its twin. Izzy and I bought them together in an Emma Bridgewater sample sale years ago. I wasn't sure whether to pack them but I had to bring something. So few of my other things have made the trip; the balding removals guy even made a joke about how little work he'd done when he took my money (he still took it though). I look for a cupboard to put them in. Most are covered with a film of dust and leftover sugar particles and the door's hanging off the one next to the fridge. That's the problem with rentals; people don't look after them. The kitchen's stuffy too, like it's been shut up a while. I tell myself it won't be long before we're putting down real roots. Especially now we've said we love each other.

But I feel more tense than I thought. It must be the pace

this move has happened at. Someone called to arrange a viewing within an hour of the estate agent hammering the For Sale sign to Rich's gatepost and because he wasn't in a chain, things moved fast. Mine and Ed's flat took longer but we knocked the price down and a childless couple who'd viewed it three times made a lowball offer in the end. A 'distressed' sale, isn't that what they call it? They'll think they've got the bargain of the century. Until they have to deal with the persistent damp in the bathroom and the terrible water pressure.

One of the removals team must have had a cheeky fag in here while they were unpacking for us – I can taste cigarettes in the air. I haven't had one since my engagement party. Standing outside with Rich. I could use one now. It's more rural here than I thought it would be. When Rich suggested Cambridge, I was picturing a smart terraced house among the spires within walking distance of the station. I didn't realize he meant out past Lode and the pockets of isolated villages towards the fenland. When I look out of the window, all I can see is the green and brown patchwork of fields. Lots of space for Missy and Tilly to run around. But our nearest neighbours are a herd of cows. The next house is the size of a postage stamp on the horizon.

'It's a bit rough around the edges, isn't it?' Rich comes up behind me. He starts testing the hinge of a cupboard, trying to work out why it's keening to one side. 'I'm sure once we're unpacked, it'll be fine.' I try to inject confidence into my voice.

'You're a terrible liar.' Rich gives up on the door and laughs. 'I promise you it won't be for long. And the good

313

news is the movers have finished putting together all the furniture upstairs. So we'll have beds to sleep in tonight. Tilly's bagsied the room with the dormered window.'

Of course she has. She's got Rich wrapped around her little finger. He tries to be firm occasionally but the second he sees her face crumple, he gives in. Bedtime's anything from seven to eleven, her diet would make a trucker reach for a salad and now she'll be sleeping in the nicest room in the house. I'm lucky if she even acknowledges me at all.

He starts for the door. 'Why don't you come upstairs and work out where you want to put things?'

'Give me two secs to finish unpacking the kitchen.' I delve into another of the cardboard boxes. 'That way I can make us all a cup of tea.'

'Hold that thought.' Rich disappears and I can hear the crunch of gravel on the driveway as he goes out towards the car. A minute later he returns, holding a wrapped, oblong box. 'A moving-in present.'

I look at the wrapped package he's holding out. It's too long to be anything symbolic like a ring and even I know it's too soon for that kind of commitment. My mind flits back to Izzy's overflowing jewellery box. It could be a necklace or a bracelet, I suppose.

'It's a milk-frother.' Rich sees the confusion on my face when I tear off the paper. 'All this talk of tea – I know you're a hot chocolate fiend. This way you can have a frothy one whenever you like. Even if it is twenty-five degrees outside.'

I can feel tears threatening to fall. He could give a necklace or a bracelet to anyone. This shows he knows who I am. 'Thanks,' I croak. I'm scared to show how much this means to me.

'I promise it won't be for long.' He wraps his arms around me. 'Just until we get back on our feet.'

'Have you heard anything from any agents yet?' I ask casually. I offered to proofread Rich's book before he sent it off but he batted the suggestion away. Artistic pride, he said. Now I wish I'd pushed it because it's been six weeks and not one of them has replied.

'Not yet.'

I hold up crossed fingers. 'I'm sure you'll hear something soon. Then you'll have to let me read it.'

'If it doesn't come to anything, I'll just do something else.' For someone who spent the best part of two years tinkering with his novel, Rich has been surprisingly unenthused about it lately.

'Like what?' I make sure to sound casual. I don't want to labour the point. He gets defensive when he thinks I'm pushing him.

'Maybe I will do the teaching thing?'

'You'd be a great teacher. You're so patient.'

'I just wish I could talk to Charlie about it. He'd be the perfect sounding board.'

I watch his face fall. I can't believe how unsupportive his family is being. Their contact is limited to the breezy WhatsApp messages Jenny sends Rich too late at night for a reply, asking after Tilly as if everything is normal. She never calls or suggests coming to visit or catching up in person. As far as I'm aware the rest of them don't even bother. The last time someone posted a message on their family group was before Izzy's funeral. 'Screw them,' I say fiercely. 'You'd be a much better teacher than Charlie anyway. He can't even sit through the trailers of a film without getting bored. You've got me. I'll be your sounding board.'

'You're right. Screw them.' Rich summons up a grin. 'Just being up here is making my head feel clearer. I feel like I can breathe again now we're not living on top of ourselves.'

I don't point out that, although it might not be penned in by a cluster of neighbours, this house is smaller than his and Izzy's place in Clapham. I don't want to spoil the moment.

6.04 p.m.

'I'd better go in search of civilization and supplies.' Rich comes into the hallway where I'm lining our wellies up under the coat rack and working out where to hang things. The movers left an hour ago, each clutching a crisp twenty-pound tip from Rich. Since then I've blitzed the kitchen and all the bathrooms. Rich has spent the time trying to connect the internet and tune the TV.

'Have you done the telly at last?' I peer into the cosy 'snug' where the movers put the television and the buttercup-coloured sofa. The floor is covered in coils of wires and extension leads.

'We don't have the right cable.'

'How about the internet? My phone's got zero reception.'

'That's hardly my fault, is it?' Rich sounds irritated. 'Sorry. Mine's the same. I'll see if I can get it sorted tomorrow. But I thought I'd do a quick food shop now before the shops shut. Any special requests?'

I look at my watch. 'Won't everything be closed by now?' Trying to keep it light, I add: 'You're not in Kansas anymore.'

'I could always go back into Cambridge—'

'Perhaps we should all go? Do a bit of exploring.' Tilly hasn't surfaced since she claimed the master bedroom but I don't think I can face more of her attitude tonight.

'It'll be quicker if I go on my own.' Oblivious to my expression, Rich grabs the car keys off the hall table. 'I'll pick up some groceries and stop for fish and chips on the way back. The one out by Barton's supposed to be one of the best in the country. Maybe you can go upstairs and see if you can get Tilly sorted while I'm gone?'

He's at the door before I can object.

6.10 p.m.

I have to collect myself before I approach Tilly. I know moving's never easy but the fact we can't even connect to the internet is grating. It makes me feel cut off. Rich and Izzy's house was slap bang in the middle of things, every appliance top of the range. I have to remind myself I don't want that. I've got Rich. That should be enough. When I've calmed down, I go in search of Tilly and find her lying spread-eagled in the centre of her bedroom, drumming her feet against the bottom of her bed. Toys and books spill out of boxes and the duvet's scrunched in the corner. It looks like a bombsite. Tilly pauses as the door opens. When she realizes it's me, she goes back to banging her legs.

'Hey, Tills, how's it going?' I refuse to rise to the banging.

If she wants to kick the crap out of her own bed, that's her business. 'Do you want to go outside and explore? It's still light out – we could take Missy and wander down towards the fields. See if there's anything exciting at the bottom of the garden.'

Tilly shows no signs of shifting so I try again. 'Or we could have a poke around in some of those boxes? Daddy's gone for chish and fips – we could unpack and set up your room while we wait for him to get back.'

I was hoping using Tilly's old way of saying fish and chips might soften her. She glowers instead.

'Perhaps I'll get on and make a start and you can join in if you feel like it.' I go over to the wall and open the flaps of the first box. 'Now, where do these teddies go?'

I take out the first one – rather appropriately, Sulley from *Monsters Inc.* – but Tilly comes over and snatches for it.

'That's mine.'

I relinquish the toy. 'It's not very nice to snatch.'

'*Sooorry.*' She says it in a sing-song voice that suggests the opposite and slumps back to the floor, Sulley clutched between her hands. She gives the bed a particularly vicious boot.

I close my eyes and count to ten in my head. Then I hunker down on the floor to make sure we're talking on the same level the way the parenting books recommend. 'Have I done something to upset you?'

'No.' She won't meet my eye.

'If I've done something that makes you sad, you can tell me. Maybe I can make it better.'

Tilly shrugs, but she does stop kicking.

'Is it because I've been spending lots of time with you and your daddy?'

Silence.

I've rehearsed this conversation a thousand times. I want to get it right. 'You must miss your mummy a lot. And that's okay. You know I loved her very much, too. And so did your daddy. I'm sorry we can't all be here together. But I think your mummy would be happy to know that I'm helping you look after your daddy, don't you?' Inwardly, I cringe. Izzy was a lot of things, but forgiving wasn't one of them. I look at the top of Tilly's blonde head. Is any of this getting through? 'Don't you think she'd want you to be happy too?'

Tilly stares at the floor and refuses to engage.

'I want you to know I love you very much, Tills. No matter what you say or do. I'll never stop loving you. And I hope that in a little while we can be friends again. Because I miss you.'

When she doesn't say anything, I haul myself to my feet. What a washout. I need to talk to Rich again about Tilly seeing someone. This can't go on. I'm running through how I can raise it in a way that won't upset him when I hear Tilly murmur something.

'What was that, Tills?'

'I don't want you to go.'

I drop to the floor again. I don't know if she means right now or permanently, but I'm grabbing hold of the lifeline. 'Oh, darling, I'm not going anywhere. Is that what you're worried about? I promise you I'm staying put.'

She considers this with her head tilted. She has this way

of looking at me, assessing me, which is straight from Izzy. I do miss her. Or some aspects of her, at least.

'Pinkie promise?' She thrusts her hand at me and our fingers curl around each other.

'Pinkie promise.' I hold on a little longer than I need to. *At last.*

We're downstairs on the carpet of the snug playing animal snap when Rich gets back, arms laden with paper-wrapped bundles, slick with vinegar. He walks into the open-plan kitchen and dumps the lot onto the island in the centre. Missy's already at his feet, nosing into his shopping. 'Chish and fips is here. Hope you're hungry.'

'I'm so hungry I could eat a house.' Tilly scampers after him.

'Horse,' Rich and I correct in unison, and she giggles. Rich hands her a plate piled high and raises his eyebrows at me. I make a thumbs-up behind her back. 'Later,' I mouth.

'And who's thirsty?' He nudges the dog out of the way and reaches into the carrier bag on the ground between his legs and pulls out two bottles; one of Moet and one of Ribena. Tilly and I react with equal excitement. 'We're celebrating.'

'Oh, Rich – did you hear from an agent?' I clap my hands together. I'd wondered whether the main reason he wanted to go was to get reception. He's been checking his phone all day.

'I'd say if I had,' he says a little forcefully as he helps Tilly pour a beaker of Ribena. I wonder whether I've put my foot in it and hurt his feelings. But he doesn't seem too fazed. He's already opening the cupboards looking for champagne flutes.

'They're in the—'

'Got 'em.' He balances two flutes between the fingers of one hand and pops the cork of the champagne with the other, shaking it a little like a Formula One driver.

Tilly shrieks as the bubbles burst out of the bottle like a liquid volcano. Then we sit up at the island, eating our dinner in a sticky-fingered, messy way. For the first time since she died, the shadow of Izzy doesn't hang over us.

Chapter Thirty-Five

Thursday 4 July

8.47 a.m.

I give Tilly's collar another tug, making sure it lies flat. I step back and squint, assessing my handiwork.

'It looks fine, Bec.' Rich smooths Tilly's hair. 'They're not going to be grading them.'

'I know, I know. I just want it to be perfect.' He's nervous too. I can tell from the way he keeps flitting around the kitchen. Although term won't start for Tilly until September, her new school is doing a welcome day for the new reception class. It might not be her first 'proper' day, but it feels like it. Getting it right is our way of proving we've steered Tilly through the worst. Judging from the way she's been since we moved and how she bounced out of bed this morning and attempted to get herself dressed, I think we have. Getting her away from Oak Tree was half the battle. But I still want this to be perfect. 'So what can I get you both for breakfast? Eggy bread?'

'Yummo.' Tilly tugs at the tie, pulling it askew again. 'Can I have two pieces?'

I pull the skillet onto the stove and dunk thick white bread into the eggs and milk that I beat together earlier. 'You can have three if you like.'

'Do you think the French just call French toast "toast"?' Rich muses as he pulls up the stool next to Tilly.

'Like the Danes call Danish pastries "pastries"?' We exchange a smile as I stick the sodden bread onto the hot skillet and listen to its answering sizzle.

'That smells good.' Rich sniffs the air. 'When are you going to tell me what your secret ingredient is?'

'Probably never.' It's orange juice, which Rich would know if he stood still long enough to watch me finish preparing it. But I like having an air of mystery. 'Can someone grab the maple syrup? The first bits will be done in a minute.'

Both Rich and Tilly jump up, jostling each other as they duck to get to the shelf under the central island stacked with condiments. Missy's snoozing in her basket next to it. This kitchen lacks the show-stopping appeal of Izzy's bone-white basement, but it's grown on me. Now that we've been here a little while, the whole place is starting to feel like a home.

I slide two plates over to them.

'You not having any?' Rich asks.

'I can't manage something that sweet in the morning.' Even looking at the French toast swimming in maple syrup is making me feel queasy. 'I'll get something later after drop-off.'

I pick up my phone instead and start snapping away as the pair of them wolf down their French toast in matching bites. 'Smile. You're on candid camera.'

Tilly pulls out an array of poses that would make Sydney proud. I make a mental note to WhatsApp some to our family group later. Impending fatherhood seems to have mellowed Rob. He's not as prickly about me and Rich as he was. I'm sure I've got Sydney to thank for that.

'Why are you taking them on that?' Rich asks. 'The DSLR is around somewhere. I got it out last night.'

'You know I'm rubbish with technology. Anyway, I've got this on portrait mode. Some of them are lovely.'

I put the phone down and start thumbing through. 'Look. There's one of you.'

Rich covers the phone screen with his hand. 'If you're going to pap us, make sure you do it properly.'

'I didn't realize you were so vain.'

'Ha ha. I'll go and get the big camera. I want to take some first-day photographs anyway.'

I can hear him as he digs around in his study. He comes back and hands me a camera that's practically the size of my head.

'I don't know what to do with this,' I laugh. 'I won't even be able to turn it on.'

'Here.' He takes it back, presses a few buttons and the screen on the back whirs to life, producing a perfect image of the top of the table it's pointed at. The quality is amazing – even I can see that.

'Wow. Okay, Tills, are you ready?'

'I was born ready,' she replies. Rich bursts out laughing and I crack a smile. I mentally gloss over the fact that it sounds just like something Izzy would say.

'Four going on fourteen.'

'Make that twenty-four. Okay, let's do this.' I hold the camera up to my eye then immediately put it down again. 'Hang on, have you put any film in?'

Rich snorts again. 'You are such a Luddite. Cameras don't use film anymore, and yes, I put the memory card in. Now hurry up before it's time for her to graduate.'

9.15 a.m.

Tilly bounces through the school gates, leaving Rich and I trailing in her wake. The school is so small there's only one reception class and it's clearly marked. She trots up to her classroom door and greets her teacher – who she's only seen a picture of in the school brochure – like an old friend.

'Hi, Miss Payne,' she shrieks. 'I like your hair.'

The teacher tucks her long dark hair behind her ears and smiles. 'Hi Mat— No, it's Tilly, isn't it?' I like that she's taken the time to remember not just Tilly's name but her preferred diminutive. It's a far cry from Oak Tree. I look down at her feet. No slippers. A trendy pair of Converse instead. I think I'm going to like her.

'Welcome to the Red Rockets reception class. Don't those words sound lovely together?' She turns to include us in her welcome too. 'It's lovely to meet you, Mr and—'

'Please call me Bec,' I jump in.

'Of course. Lovely to meet you, both.' She shifts out of the way so Tilly can duck under her arm to get into the classroom. 'Now, I'm happy for you both to stay as long as you feel Tilly needs you to. But generally I find if you prolong the goodbyes it tends to make them worse.'

'Of course.' I slip into people-pleasing mode. 'It's just that Tilly's had a bit of a—'

'The headmistress explained everything,' Miss Payne says, easily. 'And don't worry, I'll keep an extra-close eye on Tilly to make sure she settles. But today's just about learning where everything is, getting a feel for the classroom space and a chance to meet some of the other children. If any of the children feel overwhelmed, we'll call their parents. Not that your Tilly seems to be having any problems.'

We follow her gaze to see that Tilly's already plonked herself on the cushions in the corner. She's taken two books from the bookshelf next to her and appears to be reading both at the same time.

'A multi-tasker.' Miss Payne smiles. 'If you want to stay . . .' Her inflection suggests we needn't bother.

We sidestep out of the way of another set of new parents and a girl with two long plaits tied with white ribbons. Rich takes a few steps down the path, jangling his keys in his pocket. 'Ready?'

'Wait. We can look in through here.' The window is papered in a scene from *We're Going on a Bear Hunt* but there's a gap between the glass and the frame. I peer through the edge, ducking so that if Tilly looks up she won't see me. Rich rests his chin on top of my head. We watch as the little girl with plaits approaches Tilly and perches on the edge of a cushion near her. She says something and Tilly hands over one of the books. The little girl picks at the cover and says something else. Tilly pats the cushion next to her and gives the girl a mega-watt smile that's so reminiscent of Izzy, it makes me catch my breath. I look up at Rich to see if he's noticed but he's beaming at Tilly. 'She gets her confidence from me.'

I look at his profile; the proud set of his jaw, his eyes totally focused on her. I'm the one who needs to lay the ghost to rest, not him.

'I thought I might head down to London this morning,' he says as we cross the playground back towards the car park. 'I'll take the car and park at the station. You don't need it today, do you?'

I had been debating driving into Cambridge to have a mooch but it can wait. 'I can get by without it. What's in London?'

'Just thought I might have a bit of a wander. There's an open day on one of those teaching courses that I thought I could look into.' I nod. Although I'm not thrilled he might spend so much time based in London, Rich's redundancy won't last forever. I'm still hopeful I might get some freelancing work but so far all my pitches have gone unanswered. I didn't exactly leave *Flare* on the best terms.

Rich slides into the driver's seat and flicks the radio on. The sound of George Ezra fills the car. Jules loves this song. I think of how disappointed she was when I said I couldn't take the job, especially after all the groundwork she'd put in with Tina. I owe her an email but I've been putting it off.

'Perhaps I could come with you?' I say, suddenly thinking

I could talk to Jules in person, suggest meeting her for coffee, see if I could line up some work for a few months' time. 'I could check in on some media contacts, see if I can get some work out of it. We could make a day of it.'

'I thought we'd decided you were going to prioritise our family.' Rich turns the wheel sharply to avoid an overgrown hedge. The movement presses me against my seat.

My mind flicks back to a long-ago conversation about Izzy putting her career first. I don't want him to think I'm going to do the same, especially when he's talking about us as a family. 'I can do both.'

'I know you can.' He moves one hand from the wheel to squeeze my knee. 'But I think today one of us should stay here in case the school calls. And besides, I might be planning to bring you back a present.'

'Really?'

The smile now dancing around his eyes distracts me. I start to wonder if . . . but it's too soon. I can't let my mind wander down that particular path. We don't need to get engaged. We've got something much stronger.

'You'd better hurry home then,' I parry. The sun bounces off the windscreen as we turn up to the T-junction that takes us back to our house and I feel a burst of excitement. 'Who knows? I might have a present for you too.'

'Sounds good. So what are you going to do today?' He moves the subject on without acknowledging the present or my desire for him to come home early. I swallow the nub of unease about his eagerness to get back to London.

'I thought I might finally tackle the second spare room. There are a few boxes in there that still haven't been unpacked and you never know when we might need the space.' I smile to myself. 'If I finish that, I might do some online investigating about what there is to do around here in the school holidays. Perhaps we could go out to the fens or to the coast for a few nights.'

'That sounds good.' He pats my knee absently as he slides the car into the driveway. I wonder if his mind is already in London. I remind myself I don't have to compete with a city. 'Don't work too hard.'

I watch the car recede into the distance then I go into the kitchen through the side door and make myself a hot chocolate. I stand in a patch of sunlight drinking it and thinking about Rich. I have to learn to trust him, I remind myself. To trust in us. When nothing but the dregs remain, I put the cup in the sink, douse it with water and head upstairs to the second spare room.

Calling it a spare room is a bit of a stretch. It's the size of a wardrobe and it's currently crammed full of all the stuff that doesn't belong anywhere else. To be honest, I'd almost forgotten about it. But a lick of paint and a declutter could make it a nice space. I just have to get on with it. I steel myself and pull open the door. It's a cardboard city in there. But I won't be deterred. Like I told Rich, you never know when you might need the space. So I sit down cross-legged and set to work. I'm quick and efficient – it's easy to be brutal with someone else's stuff. I untangle an entire box full of wires, most of which are phone chargers for long-defunct models, and lob out three crates full of old magazines. I can tell Rich paid a company to do his packing. Another box entirely full of tablecloths and table runners. So much junk. I whistle while I work, imagining the room in pale blue or maybe pink, with white trim picking out the paintwork. I tear through the detritus, feeling lighter with each box I open and discard. Until I come to a box full of old photographs.

I pull out the first and realize right away that it's part of the stuff that should have gone to Glenda and Tony. The photograph is of a young Glenda pushing Izzy on the swing. If it wasn't for her seventies' flares and polo neck, she could be Izzy. I feel a wedge of renewed sympathy. Losing a mother is horrific, but losing your child must be worse. It's not the natural order of things. The last time I spoke to Glenda she screamed that I was a whore down the phone. I hung up before she could start on Rich. I lay the photos on the bed. I'll post these later. It's the right thing to do.

12.45 p.m.

After a few hours nose-deep in cardboard, I need a break. I know Rich bought envelopes for posting out his manuscript. They'll be somewhere in his office. I pad downstairs to the small study at the back of the house to find them. His desk is little more than a scratched-up table with a laptop in the middle, a discarded coffee mug and a stack of paper towering above it. There's a slit of a window, which looks out onto the back of the dilapidated garden wall, the end of which is little more than a pile of loose bricks. It couldn't be more different from the polished slab of a desk with the corner-office view.

There's a battered metal filing cabinet in the corner next

to the fireplace. I open the top drawer and start sifting through. It's a jumble of old bills and receipts. His accountant's going to have a field day next April. I ferret my way through what looks like a series of expensive lunches, digging down until I reach the bottom. My hands close around a pack of envelopes still in their cellophane wrapper. As I wrench them out, I feel something stuck to the back. I flip the packet over and see an envelope with my name on it.

My stomach churns. I recognize Izzy's confident flourish straightaway. Feeling like someone's walked over my grave, I slit the envelope open with my thumbnail and pull out a thick cream card with *Congratulations* embossed on the front. I frown. She was so busy organizing the party, Izzy never got round to giving me an engagement card. I didn't think anything of it at the time. I flick it open. Both sides are covered with tightly packed cursive.

Dear Bec,
I'm writing this on the eve of your engagement party. You finally got there and I think I can even take a little bit of the credit for introducing the pair of you. You're welcome!!

I almost stop reading then. The next line makes me carry on.

I know our friendship has had its ups and downs but I've been rooting for you to get your happy ending. You deserve it. At last! And now for the advice from someone older (barely!) and wiser (definitely!). Make sure you don't go to bed angry

*(or without your make-up on, as my mum would
say!!) and be prepared to take the good with
the bad. I'm not saying there won't be stacks of
good – Ed's a good guy. But sometimes people can
surprise you.*

*Just make sure you don't forget about me when
you're an old, married woman! I've always got
your back. And as we both know, I'm quite the
wedding planner!!*

All my love, Izzy.

I can almost hear her voice; how pleased she must have been
with herself when she wrote it. The multiple exclamation
marks bring out a pang of affection. She did want the best
for me. After that comes an unfamiliar creep of superiority.
Sometimes people can surprise you. She must have been
in a mood with Rich when she wrote it. She's describing a
partner I don't know. I don't have to remember not to go to
bed angry (or with my make-up on) and there are no nasty
surprises. We work in a way that they obviously didn't. Her
card reads like an admission of defeat. Which means I've
won the silent competition we've been waging ever since
our friendship began. At last I can let it go.

Something about the envelopes bothers me, though. Why
hadn't the packet been opened? I know Rich bought them
in case any agents wanted his manuscript the old-fashioned
way. A shadow of doubt crosses my mind. Is the real reason
why no agents have responded because they haven't got it? I
never actually saw him send any emails. Even thinking that
makes me feel horribly unsupportive. But his evasiveness

every time it comes up has been nagging at me. He's worked so hard on it for so long. Why wouldn't he send it now? My eyes fix on the tower of paper at the edge of his desk. I could just have a quick flick through to put my mind at rest. When I stand up, my phone starts vibrating in my pocket: *Rich*. It's like he knows I'm about to read it. I stop in my tracks.

'Hi.' I know I sound flustered. He's too buzzed to notice.

'Guess where I am?'

'Er, London.' I can't take my eyes off his desk. His manuscript is inches away.

'I'm in Kingston. At the university.'

'How is it?' Now I'm the one who sounds distracted. The manuscript is so close, if I stretch my fingers a millimetre I could just reach for it.

'The teaching course sounds amazing. And I meet all the entry requirements. They seemed really excited to have someone like me apply. Isn't that awesome?'

'That's brilliant.' I try to mirror his enthusiasm. 'You'll be a great teacher.' But I can't help pushing him on the book one more time, knowing his answer will determine what I do next. 'Does this mean you're giving up on your book?'

'That's not why I'm calling.' There's a trace of irritation in Rich's voice, mixed with something else I can't put my finger on. 'I'm calling to ask if you can pick Tilly up on your own today. Grab a cab or something? I've got a few bits and pieces to do while I'm in town. I don't think I'll be back till this evening.'

'Take your time.' I park my guilt and pull the manuscript towards me. I gave him a chance to tell me about his book and he didn't take it. He's shutting me out. And I have a right to know why he doesn't want me to read it anymore. 'I'd better go if I'm going to make it for pick-up.'

'You're a star. Back as soon as I can. Love you.'

I murmur 'love you' back automatically, barely even registering it for once. I've stopped listening. I'm too busy staring at the top page where *Unholy Alliance by Rich Waverly* is neatly typed. The night he told me about it swims into my mind. Of course. He said it was about an unhappy marriage. The whole conversation got side-lined when we kissed but I should have remembered.

My mind is starting to race. What if this book is about Izzy? A tribute to how much he loved her, or a warts-and-all account of where it all went wrong. What if I'm in there? Or worse, what if I'm not? My fingers skid across the page almost of their own accord. I try to tell myself that as far as betrayals go, this isn't a big one. That reading it now will help me edit the right response for when he does let me read it. I flip open the first page before I can talk myself out of it. I remember the other emotion in his voice that night as my eyes skim over the words. It was shame. I stop. Blink. Read them again.

I can't have read that right.

But I have. The words are there in black and white:

Sometimes I hate my wife so much I want to kill her.

My stomach spins like a tumble drier and I drop the page and back away.

Chapter Thirty-Six

3.07 p.m.

Tilly seems to be taking an inordinate amount of time to let go of her teacher's hand. I know it's a good sign that she liked the school but all of the other kids have long since scampered off. I have to physically stop myself tapping my feet.

'I don't want to go.' Tilly looks up at her teacher adoringly. 'I want to stay with Miss Payne.'

'I'm sure Miss Payne needs to go home too.' I try to keep the frustration out of my voice. It isn't Tilly's fault that after I read Rich's killer – quite literally – first line, I dropped the book and backed away like it was going to bite me. I sat there in denial for I don't know how long. Going over whether I am building a future with someone who killed their wife. It was time to collect Tilly before I had the guts to pick it up again. Now all I want to do is go back. I need to know what I'm dealing with.

Tilly detaches herself from the trouser leg she's clamped herself to sulkily. 'Fine.'

'Don't forget your awesome picture,' Miss Payne reminds her. 'It should be dry now. Can you help her find it, Mrs Hill? They're all on the drying rack.'

While we wait for the unseen Mrs Hill to produce the picture, Miss Payne tries to tell me how well Tilly fitted in at the school and how much they're looking forward to having her join them in September. It's as if her voice is coming from a great distance away. I can barely focus. Rich's first line is all I can think about.

'That's great,' I say, barely glancing at the picture when it's eventually produced. 'Now come on, Tilly, we've got to get a move on.'

'That's you and Missy.' Tilly points at a woman with abnormally long arms and a big red smile. 'We had to draw our family.'

I feel a surge of guilt. I should be grateful I'm in the picture at all. I make a conscious effort to pull myself into the present. 'And where are you?'

She points at a blob of paint above what's clearly meant to be the dog's tail. 'That's me. I'm riding Tilly.'

'And where's Daddy?' I make a clutch for normalcy. 'Is he behind that mountain?' I point at the slab of black and grey paint daubed at the back of the picture.

'That *is* Daddy.' Tilly giggles. 'He's so much bigger than us.' Despite myself, I shudder.

3.15 p.m.

Back at home I tell Tilly she can watch TV and she looks at me in confusion. Normally I would insist she does something else first before she flops down in front of the screen but I don't have the energy to supervise stickers or colouring.

'A treat for your first day at big school.' I fob her off.

'Bec?' she asks, as I thrust the Apple controller into her hand.

'What?'

'Will you watch with me?'

My heart clenches. 'I'd love to. I've got to check on something for Daddy but I'll be right back in.' I sweeten the deal. 'Why don't I get you some biscuits?'

'I could help you?'

What is wrong with this child? After the way Izzy rationed out Tilly's screen time and sugar intake during her formative years, she should be clamouring to plug herself in now. My heart clenches harder. *Izzy*. I need to find out what Rich has written.

'It'll only take a minute.' I take the remote control back and start jabbing at the buttons. 'There you go. How about *PAW Patrol*? See what Chase and the gang are up to.'

I hotfoot it out of the room and cross the hall before she can say anything else.

I've barely cracked the door of Rich's study when Tilly starts shouting again. I try to ignore her but the volume just increases until she's competing with the blare of the TV. I can't hear myself think.

I storm back into the room. 'What is it now?' She's standing on the back of the sofa with her face pressed up against the window.

'Daddy's back.'

'Don't be silly. Daddy's still in London. Now, are you going to sit down and watch telly or should I turn it off?' At this rate, Rich'll be home before I've even opened the book again. But she won't move from the window. I come up behind her to see what she's looking at. The white and blue blur of a local bus service rolls by. 'See? It's just a bus. Now you'd better get off the sofa before you bust the springs.' Izzy's prized sofa is looking distinctly rough around the edges. It's more stale-biscuit coloured than buttercup these days. I should have done a better job of looking after it.

'Behind the bus.' Tilly's staring out the window and resisting my efforts to peel her off the back of the sofa. I follow her gaze and sure enough the navy bonnet of Rich's Porsche Cayenne is glinting in the sun as it trails the bus up the lane. My pulse quickens. I don't have much time. 'You're right, clever girl. Honestly, I don't know why Daddy drove. He could probably just as well have got . . .'

A thousand facts suddenly fly at me, each one a shard of glass. In his banker days, Rich once called the bus 'a peasant wagon'. He and Izzy were equally squeamish about travelling on them. So why was he waiting at a bus stop that night? I know he said he'd been up to the common, but why did he go back to the bus stop? He should have been on his way home. Unless he'd already been home. I grip my throat, nails digging in. I think I'm going to be sick.

Sometimes I hate my wife so much I want to kill her.

Wanting is one thing. Doing is another. I need to read the rest of that book. The crunch of tyres on the gravel. I back away from the window. In a matter of minutes, Rich will spring out of the car then stride towards the front door. I'll only have a few seconds while he pats down his trouser pockets for the door key he's always misplacing. Then he'll be inside. It's amazing how you can know someone well enough to memorize their tiny idiosyncrasies. Turns out you can know all of that without really knowing them at all.

I hurry back towards the study. If I can just find out what happens next ... The front door swings open. Too late.

'I come bearing gifts,' Rich shouts as he thrusts open the door. Silhouetted in the frame, I notice again how broad his shoulders are.

'Roses for my rose.' He strides into the hall and I notice his arms are full of flowers. He leans down to kiss me but I move my face away.

'Don't. I'm all sweaty.'

'And one for my monkey for her first day of school.' He plucks a red rose from the centre of the bunch and bows as Tilly comes charging over.

'Like *Beauty and the Beast*.' She snatches it from his hand and hurries back to *PAW Patrol*.

'So how was it?' He looks at Tilly but directs the question at me.

'It was great,' Tilly shouts. 'I've got a best friend called Sasha and Miss Payne's got three cats.'

'Crazy cat lady.' Rich smirks at me. I can't bring myself to smile. I can tell he's waiting for me to ask about the course but the silence hangs.

'I'm sorry about the roses.' At last he notices something's up. 'I know red's a cliché. I was looking for white.'

He imbues his words with a special significance and I feel myself start to soften. Maybe I'm reading too much into this. Rich had started writing his book long before Izzy died. And if he did have something to do with what happened, why in a million years would he write something so incriminating? Still the doubt lingers. Him writing about wanting to kill his wife shortly before she dies is one hell of a coincidence. What if he wasn't on the common that night? My mind replays the gratitude in his voice when he told me on the doorstep he couldn't face it without me. Was he talking about a difficult conversation or Izzy's body? What if his words had more meaning than I realized? There's too much riding on this for me to jump to conclusions. I've got a family to consider. I need to see what else he wrote. I look at the roses reluctantly. 'They're beautiful.'

'Are you all right?' Rich peers into my face. 'You don't seem very enthused.'

'I'm fine.'

'You look a bit pale. Are you sure you're okay?'

I check Tilly's safely ensconced in front of the TV. Then I look him dead in the eyes. They're the same shade of chocolate with flecks of gold that they've always been. Even if everything else is different. I take a deep breath. 'I'm pregnant.'

Chapter Thirty-Seven

3.55 p.m.

The news was worthy of a better moment – this morning I'd been imagining champagne (just a sip for me) and holding hands by candlelight. Not standing anchored to the spot, wondering if the man I love killed his wife. But the words come tumbling out. I watch Rich's throat pumping. His fringe has tumbled over his eyes. He's suddenly a stranger. I can't read him.

'I thought you were on the—' Rich grapples with the middle-aged version of the teenage dilemma 'Is it mine?'

'I was.' Mostly. 'I guess accidents happen.'

I wait to see if he'll wince at my turn of phrase. He doesn't. He's holding the roses so tightly their red is leeching into his shirt like a bloodstain. Clouds scudding past the window throw shadows across his face. I wait. More hangs on this moment than he realizes.

'Well, this is amazing news. A bit of a shock, I must admit, despite all the practice.' Rich winks and his face rearranges itself so I recognize him again. 'Honestly, I'm chuffed. It's come a bit out of left field but you know I've always wanted more children.' His smile slips and I know he's thinking about Izzy. He hoists it up again. 'I'd have bought more flowers if I'd have known.'

He bends down to hug me and I'm reminded of how tall he is. He towers over me. Like he towered over Izzy. I squash the thought. Until I can see his book again, I don't really know anything. Even then I won't be sure. But I need to read it.

'I've just got a bit of admin to do.' I detach myself. 'Would you mind if I borrowed your study?'

'Oh no you don't.' Rich recaptures me and pulls me tight. 'I'm not marking this moment with admin. This has been the best day ever. So I'm going to sit you down and make you the nicest cup of hot chocolate you've ever had. You need looking after.'

He leads me into the snug and practically pushes me down onto the sofa. He pulls over a footstool for me to put my feet on. He's behaving just the way I dreamed he would. Before.

'It won't take five minutes.' I try to stand up. 'I'd feel much better if I got it out of the way.'

'Not a chance. You're a delicate flower now.' He grins. 'Now, Tills, I'm going to make hot chocolate and I'm leaving you in charge. Bec's not allowed to move a muscle. Do you hear?'

Tilly springs up, runs over and plonks herself directly on my feet. 'She's not going anywhere,' she giggles.

Where would I go anyway? The nearest house is miles

away and I don't even know if anybody lives in it. Even if I made it out of here, who would I call? The police investigation is long since closed. I binned the detective's card the moment he left. Jules probably isn't speaking to me, and Rob's a time zone away. I slump back against the sofa. I'm well and truly trapped.

6.15 p.m.

I can't take my eyes off Rich's hands as he cuts up Tilly's chicken and vegetables. He's got the kind of olive skin that only needs a glimpse of the sun to tan. Tilly's the same. Our baby might inherit that gene. I rest my palm against my stomach. Then I think of those same hands on the small of Izzy's back, giving her a quick, hard shove. I swallow.

'Are you okay?' He looks up from Tilly's plate, his eyebrows pulled together in concern.

'Just tired.' I stare at my plate. As he runs me through everything that his course will involve, the teaching placements, how he might be eligible for some sort of maths-related grant, I can't stop thinking about the possibility that he pushed her.

'Early night for all of us, I think,' he says. 'Precious cargo and all.'

I smile weakly.

6.40 p.m.

Rich reaches around me as I load the plates in the dishwasher. 'Here, you're stacking them all wrong. They can't sit flush against each other.' He rearranges them. Why have I never noticed how controlling he is? I used to think it was sweet how much he cared. I hate what these doubts are doing to me.

'Do you mind doing bath and bed?' I ask. If Rich does that, I can use the time to get into his study.

'You know she likes it when we do it together,' Rich points out. 'And you're better at doing the voices than I am. Come on, super mum. Let's enjoy it while there's only one of her. There'll be two before you know it.' He takes my hand and holds it to his heart. 'Can you imagine?'

I smile weakly and let him lead me up the stairs. If he moves his fingers a fraction he'll be able to feel my pulse tapping under the skin of my wrist like a radio distress signal. But he's busy talking about the possibility of getting work experience at Tilly's school and how he can fit his degree in with helping out with the baby. He's really excited. I listen with half an ear. I used to think the way we did these things together was a sign of how compatible we are. Now I'm not so sure.

I feel sweat trickling down the back of my neck. The bathroom is oppressively hot; the extractor fan must be playing up again but Tilly splashes away happily, completely unaware of any tension. She's got the entire plastic cast of *The Little Mermaid* and she's playing games with them underwater, giving them silly voices and making them do things that seem to involve a lot of water being splashed out of the bath. I watch how her face lights up when Rich joins in the voiceovers, mangling a French accent for one of the characters. He lets Tilly make him a beard out of suds and doesn't complain when she gets soap in his eye. Am I going mad? How could I think someone as kind and gentle as he is could do that to Izzy? But people can be capable of anything. I know that better than anyone. My head is spinning with the different possibilities. It's as though thousands of spiders are scuttling across my brain. I can't bear not knowing.

It's Tilly who provides the opportunity to find out. When she grows bored of the underwater kingdom, she starts posing, standing up and pouting at herself in the mirror over the sink. Pure Izzy.

'Tills, sit down. It's dangerous. And you mustn't pose like that.' Rich tries to swipe her arms down but she's got them up by her face like an ingénue.

'I've got to practise.'

'For what? Your portfolio?' Rich makes a face at me and I smile tightly. I'm still thinking of how I can get downstairs.

'Miss Payne says we're having our photos taken at school next week. The parents have to buy them.'

'More photos? You did an entire photo shoot this morning.' Rich finally gets her to sit down. He tweaks her chin. 'I think I've seen enough of this monkey face, thank you very much, don't you, Bec?'

I'm already halfway to the door. 'Why don't I go downstairs and download those photos?' I say. 'I can plug the card into your laptop?' I know 'looking' at Tilly's photos will buy me enough time to see some of what else he's written.

'You don't "plug" it in, you idiot. You put it in the card reader on the side. Do you want me to come and help you?'

'No,' I practically yelp. 'I can figure it out. Is the card still in the camera? How do I get it out?'

'Bring it up to me and I'll do it.' Rich mock-sighs. 'It is the twenty-first century, you know.'

6.55 p.m.

I hear Rich's voice rumbling through the beginning of a bedtime story as I close the door to the study behind me. It was all I could do to stop him coming downstairs with me. I reckon I've got about twenty minutes, give or take, depending on how many books Tilly demands. I should go through the motions of getting the photos downloaded before I read any more. That way if he comes in unexpectedly I can say I was doing the photos and happened to catch a glimpse of it. The manuscript is still lying where I left it, just to the right of the desk. I slip the card into the reader. I press the keypad a couple of times, key in Rich's password (T1llyWaves!) and a stream of photographs fill the screen. Tilly looking impossibly grown-up in her school uniform, followed by us clowning around at breakfast. Dozens of duplicate images wallpaper the screen. There's something reassuring about seeing how happy we all look together over and over again. But the final image is different from the rest. And if I think I felt sick before, that's nothing compared to how I feel now.

Thirty-Eight

Even in thumbnail size I recognise Izzy's old house. I'd know those grey walls anywhere – I helped choose the colour and lay the base coat until Izzy realized painting wasn't as fun as it looks. I feel a creep of unease. I never considered there would be anything else on this card. But this image predates me. Opening it feels like snooping, but I'm well past that now.

I click on the thumbnail and an enlarged image of Izzy's staircase fills the screen. The legs of the hall-table are in the foreground and you can only see halfway up the stairs. The camera must be at floor level. There's a date in the corner and a time. This must be a video, but nothing's moving. The seconds whir by but the screen stays still. Then I notice the plush fur of a stuffed animal. My eyes lock in on the date in the corner and my throat fills with bile. The teddy bears' tea party.

I slam the screen shut. I'm at the door to the study in two strides, almost screaming up the stairs. 'Rich?'

'What?' He leans his head over the top of the stairs. The top of his t-shirt is covered in soapsuds.

I hug the edge of the door to me, using it like a shield. 'Where did the card in the camera come from?'

'I grabbed it from Tilly's room. She seems to have adopted one of her old nanny cams. It's an—'

'Elephant ...' Now my voice is barely a whisper. The elephant that I took back to the kitchen. It must have been one of Tilly's old nanny cams. It's been sitting here the whole time. Rich wouldn't have known it was there. The police never even saw it. What if it holds the answer to what happened the night Izzy died?

I clutch at the door like the ground might give way.

'That's right.' Rich is looking at me curiously. 'Is something wrong with it? Has it been corrupted? If you give me five minutes, I can come and take a look.'

'No, don't.' I try to control the panic edging into my voice. 'It's fine. I was just curious. Expanding my tech knowledge and all.' I give a laugh that sounds fake even to my own ears. 'You get back to it.'

'Seriously, it's no bother. In fact, Tilly's almost done. Why don't I come now?'

Rich takes a step down the stairs and I freeze. For the first time it hits me that I really believe he pushed her. I don't know what to do.

'I'm not almost done.' Tilly's indignant voice saves me. 'You said you'd read five books and you've only read four.'

'Oh well. Duty calls.' Rich starts back up the stairs.

Thank God for Tilly's voracious reading habit. I wait until my heart rate has slowed down before I trust myself to speak. Then I mumble, 'Take your time,' and scuttle back into his study.

This time I lock the door. My knees rattle against the table when I sit down. I flip the laptop back open and tap the mouse pad. The desktop lights up with Rich's screensaver – a close-up of the two of us at a local petting zoo, Tilly sandwiched between us, the flared nostrils of a pony looming in the background. I feel a swell of sorrow and have to remind myself I haven't lost anything yet. I fumble with the keys. I type Rich's password twice before I get it right.

When it opens, the video starts playing automatically. But the only movement is still the timer in the corner, the seconds ticking away. I clench the inside of my cheek between my teeth, hoping against hope that I've blown this entire thing out of proportion. I can't stop looking at the patch of floor where Izzy's body lay.

Then a figure appears between the camera and the stairs. From this angle, all I can see is purple unicorn socks tapering into shapely calves. As Izzy moves further away from the camera, more of her comes into shot. Even without the socks, I'd know Izzy in a heartbeat. Rich is right behind her. My mouth fills with the taste of pennies. I've bitten through my cheek. I poke at the hole with my tongue, trying to get rid of the blood. Deep down I think I always thought he could have had something to do with it. Otherwise why would I have jumped in and defended him? And who really goes and sits on a common to think for an hour and a half with their phone turned off? There's no sound on the video but I can tell from Izzy's body language that she's raging at him. She's right up in his face, mouth wide, hair askew. He looks the definition of browbeaten. Perhaps you could argue that she's goading him into it? I can hardly even watch. She turns her back on him and walks towards the stairs. I catch my breath and wait for him to follow. He just stands there.

I lean so close to the screen that my nose is almost touching it. I can't stop picking at myself: the skin around my fingernails, the neckline of my top, my hairline. His indecision is agony to watch. Part of me just wants him to get on with it. Finally his feet start to move. But instead of following her up the stairs, he turns tail, walks the other way, past the camera towards the door.

I do a double take. It doesn't make any sense. I can't believe he just left. On screen neither can Izzy. She looks almost panicked standing on the stairs, staring after him, obviously waiting for him to come back. Clearly he's never walked away from her before.

After a few moments, she stomps down the stairs, across the hall and drains the glass of wine on the hall table. I can see the frustration oozing off her in waves. She picks up a wayward cushion and smashes it to the ground at the bottom of the stairs. I remember seeing that cushion later, lying next to her broken body, the indent of where she'd held it still visible. It makes me shudder.

Izzy picks up her mobile and starts jabbing at the keys. I'm feeling more and more nauseous. I picture my baby, only the size of a poppy seed, being polluted by my toxic waves of stress and anxiety. I want to turn this off – we must be minutes away from seeing Izzy plummet to the bottom of the stairs – but I can't stop. I need to see it.

Izzy's shouting down the phone now – I can see her face

curling up. But she starts laughing when she hangs up. It's creepy how quickly her face transforms. Before I can work out what's going on she slips her phone into her back pocket and slaps herself across the face. Hard enough to leave a mark. I squint. Surely I didn't see that right. Then she does it again. It doesn't make any sense. Izzy's never been the type to hurt herself. Then a slow smile creeps across her face and I understand. She's trying to make it look like Rich hurt her. Maybe he found out and that's what sent him over the edge. Why he killed her.

I shrink into my chair and wait for him to come back. On screen, Izzy's attention must be caught by something off screen. I watch her cross the room, feet tripping past the camera, back to the front door. Within a few minutes, she's back, her socks a blur of purple as she crosses towards the stairs. This time, a shadow falls on the ground behind her as she goes.

I press my fist into my mouth. I don't know if I can watch Rich do this. He's always been the epitome of everything I could ever want in a man; I don't know if I can bear to watch him destroy that.

But the person coming up behind her isn't Rich. They're too small; too slight. A totally different build. At first all I see is joggers and the flash of black and red trainers. Every sinew of my body is strained as I wait for the person to come directly in front of the camera. When she does, I can't help crying out. It's Sydney. Her hair might be tucked under a baseball cap but her face catches the light of Izzy's antique chandelier as she mounts the first step. And she's wearing Louboutin trainers.

She climbs after Izzy and disappears from view. The camera angle stops halfway up the stairs. Both of them are out of shot. I'm desperately hoping there will be something else to see; another explanation. Then I think back to Sydney's ex-boyfriend suddenly up on federal charges after their break-up, her story about the luckless Dionne. How furious Sydney was on the phone after she fell. Her sudden magnanimity at the party. It all makes sense. There's a sense of creeping inevitability as Izzy comes plummeting down, limbs tumbling over each other, picking up momentum as she goes. She narrowly misses the cushion and hits the floor so hard that I swear I can almost hear the thump. That beautiful face, which she was slapping only minutes ago, takes the full force of the impact. There's a gap of two or three seconds, then Sydney comes hurrying after her. I see Izzy's fingers curl out towards her. Sydney steps over her like she's a piece of litter. She stops briefly to get out her phone and dial a number as casually as if she's ordering an Uber. Then she keeps walking.

This time I can't keep the nausea down. I grab Rich's empty coffee mug and retch into it. Green watery bile trickles down the side, running between my fingers. I dump the mug back on the table and sink to the floor. I huddle with my hands wrapped around my knees, shaking. Of all the things I expected to see on that video, it was never that. All this over a stupid rumour and a false accusation. I bury my head in my hands, sick to the core. Tilly lost her mother for nothing.

I don't know how long I sit there. Long enough to realize it's lucky that Tilly is keeping Rich busy. How can I face him? I feel totally responsible. If it wasn't for me, Sydney would never have thought Izzy leaked the story. I think of Sydney's calm face picking up her phone as she left Izzy crumpled on the floor. I spoke to her that night. I wonder whether that was before or after everything I've just seen. The idea that I might have been on the other end of the line while life spooled out of Izzy makes me start retching again.

At least Rich had nothing to do with it, I tell myself. That should make me feel euphoric. Instead I'm on the verge of tears. He still lied to me about being there that night. He said they'd argued but he made it sound like it was on the phone. He never said he'd seen her. What else has he lied about? Never in my life have I wanted my mum more. An adult to swoop in and absolve me of responsibility. There are decisions to be made now, but I don't want to make them. Only now I'm going to be a mother I have to. I cup my non-existent bump and think of Sydney. So is she. I think of Rob saying she's had a lot of therapy and feel a claw of fear. What if she were to do something to Rob? Or to their baby? I need to take this video to the police.

Rich will be completely exonerated. Although he says it doesn't bother him, I know it does. It's part of the reason we're here – the two of us against the rest of the world. He's been living under a cloud since that night. This will set him free.

I slide the memory card out carefully. I could run outside and tell Rich or call him in here so he can see it for himself.

Instead, I drop it onto the floor and stamp on it.

Justice for Izzy? I think back to all the justices she's meted out over the years and I grind the card deeper into the carpet. The way she took Rich in the first place; how she hurt Rob all those years ago. Advising Ed to cheat on me. She couldn't let me have anything of my own.

I've had to watch her life soar while mine idled. Izzy the partner. Izzy the gym bunny. Izzy the super mum. She had everything. It's no wonder I was forced to visit tiny little acts of retribution on her in return: spilling my wine; buying Tilly the American girl doll; sticking my foot in front of hers on Clapham Common. Even kissing Rich. She deserved each and every one.

I think of the way she smacked herself in the face before Sydney arrived; how purposefully she arranged the pillow at the bottom. She could have been planning to throw herself down the stairs anyway. It's just the kind of over-dramatic thing Izzy would do – provided she had a safety net. But if this video comes to light, Sydney will be cruci-fied. First in the media, then in court. I think about how convenient their sudden move out of the country was. Did Rob know what Sydney had done? He could be charged as an accessory. Izzy's only just stopped ruining my life; I can't let her ruin Rob's.

I pick up the memory card and hold it up to the light. Have I damaged it enough? Just in case I haven't I reach over and lob it into the coffee cup. I hold my breath so I don't breathe in the stench and imagine my stomach acid biting into the chip, corroding the evidence. I want to believe that I'm doing this for the greater good; that I'm protecting Rob and preventing yet another child from losing a parent. Just like I want to believe Izzy did this to herself. But deep down I know it's not about that. It's about Rich.

It's always been about Rich.

Right now I'm all he's got and that suits me perfectly. We're making a life together and building our own family. This poppy seed inside me is a chance for both of us to have a fresh start. But I've seen how quickly his feelings have been swept away in the past. I love him too much to let that happen again. I take the coffee mug over to the tiny window at the back of the room. The frame sticks a little where it's been painted over so I put the mug down to force the window. Then I snatch it up again and flick the contents into the bushes outside. I lob the mug after them for good measure. Then I pat my hands down on the top of my jeans and rearrange my face into the kind of smile befitting a woman who has just found out she's having a baby with the love of her life. I know we promised to be honest with each other at the start of this but I'll just have to learn to live with it. I've been hiding things ever since I met Rich. What's one more secret?

Acknowledgements

I would like to thank all of the people who have given their time and encouragement to this novel. Firstly my early readers: Robyn Stromsoe, Piero Politeo, Celina St George, Katherine Saunt, Hannah Talbot, Helen Cleary, Susannah Okret and Fleur Moss – your insights and the mistakes you spotted, particularly about Northcote Road bus routes, have been invaluable.

Secondly, thanks to the generous writers that shared their thoughts and craft with me: Sophie Hannah, Jess Jarvli, Karen Osman, Annabel Kantaria, Phillippa East and Victoria Selman.

This book would not have been possible without the Emirates Literature Foundation. Thank you to Isobel Abulhoul, Yvette Judge, Luigi Bonomi and Charles Nahhas, for giving this novel a chance to shine at the Emirates Literature Festival.

Many others also gave me the benefit of their expertise in all things medical, magazine-based and police procedural. I'd like to thank Dan Holyoake, Tabitha Barda, Robert Vallings and Dan and Emma Mason for the amazing insights into their chosen fields. All mistakes, of course, are my own.

I owe a debt of gratitude to my amazing agent, Sarah Hornsley, who came at this book all guns blazing with a host of wonderful ideas, and my equally amazing editor, Bethan Jones, for her faith in this story, and her attention to detail.

Then, of course, there's my family. Effusive thanks to Henry Buchanan, Simon Buchanan, David Buchanan, Penny Buchanan, Lalage Buchanan and Lalage Phillips; each of you inspired various characters in different ways. Please don't sue!

Lastly, to Alaric Phillips: thank you for never wavering. Your relentless conviction that this book would be published can now be taken as evidence that you're always right. And you can quote me on that.

Don't miss

THE REUNION

**A chance to reconnect.
A chance to get revenge ...**

Emily Toller has tried to forget her time at university and the events that led to her suddenly leaving under a cloud. She has done everything she can to forget the shame and the trauma – and the people involved.

But events like that can't just be forgotten.
Not without someone answering for what they've done.

When an invitation arrives to a university reunion, everything clicks into place. Emily has a plan.

Because if you can't forget – why not get revenge?

Keep reading to enjoy an extract now ...

SIMON &
SCHUSTER

My eyes feel like they're about to burst out of their sockets. I can't breathe. Fingers that were curled harmlessly around the stem of a wine glass at dinner earlier are now crushing my windpipe and I'm just standing here. Taking it. I used to read scare stories in magazines like *Just 17* about girls being preyed upon as they got off the last train or walked home from school. I'd imagine that in their place, I would floor my attacker with a well-aimed kick and leg it. Instead, I'm doing nothing.

I'm freezing. My brain's starting to fizz from the lack of oxygen. These old buildings retain no heat and this room probably hasn't been opened in years. I no longer know how long I've been in here. I should be fighting back but my arms hang limply by my side. No kick, well-aimed, or otherwise. I haven't even screamed. In all the scenarios I ran through as an anxious teen, I never imagined knowing my attacker.

The force of his grip has knocked the strap of my evening dress off my shoulder. I can feel the satin, cool against the skin on my arm. My body might be powering down but my brain is still pumping, latching onto every detail. Hands big enough to span my entire neck. Breath on my face, sour from hours of toasting. And the look in those eyes, like they're finally getting what they wanted.

My head's lolling like some macabre parody of the kind of drunkenness that occurs at these big ticket reunions. I should have seen this coming. From the moment that stiff-backed, gold-embossed invitation dropped onto our doormat, this chain of events was inevitable. I was going to be a victim again.

I start clawing at the forearms, but my hands slide off the fabric. I can't get a hold. I open my mouth to scream but his thumbs are embedded too deeply in my voice box for me to do anything but gurgle. I try and unpeel his hands from around my neck, gouging my nails into them, scraping and pinching. All I need is one flinch and I might be able to break the hold. His grip tightens.

The fizzing in my head is getting louder, like the static of an untuned television. Black clouds edge my vision. Just as I feel my focus slipping, I hear a thumping, then the scrape and creak of the heavy oak door. Hope sparks. Someone must have seen us together and realised something was wrong. I wait for the sound of footsteps pelting across the medieval flagstones. All I can hear is my own ragged breath. This room is tiny, an annex off the college's main banqueting hall, stuffed with oil portraits of important people. Even by candlelight, there's no way we can't be seen. And that door's too heavy to swing open on its own. My eyelids flicker like lights going out. My last realization before consciousness slides away is that, whoever is at the door, they're not going to rescue me.

After what I've done tonight, I can't blame them.

One

Now

10 hours to go . . .

My 10-year-old daughter is lying face down on the floor, refusing to look at me. I've tried cajoling, bribery, even barefaced threats but nothing will shift her. If I'm honest, I'm tempted to join her. How easy it would be to slip off my shoes, sink onto the soft pile carpet next to her and forget about the reunion entirely. But for once in my life, I'm not going to lie down and submit. I look at the Cartier watch on my wrist. Nick should be home by now; he's always better with the kids in these situations than me. He's got the whole 'firm but fair' thing nailed whereas I tend to be a pushover who then explodes with resentment when they don't listen. Because he spends less time at home, he's also very much the fun parent whereas I'm the one who moans about tidying their rooms and finishing their homework.

One of the curses of being a stay-at-home mum, the other being people thinking I'm good at domesticity, rather than just doing it by default. I wish I was one of those mums who sewed and ironed, who could produce perfectly iced cupcakes and really revelled in the role. But I'm not.

'Do you want to talk about it?' I pat ineffectually at Artie, but she shrugs me off.

'No.'

My heart contracts. I wish Artie would confide in me. I desperately want us to be close, but I'm so worried she'll absorb all the mistakes I've made that I'm more distant than I mean to be. It's easier with Xander; I never worry I'm infecting him with my insecurity.

'Are you sure?' I try again. I wish there was something I could do to help her. I wasn't always like this. Before I went to university, I was a problem solver, a go-getter. Now the only problems I solve tend to be laundry related. Not quite the illustrious law career I had dreamed of. I clench my fists. That's why I need to go back. To reclaim the person I was – and the person I would have been. If it wasn't for them.

'Emily, are you ready to go?' My husband's voice drifts up the stairs.

I survey the child prostrate in front of me. She's had a lot to deal with over the last few months. I wonder if I'm doing the right thing in leaving her even though I know Nick would never consider staying behind. Why is it men who put themselves first are considered dynamic and driven, whereas when mothers do it, we're made to feel selfish?

'You're not having second thoughts about it are you?'

Nick bounds into the master bedroom, his face already lit up by the prospect of the weekend ahead. His smile slips when he sees Artie spread-eagled at my feet.

'What's going on, my love?' He drops into a crouch and strokes Artie's hair away from her face. When she doesn't respond, he raises an eyebrow at me.

'Doesn't want us to go . . .' I mouth. I can't allow myself to be sucked into staying home. I remind myself that no matter how much I think I don't want to go to this reunion, I do. I need to do this. It's been fifteen years. The shame I've worn like a cloak since I left Cambridge doesn't feel as red raw anymore, though the nagging guilt hasn't faded. Neither has the sense of injustice. It's time I evened the score.

'Nonna's going to be here any minute.' Nick scratches at his shirt sleeve, trying to glance at the Rolex beneath it without Artie noticing. I know he's keen to beat the traffic. He asked me to be ready to leave as soon as he got back from the gym.

'Is there something you want to talk to Daddy about?' He chucks her under the chin, tickling her to make her smile. 'Is it Tamara and the girls at school again?'

Artie nods. I feel a wash of remorse. If I weren't so distracted by my plans for tonight, I'd have realized straightaway it was the cold-shouldering Artie's been experiencing from her friends that was upsetting her. It's triggering for me. Normally I'm all about letting the children fight their own battles (not to mention being terrible at confrontation), but Tamara's such a piece of work and the way she's treating Artie is so reminiscent of how Lyla was with me at university that I could quite happily take Tamara and the rest of her cronies and drop them all from the nearest tall building. I step forward to scoop Artie into a hug, but Nick holds up his hand to indicate he's got it. 'You know you can tell me anything, Art. I'm always on your side.'

I watch her shuffle her head towards Nick. Some of her long dark hair splays across the carpet. If I'd had a dad like him, it might have made me better equipped to deal with things. But if anything, it was my older sister Helen who parented me. My dad was too busy 'earning a crust', as he put it, then spending what he made down the pub. He left when I was 8, and if I'm honest, I scarcely noticed the difference. With Mum working two jobs to keep all the plates spinning, it was Helen that fought my corner. I press my tongue to the roof of my mouth to keep my expression neutral. Now's not the time for me to give into self-pity.

'You know I had some trouble with my friends when I was younger too,' Nick says. 'I expect they're just jealous of you. It happens to everyone.'

'Did it happen to Mummy?' Artie's voice is muffled by the hair in her mouth.

I tense. The million-dollar question. Of course, Nick doesn't know how to respond. He pauses.

'Mummy was different,' he says carefully. 'When we were at university, Mummy was the girl that all the boys wanted to go out with, and the girls wanted to be. She wouldn't have even considered dating someone like Daddy.'

'Why not?' Artie sits up and stares at me, any sign of earlier upset wiped out by natural curiosity.

'Because sometimes we don't know what's good for us.' Nick shrugs good-naturedly. 'Besides, Daddy was far too busy cracking the books so he could get a good job and live in a nice house. It's important to always work hard and do your homework, isn't it?' He winks at me. 'Here endeth the lesson.'

I manage the smile he's expecting. He's got it all wrong. It wasn't that I wouldn't have considered someone like Nick, it's that I didn't even see him. I was too busy being dazzled by Henry, and Will and Lyla alongside him.

'She also happens to be eavesdropping on us right now when she should be getting ready,' Nick chides. 'Don't you think Mummy needs to finish packing? We want her to look and feel her best for tonight.'

'I can help.' Artie leaps to her feet, worries forgotten. Oh, to be 10 again. 'I can choose what you should wear for the dinner.'

'No, that's fine,' I start backing towards the walk-in wardrobe. Artie's tastes run spanglier than mine. 'I'm already packed.'

Actually, I've been packed for days. I've checked my suitcase so many times it's like I've developed some sort of nervous tic. If I'm going to do what I'm planning, there's stuff I can't forget. A combination of fear and anticipation is driving me on, like when you're applying for a job you want so badly you're too scared to go to the interview. Or when you like a guy too much to actually talk to them. Funnily enough, I felt like that around Henry before we started dating. I was instantly at ease with Will, ironically, given what happened, but Henry made me stumble over my words and get flustered right up until he asked me out. Then I saw how sweet and caring he could be. Or at least I thought I did.

'Well, let's give Mummy a minute anyway.' Nick puts his hands on Artie's shoulders to shepherd her out of the room. 'You can go and see what your brother's up to.'

'Xander's on his switch. Again.' Artie rolls her eyes. 'He's been on it all morning.'

'Didn't school set you some work to do?' Nick frowns. 'Given that it's technically a school day.'

'It's an inset day, Dad.' Artie's eyes tilt skyward again. 'Hardly the same.'

'Ridiculous. An inset day when you've only—'

'Why don't you go and get out some of the baking things then?' I file yet another memory away and keep my voice even to head off Nick's speech about how they've only just gone back to school after the summer holidays and the teachers are already getting a day off. I don't disagree. I could have used a morning to steady my nerves instead of refereeing between two 10 year olds. 'I know Nonna was planning to make a cake with you this afternoon.'

'That sounds like Nonna.' Nick shoos Artie away.

I keep the smile pasted on my face. Nick's mum is barely even Italian so insisting we all call her 'Nonna' is overkill, though I know better than to raise this with Nick. He's very protective of her, even more so since his dad died. They say it's a cliché to resent your mother-in-law but anyone who thinks that hasn't met mine. Besides, the acrimony goes both ways. She doesn't think I'm good enough for Nick. She's probably right.

I wish it were Helen babysitting. Last time she babysat, she took them into the newsroom she used to work in so they could watch all the journalists pounding the phones and writing up stories. Xander talked about it for weeks. Even my friend Tiff, who laughingly refers to the twins as 'the vermin', would be better than Nick's mother. All Luci does is bake or watch TV. I force myself to remember I wouldn't be able to go to this reunion if she hadn't jumped in. It's ironic that regaining my sense of self-worth depends on a woman who thinks I have very little value.

'It better be chocolate.' Artie's already at the bedroom door, hollering up the stairs to the next floor where their bedrooms and the playroom are. 'Xander, we're making a cake when Nonna gets here. And it's gonna be chocolate.'

The whole house rattles as she thunders down the stairs, Xander hot on her heels.

'Well done, team.' Nick smiles at me.

I smile back, then start fidgeting. Although part of me doesn't want to go to this reunion, I'm also dying to get going. I want to see what's become of them, the three architects of my downfall. Will they wear their crimes on their faces, be shifty around me and unable to meet my eye? I bet they won't. When it comes to keeping up to date, I've read anything I could find about them compulsively but I'm not on Facebook so other than the odd picture in the college magazine or the press, I haven't seen them for fifteen years. From those snapshots, I can tell they're all making millions: Lyla's had her teeth capped, Will's experimented with Botox around his eyes and Henry still plucks his chest hair. But not in a single shot do any of them look remorseful.

Then again, each of the three could afford an attic full of Dorian Grays. I'm sure what they did to me won't even have touched them. Especially given what they've gone on to do. I know a few things about them that haven't made the press. I run my hands through my hair, reminding myself they can't touch me now. I'm strong. 'What time is Luci getting here?'

'As soon as bridge finishes.' Nick checks his watch again. 'Good god, is that the time?' His eyes bulge. 'We really need to get moving.'

I run my hands down the front of my White Company cashmere jumper, smoothing away any pilling and wondering whether the ribbon of tension that's been under-scoring everything I do is rubbing off on him. 'I'm ready when you are.'

Nick strides over to the walk-in and starts rifling through the drawers on his side of it. 'Did you manage to—'

'Yes, I packed for you.'

'Did you put in my coll—'

'I put in your college colours socks, bowtie, the lot. You name it, you've got college stripes on it.'

'You know me too well.' Nick crosses back over and folds me into his arms. 'I know you're nervous about going back after all this time. But you'll do great. Did you pack that satin dress you bought?'

'I did.'

'You're going to smash it then.'

I rest my face against him. The top of my head fits per-fectly under his chin but even though he's a shade taller than me, he's broad and strong. He tightens his arms around me, shutting the rest of the world out. I could stay in this moment forever. I only wish he knew me as well as he thinks he does. He has no idea why I'm really so nervous.

'We can skip it,' Nick says. 'If you really want . . .'

He leaves the sentence hanging and I feel a stab of guilt. Nick doesn't know what really happened that night. He thinks I got a bit too drunk and fell over. On my own. He doesn't even realise the three of them were there. I've never told him. We had a single conversation about it, right when we first started dating, but I played it down. As things got more serious – our relationship was uncharacteristically whirlwind for both of us – I kept it to myself because I didn't want his opinion of me to change. Then it simply got too late to tell him. Even if, as every women's magazine shouts from its cover, secrets aren't good for a marriage. I nestle closer to him, taking comfort in his gym-honed biceps. I'll make it up to him when it's all over. The doorbell chimes. I try to hold onto him for one second longer, but he detaches himself gently.

'That'll be Mum.' He kisses me on the top of the head and starts leading me towards the door, leaving me no choice but to follow.

Don't miss the next compulsive thriller from Polly Phillips.

Available to order now.